DEADLINE

DEADLINE

STEPHEN MAHER

Steve,
Hope you find
this entertaining.

Steve

ISBN: 978-1-481-93893-8

Typesetting by Hale Author Services.

For my parents.

He shall come down like rain upon the mown
grass: as showers that water the earth.
In his days shall the righteous flourish; and abun-
dance of peace so long as the moon endureth.
He shall have dominion also from sea to sea, and
from the river unto the ends of the earth.
They that dwell in the wilderness shall bow before
him; and his enemies shall lick the dust.

—Psalm 72:6–9

Chapter 1 – We'll walk down

THERE MUST HAVE been something funny in the birthday cake, Captain Isabelle Galarneau liked to joke, because ever since she turned thirty her hips had been expanding.

On August 14, her thirty-first birthday, when it seemed like everything she owned was suddenly tight around the bottom, and she could imagine herself getting fatter and fatter for the rest of her life, alone and increasingly desperate, she had decided to do something about it. Every weekday morning for the past four months, she had gone jogging, listening to eighties pop on her iPod as she ran.

By December, she had lost eight pounds and was managing a slow, steady run of eight kilometres from her condo in downtown Hull, across the Alexandra Bridge, her bum jiggling with every heavy step, then along the Ottawa River on the Ontario side, below Parliament Hill, to the Chaudière Bridge, where she'd cross back to Quebec and head home to stretch, shower, eat yogurt and dress for work.

Galarneau was a registered nurse in the military, a member of the Disaster Assistance Response Team, the elite group that was ready to set up a mobile hospital anywhere in the world with 24 hours' notice. She had to be at her desk at National Defence Headquarters every morning at 8:00, so she started her run at 5:00. Today, the sky was still dark as she ran down the slope, through a copse of bare hardwoods, from the Alexandra Bridge to the system of eight locks where the Rideau Canal flows into the Ottawa River. There was a white sheet of fresh snow, and she had to lean back and choose her steps carefully to avoid slipping on the steep trail.

Of the eight locks, only the highest gate was closed this morning, so Galarneau had to jog uphill before she could cross the canal, her thighs aching as she pounded up the concrete steps. She sang along tunelessly to ABBA as she ran. She stopped singing when she put her foot on the walkway and caught sight of the body in the water.

A man floated face-down, his arms by his sides, the jacket of his blue pin-striped suit spread out in the water, right there, about six feet below her, pressed by the current against the lock door.

Galarneau froze and swore in French: "Câlisse!"

She looked around and saw a thin, grey-bearded fellow in a colourful Lycra outfit approaching the walkway, pushing a bike.

"There's a guy in the water," she shouted, and then she took a deep breath and jumped into the freezing canal. The water was only two feet deep as the canal had been drained for the winter, and she landed hard on her heels and tumbled backwards, falling onto her bum and going under.

The cold was terrible. There was already a thin crust of ice forming where the surface of the water met the stone wall of the canal, and ice on the rungs of the old iron ladder set in the stone face.

Galarneau staggered to her feet, shivering and grimacing, grabbed the body by the shoulder and flipped it over. The man was young and lightly built, with sandy hair and a little goatee. His eyes were closed and his lips blue. There was no way she could get him out of the water, so she got onto her knees, pulled him up into her lap, checked his mouth, pinched his nose and started to give him mouth-to-mouth. His mouth was cold and his skin was clammy and blue. She lifted her head to take a deep breath. Above her, the cyclist peered over the edge, a look of concern on his face.

"Hey," she shouted up to him. "You want to call an ambulance?"

He ran off and she returned to her work.

Karen Stevens arched one blonde eyebrow when the house manager, Phillipe, stepped into the sunroom at the back of 24 Sussex Drive.

Most mornings, she shared breakfast with her husband, Bruce Stevens, the prime minister, and their two teenage daughters, but this morning was different. For one thing, the girls were at a friend's house for a sleepover. For another, breakfast was a few minutes late. And Phillipe wasn't carrying the usual bowl of fruit salad, but two huge plates loaded with peameal bacon, sausage, home fries, fried eggs, baked beans and slabs of buttery toast. There was even a little pot of cretons – a pork spread made with lard.

Stevens, who had been up working for hours already, put down his briefing book and gave his wife a tiny smile as she looked in confusion from him to Phillipe to the breakfasts.

"Phillipe, did Chef decide we deserve a little treat today?" he asked.

"That's right, Prime Minister," said Phillipe, smiling as he laid down the plates. "It was Chef's idea."

Stevens watched a smile spread across his wife's face – a smile that creased the fine lines around her eyes. It had been a long time since he'd seen her smile like that.

"Did you hear that, honey?" he said, cutting into the peameal bacon. "Chef thinks we deserve a treat."

She beamed back at him. "So you've decided then? And today's the day."

He grinned at her, his mouth full, and raised his eyebrows.

Before he could answer, she was up and around the table and pulling him into her arms.

As he held her, he was surprised to feel tears running down her cheeks.

Detective Sergeant Devon Flanagan had to wait outside the ICU while the doctor looked at the floater. He wasn't at all happy about it. He had two centre-ice tickets to see the Leafs play the Senators, and after some challenging negotiations with his ex-wife, he had arranged to take his eight-year-old son, Jason. He had been sure that he'd get to the game on time, since he was on early shift this week. Then he and his partner caught the floater. Now he had the sinking feeling that he wouldn't be able to make the game. The thought of calling his son to cancel ate at his stomach, which was already feeling sour, thanks to too much coffee.

He sat for a minute, scratched his grey head, fiddled with his cell phone, put it away, took a sip of cold coffee, pulled his phone out again, and decided to call his partner.

"Hey, how's it going?"

"The same," said Detective Sergeant Mallorie Ashton. "I got some uniforms walking both sides of the canal. Pretty much finished up here at the locks. We've got Ms. Galarneau's statement, and one from the guy who called it in. Haven't really found anything that looks like evidence. I think I'm going to shut this down and head into the office, trace Sawatski's movements last night.

"I've been kind of waiting to hear from you, find out if the kid's going to make it."

"I still have no idea if we're looking at an accidental drowning or what," said Flanagan. "I'm still waiting for the doctor. Hopefully she'll be done soon."

"Did you call the family?" asked Ashton.

"Yeah," said Flanagan. "That wasn't much fun. They're likely in the air now, flying in from St. John's."

The door opened and Doctor Shalini Singh walked in.

"Oh, here's the doctor," said Flanagan. "Talk to you soon."

He stood up and reached to take the doctor's hand. She was about 35, tall and slim.

"Sorry to keep you waiting, detective," she said. "I wanted to make sure Mr. Sawatski was stable before I left him."

"I understand," said Flanagan, flipping open his notebook.

"Tell me, how is he? Is he going to make it?"

"I don't know," she said. "He's breathing on his own now, and his heart is pumping. I can't see any reason why he won't survive, but I can't make any promises. There are often complications in near drownings, and patients have been known to die several days after seeming to recover. I don't think that's likely in this case, though, because most deaths like that are caused by damage to the lungs caused by inhaling water. And this man didn't have water in his lungs. That's why he's alive."

"Does that mean he wasn't in the water for long?" asked Flanagan.

"No. In about 10 per cent of drowning deaths, the victim's airway is sealed off, which prevents water from entering the lungs. It's known as dry drowning. That seems to have happened in this case, and it likely saved this man's life. It markedly increases the chance of someone being successfully resuscitated." Dr. Singh paused. "Mr. Sawatski was lucky. His airway closed off. He was found by someone who knew that she should keep giving him mouth-to-mouth even though he appeared to be dead. And the water was very cold, which probably kept him alive."

Flanagan looked up from his notebook.

"So how long was he in the water?"

"It's impossible to know for sure. When someone's face is immersed in cold water, it triggers the mammalian diving reflex, which slows the body's metabolism. If the water is cold – and we're talking about the Rideau Canal in December – then the effect is more pronounced. The body cuts off blood flow to the extremities and focuses on keeping blood in the heart and the brain. There have been cases of children being revived after hours in very cold water. With a young man, it wouldn't be that long. Probably thirty minutes at the most."

The doctor leaned back and waited for the next question.

"So what's the prognosis?" asked Flanagan.

"Well, complete recovery is unlikely," said the doctor. "He has almost certainly suffered brain damage as a result of oxygen deprivation. The brain has ways of repairing itself, but we won't know the extent of the damage for days. Right now, he's alive and recovering, against the odds. He's a lucky man."

Flanagan looked up at her.

"I don't know whether I'd call him lucky or not to have survived," he said.

The doctor gave him a thin smile. "Where there's life, there's hope," she said.

"Is there any way you can tell how he ended up in the canal?" he asked. "We have no way of knowing just yet whether this is an accident or whether somebody tried to kill this young fellow."

"Well, that's really your job," she said. "I don't know how he ended up in the water, whether he could swim, if he was conscious when he entered the water, any of that stuff. People do drown all the time. I've sent away blood tests so we'll find out whether he had alcohol or drugs in his system."

Flanagan had run out of questions. He put his notebook away. "Can I have a look at him?"

She led him to the private room where Ed Sawatski lay underneath a white sheet and blanket. He was connected to a respirator, a heart monitor and an IV drip.

"I thought you said he was breathing on his own," said Flanagan.

"Yes," said the doctor, "he is, but we don't want to take any chances so we'll leave him on the respirator for now."

Flanagan stared down at the thin, handsome, blank face. By looking through his wallet on the banks of the canal, he had learned that Sawatski was a 28-year-old staffer on Parliament Hill, but he didn't know much more. The young man had close-cropped sandy hair and a little goatee. He was very pale. Flanagan peered at him but the face told him nothing. He took out his digital camera and took several pictures.

"Can I pull back the blankets for a moment, doctor?" he asked.

Dr. Singh walked over and felt her patient's head with the back of her hand.

"Okay," she said, "but please be quick. His temperature

is still low."

Flanagan pulled the blankets down carefully. Sawatski was wearing a hospital gown.

Flanagan took a picture, then lowered the camera.

"Tell me, doctor," he said, pointing at Sawatski's wrists, where there was a dull blue discoloration. "Did you notice those marks when you examined him?"

"No," she said. "What is it?"

"I believe those are handcuff bruises," he said. "Looks like we might have an attempted murder on our hands."

Jack Macdonald awoke with a start and sat up straight in bed when he heard the first trill of his cell phone. He opened his eyes and in a flash felt the hangover: sandpaper mouth, throbbing head, cramped lungs. He blinked his sore, dry eyes to clear his fuzzy vision, and looked around in confusion at his room, strewn with dirty clothes. He squinted. The clock said 9:30 a.m. The phone rang again.

"Lord Jesus," he croaked.

He looked down and noted with surprise that he had slept in his suit, on top of the blankets, on his back.

When the phone rang a third time, he turned his head and discovered he had a kink in his neck.

The BlackBerry was in the side pocket of his jacket. He grabbed it and cleared his throat but his voice still sounded hoarse and froggy: "Hello. Jack Macdonald."

"Hello," said a woman's voice. "I'm calling for Ed Sawatski."

"Well, you've got Jack Macdonald here," he said.

The woman was silent for a moment.

"That's odd," she said. "He left me a message yesterday, said it was important that I call him at this number, and only at this number."

Jack wanted desperately to end the conversation. His neck hurt, and he urgently needed to pee.

"I'm sorry, but he must have left you the wrong number,"

he said. "We're friends. Maybe he got mixed up, told you my number by mistake. Why don't you leave me your name and number and I'll get him to call you back."

The woman paused before she spoke. "Mr. Sawatski's message said that he works in the office of the justice minister, and that it was important that I call," she said. "Do you work with him there? I'm trying to figure out why someone from the justice minister's office would call me."

Macdonald got out of bed and shuffled toward the bathroom. "No, ma'am," he said. "I'm a reporter for the *Evening Telegram*. I have no idea why he would call you. He and I were out together last night. Perhaps he had my phone number on his mind. I'm sure he'll get in touch, though, once I let him know."

Macdonald stood in the bathroom, aching to get off the phone.

"Oh, you're a Newfoundlander," she said. "So am I. Is Mr. Sawatski also? It doesn't sound like a Newfoundland name."

"Yes," he said. "He is a Newfoundlander. We went to Memorial University together. Want me to get him to call you?"

She paused again. "Very well. Tell him, please, that Ida Gushue returned his call. I'll be out for a time this morning but I'll be in this afternoon."

"I'll let him know right away. Thanks," he said, and hung up before the conversation could drag on any longer.

He peed for a long time, drank some water from his cupped hands and swallowed three Tylenol. He barely recognized the face in the mirror, with its matted dark hair, deep bags under bloodshot eyes, its pale, blotchy, stubbly skin. He wanted nothing more than to get back in bed, but he was already a half-hour late for work and had to get moving.

He walked carefully to the kitchen, rinsed a dirty cup and filled it with yesterday's cold coffee. He choked some of it down, fumbled in his suit jacket for his cigarettes, and lit one. The smoke hurt his lungs, but he needed the nicotine. He leaned on the sill of the grimy window and looked out at the snow falling on the parking lot. He drank coffee, smoked and tentatively moved his neck, trying to work out the kink. The cheap window rattled as the wind blew the snow against it, and he could feel the cold coming in.

After his coffee and cigarette, he went back to his bedroom, where he spent a few unpleasant minutes trying to find clean clothes, before concluding that the rumpled suit he was wearing was the cleanest thing he had, despite the wine stain on the left lapel. Back in the bathroom he undressed, hung the jacket on a hanger next to the shower so the steam would take out some of the wrinkles, and stood there for a long time, letting the hot water work on his neck. After he'd towelled off and dressed in his bedroom, moving carefully to protect his neck, he picked up the BlackBerry from the bedside table to call Sawatski. He punched in his password, but it didn't work. He gaped at the screen:

Ed Sawatski
Property of:
Department of Justice, Office of the Minister
613 555-0139

Macdonald grabbed the holster on his belt and pulled out his own phone. In his foggy state, he hadn't noticed that he was in possession of two BlackBerrys. He sat down on the edge of his bed and tried to work out why he had a cell phone in each hand.

Stevens paused when they reached the last of the agenda items for the day. He looked down at his notes, and then around at the twenty-eight faces at the long oak table – twenty-seven cabinet ministers and his chief of staff. They were seated around the huge, wooden table in the cabinet room of the Centre Block on Parliament Hill, one floor above the foyer of the House of Commons.

"There's one piece of new business," he said as he looked around the table. "This morning I told Karen that I've decided not to lead the party into the next election."

For a moment all twenty-eight sat in stunned silence. He watched their expressions change from blank to surprise.

"I want to thank all of you for your work with me over the months and years," he said, raising his voice as an excited murmur spread around the table.

"Mais, c'est pas possible!"

He had been interrupted – a first in all the cabinet meetings he had chaired – by Geneviève Beauregard, the minister of heritage. She was a lightweight who had to be heavily coached by her staff for even the simplest speech or debate, but she was well-liked by her cabinet colleagues, in part because of her honesty and emotion when she was away from the microphones.

"Pas maintenant," she said, her voice pleading now, her eyes near tears. "Monsieur le premier ministre, pas maintenant. Pas déjà. Non."

Stevens smiled at the interruption and looked at Beauregard with real warmth in his eyes.

"Désolé, Geneviève," he said. "J'ai décidé. It's time to pass the torch."

The finance minister, stodgy, grey-haired Prentice Staunton, a former banker from Vancouver, interrupted him next.

"Forgive me, Prime Minister," he said. "But for the sake of the party, for the sake of the country, I think you should reconsider."

"Thank you, Prentice," said Stevens. "But no. My decision is made."

He smiled and looked around the table.

"I expect some of you have more mixed feelings than Prentice and Geneviève," he said, and he winked. "And, in truth, my feelings are mixed. There are more things I would like to have done. And it's never easy for a governing party to go through a leadership campaign. But the timing isn't going to be any better in six months, or a year, and I am convinced that we need new leadership before the next election."

He looked down and straightened the already tidy pile of papers in front of him.

"I've led the Conservatives through three elections, and we've won all three, thank goodness," he said. "And I'm pretty sure I could lead us to another election victory, even if the Liberals come to their senses and get rid of Pinsent before then."

Everyone at the table laughed, a welcome relief of tension in the room. He allowed himself another of his tiny smiles.

"But I promised Karen before the last election that this would be the last one. I was hoping she would change her mind, but she hasn't. If I'm going to go before the next election, I think now is the time to announce it," he said. "I propose stepping down at the beginning of March break. That will give us time to pass our legislative agenda – and I want all of you to push hard to get these bills through. The new leader can take over then, which will give him time --" He stopped himself. "That would give her, or him, time to reorganize the government and shuffle the cabinet before the second winter session begins. It will be up to the next leader, of course, to decide on this, but I think a new prime minister could bring in a new budget, and then campaign on it in the spring.

"This means a three-month leadership campaign, which is on the short side, but I don't think a governing party can afford a longer one. And I can't afford to lose any of you right now."

He looked around the table, making eye contact with one minister after another.

"I suspect the next prime minister is sitting at this table," he said. "It's not up to me, but I'd be surprised if anyone else can get organized in time to take the leadership, not with a three-month campaign. They're welcome to try – and anything can happen in a campaign – but I think one of you will be the next prime minister, I hope a better prime minister than I've been. But I can't afford to let any of you resign from cabinet. I want all of you to stay where you are until the end of the session."

He looked out the window at the grey sky and the broad lawn, covered with a thin blanket of fresh snow. "That's not going to be easy to balance. It's not easy to run a federal department and a leadership campaign, but then it's not as hard as it is to be prime minister."

Stevens was determined to keep his usual tight rein on his cabinet in his last months as prime minister. If his ministers had to stay at the table, they could hardly afford to defy him during the leadership race.

"If I get the sense, at any time, that any of you are neglecting your ministerial duties, I will ask for your resignation," he said, looking around the table, eyes hard now. "I have no intention of being a lame duck."

He smiled, his face suddenly softening.

"I'm sure it won't be necessary to remind any of you of that," he said. "And I don't want to discourage any of you from running. We need a good race. I intend to stay out of it, absolutely neutral, at least until I mark my ballot at the leadership convention. That goes for my staff as well.

"I'm planning on holding a news conference after Question Period, at the National Press Theatre, to tell Canadians that they won't have Bruce Stevens to kick around much longer."

They laughed again.

"Until then," he said, "I'd like you to keep this news to yourselves. All right?"

He looked around the table as they all nodded.

"Okay then," he said, and stood up. "Back to work."

Sawatski's cell phone rang again while Jack was brushing the snow off his dented Ford Focus, but he didn't answer it and he ignored it when it rang twice more as he drove. He had a potentially career-jeopardizing hangover, he was going to be an hour late for work, and he didn't need to jeopardize public safety or waste time taking messages for Sawatski as he drove, shivering, through the snowy streets, to the parking lot below Parliament Hill.

Once inside the Hot Room, a bullpen full of reporters

from different news organizations, down the hall from the House of Commons he hung up his coat, grunted hello to his colleagues, took the elevator upstairs to the cafeteria to get a coffee, and was finally behind his desk and ready to work by 10:30. He booted up his laptop and was checking the headlines on Twitter when Sawatski's phone rang in his pocket again.

His friend would have to be half mad without his Berry, he thought. They had spent the previous night drinking hard, and Ed likely thought he had left it in some sleazy bar, which wasn't the kind of thing political staffers wanted to have to tell their bosses.

He picked up his desk phone and called Ed's office. The receptionist told him Ed was away from his desk. Jack left a message asking Ed to call as soon as possible.

As soon as he hung up, the phone rang.

"Jack Macdonald, Telegram," he said.

It was Kevin Brandt, the city editor of the Newfoundland daily, and his boss.

"How's she going?" said Brandt. "I been trying to get you for an hour now. What? You just getting in?"

"No, b'y," said Jack, trying to sound nonchalant. "I was on my way in this morning when a buddy from home called me about a story, so we met in coffee shop for a little chat."

"Did he give you anything good?"

Jack's head was throbbing and he was sweating. He bent his head, which set off a painful spasm in his neck.

"Something to look into," he said. "Rumour about the search and rescue helicopter contract."

"You b'ys must have talked about the Len Ramia story, eh?" said Brandt. "What's the gossip about that?"

"Yes," he said. "We did chat about it."

As he spoke, he frantically typed "Len Ramia" into Google News. The first hit was a story from the *Globe and Mail*: Liberal Senator Charged With Expense Fraud.

He scanned the story. The RCMP had charged Senator Len Ramia, a Liberal appointed by Jean Chretien in 1998, with misusing Senate property. He was accused of taking furniture, art and computer equipment to his home.

"This is a good story," said Brandt. "Guy's been sitting on his arse up there, making $130,000 a year for twelve years, doing sweet fuck all, without anyone ever voting for him, and now we find out he's been stealing."

Brandt hated the Senate in general, and Ramia in particular. Since his appointment, he had done nothing of note, dodging committee work and public appearances, showing up dutifully when the Senate was sitting, but only because he had to do so to collect his paycheques. He would sit there until the day he turned 75, living the high life, a reward for some long-forgotten partisan service.

"Yes b'y," said Jack. "It's shocking. I wonder who tipped off the *Globe*."

"I'd like to know that meself," said Brandt. "That's the kind of thing we sent you up to get."

Jack winced. His editors complained whenever anybody scooped him on a Newfoundland story, something that happened more often than he liked, and he knew that others in the newsroom were not convinced having him in Ottawa was worth the expense. Brandt was his defender, but even he wasn't always happy with Jack.

"I want you to go after the Liberal MPs on this," said Brandt. "See if they'll defend him, attack him. It'd be good if they stick up for him. Liberal MPs Stick Up for Accused Senate Fraudster. Could be A1. Should be."

"Yes," said Jack. "I'll do a little digging, and then try to get the boys on the way into Question Period. They might want to dodge me, though."

"Will Ramia keep picking up his paycheques while he's up on charges?" Brandt asked.

"I think so," said Jack. "I think he'd have to be convicted before they could boot him out of the Senate."

"There's your angle, b'y," said Brandt. "Liberal MPs Don't Want Accused Senate Fraudster's Pay Stopped. Get me that."

When Claude Bouchard passed through the gate in the stone and wrought iron wall that surrounds Parliament Hill, he had to step back to make room for a group of men and women in expensive wool overcoats headed the opposite way. A pleasant thought struck him as he waited for them to pass, and a smile stole across his face as he strode through the falling snow up the broad walkway toward the Peace Tower, swinging his briefcase, a spring in his step. In a few months, he thought, the lobbyists and political staffers who now ignored him would make impressive efforts to get close to him. After twenty years in politics, beginning as a volunteer on a chaotic, unsuccessful campaign for the mayoralty of Montreal, his patience and experience were finally about to pay off. As the cabinet meeting ended, his boss, Public Safety Minister Greg Mowat, had emailed him the news that Stevens was resigning, and Bouchard was excited. There was every reason to think that Mowat would be prime minister within a few months, and he would be there with him, in a senior role in Langevin, at the heart of the office that runs the country. There's an old saying in politics: The people who get you there aren't always the ones who can keep you there. Too often, Bouchard had been the guy who got someone there, only to be pushed aside. But now it was he who had the sharpest elbows on the Hill and the best connection to Mowat, and he was finding it hard to stop smiling.

Bouchard paused to kick the snow off his shoes under the stone arch below the Peace Tower, walked up the carpeted steps and took the elevator up one storey to the ambulatory that runs largely unnoticed below the arched ceiling of Confederation Hall. He dipped out of sight around the corner, bent his salt-and-pepper head to his BlackBerry and sent a private message to Ismael Balusi, the prime minister's director of communications.

Bouchard viewed most young Conservative staffers with affectionate condescension, relishing their simple-minded loyalty to the boss and their idealistic naiveté, which made them predictable. In Balusi, though, he had found a young man with a clear-eyed perception of the currents of power and the cunning and courage to manipulate them.

At first, Bouchard saw him as a dangerous threat, an ideological purist who understood but disapproved of backroom power plays, but the middle-aged French Canadian backroom warrior and the media-savvy young Toronto South Asian became allies when they were thrown together to contain a potentially damaging scandal. Mowat's office had asked for PMO help to plan for the release of access-to-information documents that showed that senior RCMP officers had ignored sexual harassment in the force. While their colleagues worked on a plan to minimize the damage, Balusi and Bouchard found a way to convince the access-to-info office to "unrelease" the most damaging sections of the documents, and together they snuffed out the story, and developed a personal alliance that Bouchard was counting on now.

Bouchard looked up from his phone when Balusi stepped into the ambulatory

"Game on," said Balusi.

"It hasn't leaked yet?" Bouchard asked.

"No. And I don't think it will. Nobody wants to piss off Stevens today, or take away his moment in the sun. They all looked shell-shocked coming out. I don't think any of them saw this coming."

"How did Donahoe look?" asked Bouchard.

"Preoccupied," said Balusi. "I don't think this was in his plan. I think he wanted more time at Justice, raise his profile with the crime bills."

"Too bad he wasn't still in Foreign Affairs," said Bouchard.

"Yeah," said Balusi. "It would be a good time to send him to Africa for a review of our aid policy."

They chuckled.

As they spoke the Speaker's Parade entered the hall, and both men watched the sergeant-at-arms bearing the enormous gold mace walk past below them, followed by the Speaker and his clerks, all of them in tri-cornered hats and long black robes. Security guards in blue shirts kept the way clear for the somber procession to the House, where the Speaker would begin the day's sitting.

"Look," said Balusi. "If this leaks just as Question Period is about to start, when they're all on the way into the House, it'll be a feeding frenzy, a good old-fashioned pig fuck. They'll all look flat-footed in front of the cameras."

Bouchard looked at him. "Except my guy."

"Yeah," said Balusi. "That's what I'm thinking. You have to give him some lines, tell him to be ready for it."

"And you'll take care of the leak?"

"And I'll take care of the leak."

It was getting to be lunchtime by the time Flanagan made his way back from the Ottawa Hospital to the concrete bunker on Elgin that housed the Ottawa Police Service, so he picked up sandwiches and coffee on the way.

Ashton was on the phone when he came into the office. "I don't care," she was saying. "I don't care at all. You have to understand me. This is police business. We are investigating a very serious crime, and I need to talk to Ms. Fortin, like right now." She smiled at Flanagan. "No, I don't want to leave a message. I want to talk to her right now. I know that you are important. I know that the minister of public safety and his staff are very important. All right? I get it. But, right now, I am more important. And you are going to be in a lot of trouble unless you locate Sophie Fortin for me, immediately, and get her on the phone. Okay?"

Ashton sighed and recited her name and phone number.

"Now," she said. "Listen to me, Ms. Bourassa. If you don't get me Sophie Fortin on the phone very, very soon, I am going to do everything I can to get you fired. Est-que tu me comprends bien? Je vais te faire perdre ta job, osti! This is a police investigation and I'm tired of fucking around with you."

She hung up and turned her smiling face to Flanagan. "I've informed the kid's parents, but I still haven't managed

to get the girlfriend on the line," she said. "She is the, uh –"
she glanced at her notes "-- press secretary to Public Safety
Minister Greg Mowat. And apparently she's with the minister
and is very, very busy."

Flanagan laughed and set the food down on her desk. "I
have a feeling you'll be hearing from her soon."

Ashton reached for a sandwich. "So what have you got?"

"Well," he said, popping the top off of one of the coffees.
"I don't think we have an accident here. The kid has handcuff
bruises on his wrists." He turned on the camera and flipped
through the images, showing a closeup to Ashton. "I checked
with the boys, and none of our guys – or the Gatineau cops
– picked this guy up last night."

"Could be recreational," said Ashton.

Flanagan smirked. "Could be you got a different idea of
recreation than I do, detective. If this kid had the cuffs on tight
enough to bruise him, I doubt it was sex play."

"Seems unlikely," she said, "But you never know. In the
height of passion, people can be hard to distract."

"Something to ask the girlfriend."

"If she ever answers my call. Any chance Sawatski will be
talking soon, can tell us who put the cuffs on him?"

"Not much chance, no," said Flanagan. "The doctor is not
optimistic. Kid likely suffered brain damage from the lack of
oxygen, but maybe. That's what she said. Maybe. On the other
hand, he could die. It could turn into a homicide."

"So could she tell how long he was in the water?"

"No more than thirty minutes. Probably less. What time
did the call come in?"

"5:25. Took the guy maybe two minutes to run over to the
Chateau Laurier and call 911."

"So he went into the canal between, what, 4:53 and 5:10,
that's our window?"

"That's what I figure," said Ashton and waved him over
to her computer. She had it open to an aerial view of the
Rideau Canal.

"After you left, I walked up to the National Arts Centre

and threw a life jacket into the canal and timed it going down. It took thirty-five minutes to reach the locks. I think a body would be slower."

"I suspect that whatever happened, happened right there." Flanagan pointed at the four-lane bridge just above the locks. "That's where I'd go if I wanted to drown somebody in the canal."

"Not me," said Ashton. "Too many cameras around. The city might be pretty sleepy at 4:30, but security cameras never sleep. This is in the shadow of Parliament Hill. Must be cameras all over the place."

"I'll see if we can get some video from last night," said Flanagan. "I don't suppose we can get a diver to go in, see if there's anything on the bottom?"

Ashton shook her head.

"They don't want to pay for it," said Ashton. "Not for what might be an accident. It's too bad. I talked to Sawatski's boss. They're worried about this. The kid's BlackBerry wasn't on him when he was pulled out of the canal. There may be sensitive information on it, and they would like to know where it is."

"Well, it will soon be too late to send down a diver," said Flanagan. "The canal's already freezing up. It's supposed to go down to minus 30 tonight and stay below minus 25 all week."

NTV reporter Ellen Simms made an impression when she entered Metropolitain, a bistro a few minutes' walk from Parliament Hill. Most of the diners recognized her from the nightly news, and those who couldn't place her watched her just as closely as those who could. She had a mesmerizing quality that drew eyes to her – a blank, perfect face, with a pouty mouth and small, sharp pretty blue eyes. Everything about her was store-bought. The high, pointy breasts, the carefully cascading reddish hair, the high heels and stylish leather skirt, the Dolce and Gabanna handbag, the diamond earrings. Everything but that perfect doll's face, and the twitch in her hips when she walked. But that was enough to turn all the heads in the restaurant.

Fred Murphy, Ottawa bureau chief for NTV, stood when she came to the table. She smiled, apologized for being late, moved her head so that her hair flipped off her shoulder, and leaned in for a two-cheek kiss.

He already had a beer in front of him. The waiter appeared, in no time at all, to take her drink order. A Pinot Grigio? Fine. Great. Thanks.

Murphy almost had to tell the waiter to buzz off the way he hovered after she had ordered. Instead, he congratulated himself for being past the point where a bombshell like Simms made him act the fool.

At sixty-two, after more than thirty years of working on the Hill, Murphy was the reporter with the most juice in Ottawa. The lead political reporter for the top-rated English TV channel in Canada, he had chits to bargain with, and he knew how to play them. He was ruthless in pursuit of a story, and came up with the goods time and time again, carefully cultivating connections that could get him the stories, no matter what the camp. He was the top dog when the Liberals were in, and he was the top dog now that the Conservatives were in.

But he had a problem with Ellen.

The camera loved her. His bosses in Toronto loved her. Some politicians loved her. He feared her, though, because he couldn't trust her work. He had caught her lying to him twice in the six months since she'd come up from Thunder Bay, hungry for the big time. Once she had completely missed the obvious angle on the biggest story of the day, and blamed a cameraman – a level-headed veteran whom she should have known better than to disparage. Murphy knew the cameraman hadn't made the rookie mistake but he checked anyway, and found that she had indeed lied to him. He kept that to himself.

Then she stole an investigative story from a researcher and claimed it at as her own, even hinting who her source was, when the researcher had told a producer a week earlier what she was working on, and the producer had told Fred. Fred had kept a straight face and quietly let the researcher know that he knew whose story it was, and put something nice in her file.

He had hoped that Simms would settle down when she found her legs in Ottawa, when it sunk in that she was where she belonged and didn't have to lie or steal or cheat to get ahead, that she already was ahead, that there was no farther ahead to get, not in this country. But she hadn't changed, and if the rumours were to be believed, was even willing to sleep with sources for stories. She had broken up at least two marriages in Thunder Bay, and had managed to win a good divorce settlement just as she moved to Ottawa. Since then, he knew that she had slept with several MPs, and could only imagine that she did so for the information they could offer her.

It offended Fred's Catholic sensibility, but if she was ready to get dirty with party hacks as old and broken down as he was, well, that was her call and it was unlikely to come back on him, or NTV. It wasn't his business what she did in bed. What made him nervous was the desperation behind it. If she would do that, what else would she do?

After hearing the most recent rumour, which had her picking up a minor scoop in the bedroom of the Conservative party whip, he decided to invite her for lunch, planning to take her temperature, size her up better, and, most of all, let her know that he was damned pleased with her work, very impressed, let her know that he was 100 per cent behind her. He wasn't looking forward to it, but it was the only approach he thought might be helpful – to let her know that he had her back. Maybe, over time, this positive reinforcement would take the edge off her frantic ambition. Maybe he could show her how he worked, how he developed relationships with sources, over decades, always playing it honest. Not nice, but honest. He would put the knife in if he had to, but he would put it in the belly, not the back, explaining calmly why he had to do it as he slid it in. It was the story. Nothing could get in the way of the story. It was business, and the smart ones understood that, and the stupid ones usually didn't know much of anything anyway. He thought that if she could learn how the long game was played, he might be able to come to trust her.

"How the hell are you, superstar?" he said as she settled in. "What do you know?"

She gave him the big smile, the heartbreaker, and plopped a BlackBerry and an iPhone on the table in front of her.

"I'm great," she said, giving her shoulders a little shimmy. "You know, chasing stories, breaking hearts, having fun."

He laughed and it crossed his mind that maybe he worried about her too much.

"Take it easy on them, kid," he said. "You don't have to kill every fucking fish the first time you go to the lake."

They laughed together.

"Reminds me of a joke," he said. "It's a bit, uh, spicy, but with your permission."

"My favourite kind," she said, and smiled as if she meant it.

"Well, there's an old buffalo and a young buffalo up at the top of a bluff in Saskatchewan," he said. "And what do they see? A herd of lovely buffalo cows, real beauties, chewing on the grass, looking pretty as buffalo cows can look. Real hotties, eh. The young buffalo gets all excited, he starts prancing on the spot. The old buffalo turns to him, says 'What are you getting so excited about, young fellow?' The young buffalo looks up at him, says, 'Look at all them beautiful cows down there! Just look at them. Let's go! Let's go! Let's run down there and fuck one of them!' "

He smiled, getting ready for the punchline, when her BlackBerry rang, its screen flashed. Murphy could read the upside-down call display: Ismael Balusi.

She grimaced, showing her perfect teeth.

"Oh my God," she said. "Sorry. Shit. I really have to take this. It could be big. Excuse me."

She got up from the table and he watched her walk away, talking, gesturing with her free hand.

She looked nervous when she came back two minutes later. She took a long drink of wine.

"I've got to go," she said. "I'm *really* sorry. I just got a tip, a big story."

He put on his game face.

"What's the story?" he said.

"I've promised to hold it until 2 p.m.," she said and looked at her watch. "If I tell you, you have to promise you won't say a word to anybody."

She stared at him.

"It's big," she said.

He scowled.

"All right," he said. "I promise, goddamn it. What is it?"

She drained her wine.

"Stevens is quitting," she said. "He's announcing it today."

Chapter 2 – PINs and needles

ISMAEL BALUSI STROLLED out of Stevens's suite of offices on the second floor of the Centre Block just before 2 p.m. and the start of Question Period. He looked down over the stone railing into the foyer of the House of Commons and watched as Ellen Simms and a cameraman set themselves up in front of the elaborately carved wooden doors that lead to the chamber. Simms shooed away a print reporter who was standing in the background of her shot and started a live stand-up. Balusi slipped back into his office to watch it on TV.

Jack Macdonald didn't usually go to the foyer before Question Period, but he needed to get his recorder in front of some Newfoundland MPs for his Ramia story, and they might try to dodge him on the way out of the House. He was leaning against the entrance to the chamber when Simms came in, her hips rocking from side to side, heels clicking on the marble floor, red hair bobbing. He watched her with a slow-burning lust, a voice in the back of his head panting and growling like a dog.

He smiled at her, but she ignored him until she had stationed herself in front of the doors, checked her hair and makeup and talked to the control room in Toronto. Then she looked around, noticed Jack and frowned. She took two steps over to him.

"Hi," she said. "You're going to be in our shot there, so if you don't mind just moving to the other side that would be great."

She gave him a smile that lasted about a second and turned away without waiting for a response.

The voice in the back of his head didn't like that: *What the fuck? This is the foyer of the fucking House of Commons. I'll stand wherever the fuck I want to stand.* But Jack obeyed her. He stepped behind her cameraman and watched as she began her standup, straining to hear what she was saying.

"Jim, we can report at this hour that Prime Minister Bruce Stevens is stepping down. Sources have told NTV that he informed his cabinet earlier today that he will stay in office until the end of the year, launching a leadership race to choose his successor – the next leader of the Conservative party, and prime minister of Canada. Mr. Stevens is planning to announce his decision at a news conference this afternoon.

"The prime minister has led the party through three elections, forming three consecutive minorities. I'm told he had promised his wife that he would not fight another election, and he believes that this is the right time for a change. We're told he wants a three-month leadership campaign, so the new leader can take over in March."

She paused and listened to the host in Toronto, nodding her head at the camera.

"That's right, Jim," she said. "This news is sure to send shockwaves throughout Parliament Hill. Everybody will be wondering who will be the next leader, and you can bet the potential candidates are already planning their moves very carefully."

She again nodded and listened to the host.

"Well, Jim, it's early yet to guess who might run, but the two names we hear most often are Public Safety Minister Greg Mowat, from Swift Current, Saskatchewan and Justice Minister Jim Donahoe, from Lunenburg, Nova Scotia. We're hoping to catch them as they come into the chamber now."

MPs were starting to arrive at the Centre Block, none of them aware that the news of Stevens's decision had leaked. Simms's first victim was Emily Wong, the minister for national revenue.

"Ms. Wong," said Simms. "What's your reaction to the prime minister's announcement today?"

"No comment," said Wong. "I think I'd better leave that to the prime minister."

Simms turned to the camera. "There we have what appears to be confirmation of the news that Prime Minister Stevens has told his cabinet colleagues that he is planning to step down." She glanced to the side, "Oh, and here's Jim Donahoe."

With a chiselled jaw, aquiline nose, piercing blue eyes and greying blond hair, the justice minister had the air of an aging soap opera star, and he usually approached the cameras with the ease and comfort of a veteran performer, but he frowned in discomfort when Simms stepped in front of him and the hot light hit his face.

"Mr. Donahoe," she said. "Will you be a candidate to succeed Mr. Stevens?"

The smile on his handsome face soured. "It's far too early for that kind of decision," he said. "I have had some calls, asking me to run, but I haven't had even a moment to consider it, and would have to talk to my wife before I give it any thought at all. We're focusing on the business of government."

He seemed to realize suddenly that he had struck the wrong tone, and frowned. Simms spat another question. "Are those calls from cabinet colleagues? I'm told that so far only the cabinet has been informed."

Donahoe's smile was back.

"I think for the moment we should leave this to the prime minister," he said. "This is the prime minister's decision, and his announcement to make and I'll leave speculation to the, uh, speculators."

And he stepped around Simms and the cameraman.

Mowat was next at the door, striding hurriedly but smiling, the picture of a busy, hard-working silver-haired man with steel-rimmed spectacles, on his way to conduct important business, a faint smile on his face. He was followed closely by his press secretary, Sophie Fortin.

"Mr. Mowat," said Simms. "Will you be a candidate to succeed Mr. Stevens?"

Mowat frowned at the camera. Sophie stepped behind

him, so that she would stay out of the shot, and held her digital recorder over Mowat's shoulder. She was pretty – with a pixie face and spiky brown hair – too pretty to be in the shot with the minister.

"If we're discussing Mr. Stevens's future I think the first thing we should do is look at what he's done for the country," said Mowat, looking at Ellen with sadness, his eyes searching. "Under his leadership we have run a scandal-free government. We've cut taxes, rebuilt the military, got tough on criminals, managed the economy through a very challenging time, and made life better for Canadian families."

As Mowat spoke, reporters started to fill the foyer, rushing down to get in on the action. Jack sidled up as a scrum formed around Mowat, reporters wedging in with their digital recorders outstretched.

Behind Mowat, Sophie pulled her phone out of her holster. The last half-hour had been so frantic, as she and Mowat had worked out his lines, that she hadn't had a chance to look at it. With one hand, she flicked through her messages, holding the phone down at her hip.

"I'm very proud to have worked for Mr. Stevens," Mowat said. "He is an inspiration to us, personally and professionally. If he has, as you say, decided to step down, I think this is a good time to reflect on all he has done for the country, and not a time for personal ambition."

He smiled a sad smile at the camera and turned to go, ignoring the shouted questions.

Sophie was distracted as Mowat stepped toward the chamber, and for a moment she was on camera. She was looking down at her phone, reading a message.

Sujet: URGENT!!!
De: Marie-Hélène Bourassa
A: Sophie Fortin
La police d'Ottawa a besoin de te parler, à propos de ton chum. Il a été gravement blessé. Tu dois appeler la Detective Mallorie Ashton le plus rapidement que possible au 613 555 0376. C'EST TRÈS IMPORTANT!!!

Sophie suddenly felt terribly weak. She hadn't eaten a thing all day, and she'd had too much coffee. The news that Ed had been badly hurt sent her reeling. She took a step back from the minister. Her knees went wobbly. Her vision got dark. Her hands released her phone and digital recorder, and they clattered on the marble floor. Mowat turned at the sound just as she collapsed. Jack was standing behind her, and as she slumped, he caught her under her arms. The camera, which had turned to Simms, swung back a moment too late to catch the fleeting scowl on Mowat's face, but caught him showing concern, rushing back to take one of her arms from Jack and lift her up. Together they dragged her to a bench.

The camera zoomed in on the odd scene just as Sophie's eyes fluttered open, catching her eyes wildly searching around her.

"Tabernac," she said.

Jim Godin's heart sank when his boss, Liberal Leader Evan Pinsent, pushed his bespectacled face through the mustard curtains that separate the House of Commons from the lobby.

Godin, director of communications to the Liberal leader, was bent over his laptop in a corner of the lobby, his narrow shoulders hunched, jabbing at the keyboard as he caught up on emails. He glanced up occasionally at a closed-circuit TV that showed the feed from the House.

Godin was a veteran researcher and spinner, a servant to three Liberal leaders, each less successful than the last. A professional with a modest ego, good judgement and a boundless appetite for work, he had stayed scrupulously neutral in the internecine battles that heralded the coming and going of leaders and their chiefs of staff, and he had risen steadily as others came and went in waves of purges, becoming an increasingly powerful figure in an increasingly ineffective political organization.

While Pinsent's eyes darted around the lobby, casting

about for his director of communications, Godin fought the urge to duck out. Pinsent had spied him and strode toward him now, trailed by Liberal House Leader Wayne Dumaresque, who was holding his cell phone up like an exhibit at a trial.

Godin sat up straight and arranged his angular features to show alert curiosity as the two politicians walked up to him.

"Stevens is announcing his resignation," said Pinsent. "The news just leaked."

Dumaresque was holding up his phone, Godin supposed, to show how they had learned the news.

"Stevens is out?" said Godin.

"We need to rewrite the questions," said Dumaresque.

"This is great news," said Pinsent. "This changes everything."

"Yes sir," said Godin. "It does."

"We need to rewrite the opening questions," said Dumaresque.

"When is he going to announce it?" asked Godin.

"NTV says he's going to hold a news conference after Question Period," said Dumaresque.

"Well that's ridiculous," said Pinsent. "He should announce it to Parliament first."

Dumaresque nodded.

"We should hit him on that."

"I don't know," said Godin. "I'm not sure we should hit him today, not personally. His supporters are going to be sad to see him go. Our supporters are going to be glad to see the back of him. No point hitting a sour note."

Pinsent shook his head, blinking his eyes rapidly. His cheeks coloured.

"This fits into the pattern of his disdain for Parliament," he said. "Even now, when he's announcing his departure, he shows his lack of respect for this chamber. It goes to his hidden agenda."

Pinsent looked from Godin to Dumaresque and back.

"Can you bang out something like that?" he asked.

Godin sucked hard at his cheeks. "Sure," he said. "But I'll have to be fast. We haven't got much time."

Sophie Fortin was waiting on the steps under the Peace Tower
when Ashton pulled up in an unmarked police cruiser. Ashton
could tell it was Sophie because of her pale face and anxious
look. *Jesus*, Ashton thought. *So young and vulnerable.* She had
to be twenty-five, but she looked twelve, a tiny girl in heavy
makeup, high-heeled boots, a fashionably tailored winter
coat, looked like it was from Montreal, and a laptop bag slung
from her shoulder.

Ashton got out of the car.

"Sophie?" she said. "I'm Detective Sergeant Ashton."

Sophie stepped down to the car and Ashton opened the
passenger door for her.

"I'm so sorry to be the bearer of bad news," she said as
Sophie settled into the passenger's seat.

"How is he? How's Ed?" said Sophie, looking straight
ahead. "I want to see him."

"I'm going to take you there now," said Ashton, putting
the car into gear. "It's probably better that the doctor explain
the situation to you. Ed was pulled from the Rideau Canal
early this morning. We don't know how he ended up in the
water, but I can tell you that he nearly died and he hasn't
regained consciousness."

Sophie started to cry, her face crumpling in sorrow, tears
dripping off her nose, her makeup running as she dug through
her purse for a tissue.

Ashton drove in silence for a moment then pulled over in
front of the West Block, just before the security checkpoint.

Sophie was weeping into her tissue, hunched over, her
tiny shoulders shaking.

Ashton put her hand on her shoulder.

"I know this is hard," she said.

Sophie choked and sputtered and pulled the tissue away
from her nose, trailing a long string of snot.

"I'm so scared," she said.

"I know," said Ashton, thinking, Jesus, this never gets

easier. Then she remembered, it does get easier. During her first nights, years ago, walking a beat in the Byward Market, she'd often hauled hopeless drunks and addicts to the drunk tank, so pained by their misery that she had to struggle to let go at the end of a shift. To survive in the job, she had had to grow thicker skin, and she now observed the pain of others with professional detachment. Aware of her detachment now, with a crying girl in the car next to her, made her feel a pang of guilt, as though she had somehow let Sophie down. She squeezed Sophie's shoulder again.

"You've got to be strong right now, though, OK? For Ed. He'd want you to help the police. We've got to find out what happened. OK?"

Sophie nodded and Ashton took another tissue from the package in the girl's bag. She thought about wiping her nose, but couldn't manage that level of intimacy. She handed Sophie the tissue.

"I want to go to the hospital," Sophie said, drying her eyes and sitting up straight. "I want to see him."

Ashton put the car in gear. As they turned from the Hill onto Wellington Street, Sophie was staring ahead, her face rigid.

"When is the last time you saw Ed?"

"Last night. We had dinner at the pub, at D'Arcy McGee's. I had work to do, so I went home, but he stayed on with a friend for more drinks."

"Who was the friend?" asked Ashton.

"Jack Macdonald," Sophie said. "A reporter."

"Were you expecting him home last night?"

"Yes, of course," said Sophie. "But I expected him late. When he goes out with Jack, they usually stay out late. When he wasn't home this morning, I thought he'd crashed at Jack's."

"Do you have contact information for Macdonald?"

Sophie pulled out her phone. "What's your email?" she asked, and sent the officer Jack's co-ordinates.

"Sophie, would you say Ed was a binge drinker?" asked Ashton.

Sophie started crying again. "You said 'was' like he's dead."

Ashton grimaced. "I'm sorry, Sophie," she said. "I spend a lot of time investigating homicides, so it's a bad habit. But no. Ed is alive. You're going to see him soon."

Sophie choked back her tears. "He is a drinker," she said. "He likes to drink. Yes. And sometimes he gets drunk. Yes."

"I don't want to upset you," said Ashton. "But we have reason to believe somebody might have tried to drown him. We can't be sure of that, but it's possible. Can you think of anybody who would want to kill him?"

Sophie shook her head vehemently. "No. Everybody likes him. Nobody would want to kill him."

"Okay," said Ashton. "I suspect he had too much to drink and fell in the canal, but we have to check out all the possibilities."

They were getting close to the hospital.

"I have one more question," she said. "When he was pulled out of the canal, his BlackBerry was missing. Did he have it with him when you saw him at D'Arcy's?"

"Yes," said Sophie, "and I know that he had it with him later because he used it to send me PINs."

"PINs?" said Ashton.

"Private BlackBerry messages," said Sophie. "We exchanged PINs all night."

Ashton pulled up in front of the hospital.

"I need you to send me a copy of all the PINs he sent," she said. "Okay?"

Jack ignored the vibration in his phone holster as he made his way to his seat in the jammed gallery overlooking the House of Commons. Thanks to the leaked news, there was a full house of reporters today – rumpled print and radio reporters, carefully groomed TV reporters, freelancers and oddballs from strange newsletters – all waiting, pens poised, earpieces plugged in, as the prime minister strolled to his seat just as the Speaker, in his black robe and tri-cornered hat, rose to his feet.

"Oral questions," said the speaker. "Questions orale. The Honourable Leader of the Opposition."

The Liberal MPs applauded as Pinsent stood up to ask the first question of the day. He waited for their applause to die with a pensive look.

"Mr. Speaker," said Pinsent, "today we learned from a media leak that the prime minister intends to step down, and intends to let the country know in a news conference, rather than here in the House of Commons. Obsessive secrecy has been a hallmark of the prime minister's government, and it is plain that nothing has changed even as he leaves office. Why, Mr. Speaker, did the prime minister not plan to make his announcement in this place?"

The Liberals all applauded, but the Conservatives reacted in different ways. Some groaned in indignation. Others, who had not heard that Stevens was rumoured to be resigning, strained to look at him, their expressions uncertain.

Stevens stood and smiled blandly. "Mr. Speaker, I would have thought the leader of the Liberal Party would be delighted by the news." His MPs laughed and slapped their desks. Stevens smiled his little smile. "I can't count the number of times the honourable member has called for my resignation," he said. "At last he is about to have it, but he is unhappy with the manner of its delivery. I suggest the leader of the Liberal Party is very difficult to please."

The Conservatives laughed and applauded.

Pinsent rose from his seat. "Mr. Speaker," he said. "We have become accustomed to the prime minister dodging questions in this place, but this is ridiculous. We are discussing his own political future. We have often observed that the prime minister is pursuing a hidden agenda, because he knows most Canadians do not support his Republican-style policies. This is surely the worst example yet. He is keeping the news of his own resignation secret!" Pinsent smiled as if he had landed a good one, and paused to enjoy the moment before he continued. "Again, Mr. Speaker, I ask: Why did the prime minister not plan to make his announcement here, in the House of Commons?"

The Liberals stood and applauded, but they looked like soldiers doing their duty, and the Tories laughed.

Stevens wore a big smile as he rose to his feet.

"Mr. Speaker, I will now reveal my hidden agenda," he said. "I'd like to announce, as I had indeed planned to do in this place today, that I will step down as prime minister and leader of the Conservative Party of Canada in March."

The Tory benches erupted in groans of "No!"

Stevens held his hand to silence the backbenchers. "I'd like to take a moment to thank my constituents in Whitby for their steadfast support. And my family ... All of us in this House know that public life, while rewarding, takes a toll on our families, and I'd like to thank my wife, Karen, for her endless patience." He waved up to her, and MPs on both sides of the House turned, noticing for the first time that she was sitting in the gallery. She waved back at him, smiling.

"And I'd like to thank my children. Their dad missed a lot of skating practices, a lot of piano recitals, and that has been hard." He frowned down at his lectern for a moment. The chamber was still. "So it really does delight me to announce that I will step down on March 9, and I want to let Sarah and Leslie know that they'll soon be seeing more of their dad than they like."

As he sat down, every Conservative MP stood and applauded. Bloc and NDP MPs joined in, staying in their seats and politely clapping for little Sarah and Leslie. Eventually even Pinsent, red-faced and angry-looking, joined in the applause, followed by his caucus.

Jack's phone vibrated again, and he pulled it out of its holster. It is against the rules to talk on a cell phone in the gallery, so he clicked the do-not-answer button, and looked at the screen: Ottawa Police Service. He stepped out into the hallway and called his voicemail.

"Mr. Macdonald, this is Detective Sergeant Devon Flanagan, of the Ottawa Police Service. We'd like to speak with you as soon as possible about Ed Sawatski. Mr. Sawatski suffered an injury early this morning and we understand you were with him last night. So it's urgent that you call us."

After Pinsent's questions, when the Opposition critics stood to ask routine questions about their files, in the government staffer gallery above the floor of the House, Ismael Balusi slid down on the wooden bench to chat with Dave Cochrane, chief of staff to Jim Donahoe.

"Pretty good, eh?" he said.

Cochrane looked over at him.

"Jesus, the old guy has some moves," he said. "I can't believe Pinsent attacked him on that, today. Are we writing his lines?"

"I'm not sure we could write lines so dumb," said Balusi, and stifled a giggle. He looked nervously over his shoulder at the House of Commons constables, who were supposed to make sure everyone in the galleries listened to the debates in silence.

"Meet you in the hallway in a minute," he said.

Cochrane nodded his agreement.

Balusi was leaning against the wall in the narrow hallway that runs behind the galleries, reading emails, when Cochrane came out.

"How's Donahoe doing?" asked Balusi.

"Good," said Cochrane. "We think we're starting ahead."

"We ought to be ahead, but that wasn't great today. 'I'll leave speculation to the speculators.' Mowat looked a lot smoother. He had better lines."

Cochrane didn't respond for a minute. "We didn't think we'd need lines so early. We didn't think it would leak."

"All the rules are out the window now," said Balusi. "We've got to adjust our thinking. Who do you think leaked Stevens' announcement today? Cui Bono? Got to be Mowat. We got to be thinking the same way. It's the difference between the winner and the loser. Having the right lines at the right moment. Controlling the agenda. Looking good when the other guy looks stupid. Today our guy looked stupid and the other guy looked good."

Cochrane sighed. "You're right. We've got to pick up our game, but there's no reason to panic. We've got half the cabinet locked up, De Grandpré is going to run. You think those red Quebec Tories are going to go to Mowat in a convention? That family values shit doesn't go over so good in *la belle province*."

"Yeah," said Balusi. "I know. But De Grandpré will go with whoever he thinks the winner will be. Right now, he likely thinks he can win, the dumb fuck. Same with Thompson. In the end, these guys will go with the front runner. Right now they don't know. It would be a good time to give them a sign."

Cochrane laughed. "You're not going to get an argument from me. Got any ideas?"

"Maybe," said Balusi. He bit his lip and looked around. "Quebec. There are seventy-five riding associations there. Most of them have a dozen Conservative members at most, and each of those riding associations has as much weight in a leadership race as Calgary Southwest, which has, what, 3,000 members? It's the easiest way to get a head-start. They should like your guy. He's an old Tory, like them. They sure won't naturally gravitate to Pastor Mowat. If I were you I'd send your guy to Quebec, meet with some of the old Bleus, get them on side. You line up enough riding associations, you'll have Mowat beat before he gets started."

Ashton grimaced as she followed Sophie into the hospital room. She wasn't looking forward to this.

Ed Sawatski's parents were beside his bed, the mother looking desperate and scared, holding her son's hand. Her husband was trying to comfort her, with his hand on her shoulder, rubbing her back.

"Oh my God," said Sophie, and ran to the bedside.

Beverly Sawatski started to cry, and reached to draw Sophie to her. Tom Sawatski tried to put his arms around both of them. "There, there," he said, but he started to sob too.

It was the first look Ashton had had at Sawatski since they hauled him from the canal that morning. He was lying on his back, with a tube in his mouth, and an IV in his arm. A heart monitor pinged along steadily next to the bed.

Sophie clutched his hand and stared at his inanimate face. "Oh, Ed," she whispered. "Ed. Can you hear me?" But he just lay there, eyes closed, unmoving.

Ashton slipped out into the hallway and called Flanagan on her cell phone.

"Hey," he said. "You talk to the girl?"

"Yeah," said Ashton. "I just brought her to the hospital. She's in there now. Jesus."

"She broke up?" asked Flanagan.

"Pretty distraught," said Ashton. "I don't like her for this. No way. And the parents are in there, too. Just flew in from St. John's."

"She knows where he was last night?"

"Yeah. He was out drinking with a reporter, guy named Jack Macdonald."

"That checks," said Flanagan. "We've got a tape from the Chateau, shows two guys walking down from the Hill at 4:40 this morning, going down the stairs by the bridge. Maybe they are our two."

"Any chance of getting a solid ID?"

"The camera is too far away, and the landing at the top of the stairs down under the bridge is on the edge of the frame. You can just see two figures, for about five seconds, walking down the trail that runs along the edge of the bluff, then they disappear down the stairs."

"Did you find the cab driver who drove the kids home?" said Ashton.

"Not so far. It would have been a Gatineau taxi, so it could be couple different firms. They tell me they're asking all their drivers, but nobody has volunteered any info yet. Maybe later today or tomorrow. The night shift guys might not even be on the job yet."

"All right," said Ashton. "I'd better go in and talk to the parents. Christ."

When she walked back in, Sophie was holding one of Sawatski's hands and his mother was holding the other. The mother was talking to him very quietly.

"Excuse me," said Ashton from the doorway. "I'm Detective Sergeant Mallorie Ashton of the Ottawa Police Service, and I'm investigating your son's injury. I'm so sorry about what happened."

Tom Sawatski stood to shake her hand.

"What can you tell us?" he said. "What happened to our son?"

"Ed's an excellent swimmer," said Beverly Sawatski. "He was a lifeguard. This just doesn't make sense."

"I know," said Ashton. "We're trying to get to the bottom of it. I'd like to take a statement from one of you, if you feel you can manage it."

"I'll give you a statement," said Tom.

"Okay," said Ashton. "I'll go see if there's an office here we can use."

She turned to Sophie. "And Sophie, if you can forward me those messages now, please."

Sophie nodded and pulled out her phone.

Beverly Sawatski stayed at her son's side.

"Oh my God," she blurted. "Oh thank God."

Ed's eyes were open.

By JACK MACDONALD
Ottawa Bureau
OTTAWA – Liberal MPs stuck up for Len Ramia on Tuesday after the RCMP charged the senator with fraud for allegedly misusing Senate property by using government furniture, art and computer equipment in his home.

Newfoundland's Liberal MPs say Ramia should keep receiving his $132,000-a-year salary until the trial.

"The Senate has its rules," said Humber-St. Barbe—Baie Verte MP Loyola Quoyle. "And we have to respect the principle of innocent until proven guilty."

Ramia was appointed to the Senate by Prime Minister Jean Chretien in 1998 after working as the key Newfoundland organizer in his campaign for the Liberal leadership. At the time, critics described the appointment of the former insurance industry executive as a reward for his work as party bagman.

Since then, Ramia has been a low key senator, shunning the spotlight and avoiding committee work.

"Lord Jesus," said Jack.

He shook his head, which hurt his neck. He was sweating at his desk, struggling with the Ramia story, and finding it very difficult to concentrate. Since Flanagan had told him that Sawatski had wound up in the canal, nearly dead, Jack could think of nothing else. He had to file his story before he went to the police station, but as soon as he started to write, his mind wandered to the night before. Guilt gnawed at him, as if Ed's accident were somehow his fault, but he had only the haziest memory of the evening's events, which left him running over the few moments that he could remember again and again. He had to force himself to type up his story so he could get to the police station.

He banged out another ten inches, hit save, then send, and called the desk to make sure the file had arrived. Then he left the Hot Room, walked downstairs, and stepped out through the heavy brass doors under the Peace Tower, where he hunched against the cold wind and lit a cigarette. For the first time, as he walked toward the parking lot, he had time to think about the night before, and what he would tell the police.

He had met Ed and Sophie at D'Arcy's, where he had a shepherd's pie and the first beer of the evening. The three of them had gossiped about politics. He had tried to draw them out about who would be likely to replace Stevens if he stepped down before the next election. Since Sophie worked for Mowat and Ed worked for Donahoe, the two ministers most likely to get the keys to 24 Sussex, Jack had tried to provoke them into arguing about who had the better chance, in the hope that they would spill secrets, but they saw through him and laughed it off.

When Sophie tapped out after dinner, Jack was tempted to do the same, but Ed was in a drinking mood: animated, funny, laughing, singing, buying rounds, flirting with girls at the bar, and Jack decided to have another drink or two.

They did some shots at the bar, where they chatted up three Inuit girls for a while, bureaucrats from Aboriginal Affairs. Then there was another bar, Quatre Jeudis, in Hull, where they tried to hit on Quebec hotties, but were restrained by their increasing and obvious drunkenness and their bad French.

They ate greasy poutine at 2 a.m. Then they were in a cab, and then they were at Pigale, reeling into the strip bar in time to order two beers each at last call. After that, everything was fuzzy. Jack could remember the naked bodies of the tattooed Montreal biker chicks who danced there, and he could remember Ed going for a lap dance, while he sat and waited, drinking beer and leering at the dancers. Then there was another cab, which he remembered getting into, but after that, nothing.

It wasn't going to be fun telling the cops about it.

Tim Balfour sat in his office with the door closed, wasting time on one of his computers by trying out a new first-person shooter: blowing up aliens inside a spaceship, flicking from flamethrower to rocket launcher, expertly turning alien gunmen into chunks of meat.

The call was taking longer than he expected. The little Chinese slut must be slacking off.

Then, sure enough, the phone rang.

He paused the game. His screen instantly reverted to his desktop and he picked up his phone.

"Balfour here," he said.

"Um, excuse me, Tim," the voice said. "This is Eileen Sing-Chu. I seem to be having a problem with my computer. I can't access the network. It's rejecting my password. I've rebooted twice, but it doesn't want to work."

He grinned, and rubbed his big tummy with both hands.

"Did you make sure caps lock is off?" he asked.

"Yes I did," she said.

Of course you did, you little hottie, he thought.

"Okay," he said. "I'll be right out to have a look."

During lunch, while she was in the cafeteria, he had reset Eileen Sing-Chu's password. She was new and by far the cutest girl to work in the encryption section of Canadian Security Establishment, maybe the prettiest girl to ever work there. She wore glasses, but she was pretty and sporty, with an appealingly boyish body, and she didn't seem to know she was pretty. Perfect.

The encryption section of CSE, Canada's secretive electronic intelligence agency, employed math geeks, mostly pimply, awkward boy-men like him, the type who knew enough not to wear pocket protectors, but had to fight the impulse. Balfour, an overweight, prematurely balding, socially awkward computer whiz, was unlucky with women, a fact that was not far from his mind when he hired staff. It was at the front of his mind when he hired Sing-Chu, and he was now planning on giving her computer a series of problems that he would have to solve, giving him a chance to hang around her desk, look down her top, get to know her, see if there was any way he could get into her little Chinese panties.

He was standing up to go when his second desk phone rang.

"Balfour here," he said.

"Hello," said the deep male voice on the other end. "Do you know who this is?"

Balfour sat down.

"I do," he said. "Are you calling from a secure line?"

"I'm calling from my desk phone."

"Hold on," said Balfour, and he flicked a switch on the

side of the phone.

"Okay," he said. "We're encrypted. Go ahead."

"All right," said the voice. "I've got a job for you. I want you to try to locate a stolen BlackBerry for us. This is right from the top, and we need it in real time. Okay? We can't afford to go through channels."

"Have you got the PIN and the phone number?" said Balfour.

"I do. Ready?"

The voice read out the seven-digit code, a mix of numbers and letters, and then the telephone number.

"Got that?"

Balfour read it all back.

"Good," said the voice. "When you get a read out, let me know the location. Got it?"

"Yup," said Balfour. "On it."

The line went dead.

Shit, he thought. No time for games. He quickly reset Eileen Sing-Chu's password and called her to tell her to reboot.

Then he booted up a computer underneath his desk, and launched a program that disguised his computer's ISPN on the internal network. After it was running, he plugged the computer into the network. It would now appear to any network administrators bored enough to be watching, that an extra computer had come online in the Digital Intelligence Interception branch of CSEC.

He typed in a password and username he had previously stolen using a keystroke capture program on a computer in his office used by a visiting DII agent.

He found the cell-phone tracking program used by DII agents, opened the interface and started wrestling with the problem.

Every time anyone uses a cell phone, the unit sends a radio signal, which, in a city, is picked up by a number of towers. Those towers send each other signals to decide which tower will handle the call. By measuring the signal strength at each tower and triangulating, the network can quickly estimate the location of any cell phone, but it took 10 minutes for Balfour to figure out how to make the program do that.

Once he had it figured out, he entered the PIN number and phone number and sat back to watch it work.

Jack's BlackBerry vibrated on his hip while he was waiting for a light on O'Connor Street. It was a message from Sophie asking him to call.

She started crying when she heard his voice. "Oh, Jack. Did you hear about Ed?"

The light changed and Jack pulled into the intersection.

"I'm on the way to the police station now," he said. "It's terrible. I wish I had stayed with him. I'm so sorry. I don't know how it happened. I should have been with him. We were both so drunk."

Sophie choked back her tears and spoke just as Jack's BlackBerry beeped in his ear, the signal that the battery was running down.

"What?" he said. "I'm sorry. What did you say?"

"It's awful," she said. "He opened his eyes but he's just staring. It's like he's not even there."

"Oh God," said Jack. "I don't know. It's early days yet. He might come around yet. Jesus. I'll come see him after I go talk to the police."

"You can't get in to see him today," said Sophie. "Only family can get in until he's out of critical condition."

"Oh, Jesus," said Jack.

"What happened?" said Sophie. "Why didn't he come home last night?"

"I'm just on my way to the police station now," he said. "I don't know what happened. We were out till late, Christ, till Pigale closed. Then we took a cab. I think he dropped me off first. But it's hard to remember. Christ. We were shitfaced."

Sophie started crying. "I'd better go back in there," she sniffled, and she hung up.

"Lord Jesus," said Jack. He cursed at the horror of the situation, and at his phone, which was running down. At the next light, he remembered that he had another one in his pocket.

"Fuck," he said, and pulled over and dug it out, thinking he could use the battery from Sawatski's BlackBerry. He had a vague memory, suddenly, of Ed slipping it into his pocket when he went for the lap dance.

Jack punched at it, tried to look at the inbox, but it was password-protected.

He tried SOPHIE, but that didn't work.

He lit a smoke and thought about it, then opened the back of the phone, took out the battery and popped it into the back of his own.

The first time the cell phone that Balfour was tracking sent out a signal, it bounced off seven towers in downtown Ottawa. After about thirty seconds, the tracking program he was staring at lit up over Ottawa on a map of North America. He hit zoom and waited while the map redrew itself. The second signal came in while the map was redrawing, and Balfour's computer crunched it and came up with a fifty-square-metre signal zone, centred at the corner of Lisgar and O'Connor.

"Bingo," said Balfour. "Bingo, bingo, bingo. Take that, mofo."

He whipped out his BlackBerry and typed a message.

To: 74X93B4
From: 58K42E6
Subject: BB location
The BlackBerry in question is at the corner of O'Connor and Lisgar.

As he pressed send, Sawatski's BlackBerry sent another roaming signal, and when Balfour looked again, the signal zone had moved south, to the corner of Gladstone and O'Connor.

He sent another message.

To: 74X93B4
From: 58K42E6
Subject: It's moving
Now at Gladstone and O'Connor.

He quickly had a reply.

To: 58K42E6
From: 74X93B4
Subject: Can you set up remote tracking?
We need to follow it.

Balfour pulled on his bottom lip and thought about it. Shouldn't be too hard. Just go under the interface, find the code with the latitude and longitude, set up a little mailer program to forward it. He'd have to write a bit of code for the recipient phone, but that should be easy, an add-on for a mapping program. But just as he started to type a message saying that he could do it, the dot disappeared from Balfour's screen.

Flanagan had started a timeline on the Sawatski case, and when Ashton forwarded him the messages from Sophie, he added them to the document.

Approx 6 p.m.: Subject meets Sophie Fortin and Jack Macdonald at Darcy McGee's. They eat. Subject drinks three or four beers.

Approx 8 p.m.: Fortin leaves D'Arcy's.

10:15 p.m.:
De: Sophie Fortin
A: Ed Sawatski
Sujet: Come home
I'm finished work and I'm bored.

10:28 p.m.:
To: Sophie Fortin
From: Ed Sawatski
Subject: No way
Me and Jack are macking on Eskimo hotties.

10:32 p.m.:

De: Sophie Fortin
A: Ed Sawatski
Sujet: Enjoy them
Just have a shower before you come to bed. :-p

11:45 p.m.:
De: Sophie Fortin
A: Ed Sawatski
Sujet: Going to bed
I hope you got lucky with the Inuit ladies, cause I'm going to sleep.

12:18 p.m.
From: Ed Sawatski
To: Sophie Fortin
Subject: Going to Quatre Jeudi
You should come! We can parlez vous.

12:32 p.m.:
De: Sophie Fortin
A: Ed Sawatski
Sujet: No way!
I have an early morning tomorrow.
And so do you!
Have fun.
Bisous!

2:20 a.m.:
From: Ed Sawatski
To: Sophie Fortin
Subject: Viva le Quebec Libre
If Quebec separates, we totally are keeping poutine.
Mmmm. Poutine.

3:12 a.m.:
From: Ed Sawatski
To: Sophie Fortin
Subject: Pigale
Nonne of these bitches is hot like you.
But I'm going to get a lap dancce with this trashy little biler chick.
But don't worry. I'll get Jack to hold my bb.
Love you.
:*

4:48 a.m. Security video from Chateau Laurier shows two men walking from Parliament Hill to the Rideau Canal locks.
5:25 a.m. Sawatski discovered in canal by Isabelle Galarneau.

When it was finished, Flanagan emailed a copy to his partner and printed one for himself. Then he took a deep breath. He had already called his son to let him know that he might not be able to take him to the game. Jason had sounded quiet and sad, so he told him he was chasing some real bad guys, but he'd try to finish up in time.

While he was on the phone, he got a call from reception. It had to be Macdonald. He told Jason he loved him and headed down the stairs to fetch the reporter.

The kid looked like shit. He had a wine stain on his lapel. His face was pale and his hair was messy. They shook hands in the hallway, and Flanagan led him upstairs. He had already decided to talk to the reporter in one of the interview rooms, which had a window out into the squad room, not one of the shitty little concrete interrogation rooms. Play it nice.

He sat down with his notebook, a digital recorder and the time line. Macdonald pulled out his own notebook and digital recorder and switched on the recorder.

Flanagan looked at him over his glasses. "You recording this, too?" he said.

"I don't need a lawyer, do I?" said Jack, looking around the room with unease. "I want to help you. But this makes me nervous."

"You are entitled to a lawyer if you feel you would benefit from one," said Flanagan. "But we don't even know if there's been a crime. That's what we're trying to figure out." He switched on his recorder. "What time did you meet Fortin and Sawatski?"

"About 6:30. Me and Sophie were there first, then Ed arrived."

"And you stayed at Darcy's for how long?"

"Well, Sophie left around 8:30. She had work to do, she said, so Ed and I were on our own. We had a few more drinks, tried to hit on some girls."

Flanagan looked down at his notes. "These were Inuit girls?" he asked. "Is that right?"

Jack was surprised he knew that. "Yeah," he said. "We

chatted them up for a while, had a few more drinks, but D'Arcy's was getting dead, so we decided to go to Quatre Jeudis."

"In Hull."

"That's right. It was hopping. So we had a few more beers. We got pretty loaded."

"And then you had poutine?"

"Yes, at that greasy little place on Portage, a pizza joint."

"Then you went to Pigale?"

"It was Ed's idea," said Jack. "But he didn't have to talk me into it really. We were pretty loaded."

"And what happened there?"

"We ordered some beers. It was last call, so Ed got us each two beers and we sat down to watch the girls."

"Did either of you get a lap dance?"

"Ed did," said Jack. "He wanted me to get one, too, but I was too hammered. So he went off on his own, left me at the table."

"Did you get into any disputes while you were there? Any hassles with bouncers or other customers?"

"No, we're not those kinds of drunks. We were having fun, but low-key."

"Did Sawatski express fear at any time?" asked Flanagan. "Did he say he was worried about someone harming him?"

"No, but to be honest with you my memory of the last part of the evening isn't too good. We were really hammered. Like, really hammered. I felt terrible this morning. Still don't feel too good, as a matter of fact." Jack rubbed the bridge of his nose. "I have a hazy memory of Ed telling me something, something he thought was important, while we were at Pigale, just before he went to get his lap dance, but I can't bring it back. It's just ... gone."

Flanagan leaned in. "Did you and Ed argue at any point in the evening? Were you upset with him?"

Jack shook his head. "No way. We were having fun. We weren't upset or angry or anything. No."

"What would you say if I told you the bouncers at Pigale said you two almost had a fight? That you seemed very upset with him?"

"I'd say they were confused. Or lying. It's bullshit. Are you making it up? I think you are." He stared at Flanagan hard. "Are cops allowed to make shit up?"

"All right," said Flanagan. "Forget it. I've got to ask lots of questions." He turned back to his timeline. "What time did you get a cab?"

"I've no idea. Four? What time does Pigale kick out its customers? Whenever that is."

"Do you remember the cab company?"

Jack looked up at the ceiling. "No. Not at all. I barely remember getting into it, and I don't remember much after that."

Flanagan leaned back in his chair and looked away from Jack. "Do you remember going up to Parliament Hill?"

"No," said Jack. "I'd remember that."

Flanagan looked at him sceptically. "Do you remember walking down, you and Ed, going under the bridge by the canal, at about ten to five?"

Jack looked at him like he had two heads. "No," he said. "That didn't happen."

Flanagan stared at him, hard. "What would you say if I told you I had a video that shows you and Ed walking down there together?"

Jack stared back, just as hard. "I'd say you were making shit up again. Jesus. What the fuck is this? I'll tell you what happened. The cab dropped me off at my place. Ed didn't get out. After that, I have no idea where he went or what he did, or how he ended up in the canal. I know he lives by the canal. Was he drunk enough to wander over and fall into it, pass out? I don't know. I've got no idea. But I know I wasn't with him, at any point, near the canal, and I don't know who was." He stood up, shaking his head. "Is that clear? Jesus. Maybe I do need a lawyer."

Flanagan stood up, too. "Settle down, settle down. I have to ask all kinds of questions. Just because I ask you a question doesn't mean I'm accusing you of anything." He smiled, and gestured towards Jack's seat. "Sit down. You're making me nervous."

Jack sat down again, and then Flanagan did the same.

"Okay," he said. "I think that's everything I wanted to ask you for now. Is there anything you want to add? Anything you think might help us with our investigation?"

Jack stared out into the squad room. "Uh, I'd like to add that I had nothing to do with putting Ed in the water, and I hope you have more clues than you seem to."

"All right, wise guy," said Flanagan, thinking that if he finished the interview now, he could still pick up Jason and make it to the second period of the game. He sighed.

"Okay," he said, standing. "That'll do for now. I'll follow up with you in the next couple of days."

Jack was in the car and halfway home before he realized he still had Ed's BlackBerry in his pocket. Flanagan hadn't even asked him about it.

Chapter 3 – Triangulation

JIM DONAHOE ARRIVED at Ed's bedside at 7 p.m., sticking his handsome face in the open doorway and knocking quietly. Dave Cochrane stood behind him.

Sophie and Beverly Sawatski were sitting on each side of the hospital bed, and Tom Sawatski was next to his wife, holding her hand. They all looked up when Donahoe knocked.

"Oh, Minister Donahoe," said Sophie, jumping up. "It's good of you to come. You must be so busy."

"I came as soon as I could get away, Sophie," he said. "It's a madhouse on the Hill today, with Stevens' announcement, but I wanted to see Ed as soon as possible."

He turned to Tom Sawatski and stretched out his hand. "I'm Jim Donahoe. None of us can believe that this has happened. We are so impressed by your son's work, and we hope that he'll recover and be back in the office very soon."

Beverly Sawatski started to sob quietly.

"Well, the doctor doesn't know how soon that might happen," said Tom Sawatski. "We're hoping for the best. They don't know whether ... "

He looked away and then sat down and took his wife's hand again.

Donahoe stepped over to the bed where Ed was staring blankly at the ceiling.

"Ed," he said. "I don't know if you can hear me, but we're all pulling for you. We need you to get better and back to the office just as soon as you're able. We know what a fighter you are, and we're counting on you to fight this."

He stood for a moment, then squeezed Ed's hand and

stepped away from the bed. He took a pen and a business card from his pocket, wrote down his cell number and passed it to Tom Sawatski. "This is my number. If there's anything I can do for you, call me anytime."

He noticed Cochrane standing in the doorway. "Dave, give them your card as well, will you?" He motioned toward Dave. "This is Dave Cochrane, my chief of staff. He worked with Ed, and I want him to keep closely in touch with you. It would mean a lot to us if you could keep us in the loop."

Beverly Sawatski cleared her throat. Her eyes were red and her cheeks were wet with tears.

"There isn't much of a loop, Mr. Donahoe," she said. Then she excused herself and walked out of the room.

Donahoe looked at her husband. "I'm sorry," he said. "We just want to keep track of his progress."

"It's okay," said Tom Sawatski. "She's just very upset." Then he wiped his eyes and followed his wife out into the hallway.

Donahoe turned to Sophie. She stood hugging herself. Her eyes were bloodshot and her cheeks tear-stained.

"Sophie," he said. "I can't even imagine how awful this is for you, but I need to ask you a question."

Sophie nodded.

"The police told Dave here that Ed's BlackBerry is missing," he said. "This is a potential security breach, and we're concerned. As a policy adviser, Ed was involved with some very sensitive files, and we're worried that if his phone fell into the wrong hands, it could have serious consequences."

Sophie shook her head. "I don't know where it is."

Cochrane spoke up. "Do you know what Ed was doing last night?"

"He was out drinking with Jack Macdonald."

"The reporter?"

"Yes."

Cochrane and Donahoe exchanged looks.

"And you have no idea where the BlackBerry is?" asked Cochrane.

"No."

Donahoe patted her shoulder. "I'm sorry we have to bother you with these questions. You're being very brave. Minister Mowat is lucky to have such a great person working for him. You look after Ed and the Sawatskis."

He stepped away and started for the elevators, but Cochrane lingered.

"Sophie," he said. "This could be very important. If you get any idea of where Ed's BlackBerry is, I need you to let me know. Even before the police. It's a question of national security."

Sophie nodded, he squeezed her arm and turned to go.

In the lobby, as Donahoe and Cochrane waited for the elevator, the door opened and Greg Mowat and Donahoe came unexpectedly face to face. Mowat's face turned momentarily into a scowl, then brightened. He was trailed by Claude Bouchard, his chief of staff.

"Jim!" said Mowat. "You must have come to look in on Ed. How is the poor fellow?"

"He hasn't said a word since they pulled him from the water. His parents and Sophie were sitting with him when I arrived. They're very upset."

"I can well imagine," said Mowat. "A terrible shock. And do the doctors know how long it might be before the boy pulls out of this?"

Donahoe shook his head. "No idea when or if."

"Well I just wanted to peek in on Sophie," Mowat said. "She must be beside herself."

The Sawatskis had returned to their son's bedside by the time Mowat arrived.

"Minister!" said Sophie, and jumped to her feet.

"I'm sorry to barge in," he said. "But I wanted to see how you were doing, Sophie."

She rushed toward him and gave him a hug. He pulled her to him, and patted her back. Then she remembered herself and pulled herself away, flustered and crying. Mowat pulled a hanky from his pocket and gave it to her. Then he turned to the Sawatskis.

"I'm Greg Mowat," he said, reaching out to shake Tom

Sawatski's hand.

"I can't imagine what you're going through. My daughter Clarissa was badly hurt in a fall from a horse a few years ago. She had a broken leg, a concussion, was unconscious when we got to the hospital. Maude and I were frightened out of our wits. There's nothing worse than sitting by the hospital bed of your own child. We sure did some praying."

Beverley Sawatski looked up from her chair, holding her son's hand in her own.

"It's just so frightening," she said. "The doctors can't tell us anything."

"Well, Ed will be in my prayers," said Mowat. "And Maude's. She's been praying for your boy ever since I called to tell her what happened.

He walked over to the bed and looked down at Ed, who was still staring unblinkingly at the ceiling. "Son, we know you're a fighter. We're pulling for you."

He shook hands again with Ed's father, and held Ed's mother's hands in his. "I just know your boy's going to come through."

He turned to his press secretary. "Sophie. Will you walk with me to the elevator?"

Bouchard was waiting for them in an empty waiting room by the elevators, his laptop open in front of him. He stood and gave Sophie a hug.

"I'm sorry to do this to you right now," he said, "but I have to ask you a few questions. It's a police investigation and we have to know what's going on."

Sophie nodded sat down, quickly gathered her thoughts and professionally told them what she knew about the night before.

"That poor boy sure has a wild side, going off to the French ballet with a reporter till all hours," said Mowat, shaking his head.

"Did he send you any messages?" asked Bouchard.

"Yes," said Sophie.

"I need you to give me your BlackBerry for a minute or

two," he said.

Sophie handed it over. "They're kind of personal."

"We need to figure this out, Sophie," he said. "We might be able to find something that helps the police."

"I already gave them the messages Ed sent me last night," she said.

"All the more reason we need to see them," he said.

Bouchard plugged her cell phone into a USB cord and bent to the keyboard.

Sophie looked at Mowat. "I'm afraid of what you'll think of me when you read all my messages."

Mowat gave her a reassuring smile. "I can tell you right now that there's nothing on that phone that can change the way we feel about you and your work. You have nothing to worry about." He squeezed her shoulders. "Okay?"

She nodded.

"Now there's one more thing," he said. "Do you know where Ed's BlackBerry got to?"

She shook her head. "No. I told the police and Jim Donahoe the same thing. He had it when he went to Pigale, because he messaged me from there, but I don't know where it went. Maybe it's in the water."

"Any chance the reporter has it?"

"Maybe," she said. She looked down at her hands.

"What is it?" he said.

"You're going to read it anyway," she said. "Ed went for a lap dance. He messaged me right before. Told me he was leaving his phone with Jack for safekeeping. I don't know if he gave it back or not."

Mowat looked at her for a long moment. "You need to find out for me, okay? You need to go and see Jack, and you need to ask him to give you the BlackBerry, and give it to me. It's really important that we see that phone before the police do. It's a question of national security."

"That's what Cochrane said," said Sophie.

Mowat and Bouchard exchanged a glance.

"Well, you let us know before you tell anyone, Sophie,"

said Bouchard. "Okay?"

"Yes, of course," she said.

Mowat took hold of her by her shoulders.

"Can you handle this, honey?" he asked. "Are you strong enough?"

Sophie nodded. "Yes," she said. "I have to find out what happened to the BlackBerry."

"And don't tell anyone that we had this talk, okay?"

"No," she said. "Of course not."

"That's my girl," said Mowat. "I'm proud of you. In the years ahead, I'm going to need people who can keep cool when things get hot. I won't forget how tough you are."

Awkwardly, he hugged her again, and stood.

"Now, are you finished with that darned thing, Claude?"

The first taste of beer brought Macdonald back to life.

After his interview with Flanagan, he thought his hangover would kill him. The stress of the day settled on him like a heavy weight, and he was suddenly terribly thirsty. He drove to his little Sandy Hill apartment, left his car in the parking lot and walked straight to Chez Lucien, a hole in the wall in the Byward Market, with friendly waitresses, a jukebox with no bad songs, and a long wooden bar where you could sit and drink pints in peace.

The first pint of Griffon Blonde took the worst edge off his hangover, and Jack had a chance to think back through his long, strange day: the police interview, the chaos on the Hill following the news that Stevens was resigning, and his terrible hangover from that morning.

By the time he started his second pint, he was thinking back to the night before and how hammered he'd been to agree to go to Pigale at 2 a.m. on a Monday.

He could remember arriving, taking a table near the main stage, ordering four beers and staring at the naked, tattooed girls crawling on stage. After a few songs, they had gone out for a smoke in the cold. Jack remembered Ed babbling at him as they shivered and sucked at their cigarettes, his Newfoundland accent stronger than usual.

"B'y, I'm going to own this fucking town inside a year. Just you wait, buddy, I won't forget you. I'll hire you to be a D Comms, and you can forget about being a fuckin' reporter."

"Don't be so foolish," said Jack. "You're a just a little Newfie crackie, like me, buddy, yappin at the heels of the old bastards who run this town."

"No, I'm making a move. You don't believe me, but it's true. I'm going to be on my way to the top soon enough."

"Sure, b'y, I'm sure you'll be prime minister inside a year."

"I won't be prime minister, but I might be at the right hand of a prime minister." Taking in Jack's drunken, sceptical face, he had laughed. "Do you know the definition of a transition period? The period between two transition periods. Think about it."

After that, Jack couldn't remember much but getting into another cab.

He took a drink of beer and pulled Ed's BlackBerry from his pocket, and put it on the bar. He took the battery from his and put it in Ed's.

When it was booted up, Jack hit Unlock. The screen gave him a password prompt. He sat there staring at the screen. He had already tried SOPHIE. He tried NEWFIE then TOWNIE.

Jack drained his second pint, dropped the phone back in his pocket and headed downstairs to the bathroom.

Balfour was at home watching a porn video on his home computer, one hand down the front of his sweat pants and the other gripping a bubba cup full of Jack Daniels and Diet Coke, when his phone buzzed. He pulled his hand out of his pants, hit pause, the screen freezing on a close-up of fellatio, and grabbed the Berry. It was an automatic message from the application tracking the missing BlackBerry:

He shut down the video, made a secure connection to his office network, and signed into the application. A map of Ottawa showed on the screen, and he zoomed in on a red dot until he placed it near the corner of Dalhousie and Murray streets, in the Byward Market. He quickly opened another window and looked up the location on Google Maps. It was Chez Lucien. He switched back to the tracking program and opened a window that showed the detailed tracking information. The phone had been reactivated three minutes ago, at 8:23 p.m., and had pinged several times from the same location.

He picked up his own phone and booted up the little tracking program that he had written and installed as an overlay to Google Maps. It was working. The program showed a dot at the corner of Dalhousie and Murray.

He sent a message.

> **To:** 74X93B4
> **From:** 58K42E6
> **Subject:** BB location
> The BlackBerry is now at the corner of Dalhousie and Murray. Looks like Chez Lucien, a pub. It was reactivated at 8:23 p.m. You should be able to track it if you open the program I sent you to install on your BlackBerry.

He sat back and stared at the map on his computer, watching the little dot pulse every thirty seconds. In a few minutes, his BlackBerry buzzed.

> **To:** 58K42E6
> **From:** 74X93B4
> **Subject:** Re. BB location
> Roger that.

Balfour sat back to watch the dot blink.

Jack had just started to pee when the phone in the pocket of his suit coat buzzed. Without thinking, he grabbed it and answered.

"Hello," he said.

"Hello," said a woman's voice. "Mr. Sawatski?"

Jack recognized the voice. It was Ida Gushue.

"No," he said. "Is that Mrs. Gushue? It's Jack Macdonald here. I'm afraid Ed's had an accident. He's been badly hurt."

"Oh my," said Gushue. "What happened?"

"It's pretty serious," said Jack. He's in a coma. The police are investigating. They think someone may have tried to drown him."

"Oh my goodness," said Gushue.

Jack thought for a moment. "Is there any way there could be a connection between his call to you and what happened to him?"

Gushue was quiet for a moment. "I don't know. I'm wondering that myself now. My late husband was a member of the RCMP. I can't think why Mr. Sawatski would be calling me unless it was related to my husband's work."

"Mrs. Gushue, why don't I come see you tomorrow and we can have a chat," said Jack. "I'll tell you what I know about the case. It might help you decide whether you should contact the police."

"I don't want my name in the paper."

"No ma'am," said Jack. "I promise not to put your name in the paper."

"All right then," she said. "Call me tomorrow morning and see if I'll have time to meet you in the afternoon."

As soon as he hung up, Ed's phone rang again.

"Hello," said a man's voice on the other end of the line. "Who's speaking, please?"

"Why?" Jack said. "Who's this?"

"This is Senior Agent Thomas Endicott of the Canadian Security Intelligence Service," the man said. "I am investigating the disappearance of a BlackBerry belonging to the Government of Canada. This is a national security investigation. Please identify yourself."

Jack stammered, suddenly uneasy. He stalled. "Why don't

you give me your switchboard number, so I can be sure I know who I'm talking to."

"Sir, this is not a game," said Endicott. "Please identify yourself immediately. You are in possession of a cell phone that is at the subject of a national security investigation. You need to identify yourself and arrange to hand it over to one of our agents in the area immediately. If you fail to co-operate, you are liable to prosecution under the anti-terror provisions of the Security of Information Act. It carries serious penalties – we're talking about prison time – for obstructing a national security investigation. I ask you again to identify yourself and confirm your location."

Jack swallowed.

"I ask you again, how do I know you're a CSIS agent?" he said. "I think the Ottawa Police Service might want this BlackBerry. You can get it from them, can't you?"

Endicott barked back. "Look, kid, this is not a game. Identify yourself, or the agents will arrest you instead of just taking the phone."

Jack was confused. This didn't make sense.

"I'm not telling you anything until I know who you are," he said. "Why don't you give me a CSIS switchboard number?"

There was silence on the other end of the line.

"Look," said Endicott. "Let's try this again. Believe me, the last thing you want to do is face charges under the Security of Information Act. Please identify yourself and confirm your location."

Jack stood at the urinal, looking up at the ceiling. There was a hole in the drywall, in the corner, where two walls met the ceiling. It looked as though somebody had cut it out to run a wire and had not bothered patching it.

"What do you mean, confirm my location?" he said. "Do you know my location? Are you tracking me?"

He looked at the phone. The screen said Unknown Caller. He could hear the voice talking still, but he had stopped listening. He flipped the phone over and took out the battery, cutting off the voice. He looked around him, his mind racing.

Someone was coming for him, and he didn't know who. He jammed the BlackBerry deep inside the hole by the ceiling, so that nobody would see it without a flashlight and a good reason to go poking around in a dirty hole, then sprinted upstairs into the bar. He caught the waitress's eye, paid, and left. Once he was outside, he broke into a run.

Five minutes later, two middle-aged men entered the bar. One of them walked around the room, scanning all the customers, then followed the sign pointing downstairs to the bathroom. His companion sat at the bar and ordered a coke. He smiled at the waitress.

"Tell me, we were supposed to meet my friend here, but I think we got our wires crossed, and he might have left just before we got here. Did you see somebody leave about five minutes ago? I just was talking to him on his BlackBerry."

"I'm sorry," said the waitress. "Lots of people coming and going."

Balfour got bored of watching the dot blinking, so he restarted the video, and left the tracking map open in another window. When it stopped blinking, he shut down the porn, checked the time of the last ping, and sent another message.

> **To:** 74X93B4
> **From:** 58K42E6
> **Subject:** BB location
> BlackBerry no longer transmitting. Last transmission at
> 8:47 p.m.

As soon as he sent it, he got a call.

"We lost him," said the voice. "It looks like he turned the phone off. I've been thinking about this, and I think it's likely that the suspect has a second BlackBerry or some kind of mobile phone. Can you write a program that would match up the known movements of this phone with other phones that were in the vicinity at the same time?"

Balfour leaned back in his chair and thought about it.

"Hello?" said the voice.

"I'm thinking," he said. "You're talking about a co-location phone. That makes sense. It should be possible to find him that way. We can go through the raw feeds from the transmission receivers for the past 24 hours. It might take a while, but it should be possible."

"Well, you get on it, and message me as soon as you get anywhere," said the voice.

"Roger that," said Balfour.

He set to work, drilling down through the tracking program to the raw data feeds from the transmission towers that handled the signal from the BlackBerry over the previous 24 hours. It took some doing, but he was able to download massive database files.

He wrote some code for a database program and ordered it to search for other phones that were present that appeared more than once in the files. The program whirred quietly for a moment, then spat out a list of 3,276 numbers.

Balfour cursed and sat up in his chair. His mind set to work. If there were hundreds of thousands of numbers in his lists, then thousands of them would be doubled. Some people who worked in Centretown during the day lived in Hull, or went there for dinner, so it was natural that there would be some overlap. He needed to separate the wheat from the chaff, but if he only looked for numbers that matched all the transmission towers, he could easily miss the right phone.

He'd have to figure out a way to order them by signal strength, so that only those phones that were in close proximity to the missing BlackBerry would show as matches.

He picked up his BlackBerry and sent a PIN.

To: 74X93B4
From: 58K42E6
Subject: This could take a while
I'm doing everything I can. Will let you know as soon as I have a match.

As Jack ran down Murray Street, toward King Edward and his apartment in Sandy Hill, he realized that he was making himself stand out and slowed to a brisk walk. He suddenly felt alone on the near-empty street, so he turned left onto a side street, doubled back, crossed Dalhousie, and walked up to Rideau, where there were always people about. He wandered toward Sussex Street, lost in the crowd, and tried to work out what had just happened.

Somebody badly wanted to get their hands on Ed Sawatski's BlackBerry. It wasn't the police, and Jack doubted very much that it was CSIS. As a reporter, he had occasionally called sources back through a switchboard to confirm they were who they said they were, and officials always agreed to that as a security measure.

Whoever it was, they seemed to have the tools to track Sawatski's cell phone, which would make them cops, or the phone company. But it wasn't the cops. And maybe the guy was just bluffing, trying to convince him to cough up a name and his location because that was the only way they could get a line on the thing.

His mind spun in circles as he tried to figure out who would want the BlackBerry. Ed's boss, Jim Donahoe? The Ministry of Justice surely wouldn't like having one of its cell phones go astray, and it might have secret stuff on it, but they would likely just ask the police to find it. And the police would likely just ask him if he had it. Flanagan hadn't even done that. It seemed unlikely that they would not bother to ask and then suddenly try cloak and dagger stuff.

It occurred to him that the Liberals would enjoy looking at a smart phone full of emails to and from an aide to the justice minister, but Pinsent's shop barely seemed able to get their leader to give a coherent speech, much less run phone-snatching operations.

In any case, it didn't matter much. Jack resolved that in the morning he would tell Flanagan where he had left the

BlackBerry and he would let the cops worry about it.

He started when his own phone rang. It was Sophie.

"Hi Jack," she said. "I just wanted to hear a friendly voice. The Sawatskis are with Ed now and it's so depressing. His mother keeps crying and whispering to him and he's just staring at the ceiling, and his dad just keeps patting his hand."

"Lord Jesus," said Jack. "I can't believe this is happening. Do you want me to come down there now?"

"No," said Sophie. "I think I'm going to go home soon. The Sawatskis are going to sit up with him, but I think I should go into the office tomorrow, so I should try to get some sleep."

"That's probably a good idea," said Jack.

"Um, I was wondering, though," she said. "Do you have any idea what happened to Ed's BlackBerry?"

"No," said Jack, lying without thinking. "I don't. As far as I remember he had it when I saw him last. But, God, we were so drunk. I wish I could tell you more. How are you? Is someone going to stay with you?"

"No. Marie-Hélène offered, but I think I'll be okay."

"Call me later. I could pop by. It's not far. I'm worried about you."

Rupert Knowles, principal secretary to the prime minister, sat in his office on the third floor of the Langevin Building, fiddling with the remote control in his hand. He had an image frozen on the 40-inch TV next to the door of Greg Mowat's face at the moment he stopped walking and turned to Ellen Simms earlier that day. Mowat wore a poised, serene look, like a pastor about to begin a sermon. He hit play, and Mowat started to talk.

"If we're discussing Mr. Stevens's resignation, the first thing we should do is look at what he's done for the country," said Mowat. "Under his leadership we have run a scandal-free government. We've cut taxes, rebuilt the military, got tough on criminals, managed the economy through a very challenging time, and made life better for Canadian families. I'm very proud to have worked for Mr. Stevens. He is an inspiration to us, personally and professionally. If he has, as you say, decided to step down, I think this is a good time to reflect on all he has done for the country, and not a time for personal ambition."

Knowles hit rewind, went back to the beginning, and froze the screen again at the moment when Mowat's face took on the expression of pleasant anticipation. He stared for it a moment longer and went to the office door.

"Suzanne," he said to the middle-aged receptionist he shared with the prime minister. "Could you ask Ismael to come in for a moment?"

He sat down and waited for Balusi, staring at the screen.

"Hey," said Balusi, as he entered. "What's up?"

Knowles gestured to the screen. "I want to ask your opinion about something. Sit down." He nodded to the couch against the wall.

Balusi was nervous. He got on well with Frank Naumetz, the boss's chief of staff, who appreciated him for his hustle, his subtle communications skills, his work ethic and his partisan instincts, but Knowles made him uneasy. For one thing, they were about the same age, but Knowles had been working for Stevens a lot longer. He had worked his way from his body man – his go-fer – to principal secretary, the man who speaks for the boss when the boss can't make the call himself, the man who can walk into ministerial offices, casually, and see what's going on, asking questions that leave little doubt about what the boss wants.

Unlike Balusi, who liked to party with other young staffers, Knowles went home to his family whenever he could get away from the office early, and also unlike Balusi, he had the prime minister's personal confidence.

Knowles pointed to the screen. "What do you see?"

"Uh, Greg Mowat," said Balusi, glancing back and forth between the screen and Knowles. "The minister of public safety."

"Yeah," said Knowles. "How's he look?"

"He looks relaxed. Comfortable."

"Yup," said Knowles, and hit play. They watched Mowat gave his spiel. "What do you think? Good lines, eh?"

Balusi nodded. "Yeah. About perfect."

"The way Bouchard would write them?"

Balusi thought for a minute and nodded.

"Not like something he was making up on the spot?"

"No," said Balusi. "It looks like he had his lines ready."

Knowles rewound further, and played Wong and Donahoe's clumsy responses and Mowat's again.

He pressed pause and looked at Balusi.

"Looks like we've found our leaker," said Balusi. "Mowat."

Knowles shrugged. "Maybe. Or maybe he and his little press secretary – what's her name, Sophie – maybe they were just shooting the breeze, hashing out what Mowat should say after QP, and so he was ready for the ambush."

Balusi said: "Or maybe Mowat leaked so he would look sharp and Donahoe would be caught flat-footed."

Knowles laughed and got to his feet, signalling an end to their little meeting. "Politics is a funny business."

Mallorie Ashton opened a bottle of Pinot Noir the minute she got through the door of her condo. She finished her first glass as she drew her bath, her second as she soaked in the tub, and was making a pretty good start on the third by the time she finished warming her leftover Thai take-out in the microwave.

She flicked on the TV as she tucked into her red curry chicken and rice. The news was just starting. The lead item was the resignation of the prime minister. Ashton watched as Ellen Simms walked viewers through the news, showing Stevens addressing the Commons, then the Liberal leader's attack, which seemed beside the point. The piece continued with more gracious quotes from Lesley Nowlan, the leader of the NDP, who congratulated Stevens on his decision and urged him to use the rest of his mandate to leave a positive legacy for working families, and Bloc Quebecois Leader Richard Tremblay, who said that Canadians and Quebecers, whatever their political views, should be grateful to Stevens and his family for his service.

The piece ended with clips of Jim Donahoe and Greg Mowat, who Simms said were the most likely candidates to succeed Stevens. Ashton grimaced when Donahoe said that he would "leave the speculation to the speculators," and thought that Mowat hit the right tone, although he struck her as a bit preachy.

When Simms's piece was over, the old reporter, Murphy, did a story on Stevens's career, from his days as a Progressive Conservative member of the Ontario legislature, his decision to join the Canadian Alliance when he switched to federal politics, to his patient takeover of the party, and finally his three minority election victories.

When the anchor set up the next item, about a helicopter crash in British Colombia, Ashton muted the sound, pushed her plate away, and thought for moment.

She always voted – she had voted for the Conservatives in the last election, based on the Prime Minister's promise to put more police on the street – but she didn't follow politics they way most people in Ottawa did. She and her husband used to watch the news together, but since her divorce three years ago, she had stopped paying much attention. She picked up her phone and called Flanagan's cell number.

"How you doing?" he said.

"Good," she said. "Tired. That was a long day. How about you?"

"Not bad," said Flanagan. "Just dropped Jason off. We managed to catch the last two periods of the Sens game."

"How'd we do?"

"Lost to the Leafs," said Flanagan. "So where are we on the case?"

"Well, I just watched the news," said Ashton. "And there was a piece on about Stevens' resignation. It looks like Donahoe and Mowat are the two main contenders to take over.

Our victim works for Donahoe, and his girlfriend, Sophie, works for Mowat. There's likely not any connection, but I should probably have a chat with Sawatski's boss, see what files he was working on, get some understanding of his professional life. Did you talk to the reporter?"

"Yeah," said Flanagan. "But he didn't give me much. Said he and the victim were loaded and he could barely remember getting home himself. Said he had no idea how Sawatski ended up in the canal."

"Did the kid know what happened to Sawatski's cell phone?" said Ashton.

"Fuck," said Flanagan. "I forgot to ask him. I'll call him in the morning."

"According to a message from the victim to his girlfriend, he gave it to Macdonald to hold while he went for a dance," said Ashton.

"Christ, I can't believe I forgot to ask him," said Flanagan.

"Did you buy his story?" said Ashton.

"I think so," said Flanagan. "But I don't think we should give up on him yet. I was thinking I should go to Pigale, show their pictures, talk to the bouncers, see if I can find the girl he had a dance with, see if the reporter's story holds up."

Ashton laughed. "That sounds like a tough assignment for you, an afternoon in a strip bar."

"I will not rest in my pursuit of public safety," said Flanagan.

Jack was dog tired by the time he turned the corner to his street. He was thinking of drinking a beer, of microwaving a frozen chicken pot pie he had in his freezer and going to sleep. He glanced up at his three-storey brick apartment building from across the street and froze in his tracks. A flashlight beam was playing against the window of his apartment. He stood stock-still and stared, and then saw it again. The inside of the window briefly lit up.

Even though it was dark, he suddenly felt exposed standing

in the open. On the other side of the street was a 1960s apartment building, with a covered parking area making up the first floor. He backed into its shadows, crouched behind a car and watched his building.

It took some doing, but Balfour eventually got the number he was looking for.

First he had to write some code to sort all the numbers by signal strength winnowing by the range, which left him with 1,341 matches.

He wished that he had access to the programs the counter-terrorism boys used, instead of having to sit here scratching his head, trying to create one from scratch, but he knew he would get it if he fooled around long enough.

After he had checked his smaller list, making sure that he hadn't inadvertently scratched any phones that might be the match, he merged all the databases into one file, then sorted the list by the frequency of each phone's appearance, so the phones that contacted the same transmission towers as the target phone appeared at the top. It was immediately obvious that the phone at the top of the list was the one he wanted.

The two phones had been together from 6 p.m. the night before, first on Sparks Street in Ottawa, then pinging together at various locations in Hull, then back in Ottawa overnight, at a location in the Byward Market.

Balfour tried the matching number in an online reverse directory, but got nothing, so he connected to a database on his work computer and checked a cell phone directory maintained by CSIS. The number was listed as belonging to the Telegram Ltd., with an address in St. John's, Newfoundland.

He Googled that, and learned that the Telegram was a newspaper. The phone must belong to the paper's Ottawa reporter, Balfour guessed. Another search found him the name: Jack Macdonald. A final search gave him Macdonald's home address. He checked that against the location of the two phones overnight. It matched.

He picked up his phone and messaged those details, then entered Macdonald's number into the tracking program he had used to find the first BlackBerry. By the time his land line rang, he had located Macdonald's phone. A little dot was flashing on the middle of the block on Peel Street.

The voice on the phone was to the point.

"Have you got a location on Phone 2?"

"I do," said Balfour. "Just ran it through the search program. It's blinking on Peel Street. I'd say the phone is in Macdonald's apartment."

"Hm," said the voice. "I don't think so. I've got a team there now and there's no sign of Macdonald or his phone in the apartment or in his car."

Balfour sat up in his chair.

"Well, I don't know why," he said. "I've got it showing up right on Peel Street."

"Well, he's not there," said the voice. "It's a small apartment and my boys know how to search a place. There's no way the phone is there."

"Just a second," said Balfour.

He laid the tracking map over the Google map of the neighbourhood, and zoomed in. The dot was blinking on Peel Street, but not on 88 Peel Street. It was blinking across the street. He clicked on Satellite View, and zoomed in on the roof of the building, then hit street view, and looked at it from street level.

"Okay," he said, "I think I've got it figured out. It looks like he's actually across the street, at 85 Peel, a four-storey apartment building with parking on the first floor. I don't know why he would be there. Is his car parked there?"

"Hold on," said the voice, and Balfour heard him talking into another phone.

"Okay," he said, back on the line. "I've told my team that he's likely across the street and they're going to go look for him there. How long would it take you to load a tracker for this phone onto my BlackBerry?"

"Um, about a half an hour," said Balfour. "You'd have to download it and reboot your Berry."

"I can't do that now," said the voice. "How about you stay on the line and let me know if that dot moves?"

"Roger that," said Balfour. "Can do."

Jack hunkered down, squatting on his haunches behind a Honda Civic, and peered over the hood at his own building. He was starting to shiver from the cold when the front door opened and two heavyset men carrying flashlights stepped into the light. At first, Jack thought they were going to get into the black Buick parked in front of his building, but they walked around it and headed toward him. When one of them shone his light at the nearby cars, the hair on the back of Jack's neck stood up and his stomach dropped.

He ducked his head, turned and crawled across the dirty floor, to the rear of the parking lot into the alley behind. He took cover behind the building and ran towards the chest-high chain link fence at the back of the property. He jumped, jammed his toes into the mesh and hauled himself up and over, already out of breath. He dropped to the other side, in the parking lot of another building, slipped on the dirty ice, banged his kneecap, but kept running, limping now, in a crouch.

At the sidewalk, Jack looked over his shoulder and saw a dark figure approaching the fence he had just climbed. Cursing all the cigarettes he ever smoked, he turned right and ran downhill in the shadows of the rundown houses and shabby apartment buildings. He darted across another street and kept going, arms and legs pumping, lungs bursting. Halfway down the next block, he stumbled over the lip of a concrete path and fell hard into a shrub. He was pulling himself to his feet when headlights lit up the houses across from him.

He stayed down, breathing heavily, his face on the frozen ground, and peered out from beneath the branches of the shrub. A black Buick crept along the street and stopped a few houses ahead. When the red reverse lights went on, he pulled himself to his knees and took off in the direction from which he had come.

When Sophie got home to the little apartment she shared with Ed, she collapsed on the couch and looked around the room. She thought she had cried herself out, but as her gaze passed over their possessions, she felt a fresh wave of bitter emotion wash over her. Ed's personality was all over the place. When she turned away from his lobster trap coffee table her eyes landed on his sprawling collection of CDs and DVDs, and she couldn't help crying. Being in the place where they had spent so much time together made her realize how alone she felt without him. She wept freely. She could almost see Ed once more prancing through the apartment, waving his arms, telling a story, or cooking breakfast in his underwear. She had no idea if he would ever do that again.

When she had moved to Ottawa after she finished university in Quebec City, Sophie had been lonely and unhappy. She missed her carefree school days, missed her friends and family, missed the night life and found it hard to make friends with her new anglophone colleagues in Greg Mowat's office, who were nice but seemed bland.

When she started to go out with Ed, the whole city changed for her. He was larger than life, a blowhard and a braggart who always had to be the centre of attention, but who was also warm and funny. She liked his Newfoundland friends, who were more spontaneous and fun than the many serious westerners who had come to work for the Tories.

Now Ed was lying on his back, unable to move, staring at the ceiling, and the spark she loved was gone from his eyes. It was hard to imagine that he would ever be here with her again, animating her life with his presence.

So she sat and cried for a while, and then thought of her

mother in Rivière-du-Loup, and how she had had to go on raising six children after losing her oldest child, and only son, who died in a motorcycle accident at sixteen. Her mother had struggled with sadness and depression since then, but somehow found the strength to come back to her surviving children and raise them with joy, although Sophie had occasionally caught her with a look of deep sadness in her eyes.

"I can be tough if I have to be," said Sophie to herself. She dried her eyes, poured herself a glass of wine and turned her attention to her BlackBerry.

She lost herself reading work emails for a while, and then remembered that she should let her boss know that she had talked to Jack.

She sent him a quick message, telling him what Jack had said. Her phone rang immediately.

"Sophie," said Mowat. "How are you?"

"Okay," she said. "Tired."

"How is Ed?" asked Mowat.

"No change," said Sophie. "He was just lying there, staring at the ceiling, or at least he was until the nurses closed his eyes."

"Well," said Mowat. "It's early yet. All we can do is hope and pray. He's a tough kid."

"I know," said Sophie.

"Well, look, I should let you rest, but I want to ask you about your friend Jack. You say he told you he doesn't know anything about where Ed's BlackBerry is."

"That's right," said Sophie.

"Now in one of the messages he sent you last night, he said he was going to give it to Jack to hold on to. Did Jack tell you he gave it back to him?"

"Well, I didn't ask him about that. He just told me that he thought Ed had it when he saw him last. He said they were really drunk."

"You think he's telling the truth?"

"I think so. It was over the phone, so it's hard to tell."

"I'd like you ask him about it in person," he said.

"Sometimes people remember things better after they've had a chance to think about it. Or he might be lying. Do you think you can do that?"

"I will," said Sophie. "I understand it's important. I'll do it as soon as I can."

"Thanks," said Mowat. "Also, can you come into the office tomorrow morning? Just for an hour or so?"

"I was planning to do that," said Sophie.

"Okay," said Mowat. He hesitated before adding, "Thank you so much, Sophie. I wish I could tell you how grateful I am to you for your support, and I wish I could do more to help you right now."

"I know," said Sophie, very quietly.

As minister of public safety, Greg Mowat had an office on the top floor of the Terrasses de la Chaudière complex, a massive, ugly, Trudeau-era complex of government buildings in Hull, across the Ottawa River from Parliament Hill. The office was furnished with simple old furniture – no minister wants to risk a bad news story by blowing tax dollars on new furniture – but the office was huge and a wall of glass windows looked over the river to the picturesque neo-gothic Parliament buildings, now lit up and sparkling in the dark.

Mowat was tired. After he got off the phone with Sophie, he walked to the windows and watched the wind-driven snow swirl outside. He sat back down to go through a printout of the hundreds of PINs Sophie had sent or received in the past month. He rubbed his eyes from time to time, and made notes, struggling with exhaustion. He was relieved when Bouchard came to his door, holding another copy of the same printouts.

"I've been through these twice now and highlighted all the ones that are of concern," he said. "I'll cross-check them tomorrow with the ones you highlight, and make sure I didn't miss anything."

"That's good, Claude," said Mowat. "I think I'm about to

give up for tonight. I'm running out of gas. We should both pack it in."

Bouchard's BlackBerry buzzed then. He looked at the call display.

"It's Balusi," he said.

"Put him on speaker," said Mowat, and he walked over to the window to look out at the snow as he listened to the call.

"Hello, Ismael," said Bouchard.

"We have a little problem, Claude," said Balusi.

"What is it?"

"Knowles just called me into his office. He was watching the scrum tape from today over and over, and he's suspicious."

Mowat turned away from the window and fixed his eyes on Bouchard.

"What do you mean?" said Bouchard.

"He seems to think that someone in your shop leaked the news of Stevens's resignation. Mowat's lines were so good compared to everyone else's. I guess the boss is pissed off about the leak and he's pushing Knowles to find out who blabbed."

"Shit," said Bouchard. "Will Simms keep her mouth shut?"

"She will if she ever wants to get another story from me," said Balusi.

Bouchard and Mowat exchanged worried looks. If the leak were pinned on this office, it would be very bad news. Some governments leak like sieves, but Stevens had made it crystal clear time and time again that his government would not allow leaks. From time to time, Knowles and other top PMO staff spread false information to ministerial staffers and then watched for it to show up in a column or a blog. Mowat and Bouchard both knew veteran Hill staffers who suddenly found themselves sidelined after being caught in such a trap.

"What do you think we should do?" Bouchard asked.

"Confess," said Balusi. "Call Knowles, tell him you just learned that someone on the staff leaked the news, and assure him you're taking action."

Mowat nodded at Bouchard. He mouthed one word: Sophie.

"Okay," Bouchard said. "We can do that. Thanks."

After Bouchard hung up, Mowat tapped in a number on the desk phone and waited for an answer.

"Rupert," he said when the call went through. "It's Greg Mowat here. I hope I didn't get you out of bed."

"No," said Knowles. "Of course not. I just got home. About to look in on the kids. What can I do for you, Minister?"

"Well, I wanted to have a quiet word," he said. "I just found out that my office may have had something to do with the leak today to Simms about Stevens's resignation." He was speaking quickly, rushing to get out everything he had to say.

"I see," said Knowles.

"Yes," said Mowat. "Claude just came to me and explained what he thinks happened, and I thought I should let you know right away. If I know the prime minister, he's got you trying to figure out how it happened, and I don't want you guys chasing your tails when we already know. I know how the prime minister feels about leaks, and this one made me feel queasy. It spoiled a historic moment for him."

"How did it happen?"

"Well, I'm responsible. It was a staff member, but the person is going to get a good talking to about it, and I can guarantee that it won't happen again. I suspect there may be a more innocent explanation than it seems at first. Some of these darned reporters, you got to watch yourself or you're telling them something by mistake. It's a young staffer, and we'd like a chance to figure out exactly what happened internally, if you'll give us the chance."

Knowles was quiet for a moment.

"A young staffer?" he said. "Are you talking about Sophie Fortin?"

"Well," said Mowat. "We want to deal with it here, if you don't mind. Sophie's a great kid and she's under a lot of stress today. Her boyfriend, Ed Sawatski, young fellow works for Donahoe, he fell into the canal last night and he's in hospital in a coma, so you can imagine how upset the poor girl must be."

"I'm aware of that, Minister," said Knowles.

"Of course you are," said Mowat. "Look, the last thing she needs is to be worrying about her job at a time like this. If it was her that leaked it, I wouldn't be a bit surprised to find that she'd been a tiny bit careless in the way she dealt with Simms. It's my fault for telling any staff after the meeting.

"Anyway, can you let me and Claude handle this?" he asked. "Keep it unofficial? I mean, when it comes down to it, I'm responsible for the darned leak."

Knowles didn't say anything for a moment and Mowat and Bouchard looked nervously back and forth at one another, waiting.

"Okay, Minister," Knowles said eventually. "Thanks for calling me. I'll let you know tomorrow if we need any follow-up."

Jack's chest was heaving from running away from the Buick. Panting, he slowed to a jog on the sidewalk, looking over his shoulder every few moments, heading towards the Byward Market. He cut through the parking lot of a nursing home, keeping low enough to stay out of sight. When he got to the next street, he crouched behind a parked car and looked back. His heart sank when he saw the Buick cruising his way.

He took off again, running hard behind the cover of the nursing home, and then dashed across King Edward Avenue and up towards Rideau Street. He kept running, cutting diagonally into the heart of the market, where there were people walking to and from pubs and restaurants. He slowed to a walk and turned under a stone arch into a cobblestone walkway between two old stone buildings and into a courtyard lined by restaurants and bars. Apart from a cluster of smokers at the back door of a bar, the usually lively mall was empty. Certain that he'd lost his pursuers, Jack bent over, his hands on his knees, to catch his breath.

He was startled when his phone buzzed. It was Sophie, in tears.

"It's so hard, Jack," she said. "I'm home and I can't stop

thinking about Ed."

"Is there anybody there with you?"

"No. I'm here by myself."

"Okay," he said. "I'm coming over. See you in ten minutes."

The man was getting angry with Balfour for relaying confusing and contradictory directions, and Balfour was getting tired of sitting in front of his computer and taking abuse. He hadn't had time to put the tracking program on the man's phone, so he had to keep giving him the latest coordinates for the blinking red dot. The man yelled at Balfour and then yelled the fresh location to the men chasing Jack. Sometimes he yelled into the wrong phone.

The triangulation wasn't that accurate – only to within twenty metres or so – and it lagged behind someone moving quickly. So Balfour couldn't give precise directions, especially since Jack kept cutting through the middle of blocks. When he ran across the middle of King Edward Street, his pursuers had to go well around, wait at a set of lights and do a U-turn before they could get on his trail again.

When Jack stopped in the courtyard, though, Balfour was able to give them a fixed position, and the car pulled up outside the arch where Jack had entered. The men were getting ready to go in on foot when Balfour reported that Jack had left by the other exit, and was on Sussex now, headed south.

Jack was walking briskly up Sussex, smoking a cigarette, glancing over his shoulder every few paces, looking out for the Buick, even though he was sure he had lost his tail. He jogged across the street, and was headed for the steps to MacKenzie Avenue, when he looked back and saw the Buick turn onto Sussex. He ducked into the shadows of the stairway and peered around the corner. It was definitely the same car, and it was coming toward him. He could make out two figures in the front seats, both looking around as the car crept closer.

"How the fuck do they keep finding me?" he wondered aloud, just as his BlackBerry vibrated on his hip. He realized in a flash how they were tracking him. His phone!

The revelation stabbed fear into his guts. If they could track him by his phone, they had to be CSIS, or the cops. But if it were the cops, they would just call him, wouldn't they?

Jolted back into action, he scrambled up the steps and emerged on MacKenzie across the street from the Chateau Laurier. He ran to the corner and then forced himself to stroll toward the covered entrance, where uniformed bellboys were directing visitor traffic and ushering guests into taxis.

A portly middle-aged man was getting into the first cab in the queue. Holding his BlackBerry against his leg, Jack walked to the other side of the cab. He knelt, as if to tie his shoe, and quickly jammed the phone and its holster down behind the rear bumper of the taxi, where it stuck. He straightened up and ambled to the doorway of the hotel, where he stopped and lit a cigarette – just another guest standing outside for a smoke.

The cab drove off and signalled right at the intersection of Wellington and Sussex, likely headed to Colonel By Drive. Thirty seconds later, the black Buick went by, tailing the taxi.

Murphy was exhausted by the time he and Simms had finished their stand-ups and watched the rest of the news at their desks in the newsroom overlooking Parliament Hill, but when she proposed that they have a drink together at Hy's, he didn't refuse.

The after-work crush had died down, and they took a high table by the bar. He ordered a scotch. She had red wine and her painted fingernails clicked on the wine glass as she took her first sip.

"That was a great scoop today," said Murphy. "We were out in front of the competition all day on the only story that anyone cared about."

"I know," said Simms, and beamed. "It must be killing them at CBC."

"Your scoop is part of history now. Think about that."

"Maybe you should give me a raise."

Murphy laughed. "I was new on the Hill when Trudeau took his walk in the snow and decided to retire," he said. "I covered Mulroney's resignation, Jean Chrétien being pushed out by Paul Martin. These are the moments when things really change. Everything will be different from now on."

"Not till March," said Simms. "Stevens is still the boss until then."

"Everything changes now. Stevens is in control, but whoever wants his job has to make a move now. Soon we'll find out how good the organizations are, who has had people working away quietly for years, who has donors lined up, who has convinced some sharp customers to quit their jobs and work full time for nothing for three months."

"You think it will be Mowat or Donahoe?"

"I can't tell yet, but one of the two. Likely Mowat. Donahoe's from Nova Scotia, and he's an old Progressive Conservative. The PCs might think it's their turn to lead the party, but the Alliance types don't want to give up control, and they have a lot of money and a lot of members. Every riding association in the country is weighted equally, so Donahoe could theoretically go into a convention with a lot of support from red Tories in the Maritimes, Quebec and Toronto, but it looks to me like it would be tough."

"I like Donahoe," said Simms. "Mowat creeps me out. He reminds me of a televangelist."

Murphy laughed.

"That probably bothers you more than it concerns a lot of Tory delegates," he said. "If he came across like that in a general election it would hurt the party, but a leadership race isn't an election. Donahoe will try to make delegates think about it, but he'll have to be careful if he wants to win their support."

"There could be some great stories for us, up to and

including the convention," said Simms.

Murphy swirled his Scotch. "We want to do our best to get good sources near Mowat and Donahoe."

"I may have some ideas about that."

"Yeah? Well, whoever gave you that story today is a good source." Murphy watched her reaction carefully. He knew that Balusi had given her the story, and guessed that there was a link to the Mowat camp, because he was obviously better prepared than the other MPs during the scrums, but he didn't think she realized he'd seen her call display when the call came in at lunch.

Simms's eyes flicked to the bar and back at Murphy. "Well, it wasn't that guy," she said, and pointed with her nose at Dave Cochrane, who was leaving the dining room with Donahoe and a few other middle-aged men in suits. When he glanced back across the room, Simms's red hair caught Cochrane's eye. He did a double take and waved as he walked his boss and their companions out to the street.

"If I'm not mistaken, Cochrane and Donahoe just had dinner with Geoff Bourrie, the lobbyist, one of the old Mulroney boys," said Murphy. "I haven't seen him around in years. Probably plotting the return of the PCs. Man, those guys knew how to have fun. They make Stevens's crew look like a bunch of boy scouts."

"Some of Stevens's crew know how to have fun," said Simms, and she pointed her chin at Cochrane, who had appeared in the bar again and was walking toward their table.

He shook hands with Murphy. Simms gave him a two-cheek kiss.

"David," she said, "was that Geoff Bourrie you just had dinner with?"

Cochrane pulled up a chair. "Jesus, you don't miss much, do you?" he said. "How would you know who Bourrie is? You must have been in short pants the last time that guy was making it rain in Ottawa."

Simms winked at Murphy. "I have my sources."

"Well that's obvious," said Cochrane. "That was a good

one today."

The waiter came with a gin and tonic for Cochrane. Simms ordered another glass of wine, but Murphy decided to stop at one. "I've got to get home," he said. "I can't keep up with you kids anymore."

He squeezed Simms's shoulder affectionately when she kissed him good night.

"Good scoop today, kid," he whispered. "I'm proud of you."

After Murphy left, Simms pressed Cochrane. "So, is Bourrie organizing for you guys?"

Cochrane laughed. "Just old friends having a steak together. Last time I checked that wasn't against the law."

"No, but you guys have got to be putting together your team in a hurry if you want to have any chance of beating Mowat."

"If Donahoe, or Mowat, is going to run. Nobody's announced yet."

"No," said Simms. "Are you going to leave the speculation to the speculators?"

Cochrane laughed. "Jesus, the boss looked a bit awkward today, didn't he? I'd give my left one to know who tipped you off."

"You know I can't tell you that," she said.

"No, but you could have let me know that you were about to ambush my guy."

Simms took a sip of wine and regarded Cochrane coolly. "I could have, but I didn't want to blow my scoop. I like to get scoops."

Cochrane stared at her, smiling, drained his gin and tonic and waved for another. "Did you hear about Sawatski?"

"No. Who's that?"

"Young fellow works in our office as a policy adviser. From Newfoundland. Late twenties. Smart kid. Lives with Sophie Fortin, Mowat's press secretary."

"The girl who fainted in the lobby today?"

"Yeah," said Cochrane, taking his next gin and tonic from the waiter. "You know why she fainted? I bet it was because she just found out that her boyfriend nearly drowned. They pulled him out of the canal this morning. He's in a coma in the hospital."

"Wow," said Simms.

"I don't know if any Hill reporters have put it together yet," said Cochrane. "You might poke around, find out what happened. Could be a story there."

Simms crossed and uncrossed her legs and gave Cochrane a coquettish smile.

"Do me a favour, Dave," she said. "Don't mention it to any other reporters."

On the way to Sophie's, Jack twice reached to his hip to check his phone for messages, and felt like an idiot both times when he remembered it was gone. His mind kept turning in circles as he contemplated the events of the day. For the first time, he had a chance to think about why some scary people wanted to get their hands on Ed's BlackBerry. He thought of that menacing black Buick, and wondered if the people chasing him were the same people who threw Ed into the canal, if that's what had happened. Who would do that? Why? He ran through the day's events again, but he just ended up with more questions. It was a relief when he finally got to Sophie's and she buzzed him into the Centretown high rise. She was in her pyjamas and a robe when she opened the door for him, with bloodshot eyes and a tissue in her hand. He took her in his arms and pulled her to his chest. She immediately started to cry. Over her shoulder, he saw a box of tissues on the coffee table and a half empty bottle of red wine.

He had met Sophie better through Ed, and although they were friends, he didn't know her well, because whenever he was with her they were with Ed.

He thought Ed was lucky to have found her, though, because she was so beautiful and nice, the kind of girl you would marry, with a sharp wit, silky brown hair, big brown eyes and a slim, athletic body. She had a twinkly laugh and spoke with a light, charming French accent. She was always poised and formal when it was appropriate, but she had a saucy, earthy sense of humour when she was among friends. She didn't crowd Ed, and trusted him likely more than she should.

Jack was a little bit in love with Sophie, and he was aware of how pleasant it was to have her in his arms, even if he was consoling her because his good friend was in a coma in the hospital.

Sophie must have had the same thought, because she suddenly pulled away.

"Do you want a glass of wine?" she asked.

"Is the Pope a German?"

They sat at either end of the couch.

"So, how's Ed?" asked Jack.

"No change," said Sophie. "The doctor says there might be improvements but we can't count on it. His brain was starved for oxygen for a long time, and we don't know how much it was damaged."

Jack shook his head. "Christ. It's hard to imagine Ed spending the rest of his life on his back. I just can't believe it. I have to believe that he'll find a way to recover, that we'll see the same old Ed again someday."

"I hope so," said Sophie. She stared into her wine, then out the window. "God, I hope so. He had ... has ... so many dreams and plans for the future."

"When we were at Pigale last night, he said that he was getting ready to make some kind of a move," said Jack. "It sounded like he had a plan for a new job."

Sophie back at him. "Did he say what kind of job?"

"Not really. He said he could end up being at the right hand of the prime minister. At the time I assumed he meant Stevens, but now I wonder. Maybe he was thinking about Donahoe."

"He never mentioned that to me," said Sophie.

"He could have just been shooting off his mouth," said Jack. "So, do the police have any idea how he ended up in the canal? Flanagan seemed to be trying to figure out if somebody put him in the water."

"He has handcuff bruises on his wrists," said Sophie. "They think somebody tried to drown him." A tear spilled from one of her big brown eyes. "What happened, Jack? What can you remember from last night?"

"Well, we shared a cab together from Pigale, and we stopped at my place. He stayed in the cab. I assume he was headed home."

"He sent me a PIN late at night, saying he gave you his Berry to hold when he went for a lap dance," said Sophie. "Did you give it back to him?"

Jack felt stuck. He had already lied to Sophie about Ed's phone. He planned to tell the police that he had it, but he didn't want to tell Sophie he had lied to her. Maybe the police would agree not to tell her.

"I don't remember that at all," he said. "I don't remember him giving it to me, or giving it back to him or anything. I didn't have it when I woke up this morning."

"Did you check all your clothes and search your apartment?" she asked.

"Yes," said Jack. "But I'll have another look in the morning."

"Okay," said Sophie. "It's important. The police need to see who he was sending messages to. And his boss needs to know whether there are secrets on it that are compromised."

"God," said Jack. "Do you think somebody drowned him to get hold of his phone?"

She looked pale and her shoulders sagged. "I don't know. I don't know anything."

Jack eased over next to her and put his arm around her to comfort her.

She looked up at him. "Promise me that you'll let me know if you find the Berry, or if you remember what happened to it."

"Of course," said Jack, pulling her head onto his shoulder. "I promise."

They sat like that for a while, in silence. After a few minutes, Jack noticed that her breathing had become deep and regular, and he realized that she had fallen asleep. Soon he was asleep as well.

Chapter 4 – Scoop

JACK'S SNORING WOKE Sophie in the night and she left him sprawled on the couch. She spread a quilt over him, set her alarm and went to bed.

Her alarm went off at seven. Jack was still dead to the world when she got out of the shower, and she decided to let him sleep. She got dressed and headed to the office. As soon as she got to her desk, she called Mrs. Sawatski. Ed's mom thought that Ed may have recognized her when he woke up this morning, but he still hadn't spoken or shown any real signs of consciousness.

Sophie had worked hard to get to the Hill, sacrificing spare time during university, volunteering for the federal Conservatives and Action Démocratique du Québec, making connections, learning the ABCs of politics at street level. She had learned that the most useful people in a political organization were the ones who got things done quietly, who put in the hours when the hours needed to be put in, not when it was convenient for them, who demonstrated over time that they knew how to keep their mouths shut.

It bothered her that some people on the Hill assumed she got there because she was pretty, like some young staffers, and she took pride in her work. She made it her practice never to tell Bouchard or Mowat that she couldn't do something, or let them know what difficulties she faced, believing that they were smart enough to notice her efficiency and discretion. She had worked herself ragged for them, never complaining, but today, with Ed in the hospital, for the first time she let the strain show. She actually scowled when Mowat popped into her office and started to speak to her while she was on the phone with Mrs. Sawatski. She covered the mouthpiece.

"I'm sorry, Minister," she said. "I'm on the phone with Ed's mother. Can I have just a moment, please? I'm very sorry."

He frowned and backed out. When she hung up, he was waiting outside her little office, chatting with Marie-Hélène, the receptionist.

"I'm so sorry, Minister," she said. "I'm so stressed."

"Of course you are, Sophie," he said. "Let's get this wrapped up so you can get back to the hospital."

He put his hand on her shoulder and walked her to Bouchard's office. Claude stood and embraced her. "Pauvre Sophie. Ça va? C'est dur, n'est pas?"

Sophie struggled not to cry as she hugged him back.

Bouchard asked Sophie for her Blackberry and plugged it into his laptop. He opened up a list and started deleting files. "There are a few things on there that could violate operational security if the police take a look. We need to clean a few things out. We can't have secrets going astray."

Mowat was leaning against the door. "Did you talk to Jack again?"

"Yeah," said Sophie. "He came over last night to see me. He doesn't remember anything about Ed's BlackBerry."

Mowat frowned. "Do you believe him?"

Sophie shrugged. "Why would he lie?"

"We can't think that way. We have to assume he might be lying. He might hope to get secrets from Ed's phone."

"I see what you mean. But he wouldn't have the password."

"Okay. Keep after him, though, will you? Maybe his memory will improve."

"I will. I'll take him for drinks as soon as I can. It might loosen his tongue."

"Okay," said Mowat. "By the way, I want to ask you whether you talked to Simms before the scrum today? Someone in Stevens's office seems to think you might have leaked the news of the resignation to Simms."

Sophie was confused. Bouchard had told her that the story

was going to break, and asked her to work on lines with Mowat before the scrum.

Bouchard looked at her blankly. He was disconnecting her phone.

"No," she said. "I didn't talk to Simms."

"Okay," said Mowat. "That's what I told them. I couldn't see you leaking anything. But if anyone from Langevin asks you about that, tell them to talk to me, okay?"

Sophie nodded.

Mowat stood up and walked around his desk. "Claude, are you finished with that darn BlackBerry? We should let Sophie get to the hospital."

Bouchard returned her phone, and Mowat took her by the hand. "I don't want you to worry about anything to do with this office for the rest of the day, okay? We're very impressed by your work, and I hate like heck to have to ask you about the leak, but we have to be very careful."

"I understand," said Sophie.

"Don't give up on Jack," he said. "Keep working on him. We'll all be able to relax when we know what happened to that BlackBerry."

Jack was disoriented when he woke up on Sophie's couch. He staggered to his feet and looked around, uncomprehending, until the events of the day before came back to him, and he realized where he was. It was 9:30.

"Fuck," he said. "Fuck. Fuck. Fuck."

He went into the bathroom, took a quick shower and put his dirty suit back on.

He wanted to check his BlackBerry, but it was gone. Then he remembered where he had put it. He switched on Sophie's desktop computer in the living room, to go online to check his email. While the computer booted up, he called his editor on Sophie's land line.

"What're you at?" said his editor.

"Not much, Kevin," said Jack. "Story okay?"

"Yeah," said Brandt. "Just fine. Or at least I haven't heard anything from the publisher's office. What have you got today?"

"Well, I'm not sure. You know my buddy, Ed Sawatski, works in Donahoe's office?"

"Yeah?" said Brandt.

"Well, he got into some kind of accident yesterday, fell in the Rideau Canal and he's in hospital, still unconscious. He and I were out drinking the night he got hurt, so I think I'll have to go see him at the hospital today, and I think the police want to talk to me again. So I don't know if I'll have time to get up to much before Question Period."

"Christ. How'd he end up in the canal?"

"I don't know. Last time I saw him he was fine, drunk but fine."

"Do the police suspect foul play?"

"Yeah. They seemed to be thinking about it when they questioned me yesterday."

"That's quite a story."

"I hadn't thought of that," said Jack.

"Local boy clings to life after suspicious Parliament Hill drowning. Think about it. That's a good story."

"You're right. That's a good story."

"You're going to talk to the police today?"

"Yeah. They want to question me again."

As Jack spoke, the computer finished booting up and presented him with a password prompt.

"Okay," said Brandt. "Record the interview and see what you can figure out. Talk to the family and the doctor when you're at the hospital. You should be able to scoop everybody on this."

"I will," said Jack. "And I'll listen to the recording of the interview I did yesterday."

"You recorded it?"

"Yup."

"Good lad. You should have a great story on your hands. Front page. Let me know how it's going later."

Jack idly tried a few passwords on the computer in front of him as he talked, and then gave up. As he shut it down, he noticed a cord skirting the baseboard of living room wall. Curious, he got up to trace where it disappeared behind the computer and found that it plugged into a USB port on the tower.

"Okay," he said. "I'll get on that. But before I do anything, I've got to go to pick up a new phone. Mine fell in the toilet yesterday."

Jack traced the cord back along the baseboard to where it went into a little hole in the living room wall.

"You dropped your phone in the toilet?"

"Yeah. It fell out of the holster."

"Christ. You dropped your cell phone in the frigging toilet. Jaysus. Is it still under contract?"

"I think so," said Jack.

"Okay. Well go pick up a new one and then call in to get it activated. Call me when it's set up. And keep this one out of the toilet, will you? Jesus."

After Brandt hung up, Jack walked into the bedroom, to find where the USB cord came out. Maybe they have another computer, he thought, without password protection, and I can check my email. But on the other side, there was no sign of the cord. There was a bookshelf in the way, but no cord emerged at the far side of the case.

Jack stood next to the wall and peered behind the bookshelf. He thought he could see the cord at its base. He got to his knees and pulled some of the books out of the bottom shelf so he could see the wall, looking for the cord. One of the books, a hardcover copy of *Renegade in Power*, wouldn't budge. It was tall enough to get jammed in the shelf. Jack sat back and stared at it, then pressed his head against the wall again. The USB cord ran in a straight line from the wall to the book.

He tried to pull the book again, but it was completely stuck, as if, Jack realized, it were glued to the shelf. When he looked at the book very closely he noticed what looked to be a lens the size of the head of a pin on the edge of the spine.

A hidden camera.

Ashton was irritated. While Flanagan drove around Gatineau in search of taxi drivers and strippers, she was cooling her heels outside the suite of offices belonging to the minister of justice, waiting to speak to his chief of staff, Dave Cochrane.

He had agreed readily enough to be interviewed when she called him first thing in the morning, but she had been sitting here for ten minutes while he remained hidden in some inner office. The receptionist kept smiling and apologizing, and twice she went to check on Cochrane, but came back frowning, promising he'd be out soon.

Finally Ashton had had enough. She stood up and headed for the hallway. In the doorway, she turned to the receptionist. "I'm going step outside to make a phone call. If Cochrane hasn't got his head out of his ass by the time I come back, I'm going to go to my office – at the Ottawa Police Service – and I will send some uniforms to pick him up this afternoon to come in for a chat. All right? Capiche?"

The horrified-looking receptionist nodded and picked up the phone on her desk.

In the hallway, Ashton called Flanagan.

"Any progress?" she asked.

"Not yet," he said. "I've visited one taxi company, dropped off photos of Sawatski and Macdonald. They promised to show them to all the drivers. I'm on my way to another company now. I should be ready to hit Pigale at lunch time."

"Poor you. I'm waiting to talk to Sawatski's boss. Have you talked to Macdonald again?"

"No. I keep calling him, but he hasn't called back. I called Fortin just now. She saw him last night. Said he told her he didn't know what happened to the cell phone, but we should ask him directly."

"Okay," said Ashton. "If you don't hear from him soon we'd better track him down."

"Did you hear from Public Affairs?"

"No. What do they want?"

"Well, they put out a release yesterday, saying that we are investigating the near drowning of a young man. There's a little item in the *Citizen*. Today it looks like the news is out. A TV reporter, Ellen Simms, called. She knows the kid worked for the minister and she's pushing for an interview."

"What did you tell Public Affairs?"

"Told them they should talk to you," he said. "My instinct would be to tell them nothing, but they want to release a statement."

"I'll give them a call later. Okay. I gotta go."

Cochrane had finally appeared. He was standing in the doorway with an apologetic smile on his face.

"I'm sorry, Detective," he said. "Please come in."

He showed her into his office at the end of a long hallway. It was on the corner of the building, so it had two glass walls. Ashton stood and looked out at the snow blowing around outside, and the pedestrians below, scampering in the cold.

"What were you doing?" she said. "Sitting here admiring the view, thinking you'd impress me about what a big shot you are?"

"My apologies," said Cochrane. He stood next to a couple of couches and a coffee table, waiting for her to come and sit down. She stayed at the window, looking at him.

"I don't want you to think that we aren't willing to co-operate with you in any way that we can," he said. "I would normally never keep you waiting, but I was on the phone with the prime minister. He doesn't call me very often, and when he does I drop whatever I'm doing and take the call."

Ashton stared at him, trying to get a bead on him. He struck her as oddly passive and diffident.

"What did he want?" she asked, narrowing her gaze.

"It doesn't have anything to do with your investigation, but there's some news that will be released today, and we were discussing whether my minister should be the spokesman or whether Greg Mowat, the minister of public safety, should handle the file. It's a, uh, difficult file, so I was trying to convince him and his chief of staff that Minister Mowat should handle it."

"Okay," said Ashton. "That doesn't sound like it has anything to do with the Sawatski case."

She strolled over and finally sat down. She took out her notebook and a recorder. Cochrane did the same.

"You want to record our conversation?" she asked.

"I have to, I think," said Cochrane. "The opposition could ask about this case in Question Period, or the Prime Minister's Office might decide it has national security implications and want to know exactly what I told you and when."

"What kind of national security implications?" asked Ashton.

"I assume there's still no sign of Ed's cell phone?" he asked.

Ashton shook her head.

"Well, we're trying to figure out what kind of information might have been on it," said Cochrane. "It should be password-protected, but we can't know for sure that Ed wasn't forced to divulge the password. I assume that's still a possibility? Ed's still unconscious?"

Ashton nodded. Cochrane sighed and looked at his hands.

"Well, a security officer from the Privy Council Office is in the process of going through all the email Ed sent or received, figuring out how much of it would have been on the BlackBerry, based on its memory capacity. Then they'll analyze what the implications would be if any of the information ended up in the hands of hostile governments, or third parties, commercial entities."

"I need to have some idea of what kind of work Mr. Sawatski did," said Ashton.

"He was a policy adviser in natural resources," Cochrane replied. "The Justice Department has lawyers in all the federal departments. They analyze legislation, write opinions on government decisions, advise the government on contracts we might enter, that kind of thing. Ed was in charge of considering the policy implications of the work done by the Justice

Department lawyers in the Natural Resources Department. It's a political role, to make sure that the minister – who is accountable to voters – knows what's going on, and recommend intervention when necessary."

"What kind of files did he work on?" asked Ashton.

"Well, a lot of files," said Cochrane. "It would depend. He reviews files, does some research when necessary, checks whether the departmental staff seem to be following the law, and government policy. Usually he just sends us reports letting us know what's going on, but sometimes he identifies decision points where someone more senior should take a look, make sure the departmental staff is moving in the direction we want, the direction that the government wants."

"Give me an example," said Ashton.

"Most recently he gave us a heads-up concerning a coal mine in Sydney, Cape Breton," said Cochrane. "The entrance is on land, but the mine goes out under the sea. The vast majority of the coal is therefore federal property, not provincial, and subject to federal regulation and taxes. A German company wants to reopen the mine, but they would prefer to do business under the provincial regulatory and royalty regime. We don't have a problem with that, and we want the project to go ahead, to bring jobs to a high-unemployment community. The lawyers at Natural Resources are nervous about the implications, though. They don't like to step out of an area of federal jurisdiction without making absolutely sure it won't set a dangerous precedent, or expose the Crown to some unanticipated liability, so they've been going around in circles on the file for six months. Last week, Ed recommended that we light a fire under them, give them a 15-day deadline to produce enabling legislation so that the Germans can put some unemployed miners to work. If we force them to act now, some of those fellows might be bringing home paycheques by the time the snow melts."

"Your minister's from Nova Scotia, isn't he?" said Ashton.

"From Lunenburg, on the other end of the province."

"So I suppose he'd like to cut the ribbon."

"Politicians like cutting ribbons, but that's a pretty safe Liberal seat," said Cochrane. "We wouldn't be doing our jobs if we didn't push this project."

"Okay," said Ashton. "That gives me an idea of what kind of work Ed did. Now I'd like to have a look at all the files he was working on recently, maybe have somebody explain them to me."

"We can do that, but it would be a lot of work," said Cochrane. "Are you sure it's necessary?"

"Right now we're operating on the assumption that somebody tried to kill your Ed. He may have fallen into the canal by accident, but if somebody drowned him to steal his BlackBerry, it could be related to his work. Is there any chance it could be industrial espionage?"

"I guess we can't rule anything out," said Cochrane. "It's possible, but the scenarios are pretty far-fetched. For example, in the case of the coal mine in Cape Breton, it's theoretically possible that somebody would be trying to block its development, but I find it hard to imagine those people going so far as to drown Ed to influence the process. So far, the project's biggest opponents are some risk-averse Justice Department lawyers."

"I see your point, but you said he worked lots of files. Some of them must be more contentious."

"Absolutely," said Cochrane. "I wonder if I should arrange for you to meet with Fred Chiasson, who is looking at the security issues here. He would be familiar with the broad outlines of the files that might have been on the Berry. That would be a place to start, and he'd be better able to brief you than I am, likely. He's a former RCMP officer, if I'm not mistaken."

"That would be great," said Ashton. "Will you contact him today and explain that I need to see him ASAP."

"I'll call him as soon as we're done."

"Okay," said Ashton. "Now, how much do you know about Mr. Sawatski's private life?"

"Not that much," said Cochrane. "He was quite personable. I think everyone on the staff liked him. He worked hard, wrote good reports. That was the most important thing to me."

"Were you surprised that he was out at a strip bar with a reporter on a week night?" asked Ashton.

"Yes, I was," said Cochrane. "But I gather that he had a wild side. I do recall seeing him looking a little bleary at some morning meetings, but lots of staffers get up to mischief from time to time. They're young people with money away from home. They work hard and sometimes they need to blow off steam. We don't encourage junior staffers to go boozing with reporters, but I'm told Ed knew this Macdonald fellow from university in Newfoundland. I'd have preferred if he'd let me know they were drinking buddies, but I understand why he didn't."

"What do you know about his relationship with Fortin?"

"Sophie Fortin?" said Cochrane. "Not much. She seems like a fine young woman, and I thought he was doing quite well for himself. That's about it."

Ashton got to her feet. "Thanks for your time, Mr. Cochrane. I'll be expecting to hear from Mr. Chiasson."

Cochrane walked her out. "I want to let you know that we will give you whatever help we can. Again, I'm sorry I kept you waiting this morning."

"No problem," said Ashton as she got to the door. She turned and smiled. "Give my best to the prime minister."

On the way back to his apartment, Jack picked up a coffee at a stand in the Rideau Centre, the huge downtown mall, and popped into the shop where he had bought his cell phone. He told the girl at the counter that he dropped his phone in the toilet, and he desperately needed a new one in a hurry. She checked his contract, typed some digits into her computer, tried to sell him a newer version and when he refused finally coughed up a replacement for him.

He bought a copy of the *Ottawa Citizen* and walked home to change. His fear from the night before, when he ran flat out from the black Buick, seemed out of place, even silly, in the light of day. Even so, he was apprehensive when he opened his apartment door, ready to run back down the stairs if someone were waiting for him there. But everything looked the same as the morning before, with books and newspapers and empty cigarette packages and beer bottles strewn around. He couldn't be sure that it hadn't been searched because there was no way of knowing what if anything was out of place.

He found another rumpled suit on the back of the bathroom door and after he'd changed into it, leaving the stained suit on his bedroom floor, he went into his living room to go online.

While he was waiting, his new BlackBerry rang.

"Jack Macdonald. *Telegram*," he said.

"Mr. Macdonald, this is Detective Sergeant Devon Flanagan here," said the cop. "I've been trying to get a hold of you most of this morning."

"Uh, I was having a problem with my phone," said Jack. "What can I do for you?"

He scrambled to find his digital recorder under a newspaper on the coffee table. He hit the button and held it up to his phone to record the call.

"I have a follow-up question or two for you," said Flanagan.

"Do you want me to come in again?"

"Is your office on the Hill?"

"Yes but I'm still at home, in Sandy Hill," said Jack. "What's going on anyway? If Ed fell into the canal because he was drunk why are you investigating me?"

"Do you know that that's what happened?"

"Well, no. But isn't that what you guys think?"

"I don't want to get into that, but we're investigating. We have a lot of questions still."

"Well, if you have more questions you must think he didn't fall in by accident. That's scary and weird. You think someone tried to drown him? Why would anyone want to drown Ed?"

"That's why we're asking questions," said Flanagan. "Can you think of any reason why anyone would wish him harm?"

"No. I have no idea. Everybody I know liked him. No idea."

"Do you know what happened to his BlackBerry?"

Jack felt stuck. If he told Flanagan where the phone was, and it got back to Sophie, she'd know that he'd lied to her.

"No, I don't," he said. "Sophie told me that Ed sent her a message saying he gave it to me, but I don't remember that. I was hammered."

Now that he had lied to Flanagan, Jack felt he'd done something bad and stupid. What if the phone were the key to the whole thing, and he was keeping it from the police? Then again, he'd just lied to the police. Best to shut up about the damn thing, maybe go back to Chez Lucien, wipe his prints off it and call in an anonymous tip from a pay phone.

"So you remember what you talked about?" Flanagan said. "When I talked to you yesterday you said you had the feeling Ed said something to you, but you couldn't remember what."

"Yeah," said Jack. "I do remember. We went out for a smoke on the patio at Pigale. He said that he expected to make a move soon. That was the exact phrase. 'Make a move.' He didn't explain what he meant, but I had the idea that he meant a new job, a better job."

"What do you think he meant?" said Flanagan.

"He said he would end up at the right hand of the prime minister," said Jack. "I've been thinking about it. It looks like Donahoe is going to take a run for the leadership. Maybe he figured he'd end up with a better job if Donahoe takes the prize. He likely would. Anyway, that's only a guess, and my memory isn't too good. We were full of beer."

"I'm sitting in the parking lot of Pigale right now," said Flanagan. "I'm about to go in, show your picture, Ed's picture, see if anybody remembers anything about you two. Are you sure there's nothing else you want to tell me before I do that? Maybe you two argued? There's no point hiding the truth, because if I find out you've been lying to me it won't go well for you."

"Why do you keep trying that shit with me? I didn't argue with him, or fight with him and I don't have any idea how he ended up in the canal."

"Tell me," said Flanagan. "Do you own a set of handcuffs?"

"No. I don't. Christ. Did Ed have handcuffs on him when he was pulled from the water?"

"No, he didn't, but we think he may have had cuffs on him earlier. There are bruises on his wrists. You two didn't get into a tussle with the Gatineau cops or anything?"

"No. We were happy drunks."

"All right," said Flanagan. "That's all I've got for you now, but I think we're going to have to have another sit-down soon."

"Is there any chance that this could be connected to Ed's work?"

"Why do you ask?"

"Well, I don't know that much about his job, but there'd be a lot of money riding on some of his files," said Jack. "And his boss is probably going to run for the Conservative leadership. That's what the gossip is. I don't know how any of that could be connected, but it's worth looking into."

"You got any specific ideas?"

"No."

"My partner's looking into that stuff. She's on the Hill now, talking to the people in his office. You sure you don't have any specific ideas, anything he ever talked about?"

"Nope," said Jack.

"Okay," said Flanagan. "Stay in touch. We get uneasy when we can't get in touch with you, and when I get uneasy I get grumpy. You haven't seen my grumpy side but you wouldn't like it."

"I hear you loud and clear."

After he hung up, Jack checked his email and then scanned the *Citizen*. The front page was dedicated to Stevens's surprise announcement.

Jack found a short piece in the local briefs at the back of the first section.

Man Rescued From Rideau Canal

A young Ottawa man was pulled from the Rideau Canal

early Tuesday morning after nearly drowning.

Edward Sawatski, 28, was rescued by a jogger, who spotted him in the water next to the locks where the canal enters the Ottawa River, and dived in to administer mouth-to-mouth resuscitation, police said.

"If it wasn't for the quick thinking of the jogger, who dove into the freezing water, the young man might have lost his life," said Ottawa Police Service spokesman Dwayne Enright.

Enright said the heroic jogger didn't want to be publicly identified.

Sawatski is being treated at Ottawa Hospital.

Jack was glad there were no more details. Whoever rewrote the police news release obviously didn't know Sawatski was a Hill staffer, or hadn't bothered to Google his name. Other reporters might notice the name in the paper, and put two and two together, but Jack had to be way ahead of them. He had a great story on his hands, and he grinned as he bent to look through the rest of the paper.

His grin disappeared when he read the next item in the column of briefs.

Two Killed In Single-Car Crash

Ottawa taxi driver Abdullah Arar and his passenger, Winnipeg man Duncan Powers, were killed Tuesday night in a single-car crash on the Airport Parkway.

The Ottawa Police Service said the men were killed instantly when the taxi crashed into the concrete overpass at about 8 p.m.

A witness in another vehicle said the taxi driver appeared to swerve to avoid a black sedan that lost control in fresh snow and entered the taxi's lane.

Police are seeking more witnesses.

Claude Bouchard hadn't bothered putting on his hat for the

short walk from Centre Block to Langevin, and he was regretting it. The freezing wind felt like it was trying to rip the skin off his forehead, and he had to fight the urge to clamp his hands over his burning ears.

He wasn't having a good morning.

He had spent years quietly planning for Greg Mowat to take over from Bruce Stevens, discreetly putting together a network of organizers and supporters across the country, and he was sure that Donahoe's people had no idea how far behind they were. The race was Mowat's to lose, but there was a last tricky bit of road to cover before Bouchard and his guy got to the finish line, and Balusi and Knowles were in a position to put blocks in his path.

The thought put a knot in his guts. But he had the inside track with Balusi, who, unlike Knowles, hoped to stay in Langevin after Stevens' exit, and thus had good reasons to make himself useful to the likely next occupant of Knowles' office. But Balusi had given him no indication of the subject of today's meeting when he had summoned him by email early this morning, and he had ignored Bouchard's messages and calls since then, which wasn't a good sign.

Balusi still gave no hint of what was up when Bouchard got off the elevator on the fourth floor of Langevin. He led him straight him to Knowles's office.

Knowles, looking cool and bloodless in his blue suit, shook hands with him, thanked him for coming and invited him to sit down at the end of the coffee table.

There was a document on the table in front of each man. Knowles and Balusi both had marked up copies, with colour-coded plastic tabs sticking out the side. Bouchard's copy was crisp and new.

"You want some coffee?" asked Knowles.

"Sure," said Bouchard. "Cream and sugar."

Knowles glanced at Balusi, who went for the coffee. Bouchard picked up the document.

It was thin, with a cover of thick white stock.

The coat of arms of the Auditor General was in the

middle of the cover. It was titled: *An Audit of the Correctional Infrastructure Renewal Program.*

This can't be good, thought Bouchard. The Auditor General, Adam Duncan, was a hard ass, with a long record of delivering blunt, harsh reports without regard to the political consequences for the party in power.

Bouchard looked at Knowles, who was regarding him with a thin smile.

"The AG is releasing this today," he said.

Knowles nodded. "The journalists are in the lockup now. They'll be out just before Question Period."

"I understand it's not a, um, positive report," said Bouchard.

"That's right," said Knowles. He turned to look as Balusi came into the room with Bouchard's coffee.

"Ismael, Claude wants to know if the report is positive?" Knowles said. "What would you say?"

Balusi put down the coffee in front of Bouchard. "I'd say Duncan's fucking us in the ass today. And he's not using any lube."

Bouchard exhaled. "And you want Mowat to carry this?"

"It's not what we want," said Knowles. "It's what the boss wants."

"You have lines for us?" said Bouchard.

"Well, that's the good news," said Knowles. "We do have lines. And the boss is quite particular about them. We've worked out a two-part communications strategy. The boss will reply in Question Period to the first questions from Pinsent. From there on, he wants the minister of public safety to take all the questions on the file. And he wants the minister to stick very closely to the script."

Bouchard opened the document in front of him and glanced at the executive summary.

"Well, the boss wants what the boss wants, but I'm sure you know that the request for proposals for CIRP was set up by Donahoe when he was at Public Safety, and administered by Public Works," he said. "Our department had nothing to do with handling the contracts. We've been completely out of the loop. Wouldn't it make more sense for De Grandpré to handle the questions, since his department is actually the one that fucked this up? They have had this report for months. They've worked with that cocksucker Duncan on this!"

"As you say," said Knowles. "The boss wants what the boss wants."

Balusi cleared his throat. "Just between us, not to be repeated outside this room, the boss was upset about the leak yesterday. Until then, the plan was for De Grandpré to handle the questions today. This morning, the boss decided he wants your guy to carry the ball."

Bouchard looked back and forth at the two men. "Okay. Fair enough. But at least put on some romantic music before we get started here."

Jack was filled with dread as he approached Ed's hospital room. He was afraid of hospitals, and afraid at how he would react when he saw his old friend comatose. He felt a little better when he heard a familiar tune: "Gotta Get Me Moose, B'y," by Buddy Wasisname and the Other Fellers, wafting from Ed's room. He paused in the doorway, and saw that the music was coming from a portable stereo on a table near the bed on which his old friend was lying flat on his back, staring vacantly at the ceiling, his parents and Sophie clustered around him.

Sophie jumped up and hugged him when he arrived, and introduced him to Ed's parents.

"I'm sorry I couldn't visit yesterday," he said.

Sophie said, "Mrs. Sawatski has been talking to Ed and she thinks he understands what she's saying."

"I'm sure of it," said Mrs. Sawatski. "A mother knows her son."

She led Jack over to the bed. Jack tried to smile down at his friend's blank face, which he found terribly difficult to do. The fact that Ed's eyes were open made it worse. There was no light in his eyes. He didn't look like someone sleeping, but as blank and unmoving as a mannequin or a crash test dummy. Jack fought the urge to grimace and flee for the hallway. He felt the eyes of Sophie and the Sawatskis on him as he struggled to smile at his friend.

"Hey honey," said Mrs. Sawatski. "Look who's here. It's your friend Jack."

"Hey buddy," said Jack. "What are you at?"

Ed blinked but his eyes showed no flicker of recognition.

"See," said Mrs. Sawatski. "He blinks. That's how you can tell that he's hearing us. Tell him what you've been doing."

Jack smiled at Mrs. Sawatski and glanced at Sophie, who looked back at him blankly.

"Well, b'y," he said. "I hope they're treating you all right in here." He looked up at Sophie and Mrs. Sawatski, who nodded encouragingly. "You've got some tunes, eh, b'y? Tunes from home. That's just great."

"It was Mrs. Sawatski's idea," said Sophie. "She sent Mr. Sawatski to buy the stereo and got me to bring in Ed's iPod today."

"It perked him right up," said Mrs. Sawatski. "Ed loves music."

"He sure does," said Jack. He turned to his friend. "Remember when we saw Great Big Sea on George Street? By Jesus there was some crowd of ol' drunks out for that, eh? Thousands of people, all jumping up and down, singing along with every song. That was a time, eh?"

Ed blinked.

"See," said Mrs. Sawatski. "He's saying yes. He does remember. Don't you Ed?"

But Ed didn't blink again.

"You'd better get better soon," said Jack. "Because it looks like your guy Donahoe is going to need all the help he can get. I think he's in the race, but people think he's likely already fallen behind that arsehole Mowat."

Jack remembered who Sophie worked for and frowned at her in apology.

"Whoops," he said. "I guess I'd better watch what I say in

front of your girlfriend, here. Sorry, Sophie. I was just kidding with Ed here. Ed likes a joke, don't you, b'y?"

He babbled on for a while longer, telling Ed what little Hill gossip he could think of but he found it painful. When a nurse came in to feed Ed his lunch, Jack took it as his excuse to leave.

"Well, Ed, I got to get back to the Hill," he said eventually. "You hang tough, okay? I'll come back to see you as soon as I can. You get better, now. I got plans for us to have a bit of fun, all right."

When Jack took Ed's limp hand in his to shake hands goodbye, he pulled up his sleeve to have a look at the fading bruise on his wrist.

As he said his goodbyes, promising to visit again soon, he thought about asking the Sawatskis if they had anything they wanted to say for his story, but he couldn't make himself do it.

There was a good crowd in the press gallery for Question Period, including a gaggle of reporters fresh from the Auditor General's lockup. They had filed their initial stories on the report into the wasteful and possibly corrupt federal prison-building program, and were now keen to watch how the government would cope with the Opposition's attacks.

Jack didn't know what was in the report, and his paper would rely on Canadian Press copy for stories about it, but he still wanted to watch the action. He tucked in his earpiece and opened his notebook just as Pinsent got to his feet to deliver the first question.

"Mr. Speaker," said the Liberal leader. "When will this government realize that its approach to fighting crime is wrong? Mr. Speaker, let me tell you what the Auditor General found. I quote: 'Billions were spent without appropriate controls.' The government relied on private prison contractors with links to the government and now it can't show how the money was spent. How can the prime minister explain this?"

The Liberal MPs nodded as Pinsent spoke, and when he

finished they rose to their feet and applauded enthusiastically. The report was damning and the government was on the hook for it. Finally a scandal that might damage Stevens had fallen into their laps.

Stevens rose calmly to his feet, his hands clasped in front of him. "Mr. Speaker, the Auditor General's report has identified some administrative problems with the Correctional Infrastructure Renewal Program. The Auditor General and we have different opinions on some details of the public-private partnerships. Departmental officials have already taken the steps recommended by the Auditor General to provide a more complete accounting in the future. That's what we will do. What we won't do is go back to the bad old days, when the Liberals ran our justice system with a revolving door for criminals. This government will not turn back."

The Tories rose to their feet and applauded the prime minister; when Pinsent stood again, they jeered.

"Mr. Speaker, the Auditor General has found that hundreds of millions of dollars were spent without basic accounting. I quote: 'The contracts with service providers did not have elementary mechanisms to allow the government to ensure that money was spent appropriately.' One of these firms, SecuriTech, employs the prime minister's former chief of staff. It won $440 million in contracts. How does the prime minister explain the stench of corruption?"

The Liberals rose to applaud their leader, and the Tories shouted and heckled. Stevens sat with a small smile on his face while the Speaker rose to quiet the screams and catcalls.

"Mr. Speaker, the Liberal leader is right," said Stevens, calmly. "Our party is tough on crime. He would prefer that we follow the Liberal policy, of allowing violent criminals off with a slap on the wrist. He would rather that gangs be free to terrorize law-abiding citizens, that seniors live in fear. Well, that may be what the Liberals want, but it's not what Canadians want, and this government won't ever apologize for being tough on crime! Never!"

The Conservatives rose to their feet and applauded and

stomped their feet.

The next question was from Eileen Cross, the Liberal justice critic. It was to the point.

"Mr. Speaker, the Auditor General identifies dozens of contracts that were let to a handful of private prison construction companies for services that the contracts define so vaguely that the auditors could not determine that taxpayers received any benefit. Can the government provide this House with what it failed to provide the auditors: an explanation of where the money went?"

Greg Mowat stood to answer. He smiled at the Speaker and said quietly, "Mr. Speaker, in 1997, when the Liberals were in power, a drug dealer named Ivan Baldwin was released on parole after serving only four months of his two-year sentence on three counts of aggravated assault. He was released under a Liberal community sentencing program. Do you know what happened next? He killed a six-year-old child a week later in a drive-by shooting. That is Liberal justice, Mr. Speaker. This government will not stand by while children are murdered in the street!"

Cross rose again.

"Let's try again," she said. "The Auditor General identified one $8-million contract that went to SecuriTech. The prime minister's chief of staff used to sit on the board. The contract was for security consulting. The Auditor General found that departmental staff could provide only, and I quote, 'vague generalities,' to describe the services performed. Mr. Speaker, where did the $8 million go?"

Mowat smiled as he rose to answer.

"Mr. Speaker," he said. "Liberal justice is not justice. Consider the case of Daman Winston. In 2002 the young man was released on probation after serving only six months of a three-year sentence for sexual assault. He had received a three-for-one bonus for the time he had spent in remand. That was Liberal justice. Do you know what happened? He sexually assaulted five more women before police apprehended him. That is Liberal justice, Mr. Speaker, and the honourable member should have the guts to stand in this place and apologize to the women who were assaulted by Daman Winston!"

The Conservatives applauded as he sat down, and heckled Cross. "Apologize," they shouted. Stevens was reading though a stack of documents on his desk, but he allowed himself a small smile.

Ashton sat at her desk in the investigations unit at the Ottawa Police Service headquarters, working on the timeline of the events in the Sawatski case, and making a list of leads to pursue. After a day and a half of investigation, she and Flanagan hadn't made much progress. They had no suspects, no motives and no compelling evidence that a crime had even taken place, except for some bruises on the victim's wrists, and some inconclusive videotape.

It wasn't looking good.

She was staring at the paperwork when her phone rang. It was Captain Wayne Zwicker, the director of criminal investigations. He wanted to see her in his office.

He was waiting for her with the door open, sitting at his big oak desk, a tall, athletic man in his fifties with a bit of a pot belly that barely showed under his thick blue uniform.

"Detective Sergeant," he said, standing as she arrived. "How's it going?"

"Good, Captain," she said. "Working this Sawatski case."

He gestured for her to sit down. "That's what I want to ask you about," he said, his face neutral, his blue eyes unblinking. "Fill me in."

"We're working our leads, trying to reconstruct the hours before Sawatski ended up in the water. Flanagan's over in Gatineau, at Pigale, trying to see if any of the staff remember anything."

"Do you have a working theory?" asked Zwicker.

"There's a blank spot beginning at about 3:50 a.m., when he said goodnight to his friend and headed home in a taxi. An hour later, he was found floating face down in the canal, barely alive, with handcuff bruises on his wrists. We think someone snatched him, put the cuffs on him and held him under until he stopped struggling. They thought he was dead, removed the cuffs and let him float away, but his heart was still beating."

"Got any suspects? A motive?"

"So far, no," said Ashton. "The victim is a political staffer with no ties to crime that we've been able to find. Neither his girlfriend nor the friend he was drinking with would seem to have a motive to do him in."

"Has it occurred to you that he might have fallen into the canal?" asked Zwicker.

"Well, yeah, Captain," said Ashton. "We'd be happy to mark it down as an accident, but there are a few things that make us think that's unlikely. For one, the kid was once a life guard. Even if he was drunk, it's unlikely that he would end up drowning in two feet of water. Then there's the handcuff bruises, and we have a video. It seems to show him walking under the bridge by the canal with another man shortly before we think he went into the water."

He looked down at a notepad on his desk.

"So, tell me about your meeting today with David Cochrane."

Ashton didn't expect that. "What, the guy in Donahoe's office?"

Zwicker wasn't making eye contact. "Yes."

Ashton shrugged. "I thought I should get some idea of what kind of work Sawatski did. I guess I was, you know, looking for clues."

"Do you have any reason to think somebody tried to drown the kid because of his work as –" he looked down at his notes "– a policy adviser to the minister of justice?"

"I don't know why somebody would want to drown him," said Ashton.

Zwicker put the tips of his fingers together and looked away from Ashton. "I'm told you asked for access to the files the kid was working."

Ashton nodded at him. "Looking for clues."

"Okay," said Zwicker. "I'm told that you need the kind of security clearance that nobody in this office has to see those documents. I'm told we need a good reason before we start pressing the office of the minister of justice to release secret documents to us."

Ashton shrugged.

"They suggest that we would likely have to have our lawyers talk to the Justice Department's lawyers before any such documents would be forthcoming," he said. "And, I didn't know this, but they tell me that in the future any visits you make to Parliament Hill should be cleared with the office of the Speaker of the House of Commons, or the Speaker of the Senate, depending on where the office is."

Zwicker looked up from his notes. "We don't have jurisdiction in the parliamentary precinct. It's something to do with parliamentary privilege."

"I didn't know that," said Ashton.

"Now," said Zwicker. "As to your request to look at Sawatski's files, I'd need something in writing to show to our lawyers. That would be a lot of paperwork." He shrugged. "Go ahead if you want, but it might be better to work your other angles first."

"Okay," said Ashton. "I'll think it over, talk to Flanagan before we do anything else."

Zwicker got to his feet. "Great. Can you give me a report on the progress of the investigation by noon tomorrow?"

"That will take up some time I could spend digging," said Ashton. He returned her gaze, expressionlessly, waiting. "But yeah. Of course."

"Tomorrow we'll have to have a look, see where we are with the whole thing," he said. "Also, Public Affairs tells me they've had some calls about this. For the moment, we don't want to release anything more to the media. So don't talk to any reporters."

"Of course," said Ashton.

He escorted her to the door and held it open for her. As she walked away, he called out.

"Hey," he said. "By the way, when you get back to your desk, send up a copy of the pictures of the handcuff bruises, and the video."

Jack decided he'd better skip the scrums after Question Period and start writing his story about Sawatski. The Telegram could use the wire services to handle the Auditor General's report. He called his editor, told him he was working on his exclusive, and started to type, stopping every now and then to listen to the recordings he'd made of his conversations with Flanagan.

By JACK MACDONALD
Ottawa Bureau
OTTAWA – A St. John's man working in the office of Justice Minister Jim Donahoe is in hospital recovering from an attack that police consider to be suspicious.

Ed Sawatski, 28, a policy adviser in Donahoe's office, was pulled from the Rideau Canal early Tuesday morning when a jogger spotted him floating face down. The jogger, whom police have not identified, jumped into the water and administered mouth-to-mouth resuscitation, saving Sawatski's life.

Police have made no official comment on how Donahoe ended up in the canal, but sources close to the investigation say they suspect foul play, in part because Sawatski has what appear to be handcuff bruises on both wrists.

"We think he may have had cuffs on him earlier," said one source. "There are marks on his wrists."
Sources say Sawatski is still unconscious, having spent about a half an hour face down in the water.

Police are seeking a connection between Sawatski's near drowning and his work in Donahoe's office. Officers are interviewing his colleagues there, a source close to the investigation says.

Police are also looking into Sawatski's movements in the hours before he wound up in the canal. Sawatski was drinking at Pigale, an exotic cabaret in Gatineau, Quebec, across the Ottawa River from the capital, early Tuesday morning.

Sawatski, who grew up in Mount Pearl, attended Memorial University, earning a degree in political science, and worked in the office of Newfoundland Premier Danny Williams until he landed a job in Donahoe's office.

Donahoe and Public Safety Minister Greg Mowat are said to be the two leading contenders for the leadership of the federal Conservative Party. Prime Minister Bruce Stevens announced Tuesday that he will resign once the party chooses a successor.

Jack stopped typing when the newsroom TV showed Ellen Simms holding a copy of the Auditor General's report and standing in the House of Commons foyer, with reporters and politicians milling around behind her.

"Sparks flew here today when the Liberals accused the government of favouring its friends in prison construction contracts," she said. "Backed by an Auditor General's report that found administrative irregularities in some of the prisons the government has built as part of its tough-on-crime agenda, Liberal Leader Evan Pinsent went on the attack."

She played the clip of Pinsent sputtering in the House: "This government has wasted billions building prisons in pursuit of a dim-witted American-style policy that everybody knows does not work. And why? So they can brag that they're tough on crime!"

"Well, the prime minister didn't take that sitting down," said Simms. "He countered by attacking the Liberals for being soft on crime."

The report cut to a clip of Stevens, looking firm but calm. "Our party is tough on crime," he was saying. "The Leader of the Opposition says that our policies do not work. He would prefer that we follow the Liberal policy of allowing violent criminals off with a slap on the wrist."

Simms beamed at the camera. "But the Conservatives

didn't stop there," she said. "When the Liberals pressed further, they went on the attack. Here's Public Safety Minister Greg Mowat." She played the clip of Mowat demanding that the Liberals apologize to rape victims.

"Opposition MPs said Mowat had gone too far," she said, and played a clip of NDP Leader Lesley Nowlan talking to reporters in the lobby. "I think this is the worst I've seen since I've been in the House of Commons. Stevens and Greg Mowat should be ashamed of themselves. They're hiding behind the victims of crime."

Simms said, "But the Conservatives were making no apologies."

Next was a clip of Mowat in the lobby, confronting a noisy throng of reporters. "I will not apologize for what I said today," he said. "It's the Liberals who should apologize to the many Canadians who were victimized by their soft-on-crime policies."

Simms signed off: "For NTV, I'm Ellen Simms."

The phone on Murphy's desk rang the moment the story ended. It was Jim Godin, communications director to Pinsent.

"What the fuck was that?" he said. "That was the biggest fucking blow job I've seen in my entire life, and I've seen some doozies."

"I take it you didn't like Ellen's QP piece," said Murphy.

"Jesus Christ," said Godin. "I've never seen anything like that. We have a scathing Auditor General's report, which comes very close to proving the government's friends are getting kickbacks for their unbelievably stupid multi-billion-dollar prison-building spree, and when I watch NTV, do I see the Auditor General? Do I hear his quotes? Hold on. I have them here. Did you see his news conference? He said that he 'had no idea whether taxpayers received any value at all' for many contracts. Jesus Christ! And you guys buried him. You didn't even put his clips on the air. Instead, you made it look like we were sticking up for rapists!"

"All right, all right," said Murphy. "Take it easy. I'm listening." And as he listened, he sent Simms an email, asking her to come to his office.

"I expect you guys to pull some of your punches with the Tories, but this is different," said Godin. "I don't think I've ever seen such a slanted piece of shit. You can't tell me you think it's good. I know you better than that."

"Okay," said Murphy. "I understand you. You're expressing a concern here because the piece downplayed the contents of the Auditor General's report and, in your opinion, gave too much prominence to the government's counter-arguments. Is that right?"

"Yes," said Godin. "I am expressing that concern."

"Okay," said Murphy. "I read you loud and clear. I want you to know that I am taking your complaint very seriously, and we'll take a good look at what you've said, and keep it in mind when we put together our piece for the nightly news."

"You're going to take another look at it and consider my concerns when you put together your piece for the nightly news?"

"Which has two million viewers. As opposed to the bit you just saw, which has a viewership of, what, forty thousand."

"Okay," said Godin.

"You feel better now?"

"Yeah, I do. Thanks."

"Well, thanks for your call."

Simms stuck her head around his office door a couple of minutes after he hung up.

"Hey," he said, smiling. "Come in. Sit down. How you doing?"

She gave him a nervous look as she sat down, crossed her legs and tossed her red hair.

"You have a problem with the QP piece?" she asked.

"Yeah," he said. "I do. It's a well-put together piece of TV journalism. Lots of drama, emotion. The cuts are fast, and your stand-up bits are excellent."

"What's the problem then?"

"It doesn't communicate the substance of what the Auditor General reported today, and the piece we put on the air tonight needs to do that."

"If you say so. Did you watch his news conference? The guy's such an accountant. Couldn't give a good quote to save his life."

"I know," said Murphy. "It's true, but we have to lead with what he found. It's a lot of money and it raises real questions about the government. It looks like they might be kicking back money to their friends."

"That's not what Duncan said though."

"He can't say that, because he doesn't know that. But he does say that he doesn't know where the money went and has 'grave concerns.' That's auditor speak for a big deal."

"Okay. I can include more background on his report."

"As it is now, the piece makes it seem like the Opposition is angry because the government is locking up criminals."

Simms was unconvinced. "Look, I don't know if I want to make this too negative on the government. Last night you told me I should cultivate sources near Mowat and Donahoe. But if I do the piece the way you want, Mowat won't like it. He might shut me out."

Murphy drummed his fingers on his desk. "I'll tell you what. I'll do the AG piece, and we'll lead with that. Then you can follow up with a reaction piece, with whatever clips I don't use from QP and the scrums. That way if Mowat gives you grief, you can tell him it was me. Tell them I'm a hard ass and insisted that I do the lead piece, because I thought your piece was too soft on them."

He laughed, then stood up. "I've got to go. If I'm going to do the piece for tonight, I'd better get to work."

He looked back at Simms, who was still sitting with a perplexed expression on her face.

"I'm not joking," he said. "Tell them it was my idea, and tell them they're likely not going to like the piece."

Jack filed his article and called his editor to talk through it. They made a few small tweaks, and his editor quizzed him about some of the sourcing, but his answers satisfied him.

"That's a good fucking story, b'y," said his editor. "Them b'ys up there will be following us for a change tomorrow. Good work."

Jack made his way outside, where he stood on the steps of the Peace Tower, smoking a cigarette and smiling at his colleagues, who were heading home after filing their stories about the prison-building program gone wrong. In a few hours, when his story went online, they would learn that he'd scooped them with a juicy Parliament Hill crime story. He smiled inwardly in anticipation, and then he thought about the subject of his scoop, and chill came over him.

Back at his desk, he gave Sophie a call and asked how Ed was doing.

"It's hard to know," said Sophie. "His mom keeps saying that he can understand when we talk to him, and I almost think she's right. He blinks occasionally after someone says something, and it really seems like he's acknowledging it. Other times, though, it seems totally random. The doctor says he might be sort of fading in and out. Maybe sometimes he's registering what we're saying and other times he's not."

"That's so hard," said Jack.

"Well, it's reality, at least for now," said Sophie. "We have to keep talking to him and hope that he gets better."

"Well, I'll pop in to see him when I can," said Jack.

"It'll get easier," said Sophie. "I felt bad for you today, with his mom making you talk to him, but she has the right idea. If you engage him directly, try to communicate, we might be reaching him."

"Maybe there is reason to hope."

"There is always reason to hope," said Sophie, and she laughed. "Listen to me, the wise woman."

"So you still there?"

"No. I'm at home. I'm having a bite, then I'll sit with Ed while his parents go out for dinner."

"Sophie, I think you should let them know I've got a story on Ed coming out tomorrow. I didn't want to tell them about it today. It seemed like too much."

"What kind of story?"

"Nothing much," said Jack. "Just the facts. He's in hospital after nearly drowning. The police are investigating. I didn't want to do it, but my editors said it would be a story at home."

"Shouldn't you tell his parents yourself, give them a chance to comment?" said Sophie.

"I just really don't want to bother them."

"You don't mention me or Minister Mowat?"

"No. I didn't see any reason to drag you into it."

"Okay," said Sophie.

"Call me later if you feel like talking, after you're finished at the hospital."

Ashton and Flanagan met in the police station cafeteria when he got back from Gatineau.

"How was the ballet?" asked Ashton, when she walked up to the table with coffees for both of them

"Ah, you know," said Flanagan, laughing. "Seen one you seen 'em all."

"I bet," said Ashton, turning a chair backwards and straddling it. "Did you have time for a little grind?"

"Jesus, Mary and Joseph," said Flanagan. "I'm a good Catholic. I wouldn't dream of it. Anyway, the wife would kill me."

"Devon, you're divorced."

"I am," he said and winked. "She divorced me for being a bad husband. Think what she'd do if she caught me with a naked lady."

They laughed together.

"So did you learn anything?" Ashton asked, sipping from

her old Ottawa Police Service mug.

"Not a whole lot," said Flanagan, flipping open his notebook. "I did talk, though, to one Henri Tremblay, driver for Regal Taxi, who is pretty sure he drove Jack Macdonald to his residence and Ed Sawatski to his. Mr. Tremblay is ninety-five per cent sure that they were the two guys in question. I suspect the five per cent is just in case he has to go to court to testify and finds out some tough guys don't want him to. He was carting drunks home after Pigale closed. The time matches. He can't remember the exact addresses, but the neighbourhoods match with Macdonald and Sawatski's addresses. Said they didn't say anything, and he didn't see where either of them went once they got out of his cab."

"Shit," said Ashton.

"Shit is right," said Flanagan. "And, before you ask, he didn't find a BlackBerry in his cab."

Flanagan turned the page in his notebook. "According to the best recollection of one –" he flipped more pages "– Rejean Masouf, a security professional at Pigale, the two gentlemen appeared to be thoroughly intoxicated. He remembers them because they were so drunk. They weren't causing trouble, but apparently one of them fell down and Masouf thought about ejecting them for drunkenness. It was after last call, though, so he decided to just wait till they left."

"Did you talk to the girl?"

"Regrettably, the likely dancer in question, a short blonde with a nose ring, one Michelle Gagnon, is from Montreal and has returned to that city. I doubt that she has much to tell us, though, since she doesn't speak English, and Sawatski apparently isn't too good with the *parlez vous*. Also, Mr. Masouf does not have contact information for Mademoiselle Gagnon, and suggested that I look for her in similar establishments in Montreal, which I would be only too happy to do, if you think there's any way we can sell a road trip to Zwicker."

Ashton laughed. "I don't think that he'd approve that. Of course, should you continue your investigations after work, or on the weekend, he could hardly complain."

"I hadn't thought of that." Flanagan grinned.

Ashton frowned at him.

"Zwicker called me up to his office. He asked for a report by noon tomorrow."

Flanagan shook his head. "He's gonna shut us down."

"Looks like it. And he asked me to send him the pictures of the kid's handcuff bruises and the bridge video."

Flanagan sighed. "No sign of a crime here. No suspect. No evidence. Time to move on."

"I imagine that's about it."

"It doesn't feel like that to me."

"His call," said Ashton.

They sat in silence while a janitor pushed a broom past them.

"So I went up to see David Cochrane today, the chief of staff to Jim Donahoe, Sawatski's boss," Ashton said. "I asked to see a breakdown of the files he was working on. Cochrane said they'd kick it around, talk to a security officer at the Privy Council Office and get back to me. When I got back here, that's when Zwicker called me in."

"Said he didn't think you needed to go poking around in secret government of Canada files."

"That's right. Said lawyers would have to get involved. Said that if I really wanted to see the files, I should submit a request up the chain of command."

Flanagan whistled. "We'd better hope we get some stronger evidence tomorrow," he said.

It took Jack fifteen minutes of driving a maze of suburban streets before he found Ida Gushue's grey brick split level deep in Ottawa South. He swished the last of his coffee around in his mouth and checked his teeth in the rearview mirror.

Ida Gushue, a handsome woman in her fifties, met him at the door. She wore her greying blond hair in a bun. Reading glasses hung on a chain around her neck. She led Jack to an immaculate living room, seated him on the sofa and went to put the kettle on for tea. Jack's gaze was caught by a large framed photo a table by the wall. It was a formal portrait of a smiling man with a bristly moustache in a scarlet Mountie uniform, but the man's smile was warm, and he had a twinkle in his eye.

"Is this your husband?" Jack asked when Mrs. Gushue came back in.

"Yes," she said. "That's Earl. He passed away last year."

"I'm sorry for your loss."

"It has not been easy. Our daughter, Erin, was in her first year at Memorial when Earl passed away."

"She's still down there?"

"Yes. We thought it would be good for her to go to school in Newfoundland, but I sometimes wish that she was here."

"You're originally from Newfoundland, are you?"

"That's right. Earl joined the Mounties when we were first married, and we were posted to different communities across Canada. We moved to Ottawa in 2009. It was to be Earl's last post before retiring. We had planned on moving to our summer place in Ferryland. We were planning the renovations."

In the kitchen the kettle started to sing, summoning Mrs. Gushue, who came back a few minutes later carrying a tea tray, and they both fussed with sugar and milk.

"So," Jack said, lifting scalding tea to his lips. "Have you got any idea why Ed called you?"

"Well, my husband worked on a case that had possible political implications, and I wonder if that is why your friend was calling. But I can't be sure. Tell me what kind of work he did."

"He was a policy adviser to the minister of justice," said Jack. "Beyond that, I don't know a lot. I'm a reporter, so he was never very forthcoming with me about what he did."

Gushue blew on her tea and kept her eyes on Jack. "Can you think of any reason why he would want to talk to a retired school teacher about Justice Department policy?"

"No" said Jack. "What was the political connection to the case your husband worked on?"

She ignored his question. "Is your friend still in a coma?"

"He is," said Jack. "I went to see him today. His eyes are open and he seems at times to follow what's going on around him, but he hasn't spoken. His mother insists that he understands what people say to him, but it didn't seem like that to me."

"Poor woman," said Mrs. Gushue. "I can't imagine how terrible she must feel. Are the police investigating? Do they suspect someone may have tried to drown him?"

Jack told her how they had been drinking together, although he didn't mention where, and told her what he had learned from his interviews with police.

"It's all very mysterious," said Mrs. Gushue.

"Can you give me some idea of how your husband's case might be connected to this?" said Jack.

She opened her mouth to speak, then thought for moment while she took a sip of tea. "I'm not at all sure that I should tell you about this. I wanted to see you because I thought you might have some idea why your friend tried to contact me, so that I could forget about the whole thing. But I can't think of anything else but the case my husband handled."

"Um, I wonder ... Perhaps you could give me some sense of what you've got?"

She was suddenly all business, looking at him with her sharp pale eyes. "I want to know you that you won't reveal what I'm about to tell you, to anyone, not even your editor, unless I decide I want to go with a story."

"I'd rather go to jail than reveal a source," he said. "I swear I won't tell anyone what you tell me without your permission."

She looked at him, appraisingly. "You should know, Mr. Macdonald, that my maiden name was Sullivan. You may know my uncle, Allan Sullivan."

The Sullivans owned the *Telegram*. Allan Sullivan, the publisher, was a remote and powerful figure to Macdonald.

"Then you have the added comfort of knowing, Ms. Gushue, that if I break my word, you could cost me my job."

"Yes, Mr. Macdonald, you're right. I do have that comfort.

You probably think I'm an old fool, with no idea of how politics works. But I'm not. Before I met my husband, I worked in Brian Peckford's office."

She looked at him sharply.

"Mr. Peckford was premier then," she said.

Jack nodded, meaning to show that he knew that.

"I kept my eyes and ears open, so I know a thing or two about the business," she said.

"I'm quite sure you do," said Jack.

"Yes, well," she said. "After my husband's death I didn't have the energy to deal with all of his things. I just recently sorted through some of his papers and I found a case file, which in itself is quite surprising. My husband was a stickler for the rules. He never brought case files home. This one had to do with a murder he investigated – the murder of a prostitute in Fort McMurray. Unless I am mistaken, the information in the file would end the career of a prominent Canadian politician."

Jack stared at her blankly before he spoke. "If you have information that raises serious questions about the fitness of a cabinet minister, you have an obligation to make it public."

She laughed, and Jack saw a flash of her as a young woman.

"No," she said. "No I don't. My obligations are anything but clear. If my husband had followed the law, I wouldn't be in possession of this file, although I'm under no legal obligation to return it, not so far as I'm aware. I can't say I'm sure what to do about it. I've told you as much as I have so that you will take me seriously. I'm going to mull it over, likely over the holidays when Erin and I are home visiting family. I may seek advice from an old family friend." She smiled at Jack and placed her cup on the tray.

"I come from a Tory family, as I'm sure you know," she said. "We opposed Confederation, but eventually reconciled to it and made common cause with the federal Conservatives. That's a relationship of some fifty years. I must decide whether, in the long run, the information I have is more likely to hurt my family, the party, or the country. It's far from black and white. I need to think about it. I'll get in touch with you in the new year."

She stood up. "I want to thank you for coming."

Jack stayed seated. "If there is some possibility of a connection between a murder in Fort McMurray and what happened to Ed, and you stay silent about it, you could be letting some bad people get away with mischief."

"That is one of the things I must consider," she said. "Believe me, I don't take that lightly."

"There are some things I haven't told you," he said, making no move to stand. "I've been followed and my apartment has been searched, and not by the Ottawa Police. I have the feeling there are some dangerous people with an interest in this, so you should be very careful."

"I will," she said. "I promise you that. I'll get in touch with you."

He reluctantly stood up and she showed him the door.

Balusi got a glass of red wine at the bar and carried it over to a booth in the rear of Hy's, where Bouchard was working his BlackBerry, a double Scotch on the rocks resting on the table in front of him.

"How's it going?" said Balusi.

"I've had better fucking days," said Bouchard, and nodded at his drink. "But it's starting to get a little better."

Balusi eased into the booth across from him. "It wasn't pretty, but I think it could have been even worse."

"Have you seen the clippings?"

"Yeah. Not terrific."

"Here's one I like," said Bouchard, and read from his BlackBerry: " 'Mowat disgraced himself and his office today with his below-the-belt attack on the Liberals, an ineffective drive-by smear clumsily designed to draw attention away from the Auditor General's devastating report. The move should give pause to any Conservatives hoping that Mowat would bring a kinder, gentler face to lead a government that too often seems pointlessly vicious.' That's from Taylor, usually one of the friendly columnists." Bouchard shook his head in dismay. "At least the Simms piece was pretty good."

"Well, from what I hear NTV news is going to be tougher tonight. Murphy thought she was too easy on the government and he's doing the piece. I don't think we're going to like it."

Bouchard laughed. "I guess the Stevens leak wasn't such a great idea after all."

Balusi nodded. "I outsmarted myself there. I admit it. I'm sorry, but I won't underestimate the boss again."

"You could have called me this morning," Bouchard said. "Given me a heads-up."

Balusi shook his head. "What would've been the point? So you could lube up? If I'd warned you, Knowles would have seen it in your eyes when he told you. He doesn't miss much and he doesn't trust me."

Bouchard laughed, and held up his glass. "Well, he's smarter than me then. Here's to him."

The two men clinked their drinks.

"Hey," said Bouchard. "Look who's here."

Balusi turned to see Ellen Simms approaching, glass of white wine in hand. She had removed her business jacket and looked amazingly sexy in her tight silk blouse and pencil skirt.

"Hey, you scamps," she said. "Gossiping as usual, I see."

"We were talking about you," said Bouchard. "Have a seat."

She flopped down beside Bouchard, tossed her hair and took a weary look around the bar before focusing again on the two men.

"So, that didn't go so well today for your team," she said.

"I thought your piece was good," said Bouchard.

Ellen laughed. "I guess it was a bit too good. Murphy yanked it and he's putting a tougher piece on the air. It's a humdinger. I did the reaction piece."

"Well, you'll all be on the same page then," said Bouchard. "All shitting on my boss."

Ellen stared at him. "Did you see the brief in the *Citizen* about Sawatski?"

Both of them looked at her blankly.

"The kid who worked in Donahoe's office," she said. "They pulled him out of the canal."

"He goes out with Sophie Fortin, who works in your office, Claude," Balusi said.

"I know. I went with the minister to the hospital to see how Sophie was doing."

Ellen frowned at him. "You knew about it? You could have told me. I was trying to get the story today, calling the cops, but they wouldn't give me anything."

"I don't know if it's much of a story," said Bouchard. "Drunk kid falls in canal."

"That's not what the cops think," said Simms, and nodded to her phone.

"What's the story say?" said Balusi.

"I'll flip it to you," said Simms, and she forwarded the story to both men.

They sat there reading it while she scanned the bar.

"Hey," she said. "Is that tall guy at the bar Jack Macdonald?"

Balusi looked up. It was Jack standing at the bar, drinking with a couple of other reporters.

"Yeah," he said. "He's the guy with the Newfoundland paper. He's the guy who got the story."

Bouchard looked up. "The kid in the suit that doesn't fit? That's Macdonald?"

"I wonder how he got it," said Ellen. "I would've thought that the cops liked me better than they like him."

"What the story doesn't tell you is that he was out drinking with Sawatski the night he ended up in the canal," said Bouchard. "That's how he got the story."

Simms kept her eyes on Jack. "I wonder what else he knows. That's a juicy story." She looked at the two glum men with her for a moment, then grabbed her wine glass and got to her feet.

"I'm going to ask him," she said. "See you scamps later."

Bouchard groaned as she walked away. "I bet he tells her."

Jack was leaning against the bar, accepting the

good-natured, half-hearted congratulations of two colleagues who worked for Ontario papers when they suddenly fell silent and looked behind him.

He turned to see Ellen standing behind him, smiling at him.

"Hey, Scoop," she said.

"Uh, hi," he said, smiling and frowning and smiling again. "You're Ellen Simms."

She laughed. "I can see how you get your scoops. You don't miss much."

He leaned back nonchalantly against the bar, but with an effort. Being this close to her was making him nervous.

"I identified you from your television appearances," he said, and winked. "That's how I get a lot of my scoops."

"That's a good one today," she said. "I was chasing that, too."

"Oh, well, you know, got lucky. Really, it just fell in my lap."

"Do things often fall in your lap?" she asked, and glanced quickly down at the front of his trousers. "What kinds of things?"

She smiled and looked away as he blushed.

"All sorts of odd things," he said. "I never know what I'm going to find down there."

She giggled and took a sip of wine, then propped herself against the bar, cutting him off from his colleagues. She spoke without looking at him. "If I invite you to my place for a glass of wine, will you tell me how you got the story?"

"Well, I never talk about my sources, but in this case there's not much of a story," he said.

"Is that a no?" she asked, and she turned her head and looked at him with sad puppy dog eyes.

"Nnnnno," he stammered. "I'd be happy to accept your invitation. I'm just warning you the story might not be worth the wine."

"Well, maybe you'll find a way to make it up to me then," she said, then leaned over until her hair brushed against his cheek and whispered in his ear. "700 Sussex. Buzzer 1483. Give me half an hour. I'm going to go say goodbye to my friends"

Then she gave him a tiny kiss on the cheek and walked over to Balusi and Bouchard, her hips swaying.

Jack watched and took a long drink of his beer.

Sophie eventually managed to convince the reluctant Sawatskis to go out for dinner and sighed with relief when they left. She turned down the stereo, which was playing a Newfoundland jig, and pulled our her iPod. She paused before she plugged it into the stereo's iPod dock.

"Ed," she said. "You don't mind if I change the music, do you?"

He lay mute on his back, staring at the ceiling.

"I'm just going to put my music on for a bit. Okay?"

A Cowboys Fringants song started.

"Here," she said. "We can work on your French."

She lay next to him the bed, took his stiff hand in hers, gave him a small kiss on the cheek and put her head on his shoulder.

She started to sing along softly and sweetly, her mouth next to his ear, singing along to Les Étoiles Filantes.

"Got that?" she asked, when the tune ended.

"No? Well you never studied hard enough at French. Let's see, in English, it says, um, 'Even if we know that nothing lasts forever, I'd like if you were, for the moment, my shooting star.' "

She was quiet then, with her head on his shoulder, letting the pretty song play without singing along.

She propped herself up on her elbow and looked down at Ed's face. She smoothed his hair and kissed him on the mouth.

"That song is kind of right," she said. "Nothing lasts forever. Our lives are like shooting stars. But I thought we'd have more time together than this."

She started to cry silently, the tears running down her cheeks. She put her head back on his shoulder and her tears ran down her cheek and soaked into Ed's hospital gown.

"I never told you, but I hoped you'd propose to me

eventually. I was planning to say no, of course, because we modern Québécoise are too liberated to need a wedding ring." She laughed through her tears for a moment. "But I would have liked you to propose, and I would have maybe, eventually, said yes."

She stroked his hair back from his forehead and kissed him. "And I wanted to have your babies, not yet, but in a few years. I never told you that, but I used to think about it a lot. What they'd look like, how I'd make sure they grew up speaking French. Whether they'd be boys or girls." She stayed still for a moment. "That's why it's important that you get better."

She propped herself up again, meaning to give him a little lecture, but found she couldn't speak.

A tear was running down his cheek.

Jack found it hard to believe he was headed to Ellen Simms's apartment, in the most stylish condo building in downtown Ottawa.

After she buzzed him up, he took his time making his way up, dawdling over the subtle splendour of the carpets, admiring the lovely wallpaper, the quiet beauty of the glass elevator.

"Fix this in your mind, b'y," he said to himself. "This is where the good life is at."

When he got off on her floor, he stopped to appreciate a striking photograph hanging on the wall opposite. It was a beautifully framed, artful black and white photograph of the building.

"Very nice," he said, as if he were being escorted by a realtor. "Nice touch."

Finally, outside her door, he could think of no reason to delay any longer. He knocked, and heard the click of her shoes and then she was there in front of him, holding the door open, smiling. She was holding a glass of wine and had undone the top button on her blouse. She seemed a little drunker.

"Hello, Scoop," she said. "You going to come in or you

going to stand in the doorway?"

Jack stepped inside and she gave him the two-cheek kiss, leaning against him as she did so.

It was quite a place, with a marble and stainless steel kitchen on the right and a step down to the living room straight ahead. A buttery-looking leather couch and armchair were arranged around a steel and glass coffee table, where there was an open bottle of red wine and two empty wine glasses. A big TV hung on the wall. The art – expensively mounted photos of flowers – reminded Jack of the art in the building's hallways: expensive and tasteful but bland. Behind the furniture was a glass wall and sliding door leading to a balcony.

"So, are you inviting me just for a glass of wine, or are you looking for a roommate?" Jack asked, as he followed her to the leather couch.

Ellen laughed and looked over her shoulder at him. "I don't know if you could afford it."

"Not yet," he said. "Give me time."

Jack went out onto the balcony to admire the view of Parliament Hill and the snowy Ottawa River. The arctic wind blasted him the moment he pulled the sliding glass door open, and the drapes went flying. She stepped out with him, and they stood there, shivering and gazing at the glittering scene.

Ellen hugged herself with one arm and smiled up at Jack.

"Were you married before you moved to Ottawa?" he asked.

Her smile turned to a frown in the blink of an eye, and her eyes narrowed and glittered.

"You mean, is that how come I can afford a place like this?" she said. "I thought I was supposed to be the one asking the questions."

Jack laughed. "It's okay. I know the answer anyway. I know more about you than you might guess. Sometimes it seems like all we ever do in the gallery is gossip about you."

The smile was back.

"Reaaaally?" she said. "What do they say?"

Jack smiled at her, and brushed her hair off her face.

"They say you're dangerous," he said. "A femme fatale."

He leaned in to give her a kiss, but she stepped back and slapped him, very softly.

"Easy, tiger," she said, and stepped away. She looked back over her shoulder.

"Time for you to keep your side of the bargain. I want some info."

Jack followed her inside and poured them both a glass of wine. Ellen curled up in the armchair, tucked her knees under herself and cradled her wine glass in both hands. He sat on the couch with his legs crossed and swirled the wine.

"Shoot," he said.

"Tell me how you got that story today," she said, measuring him with her eyes. "The police wouldn't tell me anything."

"Well, like I said," said Jack, "it fell into my lap. Ed and I are friends, and we were out drinking the night before he wound up in the canal. So the police have questioned me several times. You'd have to be stunned not to realize what they were getting at."

"So you interviewed them while they were interviewing you?" said Ellen, squinting at him. "Smart. I'm impressed."

"I don't think they're likely impressed. They had no idea the story was coming."

"Stupid," she said. "You should have tipped them off after you filed. Give them a chance to prepare themselves for the fallout."

Jack shrugged. "You're right."

"So, how do you think Ed ended up in the canal?"

"I don't know," said Jack. "He was pretty hammered. I think it's possible that he fell in. I can't figure out who would want to kill him."

Ellen studied his face.

"You know more than you're saying," she said. She got up and sat next to him on the couch, resting her hand on his thigh.

"You have a secret theory," she said. "Don't you, Scoop?"

Jack smiled. "I might. But if I tell you it won't be much of a secret."

He leaned in and kissed her, and she let him for a moment.

His head swam. Then she put her hand on his chest and pushed him away.

"Tell me," she said.

"No," he said, and leaned in to kiss her again.

She pushed him away and jumped to her feet.

"So," she said, smoothing her skirt, "do you want to see the rest of the place?"

Jack, deflated, got to his feet and followed her back to the kitchen.

"This is the kitchen," she said, and did a little spin in the middle of it, then frowned. "I don't use it much."

He followed her down a hallway to her tidy little office, with a computer and a file cabinet and more bland art prints.

"This is my office," she said, and gestured like a car show model. Then she led him to the last door.

"And this," she said, as she pushed it open, "is my bedroom."

She stepped inside and stood at the foot of her king-sized bed, waiting for him, saying nothing.

He stepped forward and took her in his arms. She returned his kiss this time, and pressed her body against his. He was so aroused that he felt that he might fall down.

He pulled back and stared at her. She smiled at him mischievously, turned and pushed him down on the bed, so that he lay on his back.

"Tell me, Scoop," she said. "Do you know how to keep your mouth shut?"

"Oh my God," he said. "Yes. Yes. Yes."

She climbed on top of him, her legs straddling his waist, and leaned down so that her hair fell in a curtain around his face. She kissed him very gently on the mouth. He put his arms around her and pulled her in closer.

"No," she said, sitting up. She pushed his arms down and held them above his head. Again she leaned down and kissed him gently. Then she sat up and removed her blouse. She was wearing a tiny, purple, lace bra. Jack moaned with desire and reached for her breasts.

"No," she said, sharply, and pushed his hands away.

She unbuttoned his shirt and leaned down again, her bra rubbing against his bare chest, and kissed him lightly.

Jack moaned and reached for her back. Again she sat up.

"Tsk tsk," she said, waggling her finger at him, and ground herself on the front of his pants. "I like to be in control."

Jack was overwhelmed by lust.

"You're so hot," he said. "I can't stop myself from touching you."

Ellen smiled at him. "We'll just have to do something about that then."

She pulled herself off him and opened a drawer in her bedside table. She pulled out a condom and a pair of handcuffs.

Jack moaned.

"I think this will be better," she said, and she cuffed one of his wrists. She straddled him, ran the cuffs through a bed post, and snapped the other cuff to his other wrist, so that he was pinned on his back.

"Oh my God," said Jack, and ground himself against her.

"Easy Tiger," she said, and got to her feet. She stood staring at him and took off her skirt and her bra. She climbed back on top of him and kissed him again, rubbing herself against his bare chest. She teased him, pulling away when he rubbed against her too aggressively. She nibbled at his ear, lightly scratched his chest and kissed him again, then teased him with her breasts. Jack was a frantic lustful mess.

She slowly took off his shoes and pants, straddled one of his legs and toyed with the waistband of his underwear. Jack held his head up, staring at her, willing her to touch him.

"Now," she said, tugging on his underwear. "Tell me about your secret theory."

Jack groaned in frustration. "That's not fair."

She laughed and took her hand off of him.

"No," she said. "That's right."

She put her hand back on him.

"Tell me," she said.

"It's his phone," said Jack. "The cops think maybe somebody wanted his BlackBerry. It wasn't on him when they pulled him from the canal."

Ellen leaned down on her hand, then pulled it away.

"What could be on it?"

Jack twisted his hips in frustration.

"I have no idea. Honestly. Something to do with his work? He was a policy analyst. Something to do with Donahoe's leadership run? I don't know."

"Did he have it with you when you were drinking together?"

"Yes," said Jack. "But we were fucking hammered. I have no idea what happened to it. He might have lost it in Pigale."

"Hm," said Ellen. She grabbed the waistband of his underwear and pulled it down to his knees. She touched him very lightly.

"Where is it?" she said.

Jack almost bellowed with lust.

"I have NO IDEA," he said. "Jesus. Stop."

Ellen laughed and stood and removed her thong, and climbed back on top of him.

"I believe you," she said, and reached for the condom.

She put the condom on him and settled down on him with a gasp of pleasure. But Jack was overexcited and as she started to move against him he lost control.

"No," he said. "No. Stop."

She did, but it was too late.

She ground against him as he spent himself, and then flopped on to her back with a sigh of disappointment.

Jack's chest heaved.

"I'm sorry," he said. "You're too much for me."

"Story of my life."

"Oh my God," said Jack. "Just give me a few minutes and I'll try to redeem myself."

Ellen jumped to her feet.

"I'm going to have a shower," she said, and headed for the bathroom.

"Hey," said Jack, still cuffed to the bed. "Let me loose."

She turned and gave him a good look and started laughing.

"You look so pathetic right now," she said, nodding at the

condom. "Why don't you take that thing off?"

"Come on," said Jack. "Let me loose."

"Maybe I should leave you cuffed up until you're ready to go again," she said, and kissed him on the mouth, running her hand through his hair.

He kissed her back. "Might not take that long."

"Look," she said, and showed him the switch on the cuffs that popped the lock, and headed into the bathroom.

"Try to stay out of trouble," she said.

Jack picked up his BlackBerry while he waited for her to shower.

There was a new message from Sophie, sent two hours ago.

> - Jack! Ed is alive in there!!! I'm soooo happy!
> - He typed back: Wow! Is he talking?

She responded immediately:

> - No. Not talking. But his mom was right. He can understand what we say to him. You can tell by his eyes. I was with him tonight alone, and talked to him for a while, and he started crying.
> - Wow. Wow. That's intense.
> - So intense.
> - You sure he understood you?
> - Absolutely. I chatted with him after he started crying and he blinked in response, and his eyes were following me.
> - Wow. Amazing.
> - It's a breakthrough.
> - Is he still communicating now?
> - No. :-(After a while he seemed to get tired and stopped responding. The doctor said it can happen like that, but we have to keep trying.
> - Wow.
> - :-)
> - U still there?
> - Yes. Going home soon. He's sleeping.

Jack heard the shower stop.

> - k ttyl

- bye
- so happy about Ed!!!
- :-)

Ellen came out of the bathroom in a short silk robe, with a towel around her hair. She was still wearing her makeup.

Jack tossed his BlackBerry on the bedside table.

"Just got some amazing news," he said.

"Tell me," said Ellen.

"Ed's showing signs of life," he said.

"Wow," said Ellen, and she sat on the bed. She looked at his BlackBerry on the table. "Who texted you?"

"Sophie. His girlfriend. Works for Greg Mowat."

"Pretty but kind of mousy? Brown hair?"

"I don't think she's mousy," said Jack. "She's the one who fainted in your scrum the other day."

Ellen pointed her chin at Jack's phone, which sat face up on the table. The automatic lock, which kicks in after five minutes, hadn't gone on yet, and there was no password prompt.

"She said she was talking to him at the hospital," said Jack. "She thought he was in a coma, but he started to cry, and then she was chatting with him and he was responding by blinking."

"That's amazing. Did he, uh, say anything?"

"No. Sophie said he seemed to get tired, but it's a start."

"That's great."

"Yeah," said Jack, grinning. "I can't believe it. You can't believe how depressing it is to see him lying there staring at the ceiling. His face is so blank."

"I bet," said Ellen, turning to the mirror over her dresser and removing the towel from her hair. "You gonna hit the shower?" she said.

"Yeah," said Jack. "I guess I'd better."

He noticed her glancing at his phone in the mirror.

He went over and put his arms around her and tried to slide his hand up the back of her robe.

"But maybe I should wait until I'm sure we're through."

"Gross," she said, turning around and shoved him toward the bathroom. "Nothing for you until you're clean." She slammed the door shut.

Jack turned on the water in the marble tub and stepped into the hot stream. When he reached for the soap, he noticed with a start that his wrists looked like Ed's. There were blue handcuff bruises coming through.

"Wow," he said.

He got out of the tub and opened the door to the bedroom.

"Check it out," he said. "You bruised me."

Ellen was sitting on the bed reading a BlackBerry. She looked up, startled, and tossed the phone behind her on the bed.

"Oh, you poor thing. Think you'll live?" she said and stuck out her tongue at him. "Now get cleaned up. Maybe we can play doctor when you're done."

Jack looked down at his wrists and then back at her. "They look like Ed's wrists."

"Come on," she said. "Hit the shower, Tiger."

He looked over at the bedside table. "Where's my BlackBerry?"

Ellen looked up at him blankly.

He walked around her, trying to see behind her.

"Come on," she said. "Get cleaned up. I want you clean so we can have more fun."

She was half sitting on his phone.

"Were you reading my BlackBerry?" he said, and reached for it.

For a second she looked vicious, and he shied away, afraid she was going to scratch at him. Then she rolled her eyes and got up.

"Oh," she said, nonchalantly. "I thought it was mine. I just picked it up."

He picked it up and looked at the blank screen, then smiled at her.

"You little snoop," he said. "You were trying to read my BlackBerry. What are you looking for? My sources on the Sawatski story?"

She walked to the bedroom door.

"Okay," she said, and nodded toward the hallway. "Out. I don't appreciate being accused of something I didn't do. Get out."

"What?" said Jack.

"You heard me. Fun's over. You're pissing me off. Out."

"You are bad news," said Jack.

Ellen raised her voice. "I've had enough. Out. *Out.* Get dressed and get out."

Jack pulled on his clothes and walked past her. She followed him in silence down the hallway.

"I think the things they say about you might be true," he said when he got to the door.

She held it open for him and pointed at it with her a gesture of her chin.

"I'm not interested in your opinion," she said.

He stepped outside and turned to say something to her, but she slammed the door in his face.

After an hour at the computer at home, Sophie knew a lot about brain damage and comas. There was not a lot of reason to be encouraged by Ed's temporary apparent recovery. Some patients stayed locked in for years, intermittently communicating with blinks, but fading slowly over time, as their bodies atrophied and their minds ground down.

That didn't mean that there was no hope, though. The medical literature was full of examples of people who had made surprising recoveries, their brains forming new pathways around dead and damaged issue. It was hard to believe that Ed would ever be as he was, but she reminded herself that the bruises on his wrists still weren't healed. That meant that the tissue in his brain wouldn't have healed yet. There was reason to hope.

Sophie sighed and shut down the computer. She knew she needed to sleep so that she could get back to the hospital in the morning and try to encourage that spark of life that she'd seen today. She was getting ready to go brush her teeth when she noticed the messenger light blinking on her phone. She picked it up. It was a fresh message from Jack, asking if he could pop by

When he arrived, Sophie thought there was something odd about him, but she couldn't figure out what it was. He was rumpled-looking, but he was always rumpled-looking, and his smile was crooked, but it always was. She poured him a glass of red wine and he asked about Ed, and listened, entranced, as she told him about the tear. After she was sure that Ed was really hearing her, she had got him to blink for her, so she was sure he was really responding, and they had a little chat, with him responding by blinking, once for yes, twice for no.

"Wow. You must have been freaking out."

"Oh, I was a scene. I was crying and talking really loud. Then I asked him if I had to talk loud for him to hear me, and he blinked twice. And then I was laughing and crying. Oh my God." She cried and giggled a little as she talked. Then her face grew serious. "I asked him if he could move his arms or legs, and he blinked twice. And then his face grew kind of still, and I couldn't get him to respond at all."

Jack pulled her into his arms to comfort her.

"Hey," she said. "What happened to your wrist? It looks like Ed's."

She sat up and took his hands in hers and examined them closely. "Are those handcuff marks? Did you get arrested?"

"No. I didn't get arrested. Sort of the opposite." He chuckled. "I want to talk to you about it. But I need you to promise me you'll keep it secret."

"What is it?" she said. "I promise."

"Well, it's kind of weird."

He told her in a rush, everything except how he had lost control during sex. Sophie listened with wide eyes.

"Oh my God," she said, and she got up to get more wine for them.

"I hope you used a condom," she said. "Ugh. She probably has herpes on her herpes."

Jack laughed.

"Yes, we did," he said. "Although she didn't have any extra large."

Sophie laughed and smacked him lightly on the head.

"Idiot," she said. "Quel gros con."

"It seemed like a good idea at the time."

"I bet," said Sophie. "Ed will be jealous. He always said he wanted to 'fuck the shit out of her.' "

She made air quotes with her fingers.

Now it was Jack's turn to be surprised. "He told you that?"

"We don't keep secrets from each other.'

"Well," said Jack. "You promised you'd keep this a secret."

"I will," said Sophie. "Believe me, it's not the first thing I want to share with my boyfriend while he's in a coma. Honey, guess what? Your friend fucked that slut Ellen Simms. Blink once if you're jealous, twice if you're happy."

They laughed together.

"I bet it was fun," said Sophie.

"Until she kicked me out, yeah," said Jack. "So, the reason I told you, aside from wanting to brag, is that I wonder what it means. Should I tell the cops? Is there any way that she had something to do with Ed ending up in the canal? I mean, did he sleep with her?"

Sophie thought about it. "No," she said. "I don't think so. He would have told me."

Jack cocked an eyebrow at her. "I don't know if you can be so sure," he said.

She gazed at him coolly. "Yes I can. He always told me the other times he slept with someone. We had, uh, have, kind of a deal about that."

"You have an open relationship?" asked Jack.

"Yeah," said Sophie. "You could say that."

Jack whistled.

"Don't tell anyone," said Sophie. "It's a secret. I shouldn't have told you. Shit."

"Anyway. The point is, he would have been back here bragging about it in about a minute if he had 'fucked the shit out of her,'" she said, making air quotes again.

"So do you sometimes tell him about your adventures, too?" asked Jack. "Do you have adventures?"

"None of your business," she said. "She was really curious about Ed's BlackBerry, eh?"

"Yeah. I won't tell you how she got me to tell her about it, but she seemed like she really wanted to know."

"But you don't know where it is."

"Nope."

They sat in silence, and for a moment he thought he was going to tell her the truth, and tell her about the men who chased him, and about the dead taxi driver and businessman from Winnipeg. And he'd ask about the hidden camera in her bookcase, put all his cards on the table. He opened his mouth to speak, and then she got to her feet.

"Well," she said. "I'm tired and I have an early morning tomorrow. I'm going to go to bed. You can stay here if you want. Did you sleep okay here the other night?"

"Yeah," he said.

Sophie kissed him on the cheek. "Good night."

She went to the bathroom. Jack took off his suit and wrapped himself in a quilt.

When she left the bathroom for the bedroom, he went in and used the bathroom.

When he came out, her bedroom door was open and the light was on. He went and stood in the doorway. She was under the covers, staring at the ceiling.

"Can I stay in here with you?" he asked.

"Hm," she said. "Do you promise to behave?"

"Yes," he said. "I don't know if I mentioned it before, but I fucked the shit out of Ellen Simms tonight, so I think I'm good."

He crawled in next to her and they lay silently beside one another for a long time before falling asleep.

Chapter 5 – Pool report

ZWICKER HAD ASHTON and Flanagan in his office at 8 a.m. "Sit down," he said, his face completely blank. He strode back and forth behind his desk for a while without saying anything, and stopped a couple of times as if about to begin, only to start pacing again. Finally, he sat down and opened a notebook.

"Detective Sergeant Ashton," he said, looking down at the paper in front of him. "What did I say to you yesterday about talking to reporters?"

"Uh, you told me not to talk to any reporters."

He laughed, a short bark with no humour. "Right. That's what I thought I said. So then I have this story here, from a Newfoundland newspaper, with all kinds of inside details about the investigation. It doesn't quote anyone by name, but refers to 'sources close to the investigation.'"

"It was me," said Flanagan. "I interviewed Macdonald twice, once in person and once over the phone. He is a friend of the kid, Sawatski. He was drinking with him the night before he was pulled out of the canal."

"And did you tell this witness, this possible suspect, that we were investigating personnel in the office of the federal minister of justice?" said Zwicker. "Am I right in thinking that?"

Flanagan was silent for a moment. His expression was pained. "I believe I told him that Detective Sergeant Ashton went up to the Hill to talk to Sawatski's colleagues."

Zwicker's face was crimson. "I find that surprising."

He cradled his head in his hands and stared down at his notes. "So, do either of you have any further evidence, aside from the photo and video you sent me yesterday, that points to the idea that this is anything but a story about a drunk kid falling in the canal?"

Flanagan and Ashton looked at one another.

"Nothing definite," said Ashton.

"Nothing definite," said Zwicker. "Would you agree with that assessment, Detective Sergeant Flanagan?"

"Yes sir," he said.

Zwicker glared at the two officers in front of him.

"I doubt that you two really appreciate how delicate this situation is. We have a story here," he jabbed the printout on his desk, "that's drawing a connection between a serious crime and the highest officials in the federal government. This is a matter of grave concern to those officials. They function in a very challenging environment, scrutiny-wise. This makes them very sensitive. So they are saying, reasonably enough, I think, 'What is this? What is this crime we hear about? What is this crime, to which we are linked, in a very painful way for us?' "

Zwicker picked up the notebook then slapped it down with a crack. "What shall I tell them?"

Neither officer spoke.

"I am not impressed by your evidence," he said. "Not at all. I am not convinced there is a crime here. You understand?"

They both nodded.

"I was going to shut the investigation down unless I saw something in your report that gave me reason to reconsider. I think you two probably guessed that."

"Yes sir," Ashton said.

"If I thought you had leaked anything to this reporter on purpose, I would express my frustration more fully," he said, and he smiled at them in a distinctly unfriendly way. "That would be very pleasant for me. Do you understand that? It would be very pleasant for me to express those feelings, but not for you two," he said, and his face was distorted with a flash of rage. "Sadly for me, I don't think you are quite stupid enough to have planted this story on purpose. I think you are stupid enough to have done so by mistake, which is still pretty stupid. Would you agree with me, Detective Sergeant Flanagan?"

"Yes sir," he croaked.

"Okay," said Zwicker. "So because of this story, I am not going to ask you to shut down the investigation today, as I had planned to do. That would be my preference, but others feel that that might leave in the public mind the impression that something is being covered up, that political influence was being exerted to shut down a police investigation. You follow me?"

He stared at them until they nodded.

"I find it ironic that, in fact, looking at it one way, there is now political pressure to continue a police investigation that is embarrassing to senior government officials. So, I was tempted to tell you to continue the investigation in such a way that you don't talk to anyone. You two could look for clues at your desks, write reports about it. On reflection, though, I don't think the director of investigations can order you not to investigate, even though that's what I want to do. So carry on. If, though, at any point, you are tempted to take an investigative step that might subject the Ottawa Police Service or the federal Department of Justice to scrutiny, I want you to report to me before you take that step."

He glowered at them and said with painful slowness, "Do you understand?"

"Yes sir," they said.

"Okay," said Zwicker. "Now get the fuck out of my office."

Jack was drinking coffee in the Hot Room, reading the day's headlines on his laptop when his editor called.

"Hey," said Brandt.

"Morning," said Jack.

"I just had a call from a Detective Sergeant Ashton from Ottawa Police Service," he said. "And I have some questions about your story today."

Shit, thought Jack.

"According to her, the information about the investigation, and the quote, all came from interviews in which you were being questioned by a Detective Sergeant Flanagan. Is that right?

"Yeah," said Jack. "He asked me questions. I asked him questions. I wrote the story. Why? He knew I was a reporter."

There was quiet on the line before Brandt spoke. "Well, for one it would have been good if I'd known that. We would never pull a trick like this with the Royal Newfoundland Constabulary, because they'd never give us a fucking thing again, but the Ottawa Police Service doesn't have too much juice around here."

"So, we're okay then. I mean, did Ashton complain about the facts in the story?"

"Not really. She didn't like the stuff about police investigating officials in the federal Justice Department, but she couldn't deny that she did personally go there for interviews. She asked me for the assurance that if she needs to interview you again in the course of the investigation, she can do so without you quoting her. Seemed reasonable to me, so she got that assurance. She can't do her job if she's worried that she'll get quoted."

"Okay," said Jack. "I'll continue to co-operate with their investigation, but I won't quote them again."

"All right," said Brandt. "Got anything for tomorrow?"

"Not yet," said Jack. "I'll let you know when I get organized."

When Jack hung up, he had a fresh email.

From: 1officer123@gmail.com
To: Jack Macdonald
Subject: Good story today
I've got a document that links a Minister to a crime.
Send me your cell phone and I'll call.

Jack searched the email address, but nothing came up on the internet. He thought for a moment and sent his cell number. His phone rang almost immediately.

"Jack Macdonald," he said.

"Mr. Macdonald, this is Detective Sergeant Mallorie Ashton."

Fuck. "Hello detective," he said. "How can I help you?"

"I have a few questions for you, and I'd like to have a chat with you today."

"Sure," said Jack. "I'm glad to help."

Ashton laughed. "I bet you are. Can you be here, at OPS headquarters, at one?"

"You want me to go in there?" he said.

"That would be a help to us, yes," she said.

"Fine," said Jack.

"See you then," she said.

The phone rang again.

"Jack Macdonald."

"Hey," said a male voice. "This is the guy who sent you an email. You know what I'm talking about?"

"Yeah," he said. "Just a minute."

Jack dug his recorder out of his pocket and held it next to the phone.

"I'm back," he said.

"Got your recorder going?" The voice was muffled, as if somebody were holding a towel over the handset.

"Yeah," said Jack. "That's right. Go ahead. What have you got? I'm interested."

"Would it interest you to know that a current cabinet minister once tried to drown somebody?"

Jack sat up straight. "I find that very interesting."

"There's a police report," said the voice. "You want it?"

"Yes," said Jack. "Yes I do."

"Okay," said the man. "Are you prepared to make an undertaking that you will never reveal my identity to anyone, under any circumstances?"

"Yes," said Jack. "I undertake to never reveal your identity to anyone, under any circumstances."

"I don't want to say my name over the phone," he said.

"But I'll meet you in thirty minutes, and I'll have the police report with me."

"Where do you want to meet?"

"You know the cab stand at the corner of Sparks Street and Metcalfe?"

"Of course I do."

"See you there in thirty," the man said.

Balusi sat on a couch in the corner window of the Bridgehead Coffee Shop, on the corner of Sparks and Metcalfe, and sipped at his Americano. He paged through documents on his BlackBerry while keeping an eye peeled for Simms. When he spotted her, strolling down from the Hill, he sat back to watch. He liked to watch the effect she had on crowds, the way people stopped to watch her pass, men especially, but women, too. As she passed the RCMP bodyguards outside the entrance to Langevin Building, all of them in their shades and earpieces turned, as one, to idly look down Metcalfe Street – all of them super casual, just looking around, at the exact moment that she passed them – and checked her out from behind.

She came in, shrugged off her heavy winter coat, and took the chair opposite him.

"Oh my God," she said. "What a day. And it's only eleven."

"Want a coffee?" said Balusi.

"Yes thanks. A soy latte with cinnamon sprinkles, but not too many."

Balusi went up to the counter and returned moments later with her order.

"I've got something else for you, too," he said.

She winked at him. "Is it big and brown?"

"Enough of that or I'll never be able to focus on the business at hand."

She frowned. "Fine. All business. What have you got?"

"Well, it is brown, and I think it's big," he said, and he

tossed a manila envelope on the table. "It's a story."

She opened the envelope and pulled out a transcript. "This is in French," she said. "My French isn't great. What's it say?"

Balusi laughed. "What it says is Jim Donahoe said some things in Montreal last night that he should not have done. It's a transcript of an off-the-record talk he had with some heavyweight Quebec Tories, at the Champlain Club. It was a fundraiser, get-to-know-you session. Open it up. I had it translated."

Simms flipped through until she got to the English. She skimmed it.

"Looks boring," she said. "Quebec's place within Confederation, renewal, blah blah blah."

"Check out the bit I highlighted."

It was the last paragraph of the transcript. Simms read it aloud. "Ever since the repatriation of the constitution in 1981, against the express wishes of the voters of this province, Quebecers have been governed by a constitution that the province's elected representatives did not ratify. Many Quebecers think this keeps them from embracing their place in Canada. That's why Quebecers continue to support, at best, nationalist parties, and at worst, sovereigntist parties, parties led by people who would tear our country apart. To mend this rift, they say, we need to make a new place for Quebec in the Constitution, and formally recognize what is a fact of life, the distinct and rich cultural life of the province. Call it Meech II. I am with these people. We can't campaign on this kind of risky business, it would be divisive and destructive, but a majority Donahoe government could succeed where Mulroney failed."

Simms looked up.

"This is boring," she said. "Constitution. Blech. Where's the channel changer?"

"No," said Balusi. "It won't be boring to anyone who lived through Meech Lake. When Mulroney tried and failed to recognize Quebec as a distinct society, the country almost fell apart."

She looked at him impassively.

"Remember the referendum in 1995?" he said. "That was in reaction to the collapse of Meech Lake and the Charlottetown accord. This stuff will drive the western Conservatives nuts. Especially since he says that he'll do it without campaigning on it. It's secret backroom politics, and it will explode in Donahoe's face."

"Okay," she said. "I see. It is a story. Donahoe proposes secret deal to appease Quebec."

"Yeah," said Balusi. "If you don't want it, I'll give it to someone else. This is big. This could lead the news."

"No," she said. "I get it. I want it. It's good. I was wrong."

"You have the audio file?" she asked.

"Yeah," he said. "I can email it to you later. But in no way must this be linked to me. Very important. Would cost me my job."

Simms smiled. "Don't worry. I get it. Won't say a word to anyone, ever."

"Hey," she said, looking out the window. "Look. It's Macdonald."

Macdonald was getting into a cab.

"Oh yeah," said Balusi. "The Newfie."

"He creeps me out," said Simms.

"Yeah?"

"You remember how I went to talk to him the other night at Hy's? I asked him about his story."

"Yeah?" said Balusi.

"He was weird," she said. "Creeped me out." She shivered and wrapped her arms around herself.

"Did he say anything scary?"

"Not really," said Ellen. "Anyway, who recorded the tape?"

Jack's BlackBerry rang when he got to the corner.

"This is your new friend," said the same male voice. "I want you to get in a taxi and meet me in Vanier, just in case someone's watching you."

"Are you sure that's necessary?" Jack asked.

"We can call this off," the man said. "I can give this to someone else."

"No," said Jack. "What's the address?"

"Tell him to take you to Xcitement Lanes, in Vanier, on Cartier Street."

"You want to bowl?" Jack asked.

"There's a snack bar."

"Okay," said Jack. "On my way."

It was a sad bowling alley, across the street from a sad mall. The owners had spent some money to spruce it up, installing flashy neon signs and a big sound system, neither of which were geared up during the day, to Jack's relief. A francophone seniors' group was quietly bowling in the lanes nearest the snack bar. He ordered a cup of bad coffee and watched them.

By the time he started to get interested in their competition, admiring the footwork and accuracy of one blue-haired woman, he was pretty sure that someone had sent him on a wild goose chase. Maybe Detective Sergeant Ashton.

Then the man arrived.

He was a big guy with a bushy black moustache, and short salt-and-pepper hair. He had a deep scar on his right eyebrow. He wore a dark blue wool overcoat and carried a briefcase. He looked like a cop.

"Jack?" he said.

"Hi," said Jack, and stood to shake the guy's hand.

"Easy there, big fellow," he said, and shook his crushed hand in the air. "Quite a grip you got there."

"Sorry," said the big guy, and sat down. He smiled and nodded at the server behind the counter.

"Un café, s'il vous plaît, madame."

He put his briefcase on the counter, rubbed his hands together and waited for his coffee.

Jack introduced himself.

"I'm Sergeant Michel Castonguay," said the guy, and he dug into his breast pocket for a business card. It identified him as an investigator with the RCMP's commercial crime unit.

"Commercial crime?" said Jack

Castonguay laughed. "You are an investigative reporter. Let me save you some time. I wasn't always here in Ottawa."

He opened his briefcase and removed a tan envelope and rested it in front of him on the counter.

"Fifteen years ago, I was stationed in Swift Current, Saskatchewan," he said. "I was a constable, doing routine small town policing: highway patrol, breaking up fights, and, of course, every cop's favourite call, domestic disputes."

He slid the envelope in front of Jack. Jack opened it.

"One summer night, I forget the date, but it's in the report, I went to a nice suburban house, really nice place, to respond to a domestic dispute. There was a lady there, and, oh boy, she was upset. She was soaking wet, fully dressed, sitting on the front step, and she started talking to me as soon as I got out of the car. She said she and her husband had been sitting by the pool after dinner, having an argument about her daughter, who was dating a boy that they didn't like, and her husband got so mad, he grabbed her by the neck and threw her in the pool. She said it was like he was a stranger suddenly, and he held her under for a long time. She was kicking and scream-ing and waving her arms, but he held her under until she ran out of air and gulped water. She said she started to black out. Said she saw stars. That's what she said. 'I saw stars.' I guess the husband must have realized then what he was doing, and he pulled her out of the water and she got a breath of air. He hopped in his car and drove off."

Jack was looking at the report while the guy was talking.

"Her name was Maude Mowat," said Jack.

"That's right," said Castonguay. "And her husband was Greg Mowat."

The two men sat there looking at each other for a minute.

"Scary, eh?" said the cop. "Long story short, I took a state-ment right there on the front stoop, got all the details, then I asked her to change into dry clothes, so we could go down to the station and sign an affidavit. She said she'd be right back.

Then I guess while she was getting changed, she started to have second thoughts. She comes back, says, what will happen? I don't want my husband to go to jail."

"She decided not to press charges?" asked Jack.

"That's right," said Castonguay. "I'm talking to her, asking if she's sure, and then the husband comes back. Oh boy he was sorry. He was really sorry. They got down and prayed together right there. It was really something. I did my job, told her that we couldn't do anything to protect her if she didn't press charges, but she told me no, and he was still apologizing. I had no choice but to get in my car and go back to the station and type it up."

"Did you know who Mowat was then?" asked Jack.

"He was in the insurance business," said Castonguay. "And he was deputy mayor. Not the big shot he is now."

"Why did you decide to go public now?" asked Jack.

"Well, I've thought about it over the years, and watched his career, and it made me uneasy to think that a man who could almost drown his wife would be in a position of authority, but when I joined the force I took an oath to follow the law," he said. "The law says that report in your hand is not to be made public. Obviously, I'm breaking that law now, but I don't think I have any choice. I mean, someone tried to drown that young man. I'm afraid it might be Mowat. I mean, look at it."

He was quiet for a minute. "You know, I don't make a big fuss about it, but I'm a proud Canadian. I get a lump in my throat when I stand for the anthem. I take pride in my country. Even if Mowat didn't have anything to do with trying to drown this boy, I don't like the idea of my kids living in a country governed by a prime minister who would do that to his wife."

Jack stared at him. "You're doing the right thing," he said. "I admire you. Jesus."

"I hope I'm doing the right thing," said Castonguay. "And I hope it doesn't cost me my job."

"It won't," said Jack. "Nothing will make me say where I got this. I'll go to jail before I give up your name."

Jack called his editor on the cab drive to the Hill.

"I've got a big one," he whispered, so the driver wouldn't hear said.

"What is it?"

"I just met with a source, a Mountie, and he leaked me a police report that says Greg Mowat, the public safety minister, tried to drown his wife in 1996."

"Fuck," said Brandt.

"He held her under the water until she blacked out," said Jack. "She called the cops, described the whole thing, but then the husband came back and she had a change of heart, wouldn't press charges."

"Jesus. It makes you wonder if he had anything to do with putting the kid in the canal."

"I know," said Jack. "It's a fucking doozy. But I don't think we even have to hit that, maybe mention the Sawatski case at the bottom, but don't even draw the link."

"Readers will do that on their own."

"Exactly. It's an amazing story even without the Sawatski angle. Mowat won't be prime minister. I think he'll have to resign. I think this will put him out of politics."

"Shit," said Brandt.

"Exactly," said Jack.

"Okay," said Brandt. "Any way to confirm this?"

"No. But I have the original police report. And I interviewed a Mountie who is familiar with the case. I don't see how they can go after us on this."

"Sounds pretty tight. You'll have to get comments from the Mounties and from Mowat's office."

"I know. But I want to do that just before we go with the story. I think we should get the denials, and bang, put it online."

"Before they can go after you, or leak another version of the story to someone else."

"They'll be desperate. I don't know what they might do.

Fuck. Might throw me in the canal."

"Okay," said Brandt. "You in the office?"

"Headed there now."

"Bang out a first draft and send it to me, with lots of quotes from the police report."

Balusi sent Simms the audio file once he got back to the office, and she listened to it right away, following along in the English transcript. It was hard work, since her French wasn't very good, but she got the gist. A group of Quebec Tories was asking Donahoe about his plans for the country if he were to become prime minister, and he was answering, in his accented but serviceable French. They would clap after each of his answers.

She found it boring, but went through it all to make sure that she didn't overlook an angle that would make her look stupid later. Her mind drifted off at times, but by the time she got to the end, she was pretty sure that she hadn't missed anything important.

She was listening to the bit about Meech II quite closely, reading along with the transcript when she got a PIN from Balusi saying that he'd sent her the wrong file and asking her to delete it. The right mp3 file was attached. She saved it on her desktop, next to the first file and sat back to look at them.

She sent Balusi a PIN saying that she's deleted the first and was listening to the second. Then she sat back and wondered how to find the difference between the files.

Jack sat at his desk with the police report next to his keyboard and started typing.

Eds: Raw version. Not for publication.
By JACK MACDONALD

Ottawa Bureau Chief

OTTAWA – Public Safety Minister Greg Mowat held his wife under the water until she "saw stars" in a 1996 domestic assault, according to an RCMP incident report obtained by the Telegram.

After an argument about their daughter, Mowat threw his wife, Maude Mowat, into the pool in the backyard of their home in Swift Current, Sask., and held her under water until she blacked out, the report says.

"The victim reported that she struggled violently until she swallowed water and lost consciousness," the report says. "Victim said she 'saw stars.' When she recovered, she was alone on the ground next to the pool. She went to house and called police."

Mowat pulled his wife out of the pool and drove away in anger, the report says, at which point an RCMP officer arrived to take her statement.

"Victim was in wet clothes, very distressed and frightened when officer arrived," the report says. "She said her husband wanted to kill her."

But after Mowat returned, Mrs. Mowat decided not to press charges.

"Suspect apologized profusely to wife and begged her to pray with him," the report says. "Suspect and victim got on knees and prayed for guidance."

The report says the officer tried to convince Mrs. Mowat to press charges, but she refused.

"Victim said she didn't want her husband to go to jail," the report says. "Victim said the Lord would help them."

At the time, Mowat was an executive with Great Canadian Farm Assurance, an insurance company headquartered in Swift Current, and also deputy mayor of the town.

Because Mrs. Mowat did not press charges, the police report was not made public until now. In 2000 Mowat was elected as a Member of Parliament for the Reform party. In his first term, he was forced to apologize to women's groups after referring to a Regina

women's group critical of his party as a "a gang of radicals and lesbians."

Mowat was an important backer of the Conservative
leadership campaign of Bruce Stevens. Stevens
appointed Mowat as president of the Treasury Board in
his first cabinet and as public safety minister in 2008.
Mowat is a strong advocate of tough law-and-order
policies, spearheading the Conservatives' legislation to
provide for mandatory minimum sentences for violent
crimes.

Earlier this week, he was heavily criticized by pun-
dits and opposition critics for calling on Liberal MPs
to apologize to victims of violent crime under their
government.

Mowat is thought to be the front runner in the campaign for the Conservative leadership.

In a more recent near drowning, early Tuesday
morning, in Ottawa, Ed Sawatski, an aide to Mowat's
leadership rival, Justice Minister Jim Donahoe, was
pulled out of the Rideau Canal, near death, and taken to
hospital. Sources close to the Ottawa Police Service's
investigation say they suspect foul play, and have been
interviewing witnesses on Parliament Hill.

Sawatski is originally from Mount Pearl.

Jack read over his story and emailed it to his editor. In a
few minutes he had a response, asking him to fax the police
report to the newspaper. He sent it immediately, then sat
nervously at his desk until his editor called.

"Jesus Christ, b'y," said Brandt. "This is a crackerjack."

"It's strong, eh?"

"By Jesus, I guess so," said Brandt and laughed. "Christ,
that sanctimonious fucker will have to go, like today, when
we put this out."

"Did you lawyer it?" asked Jack.

"No b'y, I'm not even going to bother. This is rock solid.
We've got the frigging police report. What I will do, though,
is put Mowat's denial at the top, if he does deny it, which I
suspect he will. I would." He laughed again. "So, I'm sending

this to the copy desk. I'll have it ready to go. You need to call the Mounties and Mowat's office and get the denials. Tell them we're going on line with this, and if they won't give us a comment, we'll print that."

Simms started by examining the properties of the two files. They were the same length and the same file size. She sat for a while, chewing on her pen and staring at the screen. Then she opened them both in an audio editing program. Both sound files appeared on the screen as sound wave files, with an undulating line showing the pitch of the sound. They looked the same.

She enlarged the .wav files and scrutinized them. They seemed to be an exact match. She clicked along the bar, zipping to the end, to look at the Meech II section. It appeared to be the same.

Her eyes were about to cross when she spotted the difference. The original file ended after the second file did. She put on the headphones and listened to the end of the second file. There was a hiss of white noise. It was two seconds shorter.

She was swivelling in her chair, thinking about it, when Murphy caught her eye. He was walking across the newsroom to her, moving fast.

"Ellen," he said. "Did you see National Newswatch?"

"No," she said, and immediately minimized her sound files in the background and pointed her browser to the popular news aggregator site.

"It's a hot one," said Murphy.

There was a picture of Greg Mowat looking smug – it was a shot from Question Period from Tuesday – and a big headline: Mowat Tried To Drown Wife.

She clicked on the link and quickly scanned the story.

"Holy fuck," she said. "This will kill him."

"I need you to get down to the Hill now and cover the reaction to this," said Murphy. "But be careful. We haven't seen the report. Every time you mention it, call it unconfirmed."

Jack's phone started to ring as soon as the story went up online. Most of the calls were from other reporters, congratulating him and asking if he would give them the report. He enjoyed accepting their congratulations and telling them that he couldn't give them the report, although the appeal started to wear thin after a while, and he started to begin the conversations by saying that the paper was not, at this time, sharing the report.

Simms was the first TV reporter on the story, standing in the lobby, ready to interview MPs as they arrived for Question Period.

Jack watched from his desk, with his digital recorder next to the TV, to gather quotes for a reaction story.

"Lorne, we're waiting for MPs to arrive to get their reaction to an explosive story that has just gone up on the Internet," said Simms, looking serious but beside herself with excitement. "A Newfoundland newspaper is reporting that Public Safety Minister Greg Mowat tried to drown his wife in a domestic dispute in 1996. The paper, quoting an RCMP report, says that Mowat held his wife, Maude Mowat, underwater in the pool in the backyard of their home until she saw stars." The screen showed a picture of Mowat and his wife holding hands at a fundraiser. "According to the report, Mrs. Mowat called police after the attack, but decided not to press charges after the two got down on their knees and prayed together."

"Ellen, is this a confirmed report?" asked the anchor.

"No, Lorne," said Simms. "I should point that out. The *Telegram*, a Newfoundland daily, claims to have a copy of the police report, but Mowat's office is denying the allegation, saying it is totally and completely false and without foundation."

"What's the reaction so far, Ellen?"

"Well, we're waiting now for MPs to arrive for Question Period," she said. "As minister of public safety, Mowat is the man in charge of the RCMP and other security agencies, so we anticipate that the Opposition will call for his resignation. Mowat is also rumoured to be in the running to replace Prime Minister Bruce Stevens, but this report would likely pose severe problems for his candidacy."

"But there is no independent confirmation of this report?"

"No, Lorne, that's quite correct," she said. "The report is unconfirmed. It is being reported by a Newfoundland daily, but the minister's office says the story is totally and completely false and without foundation."

Simms turned to look at Eileen Cross, who was approaching the doors to the House of Commons.

"Here's Liberal justice critic Eileen Cross, Lorne, with reaction. Ms. Cross, what do you have to say about this news?"

"Well, I haven't seen the police report, Ellen," she said. "But if this is true, it will make it impossible for him to continue as Minister of Public Safety. Remember this is the politician who once referred to feminists as 'radicals and lesbians.' We think the prime minister has no choice but to remove Mowat from his post immediately."

Jack took his phone off the hook as he watched Simms. He was sweating heavily and his heart was pounding. He chewed on his pen. He was at the centre of a whirlwind, and it was exciting and stressful. He wondered if he should ask his editor what to do if TV wanted him to do interviews. No. He should just do them. Let his editor find out when he saw him on TV. He looked down at his rumpled suit. Maybe he should rush home and change. But his other suit was dirty.

He glanced at his BlackBerry. There were dozens of messages. His eye jumped to one from Sophie. Without opening it, he called her.

"Jack, what's wrong with you?" she said.

"Hey Sophie, how are you?"

"Jack. Your story is wrong. I'm sure of it."

"What do you mean?"

"I know Greg Mowat," she said. "He wouldn't do that. It's not true."

Jack switched on his recorder.

"Sophie, are you speaking on behalf of the minister?" he asked.

"No. I'm calling as a friend, and you cannot quote me. I'm at the hospital, with Ed. I haven't even talked to the office about this."

"How's Ed?"

"Never mind," said Sophie. "Listen to me. That story is wrong. I know it's wrong. Mowat wouldn't do that."

"How do you know?"

"He's just not like that. He wouldn't lose control like that. He's very ... I don't know the word for it. It's wrong, that's all. If you're smart you'll take it down right now."

"I can't do that," said Jack. "I've got a police report. I have no choice but to report on this."

On the TV, Pinsent was approaching the camera.

"Sophie, I've got to go," said Jack. "I'll call you later."

Pinsent faced the camera: "This is shocking news. We have long known that this is a government that shows no respect for women, but now we find out that one of its ministers – the minister in charge of our police – himself tried to drown his wife. It is the prime minister, Bruce Stevens, who appointed this man to cabinet, and this reflects on his judgment. We warned the prime minister. Greg Mowat once referred to feminists as 'radicals and lesbians.' Stevens knew that. Did he know about this attack on Mrs. Mowat? We need to find out."

Pinsent walked off, entering the open doors of the House of Commons, and Simms came back on camera.

"NTV has now learned," she said, "that the Swift Current RCMP detachment has issued a statement saying that they have thus far found no record of a police report alleging a domestic assault by Greg Mowat, but they are still searching. We go now to live coverage of Question Period, where this is sure to be on the agenda. I'm told Greg Mowat is in his chair in the House, as usual."

Jack looked down at his BlackBerry. He had a fresh email from Brandt, subject: Call Me. He decided to wait until after the first few questions at QP.

Pinsent rose in his seat, looking impatient to begin.

"Mr. Speaker," he said. "Today we learned that the prime minister's hand-picked public safety minister was investigated for a domestic assault on his wife in 1996. We are told that the minister tried to drown his wife."

The Conservative MPs howled at this, and pointed to the entrance: "Say it outside." The Speaker quieted them and Pinsent continued. Stevens sat stone-faced on his side of the chamber.

"Mr. Speaker, the RCMP conducts extensive background checks on ministers before they are appointed to cabinet. What happened here? Did they miss this, or did the prime minister know about this attack and still appoint the member for Cypress Hills-Grasslands to his cabinet?"

Liberals applauded and Conservatives heckled and shouted. Stevens rose.

"Mr. Speaker, I would merely caution the Opposition leader that he ought to be careful about what kind of allegations he makes in this House," he said. "My colleague may be protected from legal sanction by parliamentary privilege, but Canadians are right to judge him for making wild accusations when he does not have the facts in front of him."

He sat down. This cautious, legalistic answer was greeted by polite applause from his side of the House, and by muted derision from the Liberals.

He isn't sure of the truth yet, thought Jack. The story broke too soon, and they haven't got their hands on the report so they will stonewall the opposition until they get it. They'll wait until after QP, and then fire him by news release.

Pinsent stood again.

"Mr. Speaker, the prime minister's blasé response is absolutely unacceptable," he said. "It is unacceptable to Canadian women, and unacceptable to anyone with a shred of decency. According to the police report, the minister in charge of public safety committed a very serious crime. He is the minister in charge of keeping Canadians safe. And there he still sits, in spite of this revelation. How can the prime minister have confidence in a minister who would hold his hands around his wife's neck –" Pinsent mimed the motion "– and hold her under water until she blacked out? According to the report, she told officers she 'saw stars.' Has the prime minister taken leave of his senses?" He sat down, shaking his head.

Stevens didn't stand to respond, but looked down his side of the House and nodded at Mowat, who rose to his feet, holding a piece of paper in his hand. A hush fell in the House.

"Mr. Speaker, I scarcely know how to answer these allegations," he said. "I am a public servant, and I thought I had developed a pretty thick hide. But I admit I am finding this hard to take. I have just got off the phone with my oldest daughter, who is at university, and I can tell you I did not enjoy that call. But I told her what I will tell you, and what my office told the journalist who called today. This is totally and absolutely false. This is untrue. It is absurd."

He looked around the chamber, started to speak, stopped, shook his head and continued. "I can't believe I have to say this. I have at no time assaulted my wife, and would not dream of doing so. The story is an invention, a ridiculous, damaging invention. We don't have a pool. We have never had a pool. I have never kneeled to pray in front of a police officer.

"I have instructed my attorneys to do everything they can to respond to this as quickly as possible. I anticipate that we will be commencing legal action against the newspaper in question, and against the leader of the Opposition for his comments in the lobby. I would ask all of you in this place, if you have a shred of human feeling for me or my family, or for the truth, to stop repeating these false and defamatory stories about me until the facts are as plain to you as they are to me."

As Mowat sat down, Stevens rose and started to applaud. As one, the rest of the Conservative caucus rose to its feet and applauded Mowat, who sat in his chair and looked at his notes. Some New Democrats joined in, and then all of them did. Seconds later, the Bloc Quebecois stood, and, after a hurried whisper between Pinsent and Dumaresque, so did most Liberals.

Jack picked up the phone and called Brandt.

"We have some problems here," said Brandt. "We pulled the story down. Our lawyers advised us to do so. In very strong terms. And they sent a copy of the police report to Mowat's office."

"What?"

"They didn't ask our permission, which we would, incidentally, have given. They were sufficiently impressed by whatever they heard from Mowat's lawyers to make that decision unilaterally."

"But ..." Jack sputtered.

"But nothing," said Brandt. "We're in a world of shit, b'y, you and me both. Did you check to see whether Mowat had a pool, had ever had a pool? I think I asked you to check that."

"No," said Jack. His stomach was cramping and he was sweating profusely. "You didn't ask me to check that. And, no, I didn't check."

"I'm pretty sure I did," said Brandt. "Anyway, apparently he doesn't have a pool, and never has. Apparently we printed a big load of shit."

Jack didn't say anything. He dug into his pocket and pulled out Castonguay's business card.

"I'll call my source right now," he said.

"Okay," said Brandt. "Good idea. Find out if it was a wading pool. Please, sweet Jesus, let it be a wading pool."

"I'll call right now."

He turned on his recorder and dialed the number.

There was a little blast of music, and then an excited male voice. "You've reached Xcitement Lanes! Vous avez rejoint Xcitement Lanes! For English, press one. Pour le français, appuyer sur le deux."

Jack stared at the phone in his hand, refusing to believe what he heard. He double checked the number on the business card and dialed again.

When he heard the music again, he bent down and noisily vomited on the floor beneath his desk. The vomit splashed onto his right shoe and sock.

He sat back up, gasping, and wiped his chin.

A middle-aged female Radio Canada reporter stepped around the corner to look at him.

"Are you okay?" she asked.

Jack just stared at her, and then looked at the TV.

Simms was talking. "We go now, to Swift Current, where RCMP Sergeant Andrew Grant is about to make a statement about the Greg Mowat story, and the allegations that he tried to drown his wife."

A middle-aged man in a Mountie uniform stood in front of the detachment, in front of a small group of reporters. He cleared his throat and leaned into the microphones.

"Good afternoon," he said. "I'm Sergeant Andrew Grant, public affairs officer for the Swift Current City RCMP Detachment." He looked at his notes and then back at the cameras. "After media reports earlier this afternoon, our detachment conducted a thorough check of our files to determine if there was any truth to a story alleging that Public Safety Minister Greg Mowat assaulted his wife. We have found no such record. About an hour ago, the minister's office provided us with a copy of the alleged police report. I have it here." He held it up.

"We have copies for all of you," he said. "After looking through our records from that period, we determined that this appears to be a forgery. It is a real police report from the summer of 1985, but the name of the suspect and victim in this case have been replaced with the name of the minister and Mrs. Mowat."

Jack's phone was ringing. He picked it up and put it down again and looked at the screen in a daze.

Simms was standing in the lobby. "So there you have it," she said. "The Swift Current RCMP is saying that the police report in the Greg Mowat story is a forgery. This seems to make it clear that the story is, as the minister said, completely false."

The anchor asked, "Ellen, is there any other evidence to suggest that Greg Mowat did anything wrong?"

"No, Lorne," said Simms. "This story was broken by a Newfoundland paper, the *Telegram*, which was the only media outlet to have a copy of the forged police report. It was on the paper's web site for about an hour, and has since been taken down. In its place, there is now an apology."

The screen filled with the *Telegram*'s web page. The main headline read: "Apology and Retraction."

"So it looks like somebody had the wool pulled over their eyes here?"

"That's right, Lorne," said Simms. "We're told that the *Telegram* has suspended both the reporter who wrote the story, and the paper's city editor."

"What's the reaction on the Hill, Ellen?" said the anchor.

"Well, apparently, we're about to have a statement from Evan Pinsent," she said. "He's expected to apologize for his comments about the Mowat allegations earlier today."

Jack dialed Brandt.

"Hey b'y," said his editor. "Lucky you got me. Just clearing out me desk."

"Am I suspended?" asked Jack.

"Until further notice," said Brandt. "We both are."

"Fuck," said Jack.

Brandt laughed. "Yup. I'm off to the pub. But hold on a minute, I'm going to transfer you."

A moment later, a male voice said, "Good afternoon, Mr. Macdonald. This is Paul Dexter. I'm a lawyer for the Telegram Ltd. I'm sure this is a difficult time for you."

"I just puked under my desk," said Jack.

"I'm sorry to hear that," said Dexter. "Do you need medical attention?"

"No," said Jack. "Go ahead."

"I'm calling to let you know that you are suspended until further notice. We ask you to leave the office after this call, and leave anything belonging to the Telegram Limited there."

Jack was silent. He looked down at his feet and noticed he had stepped in the puddle of vomit.

"Are you there, Mr. Macdonald?"

"Yup," he said. "Anything else?"

"I'm sure this seems terrible to you right now," said Dexter, "but I would caution you not to jump to conclusions. We suddenly find ourselves in a very awkward legal position. We have to demonstrate that, having defamed Mr. Mowat, that we are doing everything we can to remedy the situation. That means we have to get to the bottom of how it happened, and show that we're taking appropriate actions. That means we have to suspend you."

"And you may or may not give me a job again when the process is complete," said Jack.

"That's right," said Dexter.

"Is there any chance at all I'll stay on here in this current position?"

"None of that has been decided"

"But don't bet on it," said Jack.

Dexter didn't say anything.

"Well," said Jack. "Can I keep the BlackBerry, for now, until the suspension is lifted or whatever, or I'm fired?"

"Sure," said Dexter. "We need to be able contact you in the coming days, for information about the libel suit."

"Okay," said Jack. "Thanks."

"Mr. Macdonald, on a personal note I just want to tell you not to take this too hard," he said. "These moments are very stressful, but I want to assure you that things will look a lot brighter in a day or two, and in the future you may look back on this very difficult moment and see if for what it was, a new opportunity."

Jack laughed and hung up

"In the future, I may be very drunk," he said.

He walked out of the Hot Room.

Ashton realized why Jack had missed their meeting when she got to Sophie's apartment.

Sophie invited Ashton to sit down and went to the kitchen

to pour them both a cup of coffee. The TV was tuned to an interview with Maude Mowat, an attractive middle-aged blonde, in the backyard of the Mowats' home. Mrs. Mowat was pointing out that there was no pool, and saying how painful she found the brief furore surrounding the allegations that her husband had tried to drown her.

"I know it's silly," she said, "but I keep thinking about people who may have seen the story saying that Greg attacked me, but haven't seen the news since then. I hate to think that some of my neighbours might think that my husband would do such a terrible thing."

Sophie turned the volume down when she brought in the coffee.

"Isn't that your boss's wife?" asked Ashton.

"Yes," said Sophie. "That's the minister's wife. They've played the same interview three or four times now."

"What's she talking about? I haven't been following the news."

Sophie quickly explained how Jack had broken the story based on a forged police report, and how it had been discredited.

"So that explains why he didn't show up for an interview I had scheduled with him this afternoon," Ashton said. "And why he hasn't answered my calls."

"Poor Jack," said Sophie. "He's been suspended, and his boss, too. I think the minister is going to sue them."

"Do you know where Mr. Macdonald is?"

"Not exactly, but he's probably in a bar."

"Do you think he forged the document?" asked Ashton. "You're pretty good friends, aren't you?"

"I don't think he did. But I really don't know. If he didn't forge it, who did? I can't figure it out. I've been trying to get in touch with him, but he's probably ignoring everybody now."

"So, how did you get to know him?" asked Ashton.

"I didn't know him until I started going out with Ed," said Sophie. "They were friends at university, and after Jack moved here last year, they used to go out drinking every couple of weeks. I would sometimes have dinner with them and then they'd go off on their own."

"Was there ever any tension between them?" said Ashton.

"No," said Sophie. "Not that I saw. Ed never talked to me about anything like that."

"Would he have?" asked Ashton.

"I think so," said Sophie. "Ed didn't keep a lot of secrets from me."

Ashton took out her notebook. "What files was Ed working on?"

"You mean at work?"

Ashton nodded.

"Well, his colleagues could give you more detail than I could," she said.

"Yes. I've talked to them about that, but I'm interested in knowing what files he talked about with you."

"Well, natural resources files. Mining. Oil. I didn't find it very interesting."

"Oil?" said Ashton.

"Yes. A lot of oil sands projects. He would talk about those sometimes, mostly just to complain about how much work they were, or the way Environment and Natural Resources would be fighting."

"What would they fight about?"

"The guys at the Environment Department – Ed called them ecofreaks – would be trying to slow down the approval process, complaining about water or wildlife or whatever, and Natural Resources would be pushing for projects to be fast-tracked. Ed would have to write briefing notes for the minister advising what course the government should take."

"Were any of the fights particularly nasty?"

"Not really. Not that he said."

Ashton got up off the couch and walked over and looked out the window, then leaned against the computer desk.

"You still have no idea what happened to Ed's BlackBerry?" she asked.

"No," said Sophie. "Jack says he can't remember. Could it

still be in the canal?"

Ashton ignored the question.

"Did Ed have a personal email account as well as his work account?" she asked.

"Yes," said Sophie. "Gmail."

"What was his email address?"

"Mountpearled@gmail.com."

"Do you know his password?"

"No," said Sophie. "Can you get it from Gmail?"

"Did he use this computer?"

"Yes, that's where he would play games, or cruise the Internet."

She got to her feet. "Excuse me for just a second. I have to use the bathroom."

Ashton turned on the computer and waited for it to boot up. When it started up, it presented her with a password prompt.

Sophie looked surprised to see her fussing with the computer when she came back from the bathroom. "Excuse me. What are you doing with the computer?"

"Do you mind?" said Ashton, turning to look at Sophie. "There might be something on it that would help us figure out what happened to Ed."

"No," said Sophie. "I don't really mind, but that's Ed's computer. I don't have the password."

Chapter 6 – CRACKIE

JENNIFER, THE BARTENDER at Brixton's, a Sparks Street pub, was happy to see Jack, a frequent customer, a casual friend and happy drunk. He walked up to the wooden bar and she beamed at him from behind the bar and leaned over to give him a kiss.

"You want a pint of Keiths Red?" she asked him, reaching for the glass.

"You bet," he said. "And a shot of Jameson."

"Oh," she said. "Celebrating?"

Then she registered the sickly smile on his face.

"No," he said. "Not really. Give me the whisky first."

He knocked back the shot and chased it with about half a pint of beer, then looked up and grimaced.

"That's better," he said. "I just got fired, or at least I think I did. And to make matters worse, a lot worse …"

He stopped there and thought for a second.

"I want another Jameson, please," he said and waited until he had it in his hand. "To make matters worse, they did the right thing. Suspending me, I mean."

"Oh my God," said Jennifer. "No."

He winked and knocked back the second shot of Jameson. Then he drained the pint. "I'm going to need another pint of that stuff."

"What happened?" asked Jennifer as she poured.

"Well," he said, "I fucked up a really, really big story, and my paper's getting sued, and I've been suspended. I expect they'll fire me soon, or maybe offer me a job back in Newfoundland. And nobody here will want to hire me."

"Well," said Jennifer. "I think you should get drunk. Why don't I buy you a drink?"

"That sounds like a good idea," he said.

As soon as Jack had two fresh pints in front of him, Jennifer picked up her iPhone and sent a few emails to people who knew him. Before long Jim Godin showed up.

"Hey," said Godin, slapping him on the back. "It's the fuckhead of the hour."

"Hey Jim," said Jack. He shouted to Jennifer, "Jim's gonna buy me a beer, and get him one of whatever he wants, too."

Godin sat next to him. "So, what the fuck happened?"

Jack took a drink of beer. "I screwed up really bad. I didn't check the story out."

"Yeah, I know," said Godin. "I had to write the boss's statement apologizing, very sincerely, to Greg Fucking Mowat. Well, basically the lawyers talked and I wrote down what they said. I know you fucked up. I'm wondering why."

Jack shrugged and stared at the line of bottles behind the bar. "I don't know," he said. "Guy gave me the police report. It looked legit. I wrote it up."

Godin spoke very quietly. "Who gave it to you? Was it Donahoe's people?"

Jack looked at him and laughed. He shook his head to stop himself from crying. "The terrible truth is I haven't got a fucking clue."

A couple of reporters arrived then, and came over to slap Jack on the back and buy him a beer. Jack was already a little drunk, and the free drinks pushed him quickly over the edge. Before long he wasn't really capable of talking about his day. He sat there smiling drunkenly, not saying much. Eventually, he started proposing toasts. "To all the cocksuckers on the Hill," he shouted, more than once, and lifted his shot glass. His colleagues drifted off after he started with that, and he ended up at the bar alone, unable to speak clearly.

The bar was full of Parliament Hill types by then, some of whom knew who he was. He ignored their looks and whispers and focused on getting more beer into his belly. Then he heard some young staffers talking at a nearby table. He thought he heard the phrase "Jack the Hack" and then they all laughed, and suddenly Jack was very angry.

He jumped to his feet and turned to the group, swaying. "Who said that?" he said, glaring at them. "Who the fuck said that?"

They looked at him with surprise. He balled his fists and stepped unsteadily toward them, teeth gritted, face red.

"One of you motherfuckers call me Jack the Hack?" he said. "Is that what I just heard?"

Jennifer rushed over and stepped between him and the guys at the table. She placed her hands on his chest and pushed him back. Then she put her arm around his shoulder and turned him. "Hey buddy," she said. "Let's go for a little walk."

She walked him through the bar and right out the door.

"You kicking me out?" he said, once they were both on the sidewalk.

"You can look at it that way," she said, and she gave him a kiss on the cheek. "Or you can decide that you've had enough to drink and it's time to go home and go to sleep."

Jack stood there and thought about that for a minute.

He hugged her.

"You're a good friend, Jennifer," he said.

"I'm going to call you a cab."

"I'm all right," he said, and he staggered down the street.

It was bitterly cold outside. The wind whipping down Sparks Street was full of snow. Jack wanted another drink, and he wanted to find out who had set him up.

Ellen Simms was surprised when Jack came into Hy's, surprised and alarmed. She was seated at the bar with Balusi and Bouchard, and they had had a few drinks, but not nearly as many as Jack.

He staggered into the bar and stood there with a dark expression on his face, looking around.

"Oh my God," said Ellen, and Balusi and Bouchard turned to look. "I hope he's not looking for me."

He was, though, and he started towards her.

"Hi," he said. "How you doing, Ellen?"

He leaned against the bar and asked Wayne, the bartender, for a beer.

"How about a water?" said the bartender.

Jack smiled, as if he and Wayne were sharing a joke, took the water and turned to Ellen.

"What's that smell?" said Balusi. "What's that on your shoe?"

Jack looked down at his foot and forced a laugh, then he took a drink of water and looked at Ellen.

"Ellen, I was just wondering if you knew who set me up?" he said. "I mean with the story today. I fucked it up, but somebody fucking set me up. I don't think it was you, but I wonder if you know who."

Simms looked at him with real alarm. "I have no idea," she said. "And I think you should go home." She turned to Bouchard. "He's scaring me."

Balusi stepped between them.

"It's time for you to go," he said. "Ellen doesn't want to talk to you."

Jack could see Ellen watching him, to see how he'd react. Balusi stepped closer to him.

Jack took a step back.

"It's puke," he said to Balusi.

"What?"

"On my shoe. I puked on my shoe today when I saw my story, my story was shit. It's puke."

Balusi tried not to laugh. Ellen snorted. "This is pathetic."

"Kid," Bouchard said. "There's times you gotta know you're beat. Tomorrow's another day. You should go home."

Jack nodded and took another drink of water and walked out into the cold.

Sophie, he thought. I want to see Sophie. I don't want to go home.

It took a long time to get to her place. He was walking slowly, and at one point he got lost and walked the wrong way for a while. When he finally reached her apartment building he waited until he saw someone leaving, and entered as they were on their way out. He rode the elevator up and knocked on her door.

"Sophie," he said.

He heard her move around and then he could tell she was looking at him through the peephole. He was suddenly self-conscious.

"Can I come in?"

"Jack," she said from behind the door. "I'm sorry. You can't come in."

He frowned. "Please let me in" he said. "Just for a minute. I just want to talk to you for a minute."

"No," she said. "You need to go."

Jack heard the indistinct rumble of a male voice from behind the door.

"Jack," she said. "I'm sorry. There's somebody here."

He frowned again. He opened his mouth and closed it without speaking.

"Okay," he said.

He turned to walk away, then stopped.

"Sorry to bother you," he said.

Jack was suddenly very hungry, so he walked to the McDonald's on Elgin Street and ate a Big Mac with fries. He was a bit less drunk after he finished eating, but felt worse: depressed and tired. So he went outside and got in a taxi.

It was hard to dig the keys out of his pocket and hard to get them in the front door of his building. It was hard to walk up the stairs to his apartment and it was hard to open his apartment door.

"Fuck," he said, when he pushed the door open at last.

He turned to switch on the living room light and suddenly

he was falling down, convulsing in the darkness, all his muscles cramped, his teeth jammed shut and his heart pounding. He had no idea what had happened to him, but he was sure he was going to die. He was face down on the floor of his apartment. His muscles twitched.

Someone turned on the lights and he could see a pair of boots in front of his face. Someone else grabbed him and flipped him onto his back. He was looking up at Sergeant Michel Castonguay, who was holding a stun gun in his hand.

Castonguay was squatting down, next to Jack. He was wearing black pants, black turtleneck, a dark blue ski jacket and black leather gloves. He snapped his fingers in front of Jack's eyes. Jack blinked.

His muscles had stopped twitching but he still couldn't move.

"How we doing?" said Castonguay. "Bit tired? Bit drunk?"

Jack spluttered.

"Easy now," said Castonguay. "It takes a minute."

He held up the stun gun. "This is the Taser 3000. It's designed to immobilize an attacker for several minutes."

He looked behind Jack. "I told you it was stronger than the old ones," he said.

"You're right," said another man. "You're usually right."

The second man came around and stood next to Castonguay. He was a bit younger, with dark brown hair and bushy brown moustache. He was dressed the same as Castonguay, except his ski jacket was black.

Castonguay said, "Are you sober enough to understand what I'm saying?"

Jack nodded.

"If you start screaming or moving or doing anything I don't like, I'm going to hit you again with this." He tapped the stun gun with one gloved finger. "Okay?" He peered at Jack intently, trying to see if he really understood.

Jack nodded.

"Okay," he said. "I'm going to ask you a few questions, and you're going to answer them. Then we're going to leave, and you are going to move to Newfoundland and never bother us again. Got it?"

Jack nodded.

Castonguay looked at his partner and then back at Jack. "Okay, question one. We are looking for something. Do you know what that is?"

Jack nodded.

"What?" said Castonguay.

Jack tried to speak. "BbbbbbBlackBerry," he said.

"That's right," said Castonguay. "Whose BlackBerry?"

"Ed's," said Jack.

"Good. Now, do you know where it is?"

Jack nodded. "Taxi," he said.

Castonguay narrowed his eyes. "It's in a taxi? What taxi?"

"Chateau Laurier," Jack said. "Taxi from Chateau Laurier. Blue Line. Two Four Five."

Castonguay bit his lip. "You put Ed Sawatski's BlackBerry in Taxi 245, outside the Chateau Laurier?"

Jack nodded. "Scared. I was scared. You were chasing me. I jammed my BlackBerry and his in the bbbbbumper."

"Oh boy," said Castonguay.

He got to his feet.

"Watch him," he said to his partner, and he handed him the stun gun. Castonguay took out his cell phone and walked over to the corner of the room. He entered a number and held the phone to his ear.

Jack could hear him.

"Dupré reporting," he said. He listened for a few seconds. "The kid says he put the target in the taxi with his own BlackBerry. Blue Line Taxi 245. At the Chateau. He put them both in the same cab."

He listened. "That's right. I know." He paced and listened some more. "Yup. With the Taser. He is co-operating." He listened again. "Yup," he said. "I think so."

Jack tried to flex his hands, and found that he could move them again. He twitched his legs and found that they were also coming back to life.

"Yeah," said Castonguay. "Okay. Roger that."

He put the cell phone in his pocket and came over and bent over Jack again.

"Don't move," he said to Jack, and opened Jack's overcoat and suit coat.

He opened Jack's BlackBerry holster, took out his Berry and walked over and sat down on the couch. He poked at it and then looked down at Jack. "Password?"

Castonguay's partner tapped the stun gun.

"Crackie," said Jack. "C R A C K I E."

Castonguay typed it in.

"Okay," he said.

Jack looked up at Castonguay's partner. "It's what we call dogs in Newfoundland. Like mutts."

"Shut up," said Castonguay's partner.

Castonguay dialled again.

"Okay," he said. "I'm in."

He listened for a few minutes, then wedged the phone between his ear and his shoulder and fiddled with Jack's Berry for a few minutes.

"Sorry," he said into the phone. "It's taking longer than it should because of the gloves."

He flicked through pages on the Berry.

"They are clean," he said. "Nothing from our friend."

He put the Berry down on the coffee table and held the phone to his ear. "Okay," he said. "Got it. Yeah. Good idea. Okay. I'll call you in a few."

He walked into the kitchen, returned with a beer and squatted in front of Jack. "Have a beer. Go on. Sit up. You should be able to sit up now."

Jack sat up. He was very confused. Castonguay handed him the beer. "Go ahead," he said. "Open it."

Jack unscrewed the cap.

"Go ahead," Castonguay said. "Have a drink."

"Why do you want me to drink a beer?"

Castonguay smiled. "Have a sip and then I'll tell you."

Jack took a swallow.

"Okay," said Castonguay. "We're going to give you some sleeping pills."

He reached into the pocket of his coat and brought out a little stainless steel pill container and unscrewed the lid.

"These are not very strong," he said. "So you have to take a few. You need the beer to wash them down. These particular pills may also make your memory a little hazy in the morning. So we're going to give you a few extra, because we would be happy if you can't really remember our little visit too well."

He poured two pills into his hand. "Open up."

Jack opened his mouth and Castonguay popped in the pills. He nodded at the beer. Jack took a slug. Castonguay shook two more pills out of the container. "One more time."

Jack shook his head. "That's enough. I'm already sleepy."

Castonguay smiled and stood up. "Hit him," he said to his partner.

This time Jack actually saw the blue spark from the stun gun. He made a small yelp and then he was convulsed again, all his muscles twisting and twitching. He spasmed on his back and passed out.

When he came to, his head was in Castonguay's lap. He could open his eyes, but he couldn't make his limbs move. Castonguay was holding his mouth open. He dropped a handful of pills onto Jack's tongue and then poured in some beer. He closed Jack's mouth and pinched his nose shut. Jack was suddenly unable to breath. He tried to struggle, but all he could do was flop his arms around. He had no choice but to swallow the pills. He choked them down and then opened his mouth to gulp for air.

"Good boy," said Castonguay. "Sweet dreams."

Castonguay moved away and dialled the cell phone. "All done," he said. "I just gave them to him now."

He listened for a moment and picked up Jack's BlackBerry. "All ready," he said.

Jack felt very strange. He still couldn't move his arms or legs but he didn't feel much of a desire to do so. He closed his eyes and listened to Castonguay talk on the phone.

"Okay," he said. "Sophie Fortin. Got it. An email or a PIN message? Okay."

Castonguay typed as he repeated the instructions he was getting over the phone.

"Subject: Too much. Okay. Done. Next? I fucked up so bad. Sorry. It's better this way. Okay. That it? You sure? No. I think it works. Okay."

He's writing my suicide note, thought Jack. He felt a deep stab of sadness at the prospect of dying. He forced his eyes open and tried to move, but only managed to twitch.

I have to accept this, he thought.

"What do you mean?" Castonguay said. "No. No. I hit send already."

He turned and glared down at Jack.

"Fuck," he said. "I misunderstood. I'm sorry. I thought you wanted me to hit send. No. It's too late. I did it."

He paced as he listened, then stopped in front of Jack's face. "Yes," he said. "Okay. We'll get out of here then. No. You're right. It was stupid."

Jack could see his reflection in the shiny black polish of Castonguay's boots. It looked funny to him the way his face was all twisted and smooshed into the hardwood floor. He smiled, and that was funny too, seeing his smooshed-up face break into a smile. And then he closed his eyes.

Sophie was trying not to let herself worry about Jack. It wasn't her fault that he had lost his job. She told him the story was bullshit. But when she closed her eyes the thought of his sad face in the hallway came back to her. At the time, she had been relieved when he had apologized for bothering her and left, but now it struck her as depressing. He had worn an expression of such defeat when he realized that she had someone else with her.

Jack had lost his job in the most humiliating way possible, she thought, and when he came for help, she sent him away.

He must feel like he hasn't got a friend in the world.

She tried to think of other things, of Ed's first steps toward recovery, of the great sex she'd just had, of the work that she was neglecting by spending all her time at the hospital, but her mind kept turning back to the thought of Jack's sorrowful face when she sent him away.

Eventually she realized she wouldn't be able to sleep. She got up, went into the kitchen, poured herself a glass of wine and sat down on the couch. She checked her BlackBerry.

> **From:** Jack Macdonald
> **To:** Sophie Fortin
> **Subject:** Too much
> I fucked up so bad. Sorry. It's better this way.

She hit reply.

> **To:** Jack Macdonald
> **From:** Sophie Fortin
> **Subject:** Too much
> What are you talking about? Can you call me right now???!!!

She sent the message and then dialled Jack's number. He didn't answer.

She jumped to her feet. Was it a suicide note or was she imagining things? She considered the facts and quickly decided there was a reasonable chance that Jack was trying to kill himself. If she didn't do anything and they found his body in the morning, she would be haunted forever by the thought of how she could have saved his life and hadn't.

She tried him one more time, then called 911.

She told the dispatcher her friend had sent a suicide note, bullied her into sending an ambulance to Jack's address, pulled on her jeans and coat, rode down in the elevator and ran to Elgin Street and waved down a cab. "Please hurry," she told the driver. "It's an emergency." She repeatedly tried Jack's number again in the car but it kept going to voice mail.

There was a police car in front of Jack's building when she

arrived and a middle-aged man standing in the lobby with a coat over his bathrobe.

Sophie ran to the door. "Are the police in there?" she asked.

"They just went in," said the man. "I opened the door for them. I'm supposed to let the paramedics in when they arrive. What's going on?"

"Please let me in," said Sophie. "I'm a friend of Jack's."

The man looked at her frightened face for a minute, hesitated, then opened the door for her.

"What's going on?" he asked.

She ignored him and ran upstairs. A uniformed officer was standing in the doorway.

"Can I help you?" he asked.

"I'm Sophie Fortin," she said. "I called 911." She handed him her business card. "Is Jack okay? Is he in there?"

"Can you wait downstairs please ma'am?" said the cop. "We're doing everything we can."

As the cop bent to look at the business card, Sophie tried to wedge herself through the door. The cop grabbed her and pushed her back, but not before she saw Jack sprawled on his back and a second cop rhythmically pressing on his breast bone. There was vomit on the floor.

"Oh my God," said Sophie and she stepped back. "Oh my God."

"We're doing everything we can," said the officer. "And you're not helping. Please wait downstairs."

Sophie looked up at him and nodded, her hand covering her mouth.

She paced the sidewalk, feeling scared and frantic, and when the ambulance arrived, she told them which the apartment to go to.

The paramedics ran in with a stretcher and in a few minutes they came back down with Jack strapped to it and wheeled him to the ambulance. His face was blank and his skin was slack.

"Is he okay?" she asked.

"He's breathing," said one of the paramedics as he slid the stretcher into the ambulance. "We're taking him to

Ottawa General."

The police officer who had prevented her from entering Jack's apartment walked up to Sophie as the ambulance drove away.

"I think you may have saved your friend's life," he said.

Chapter 7 – Stay where you're at

JACK'S FIRST THOUGHT, before he could open his eyes, was dread of a horrible hangover. He didn't know where he was, but he knew that being fully conscious would be unpleasant. He tried not to wake up, willing himself back into inky oblivion, but he was terribly thirsty, his head was pounding and his bladder was bursting.

He opened his eyes a crack, to take a small peek to orient himself so that he could stagger to the bathroom, pee, drink some water, eat some aspirin and go back to bed. He moaned in distress when he realized he was in a hospital.

He closed his eyes again and tried to pull the covers over his head, but it was no use. With considerable effort, he lifted his head to look around, dazed. He was in a room with four beds. Bright sunlight poured in through the window. The curtains were drawn around two of the beds, but a grey-haired man was sitting in the bed straight across from him, watching a little TV with headphones on. He noticed Jack's movement and yanked out the headphones.

"Well good morning," he said, smiling. "Your girlfriend will be glad to see you're awake. She'll be back in a minute."

Jack stared at him, blinking. He felt terrible, totally confused and savagely hung over, with a dry mouth and a terrible pounding at the base of his skull.

"I don't have a girlfriend," he said.

Jack threw off the blankets and got out of bed. That's when he noticed that he was wearing a hospital gown, and that he was attached to an intravenous drip. He peered down at himself in confusion.

"I don't know if you're supposed to be getting up," said the man. "Wait for the nurse. I'll buzz her."

The man pressed a button attached to his bed.

"Where's the bathroom at?" said Jack. He spied it then, and tried to get out of bed, forgetting about the IV rack. He sagged back onto his bed and tried to remember why he was in the hospital.

His heart sank when he remembered his story gone wrong. He flashed back to vomiting at his desk, and he felt suddenly very tired, so he closed his eyes. Then he remembered his humiliating encounter with Simms at Hy's, knocking on Sophie's door, his late night Big Mac, and the taxi ride home. He couldn't remember anything after that.

He was trying and failing to pull down the blankets to look at his limbs to see if he was injured when Sophie and a red-haired nurse appeared at the door.

Sophie looked rumpled in jeans and a sweatshirt with no makeup and her hair in a ponytail.

Jack felt suddenly a little better to see Sophie, and he tried to smile.

"How you feeling?" said the nurse.

"Not too good," he said. "Can I have some aspirin? What am I doing here?"

"You had a bad time last night," said Sophie.

"What do you mean?" said Jack. "Can I have some Aspirin please? My head hurts."

"You'll have to wait to see the doctor for that," said the nurse, checking his IV hookup. "I'll see if she can pop in to see you."

Jack turned to Sophie. She wore an expression of tender concern.

"What happened to me?" he asked.

She wore a pained expression.

"The doctors think you took some pills last night. They think you were trying . . ."

"Pills?" said Jack. "I took pills? What kind of pills?"

"Tranquilizers," said Sophie. "They think you overdosed

on tranquilizers."

Jack frowned in confusion.

"Jack, you sent me an email at 2:30," said Sophie. "You said that you fucked up, that you were sorry."

"You think I tried to kill myself?"

Then the doctor arrived to examine Jack. She was Indian, young, businesslike, pretty and introduced herself as Doctor Shalini Singh.

"I don't think I tried to kill myself," said Jack.

She smiled. "We can talk about that later," she said. "You are still affected by the tranquilizers and your memory is likely a bit scrambled."

"I'm not the type," said Jack. "I don't feel very good."

"What's the matter?" she asked.

"I have a terrible headache," he said. "I feel muddled."

Singh flashed a light in his eyes, tested his reflexes with a rubber hammer, asked him to count to ten, asked him his name and age.

"You seem to be doing okay," she said as she finished.

"I don't feel okay. I'd like some aspirin, and I'd like to go back to sleep."

"I think we can give you a couple of Tylenol. And I think you need a bit more sleep. I'll come see you later, and a counsellor will come to talk to you about how you ended up here."

"I didn't try to kill myself," said Jack.

"Well," said the doctor, "that's not what the police say."

"The police?" said Jack. "What police?"

The doctor smiled and patted his hand. The nurse arrived with some headache pills and a paper cup of water. Jack gulped them down greedily and laid back to wait for sleep.

"All right," Murphy said at the morning NTV story meeting in his office overlooking Parliament Hill. "Before we get started on the news, does anybody have any ideas about who was behind the Greg Mowat story?"

There were five reporters and four producers in the room, and Murphy went around one by one. Timothy Duncan, a veteran who went back to Diefenbaker's era, went first.

"It had to be Donahoe's people," he said. "It reminds me of a story about Lyndon Johnston. He was facing a tough Senate battle in Texas, 1960, looked like he might lose. He told his people to spread the rumour that his opponent had been caught having carnal knowledge with a pig. They said, 'LBJ! We can't do that! It's not true.' He said, 'I know. Just make the bastard deny it.' And he went on to win."

"I don't know," said Luce Politi, an energetic young reporter with a shock of gelled black hair. "I think the story makes Mowat look good. People will be sympathetic to him now. Did you see his wife yesterday? That's gold. Standing by her man. If it was Donahoe's people, they've got to be kicking themselves, because Maude Mowat knocked the ball out of the park. I don't think they're that dumb."

"Don't be too sure," said Duncan. "Who the heck are they? A bunch of old Tory warhorses been out of the game too long."

Murphy looked at Tamara Johnston, a careful young reporter who kept getting elbowed out of the way by the more aggressive and glamorous Simms.

"I think it was the Liberals," she said. "Some Liberal rat fucker, rattling the Tory cage."

"Aren't they usually too busy ratfucking other Liberals?" said Politi.

"Or it could be Mowat did it himself," said Johnston. "Figuring he'd end up with public sympathy, raise his profile."

Duncan barked a laugh. "If he's smart and ballsy enough to do that, we're all in trouble"

Jasmine Bagnell, a researcher and producer, spoke up: "Do we know for sure that somebody leaked this to Jack Macdonald?" she asked. "I'm kind of assuming that he got out his own whiteout. He enjoyed the story about the drowned staffer so much that he got carried away."

"Could be," said Murphy. "Personally, I suspect that Mowat was banging some Mountie's wife and the guy decided to screw up his week. Anyway, we've all got theories. If you hear anything that is more than a theory, I want to know about it. This is a weird story, and I won't be satisfied until I know what started it. Whether we can put it on the air or not, I want to know. What do your sources say, Ellen?"

Simms didn't know what to think. She had had drinks with Balusi and Bouchard the night before and they seemed honestly confused by the whole thing. She wasn't prepared to say much without more information. "My sources are as confused as we are," she said. "I like your theory, boss."

After the meeting, she went to her desk and took up where she'd left off the day before when the Mowat story broke. She opened both sound files and looked at their wave forms carefully. The second one had been edited, and was about two seconds shorter. She thought about going to a sound technician, who would likely be able to spot the edit in two minutes, but decided she didn't want to share whatever she had.

She sighed, put on the headphones and started to listen.

When Jack awoke, there was an attractive blonde woman sitting in the chair next to his bed.

He lay still for a moment, taking her in. Mid-thirties, with a womanly figure, a wedge of frizzy blond hair and a wide, beautiful face with a strong, sensual mouth. Dressed in a black blazer, white cotton blouse and jeans, she was fiddling with her BlackBerry.

"Good morning, Jack," she said. "How you feeling?"

"Not bad." He tried and failed to sit up. "I'm thirsty."

She filled a plastic cup with ice water from a pitcher by the door and gave it to him, then helped him adjust the bed so he could sit up.

"You must be the counsellor," he said.

She smiled. "I'm Mallorie."

"I don't know if there's much point to us talking," he said.

"What do you mean?" she said as she sat back down.

"Aren't you feeling well enough?"

Jack looked around the room, clearing his head.

"No," he said. "I feel pretty good now. It's just that I don't think I need to talk to you. I didn't try to kill myself, I don't think. I'm not suicidal. It was an accidental overdose."

The woman looked at him and didn't say anything for a moment. She put her fingertips together in front of her face and looked up in the air.

"Well, good," she said. "That's good news. Um, but, why did you take so many pills?"

Jack stared at her and scratched his head. "What time is it?"

"Eleven fifteen."

"You don't know how long I slept, do you?"

"Not exactly. About two hours, I think. So why did you take so many pills?"

"Well," he said. "I'll be honest. I don't remember."

Jack was telling the truth. His last memory was a hazy recollection of wolfing down a Big Mac.

"I was totally hammered," he said. "What I think likely happened is that I took some pills, to help me sleep off the hangover that I knew was coming. Then I was so drunk that I forgot that I already took some. I usually have a high tolerance to drugs, and I was upset and really wanted to zonk out for a while. So maybe I took too many."

He stopped and neither of them said anything for a moment. She was looking at him with a small smile and nodding.

"I feel like an idiot," he said. "It's embarrassing. I'm lucky that I didn't kill myself by mistake. I've learned my lesson. I'll never make that mistake again. Now, I want to get out of here. I have things to do. I feel like an idiot for causing all this trouble, but there must be actual suicidal people in the hospital you could be helping. I bet some poor bugger in another ward is this minute plotting to do away with himself. He's probably perched on the window sill as we speak, working up the nerve to jump."

She laughed a little. "You're funny," she said. "That's great. But, I have to ask you, if it was an accidental overdose, why did you send that note?"

Her clear blue eyes were on him. She had a way of watching that he found disconcerting, a cool intelligence in her gaze that made him feel that if he lied she would catch him.

"Right," he said. "I sent an email, did I? Shit. What did it say? I have no memory of that."

She looked at her BlackBerry and read aloud. "Subject: 'Too much.' Message: 'I fucked up so bad. Sorry. It's better this way.'"

Then her eyes were back on Jack. "What do you think you meant?" she asked.

"Shit," said Jack. "It does sound like a suicide note, doesn't it? Shit." He looked around. "Do you think you can get me some more water please?"

She refilled his cup, then stayed standing next to his bed after she gave it to him, looking down at him.

"What did you mean?" she asked.

"Well," he said, "I lost my job yesterday, in a very, uh, I guess you could say humiliating way."

"I know about that," she said.

"I went to see my friend Sophie, who I may have a crush on." He shrugged. "I wanted some sympathy from my friend. And she was busy. She was with somebody in her apartment, a man, and wouldn't let me in, and I took that hard. I think I wanted to hurt her, to let her know that she had hurt me. I can't be sure that I really wanted her to think I was killing myself. I hope not. Because that's a pretty shitty thing to do. What's it say again?"

She read it aloud again.

"I would like to think that maybe I was going to write more, and drunkenly hit send by mistake," he said. He had to look away from her eyes. "But it's possible I wanted her to worry about me. I know that must seem childish."

She sat back down. "What's the last memory you have of the night you and Ed were drinking at Pigale?"

Jack stared at her. "Did Sophie tell you about that?"

She shifted in her seat.

"Well?" she said.

He realized his mistake.

"You're not a counsellor," he said. "You're Ashton."

She gave him a big smile. "Yes," she said. "That's right."

"Wow," he said. "You just lied to me, gave me the impression I was talking to a counsellor, so I would open up to you."

"I didn't say I was a counsellor," she said.

"No," he said. "You didn't, but you let me think that. I could lose my job if I did that."

Then he laughed. "Or I frigged up a really big story," he said. "I could lose my job for that, too. Anyway, you police can get away with lying. I can't ever misrepresent myself. The first thing I have to do when I talk to anyone on a story is identify myself as a reporter. It's interesting that you don't have to do that."

She looked at him hard for a moment. "We are trying to catch killers. It's different. We can't say just anything, because we could run into problems in court, but there's a different, um, onus on us."

"I guess that's right," he said. "But you should be careful. When Flanagan interviewed me the first time he kept telling me lies and it made me defensive. Anyway, my last clear memory of Ed is having a smoke with him outside at Pigale. It was cold. He was bragging about how he was going to make a move, how he would hire me to be a d comms – director of communications – after he got his next job. Just drunk bragging, I think. He's like that. Part of his charm.

"I remember one funny thing he said to me. He said, 'The definition of a transition period is, the period between two transition periods.' I think he was counting on a promotion if Donahoe wins the leadership."

"You don't remember anything after that?" said Ashton.

"Not much," said Jack. "I remember little flashes. Sitting down watching the strippers. I remember him leaving to go for a lap dance. I remember staggering out to a cab. That's about it."

"You don't remember taking his BlackBerry?"

"No. Not at all. I don't remember if I had it or not."

"Did he talk to you about his files?"

"Not much. I'm a reporter, remember? He wasn't supposed to talk to me about his files. We would talk about politics, though. The upcoming leadership race, that kind of thing."

"How did he get on with Sophie?" she asked.

"Great," he said. "She was good for him. They were happy together. I saw them a fair bit and there was a kind of mutual respect between them that I admired."

"Did you spend time at their apartment?"

"Yeah. Scattered time. Stop by for a drink or whatever."

"What did Ed use the computer for?"

"Email. Porn. Warcraft. The usual. Sophie would read celebrity gossip blogs, Perez Hilton, check the weather."

"So they both use it?"

"Yeah," said Jack. "Why?"

"Never mind why. Last time it ended up in the newspaper."

Jack laughed. "No danger of that now."

"Have you seen Sophie use the computer since Ed got hurt?"

"Yeah. The other day I slept there. In the morning, she booted it up to check the weather. And ..."

"What?"

"After she left, I was kind of snooping around, and I found a line to a web cam hidden in a bookshelf in the bedroom."

She stared at him for a moment. "Are you and Sophie having a sexual relationship?"

"No," said Jack, shaking his head. "No. We never have. I do have a crush on her, but I've never made a move. She's my friend's girlfriend."

"Okay," she said. "Any idea who was there the other night?"

Jack shook his head. "Nope. Some lucky dude."

She sat back, exhaled and thought. "Do you have any idea who might have tried to drown Ed?"

"No," he said. "Some bad dudes."

He thought for a moment. "Look, there's something I should tell you. The night after Ed wound up in the canal, when I went home, I saw these guys near my apartment. They were dressed in dark, like black boots, dark ski jackets. They both had moustaches. They were in a black Buick. Something about them spooked me, so I took off running and it seemed to me like they were pursuing me. I would run and hide and then the Buick would go by. Eventually I shook them off and went to Sophie's.

"They looked like cops, big guys, all in black, but I didn't figure they were with you guys. They made me nervous. I had the creepy feeling that they were tracking me by my BlackBerry."

"What made you think that?"

"Because I couldn't shake them. I'd think I'd lost them and then I'd see the Buick again. Might be paranoia. But when I powered down my Berry, I did finally lose them."

"You haven't seen them again?"

"No."

"Well, if you do see them again, I want you to call me on my cell as soon as you can and get away from them. And I'm going to need a more detailed description."

"I'm pretty sure I won't see them again," he said.

"Why?" said Ashton.

"Because I'm leaving for Newfoundland just as soon as I can get out of this hospital. I'm finished with Ottawa."

Simms didn't have to listen for long to find the edit. It was in the highlighted bit.

In one file, the French recording matched the English transcript. "To mend this rift, they say, we need to make a new place for Quebec in the constitution, and formally recognize what is a fact of life, the distinct and rich cultural life of the province. Call it Meech II. I am with these people."

In the other file, there were an extra two words: *ne pas*. "Je ne suis pas avec ce monde," said Donahoe, quite clearly. Someone had edited the clip to reverse Donahoe's message. He was actually saying that he would not attempt a Meech II, and then the tape ended. He likely went on to say what he would do instead. But whoever had edited the clip cut it off there.

So Balusi and company were trying to derail Donahoe's leadership campaign with a fake tape, thought Simms, which would hand the leadership to Mowat. That would be an explosive story. PMO Operative Behind Dirty Tricks Campaign. She briefly thought about going to Murphy with the audio files. She would get a great scoop, but she would lose her best source.

Or she could try to use the secret to get leverage over Balusi, and get lots of scoops.

She sent him a PIN.

> **To:** Ismael Balusi
> **From:** Ellen Simms
> **Subject:** Bullshit
> You doctored the tape. Tsk tsk tsk.

He responded immediately.

> **From:** Ismael Balusi
> **To:** Ellen Simms
> **Subject:** Bullshit
> I can explain. Free for lunch?

After Ashton left, Jack had to sit through a session with a real suicide prevention counsellor but he was able by the end to convince her that whatever had happened the night before, he was not suicidal. After waiting for what felt like hours, the doctor came back, checked him over and he was able to remove the IV, get dressed, check himself out and smoke two cigarettes in the hospital parking lot.

Then he went back inside, found out where Ed's room was, and went in for a visit. The Sawatskis and Sophie were there.

Jack said hello, then went over and said hello to Ed, who lay staring at the ceiling blankly.

The Sawatskis greeted him so solicitously he figured Sophie had told them what happened the night before. They didn't say anything, but they looked concerned and were watching him closely. He decided to bring things out into the open.

"Look," said Jack. "Sophie probably told you what happened last night."

The Sawatskis nodded.

"I thought they should know," said Sophie.

"Yes, b'y," said Mr. Sawatski.

"Jack, you have so much to live for," said Mrs. Sawatski, and she gave him a hug.

"Well. I understand why Sophie told you, but I have to ask you now to keep it to yourselves. I was pretty upset, and very drunk, and somehow I took more sleeping pills than I should have, but I don't think I was really trying to kill myself. It was an accident that could have killed me, but Sophie here saved my life." He paused, momentarily overcome by the idea that he might have died. "Anyway, I don't want you to worry about me, at all. Whatever happened last night is behind me. I just had a talk with the suicide counsellor, and I told her what I'll tell you. I've got plans now. I'm not the least bit depressed. I'm looking forward to getting home to Newfoundland and getting on with my life. I'll leave today if I can. But the last thing I need is for people down there to be worried about me. So please don't mention anything to my parents, or anyone. It's going to be hard enough to get a job in the business already. The last thing I need is people thinking that I'm cracked."

"What you going on about?" said Mr. Sawatski. "Everybody home already knows y'er cracked."

They laughed then, and Mrs. Sawatski hugged him. Then the Sawatskis went for lunch.

Sophie stayed behind.

"You really are better?" she said, looking at him closely.

"I told the truth," he said. "I really don't think I tried to kill myself. I can't remember what happened, but it must have been an accident. I don't remember emailing you, but I was probably trying to hurt your feelings. I'm sorry, but there it is. When I went to your place and you were there with somebody, I ... "

He looked away.

"Oh Jack," said Sophie. "I'm glad you did send me an email. Otherwise ..."

They hugged then. He held her in his arms and looked down at her.

"You saved my life," he said. "I owe you."

He felt the urge to kiss her, and then felt guilty about that urge. She saw something odd in his eyes, and pulled him close into a hug again.

"I'm just so glad you made it," she said. "I was so scared."

Jack held her close and closed his eyes. He buried his nose in her hair and inhaled the clean, intoxicating scent of her. When he opened them again, he glanced over to the bed where Ed lay.

"Hey," he said. "How you doing, b'y? Ready for a little visit?"

Sophie pulled away and turned to the bed.

"Oh my God," she said, smiling.

Ed was staring at them.

"So I think you gave me quite a story," said Simms, cradling a glass of Pinot Grigio in both her hands and peering at Balusi. "But I don't think it's the story you thought you were giving me."

Balusi smiled back at her but his eyes were guarded. "What story is that?" he asked.

They were seated in the dining room at Hy's. Around them, lobbyists, politicians and staffers were lunching, eating steaks and salads, drinking wine, looking prosperous and powerful.

"I don't think you'll like it," said Ellen. "But I know Murphy will."

"Okay," said Balusi. "I give up. Tell me the story."

"Stevens' Aide Doctors Tape to Discredit Donahoe."

"Well, I don't think that's a very good story," he said. "For one thing, it's not true. I've never doctored a tape in my life."

"No?" said Simms. "Well, somebody doctored it. You sent me two files, one doctored, one not doctored. Sure looks like you were trying to sandbag Donahoe."

"It looks that way, but I really didn't know the tape had been edited until you PINed me."

"That's interesting. It's still a good story. We could put you on camera saying that. And then I could ask you who did doctor it."

Balusi laughed with discomfort. "You're right," he said. "That would be a good story."

Simms smiled broadly. "I told you!"

"But I don't think you should do that story," he said, smiling back at her. "Because then I would lose my job, and then I wouldn't be able to give you any more stories ever again."

Simms took a sip of wine. "I know," she said. "That's why I'm not going to do it."

Balusi's shoulders sagged with relief.

"But you owe me a really good scoop," she said. "Something really juicy."

"How about this?" he said. "Donahoe's going to launch his campaign tomorrow. He's going to be first out of the gate."

"Wow," she said. "They must think you're on their side."

"They might."

"That's a good start," said Simms, "but not good enough. We can call it a down payment."

Balusi nodded. "But you have to go with the tape story."

Simms shook her head. "I can't. I know it's bullshit. If you hadn't sent me two tapes, I could have, but now that I know it's a setup, I can't do it."

Balusi took a deep breath. "Well, I'll have to give it to someone else then. I need that story to break as Donahoe's launching his campaign. We need to kneecap him as he leaves the gate. We want this race to be over before it begins. If Donahoe is obviously compromised from the get-go, then it makes it easier for Mowat to twist arms in caucus. He can lock it up. So you can do it, or I can leak it to someone else.

Luce Politi maybe."

Simms stared at him. "How many people know it was doctored?"

"You, me and the guy who doctored it," he said, "who obviously has excellent reasons to keep his mouth shut. I didn't even know that it was doctored until you messaged me today. You are covered. Nobody will ever know."

"It's a good story," she said.

"You'll have the scoop of the day," said Balusi. "It will be just like the drowning story. Everybody will have to watch you all day to know what's going on."

Simms looked at him through narrowed eyes.

"And you'll still owe me a really big scoop," she said.

He smiled at her. "And I'll still owe you a really big scoop."

Sophie smothered Ed in kisses while Jack stood behind her, beaming down at his friend.

"How you doing, buddy?" he asked. "Feeling better?"

Ed blinked twice.

"That means no," said Sophie. "What's the matter? Do you want me to get the doctor?"

He blinked twice again.

"Well, she says it may be a while before you start feeling better," said Sophie. "She said your brain is healing itself right now, and the more time you spend communicating with us the better it is. She says it's likely really hard for you, but you need to do it so you can get better."

Ed's eyes flicked back and forth from Sophie to Jack.

Sophie said to Jack: "The doctor said that in the early stages, it can be terribly painful and depressing to come out of a coma, so patients will often prefer to stay unconscious. She said it's a lot of work to fight back."

She bent over Ed. "Is it painful and depressing, honey?"

He blinked once.

"Well I need you to fight harder," she said. "We need to

spend more time communicating."

Ed didn't respond.

Jack spoke up. "Ed, do you remember what happened after you dropped me off in the taxi after we went to Pigale? The police are trying to figure out who tried to drown you. Do you remember?"

Ed blinked twice.

Sophie said, "He doesn't remember anything from that night."

"Ed, do you know a guy with a black moustache and a big scar on his right eyebrow?" asked Jack.

Ed looked at Jack, then blinked once.

"Who's that?" said Sophie.

Jack ignored her.

"Do you think he might have tried to drown you, Ed?" asked Jack.

But Ed's eyes were blank again.

"That's how it is," said Sophie. "It's like he only has enough energy for a little chat, then he tunes out again."

Jack put his hand over his friend's. "Ed, b'y," he said, raising his voice. "You get better. I'm going back to Newfoundland. I hope to hear soon that you're on the mend. After you're up and around, we'll go out on a tear and celebrate, eh?"

"Talking louder doesn't help," said Sophie. "What are you going to do in Newfoundland?"

Simms was wearing a mischievous smile on her face when she knocked on Murphy's door. She dangled a memory stick in her hand.

Murphy looked up from his computer. "Here's trouble," he said.

"You know it," said Simms as she sashayed in. She put the memory stick on his desktop. "Have a listen to this."

Murphy took the stick and plugged it into his computer. "Something good?" he said.

"Not bad," she said, and stretched out on his office couch. "It's a recording of a Q-and-A session that Donahoe had with some Quebec Tories in Montreal on Wednesday. Nobody else has it."

Murphy clicked on the file, and Donahoe started to drone on in French.

"Anything good?" he asked.

"Click ahead to the eighteen-minute mark."

Murphy listened to it, then hauled the cursor back to listen to it again.

"That is good," he said. "He's proposing a Meech II, a constitutional change. That would be hard to sell to the rest of the country. Where'd you get the recording?"

"I promised my source anonymity," she said.

"Of course," he said. "I will respect it, but I need to know before we put it on the air."

Simms frowned. She had no choice.

"Ismael Balusi," she said. "He'll lose his job if we reveal where we got it. Stevens's office is supposed to be neutral in the leadership battle."

"But they lean to Mowat."

"Well, Balusi seems to. But I don't really know what he's up to. He told me he got this from the person who taped it, a Quebec Tory who was in the room. He wouldn't tell me who. He said if we don't use it, he'll give it to someone else."

"Oh, I think we'll use it. This is good stuff."

"Donahoe's announcing his candidacy tomorrow," said Simms.

"And you should be there to ask him whether he would consider a constitutional change to acknowledge Quebec's distinctness."

"Smart," said Simms. "If he says yes we have a good story. If he says no, we have a great story."

"C'est exact," said Murphy. "C'est ca."

Jack checked himself out of the hospital, got a taxi back to his apartment, where he was confronted by the mess left from the night before.

He cleaned up his vomit, changed into jeans and a sweater and packed a duffle bag with clothes. He put his laptop, his voice recorder, a notebook and a few books in a backpack. Then he got in his car and drove to Ida Gushue's house.

She was startled to see him at her door.

"Jack," she said. "Hello. What brings you back?"

"I'm sorry to bother you," he said, "but I'd like a quick chat."

"What about?" she said. "I understand you're not with the paper anymore."

"That's right. I've been suspended, and I'm moving back to Newfoundland. I don't know whether I'll get back on the Tely or not."

She frowned. "Well, if you want to ask me to intercede with my uncle to save your job, I'm afraid I can't. From the sounds of things the lawyers are calling the shots on everything to do with the Mowat story."

"No," he said. "It's not that. I made a mistake. I'll accept the consequences. I just want to ask you about something. It's related to the Mowat story. It won't take long. If you'll give me five minutes, I have a proposal for you."

She looked at him coolly.

"Please," he said. "I'm at the end of my rope and I just want a few minutes of your time."

She opened the door wide and let him in.

Zwicker greeted Ashton and Flanagan with a not very friendly smile and motioned for them to sit down.

"Thanks for coming," he said. "I want an update on the Sawatski case. To start with, I take it neither of you have been pestering Justice Department officials for secret files."

They both shook their heads.

"And you haven't conducted any accidental interviews

with journalists?

They shook their heads again.

"Good," he said. "What have you been up to?"

Flanagan started. He whipped out his notebook. "I went for a drive today with the taxi driver who drove Macdonald and Sawatski to their homes. Name's Henri Tremblay, works for Regal Taxi in Gatineau.

"We retraced his route, but he really doesn't remember anything much about these two in particular other than that they were both very intoxicated. I also tracked down Michelle Gagnon, the *danseuse* who gave Sawatski his lap dance. I found her, via telephone, at Chez Parée, a Montreal establishment for dance enthusiasts. I emailed her his picture, but she said she could remember *rien*. Has many customers. Does not recall. And that's about it."

"Okay," said Zwicker, turning to Ashton. "How about you?"

"I interviewed Sophie Fortin again, and then Jack Macdonald again," she said, flipping through her notebook. "He is no longer working as a journalist, so there is no danger that he could report on our conversation. I did come up with something interesting that I think warrants follow-up. Mr. Macdonald went to see Ms. Fortin late Thursday night. He was upset over losing his job and wanted to commiserate with her. He found that she had a gentleman caller and didn't want to let him in.

"Also, he reports that there is a hidden camera in the bedroom of Ms. Fortin, connected to the computer she shared with Mr. Sawatski. He also reported that he witnessed her using the computer after Mr. Sawatski's injury. But when I interviewed her, she told me it was Sawatski's computer, and she didn't have the password."

"A hidden camera?" said Zwicker.

"Yes," said Ashton. "It's hidden in a bookshelf. Likely a small web cam."

"And she said she didn't know the password."

Ashton nodded.

"Do we know who she's been sleeping with?" he asked.

"No," said Ashton. "And it seems to me we need to know that."

"Okay," he said. "Tomorrow morning, get a warrant for the computer. Grab it and ask her why she lied to you. Ask her who her gentleman caller was. Tell her that you may have to treat her as a suspect. She's an aide to Greg Mowat, right?"

Ashton nodded. She was taking notes.

"Tell her you don't want to alert her employer to your investigations, but her lies are causing problems for the investigation. Then bring the computer back here and tell me what she said."

He looked at them. "Anything else?"

"No," said Ashton.

"Well, get the fuck out of my office then," he said.

Ida Gushue again brought Jack tea.

"Thanks for taking a minute to listen to me," he said. "I want to ask for your help."

He paused and took a cup of tea.

"I think you know about my Greg Mowat story yesterday," he said.

She nodded.

"Well," he said. "It was a set up. A man posing as an RCMP officer leaked me a forged report. He was very persuasive. He even gave me a fake business card." He pulled it out and put it in front of her.

"I believe they did this to discredit me as a journalist," he said. "They have succeeded in doing so. I'm finished. I'll be lucky to get the Tely to give me a job in Port aux Basques now."

She said nothing.

"I don't know who this man is, or why he is trying to destroy me, but I think it has something to do with the near death of my friend, Ed Sawatski, who as you probably know, is an aide to Jim Donahoe. They think I have his cell phone, which I don't. I won't bore you with the details, but they have been tailing me. I think they are police of some kind, or intelligence agents, and I think they are being directed by someone senior in the government. I can't prove that, though. I can't prove anything."

"Have you told the police?" asked Gushue.

"A little bit," said Jack. "Not everything. I'm afraid. I know this sounds completely insane, but I assure you I'm telling the truth."

"It doesn't sound that insane," said Gushue. "What do you want me to do about it?

"Well, when I was last here, you told me you had information about an old case – the murder of a prostitute in Fort McMurray – that could end the career of a senior cabinet minister. I want to persuade you to give me the file." He stared at her, willing her to be moved by what he was saying but he could see the toughness in her eyes. "The only way I can save my career now is to nail a really good story," he said. "I worked hard to get here and now my career has been destroyed by some ruthless people. I'm begging for your help."

Gushue smiled warmly, then looked away.

"I'm sorry," she said, "but I don't think I can do that. If I decide to use the file, it will be because … because I have decided it's necessary, that it's the right thing for the country, for the party, and for me and my daughter. I am far from reaching such a conclusion. I wish now that I hadn't mentioned the file to you at all."

Jack sighed and put his head in his hands.

"I am truly sorry for what's happened to you, and I believe your story, but I simply can't give you the file," she said. "Maybe I can eventually, but not now. Maybe never."

Jack lifted his head from his hands. He finished his tea.

"Okay," he said, and got to his feet. "Thank you so much for agreeing to let me try to persuade you. I really am at the end of my rope. I would ask you to please not share my story with anyone."

"Of course," she said, rising with him.

"You are actually the only person I've told about this. If

I turn up dead, you might want to tell Detective Sergeant Mallorie Ashton, with the Ottawa Police Service."

She didn't say anything.

"I don't want to tell my family or friends about this," he said. "Anyway, I doubt they'll come after me in Newfoundland. I don't mean to be melodramatic."

"I understand," she said, walking him to the door. "I really do wish I could help. You should think about telling the police everything you know."

He thanked her again and went out and got in his car, lit a cigarette and started the engine then realized that he didn't know where he should go. He had hoped she would give him a place to start digging, to find some way to get himself out of the mess he'd made of life. What should he do now? Drive to Newfoundland? He supposed that made sense. No point flying, spending money he didn't have. But it was getting late to start a long drive, and he was tired.

He thought about going back to the apartment. He could get a good night's sleep and pack up more stuff, leave in the morning. Get as far as Edmundston tomorrow night. Maybe Fredericton. Might get on a ferry to Port Aux Basques in Sydney the following afternoon. He'd better call his parents and let them know he's coming.

The thought of the call, and the drive, was too much. He put his head on the steering wheel and closed his eyes for several minutes, breathing deeply. Then he opened his eyes, got out of the car and knocked on Ida Gushue's door again.

When she opened it, he tried to smile.

"I'm sorry to bother you again," he said. "But I just had a thought. Why don't you just tell me the name of the prostitute? It would give me a place to start digging. If I find anything I'll come back to you and you can decide whether you want to share your file. I might find the story without your help, in which case nothing would be linked to you. In either case, I swear not to drag you into it without your permission."

She stared at him, and he saw her eyes harden. He thought he had pushed his luck too far and she would slam the door in his face.

"Rena Redcloud," she said.

"Thank you," he said. "Thank you so much. I swear I won't drag you into this."

"See that you don't," she said. "And let me know what you find."

Jack got $3,200 for his car. It was a 2003 Focus with 190,000 kilometres on it, so he hadn't expected to get much, but he thought he'd get more than $3,200. He could have got more, he knew, if he had had the time to sell it online, but he needed the money right away. So he'd gone to the suburb of Vanier, and driven it back and forth from one used car lot to another for an hour. The best offer he got $3,200, from a guy who wrote Jack a cheque on the spot.

He took a taxi directly to the airport and called his parents from the departures terminal. He explained that he'd been suspended, which they had heard on the news.

"I told you to be careful around them politicians," said his mother. "Well, we been right worried about you. Good to hear your voice."

"How's Dad?" he asked.

"Good, b'y," said his mother. "Worried about you."

Jack could hear the rumble of his father's voice in the background: "Worried about what foolishness he'd get up to next."

"Tell him I'm gonna take it easy on the foolishness for a bit," Jack said.

"What are you going to do now?" said his mother.

"I've decided to go out to Fort Mac. Might get a job out there. I'm at the airport now."

"Fort Mac?" his mother said. "Well, Vern and Peggy are out there, just like everybody else these days. I bet they'll put you up for a bit. Let me get their number." She read it to him. "That's a cell, now. They haven't got a home phone there."

"Thanks, Ma," said Jack. "Don't worry about me now. I'll

call in a day or two. You look after the old fellow now."

He called the cell number next.

"Aunt Peggy," he said when his aunt answered.

"Yes," she said. "Who's that?"

"Jack," he said.

"What do you know?" she said. "What are ya at, b'y?"

"Well, I'm coming where you're to, Aunt Peg," he said. "Coming in at eleven tonight on WestJet. Any chance I can stay with you for a day or two?"

Jack slept deeply from the moment he buckled his seatbelt until the moment the plane started its descent into Fort McMurray, when the flight attendant gently woke him to ask him to put his seat into an upright position for landing.

Jack started in fear at the man, and actually squealed in fright. He stared around him, wild-eyed and disoriented for a moment. The steward had a bushy black moustache.

"Are you all right, sir?" he asked.

Jack tried to calm himself. "Yes. I'm okay. You just startled me."

The moustache made Jack think of Castonguay and he felt a stab of terror, without knowing why. Then he remembered why, and the events of the night before came back to him in a rush.

"Holy Christ," he said aloud, and his seatmate looked at him with concern.

Jack perspired with fear as the plane descended to Fort McMurray.

Chapter 8 – Fort Crack

A SHTON CALLED SOPHIE at 7 a.m., when she was in the shower. Sophie called back as soon as she got the message. Ashton said she had news for her and would drop by at 8:30. When she opened the door at 8:34, Sophie was surprised that Flanagan was with the policewoman. She invited them in and poured them both coffee. The officers sat on the couch and Sophie swivelled slowly on the computer chair. Ashton handed her a folded document..

"This is a warrant," she said. "It gives us the authority to take Ed's computer, to search it for information that might help in our investigation."

Sophie frowned. "I don't know if you'll find anything on it that will help you with your investigation. And you won't be able to get access to it without the password."

Ashton looked at Sophie and spoke sharply. "We have a computer forensic investigator at the department who's pretty good at cracking passwords. Or you could tell us what it is."

"But I don't know it," she said.

"I think you do," said Ashton. "Jack told me that he saw you boot it up when he was here."

Sophie looked away.

"Sophie," said Ashton. "Why did you tell me you didn't have the password?"

"I'm sorry. I was afraid of what you might find on it, nothing to do with the attack on Ed, but other things."

"What kind of things?" asked Flanagan.

"I don't know," said Sophie. "It just seemed easier this way. I don't know everything's that's on there. There might be stuff, personal things. And I didn't see how it would help you find whoever attacked Ed."

"Do you know who attacked Ed, or why?" asked Ashton.

Sophie shook her head.

"Then how do you know what will help us find whoever did it?"

"I'm sorry. You're right."

"What's the password?" asked Ashton.

"Gaspesie," she said.

Flanagan spelled it out and wrote it down.

"Did you install the web cam?" he asked.

"What do you mean?" she asked.

"Did you run the wire into the bedroom and hook up a web cam there?"

Sophie blinked at him.

"I don't know what you're talking about."

Flanagan got up and walked over to the computer. He pointed to the USB wire that ran to the wall.

"Come on," he said.

He walked into the bedroom with Sophie and Ashton following him.

"It's in the bookcase," he said, and started removing the books, until he found the one that wouldn't move.

He got to his knees and pulled out a flashlight and a pocket knife.

"There it is," he said, and pointed to a pinhead-sized lens sticking out of the binding of the book.

Sophie's mouth dropped open. Ashton was watching her reaction very closely.

"What is it?" said Sophie.

"It's a little tiny camera, hooked to your computer," said Flanagan. He poked at it with the head of his knife, then photographed it with his digital camera.

Sophie gaped. "Oh my God," she said. "I had no idea that was there."

"Is that right?" said Ashton. "How do I know you're telling us the truth?"

Sophie's eyes went wide. "Oh my God. I had no idea."

Ashton stepped toward her. "Who did you have over on Thursday night? Jack said you had a guest, a male guest, and that's why you wouldn't let him in."

"I did have a guest," said Sophie, stepping back. "But I'm sure it had nothing to do with your investigation," she said.

"We like to make those kinds of decisions," said Flanagan. "Your boyfriend might spend the rest of his life on his back, and you don't seem to want to help us find out who did that to him."

"I'm sorry," said Sophie. Her lip started to quiver and she turned away from Ashton, trying to hide her tears. She stood looking out the window, her shoulders shaking.

"We need to know who was here," said Ashton, her voice hard.

Sophie turned back to her. Her cheeks were wet with tears. "I can't tell you," she said. "But it had nothing to do with this."

"You need to tell us," said Flanagan. "If it had nothing to do with what happened to Ed, then we won't do anything about it. But we need to know."

"He's married," said Sophie, and looked pleadingly at the two of them, seeking understanding.

"So?" said Ashton. "We don't care about that."

"I can't," she said. "I promised I wouldn't tell anyone, no matter what."

Ashton was stern. "Sophie, this is not good. We don't want to have to go up to the Hill, and start interviewing your colleagues and friends, asking them who you're fucking. I bet you don't want us to do that, do you?"

"Oh God," said Sophie. "Let me talk to him. Give me the day. Let me tell him that I'm going to tell you, give him a chance to tell his wife."

Jack had breakfast with his Aunt Peggy and Uncle Vern in their mobile home on the outskirts of Fort McMurray.

Vern was a pipefitter who spent twenty-five years working at the pulp mill in Grand Falls, until they shut the damned thing down. The severance and pension weren't enough to live on, and there were suddenly two thousand other people looking for jobs there, so he went to a recruitment session put on by Syncrude, where they told them about Fort McMurray's rinks and churches and a bunch of stuff Vern didn't care about. Afterwards, in a one-on-one session, they told him they'd give him $125,000 for a one-year contract, plus four flights home. He signed the next day and flew out and started fitting pipes on a massive new project Syncrude was building, digging up millions of tonnes of bitumen-impregnated sand, and processing it in a massive upgrader.

Vern found the work more interesting than maintaining the old pulp machines in Grand Falls, but he missed Peggy and didn't like spending his nights in a work camp with a bunch of other fellows, some of whom he didn't like or trust. So he hitched a ride to Edmonton and bought the motor home and asked the human resources department if he could use one of his tickets home to fly Peggy out. She got a job quick enough, at a coffee shop downtown, and they found a tidy trailer park, full of other couples like themselves.

They told Jack about this as they had breakfast, and told him he was welcome to stay as long as he liked.

"B'y, you wouldn't be the first fellow from home to camp out on that couch," said Vern. "Some mornings I don't know who I'm gonna find out here, 'cept he's a bayman with a job but no place to stay. Seems like half the young fellas from home are here, with a pocket full of money and no place to lay their heads. And the ones that aren't here are in Red Deer, or Grand Prairie."

"Fort McNewfie," said Peggy.

"That's very kind of you," said Jack. "I don't know what I'm going to do, really, but I hope it will only take me a few days to do my research."

"What's it about, b'y?" asked Vern.

Jack had thought about what he would say. "I'm working

on a story that might be connected to federal politics, but I don't know if it is or not. A girl, a prostitute named Rena Redcloud, was murdered here two years ago. I'm going to poke around, see what I find."

"Redcloud," said Vern. "There's a Redcloud works on the project with me. Mike. Nice fellow. Cree, is he? No. Dene. From Fort McKay. Young fellow. Always on time and that. Always ready to work."

"Sure, he must be related to the girl," said Peggy.

"I imagine I should talk to him," said Jack. "But do me a favour, Uncle Vern. Don't mention my project to him until I do a bit of research."

"What project?" said Vern.

They all got in Vern's company truck – a white extended-cab Dodge with a buggy whip antennae sticking up from the cab, with an orange flag on top. As they drove to town, they joined a stream of similar vehicles.

"Why do all the trucks have the antennas?" asked Jack.

"That's so the big Jesus trucks can see them," said Vern. "The sand trucks are so big they can crush a pickup like this and the driver won't even notice."

They dropped him off at the town library, and he sat down to go through the electronic archives of *Fort McMurray Today*.

The first mention of Rena Redcloud was a picture of her – published July 18, 2002 – dancing in a powwow in Fort McKay, a Dene community north of Fort McMurray. She was fourteen then, one of a group of teenage girls in buckskin dancing in front of a group of men beating a big drum with sticks. One of the drummers was Dennis Redcloud, who Jack guessed was her father.

The next item was the death notice for her mother, Sara Redcloud (nee Augustine), who died after bravely fighting cancer in 2004. Rena had an older brother, Mike, and a younger sister, Karen.

The next item was a story about a prostitution bust, in 2006. Rena was one of a number of women who had been arrested after the RCMP launched an operation to put an end to street prostitution in Fort McMurray. The paper quoted Sgt. Earl Gushue saying, "Operation Clean Sweep is aimed at finding the women working as prostitutes and trying to get them off the streets. It's unfortunate that the only way we are able to do that is by arresting them and charging them, but we've worked with the Fort McMurray office of Alberta Social Services to try to divert at-risk women into a program designed to get them off the street."

Apparently the program didn't work for Rena Redcloud, because she was mentioned in two court briefs a year later, the first a prostitution conviction, the second a conviction for theft, resisting arrest and possession of cocaine.

The next item was a story about her death.

August 14, 2008
Fort MacKay Woman Killed in Motel
Chinese Oil Executive Arrested
By Todd Prosper

A Chinese oil executive was charged early Tuesday morning with first-degree murder in the death of Rena Redcloud, 24, of Fort McKay.

Ling Cho Wi, of Beijing, China, was arrested at about 5 a.m. after police were called to investigate noise coming from a room at Great Western Motel, on Highway 18. They found the body of Redcloud and arrested Wi.

"Our officers were called to the scene and quickly ascertained that a homicide had taken place," said RCMP spokesman Wayne Rogers. "They apprehended the suspect, secured the crime scene and the officers from our Major Crimes Unit began their investigation."

Wi is a representative of SinoGaz, a Chinese oil company. He came to Fort McMurray to lead a team negotiating the acquisition of a 120-hectare oil sands development from Tallahassee, Fla.-based PanPetroDev.

In December, Wi told Fort McMurray Today that his company expected to eventually hire about 4,000 Canadians who would work side by side with Chinese workers to establish a large oil sands extraction operation.

"SinoGaz wants to establish a mutually beneficial relationship with Fort McMurray," he said. "We're excited by the opportunity here."

Redcloud had been arrested for prostitution several times, and was convicted last year for prostitution, theft and cocaine possession.

Her father, Dennis Redcloud, told Fort McMurray Today that his daughter will be sadly missed.

"We are very sad," he said in a telephone interview. "We have lost our daughter."

Redcloud said he blamed drugs and alcohol for the death of his daughter.

"They made her a different person," he said. "We will try to remember her as she was before she started with the drugs."

Jack read the story three times.

The next story was three days later.

August 17, 2008

Social Worker Heartbroken by Redcloud's Tragic Death

By Todd Prosper

The women who worked closely with Rena Redcloud in a program designed to get prostitutes off the streets are devastated that their efforts couldn't prevent the troubled woman from returning to the sex trade.

Irene Faulkner, director of the Second Chance program, which was established by the Alberta Human Services Department to try to encourage prostitutes to get off the street, said she keeps wondering if she could have done something more to help Redcloud.

"We're very upset," said Faulkner. "We really thought we were making progress with Rena. She was doing so well. She was talking about going to community college in the fall, but it seems that her drug and alcohol addictions were just too strong."

Faulkner said that Redcloud was fun-loving, intelligent and artistic, with a passion for music and

Aboriginal dance.

"She was very interested in First Nations culture," said Faulkner. "We talked a lot about careers she could pursue if she could get out of sex work. She was still working the streets occasionally, but I think she had made up her mind to try to get out of the business. Then we read in the paper that she was murdered. It's heart-breaking."

Faulkner said her program had succeeded in getting some prostitutes off the streets, but it could never solve the problem.

"There are thousands of single men in the camps," she told the paper. "They have pockets full of money and no family here. That creates a large market for sex trade workers, and that demand is going to be met."

There was a picture with the story, showing Faulkner sitting at a crafts table, making a dream catcher with Redcloud. They were both smiling. Redcloud wore her hair in two long braids.

There was a short story from a few days later, when Ling Cho Wi had his preliminary hearing, was denied bail and transferred to the Edmonton Remand Centre, to await trail.

The next story appeared two weeks later.

August 30, 2008
Murder Suspect Found Dead in Remand Centre
By Todd Prosper
The Chinese oil executive charged with the murder of a Fort MacKay woman was killed in the Edmonton Remand Centre on Friday.

Ling Cho Wi, an executive with SinoGaz, was found dead at 5 a.m. in a bathroom at the jail. A news release from Alberta Correction Service said Wi was stabbed repeatedly with a knife made from a juice can. The knife was left at the scene of the attack.

Wi was charged with first-degree murder two weeks ago after the body of Rena Redcloud, a Fort MacKay woman, was found in his motel room in Fort McMurray.

Correctional Services plans to review its security

procedures in wake of the attack.

The Edmonton Police Service is investigating the homicide.

"Officers from our homicide unit have examined the crime scene," said spokesman Const. Sheila McDonough. "They are interviewing possible witnesses and following leads inside and outside the correctional facility."

Simms flew into Toronto Island, took the shuttle to Union Station and got a taxi to NTV's Toronto studio, where she joined a camera crew and set off for Goodson Fields, a public housing project near the intersection of Jane Street and Finch Avenue in the northwest of the city.

She looked up from her BlackBerry and wrinkled her nose at the grim neighbourhood when the van arrived at the community centre where Donahoe was supposed to be making his announcement. The community centre was cheerful and well looked after, with a brightly painted mural on its concrete wall, but the surrounding high-rise apartment buildings were ugly and run down. Aside from the media vehicles and a couple of police cars, the cars in the parking lot were cheap and old. There was garbage in the street, and a group of young black men in baggy pants and ball caps was hanging around on the corner. Normally a Toronto reporter would have handled the event, but Simms and Murphy had agreed she should fly in to ask Donahoe about Meech II.

There was already a good-sized group of local reporters assembled on a riser in the common room of the cheerful little community centre. Donahoe's advance staff had set up a backdrop in a corner of the room: Taking Action to Help Crime Victims.

Simms ignored the local reporters and made a beeline for Dave Cochrane, who was chatting with some local reporters next to the backdrop.

"Hi Dave," she said, and gave him the smile. "I want to have a word with you." She turned to the other reporters saying, "Do you mind?" as she turned her back on them.

"Sure Ellen," said Cochrane, stepping closer so that they could whisper. Ellen put her hand on his arm.

"Is Donahoe going to announce today?" she asked.

"Ellen, does this look like a campaign launch?" he said. "No. This is an announcement of a program, which we're very proud of, to help victims of violent crime."

"I hear he's going to announce," she said.

"Well, I don't know about that. There will be a Q-and-A afterwards."

"So he's going to announce then?"

"We don't want to take away from the announcement, but if someone asks him whether he's getting calls, asking him to enter the race …."

He looked up as a middle-aged black woman entered the room, following a little girl in an electric wheelchair.

"Oh," he said. "I've got to go."

He hurried over to shake the woman's hand, and bent to chat with the little girl. They made their way to stand in front of the backdrop.

A few minutes later, Donahoe came into the room and greeted the little girl and her mother, then lined up with them in front of the backdrop. A press assistant moved through the reporters, handing out a backgrounder. Donahoe stepped to a podium and cleared his throat.

"Good afternoon everybody," he said. "I want to introduce Myra Manchester, and thank her for agreeing to keep her daughter Grace out of school for the afternoon, to be here with us. I bet you don't mind, do you Grace?"

Donahoe knew Myra and Grace well, and he took his time with their story, telling the audience how Grace had lost the use of her legs in a drive-by shooting, and how her mother and neighbours had held fundraisers to get her a wheelchair so that she could play basketball with her friends.

"You have a lot to be proud of, Myra Manchester," he said, and led a long round of applause. Myra had to wipe her eyes.

Donahoe continued with a lump in his throat.

"Well, I want to tell you," he said, "when Myra told me her story I was inspired, truly inspired by her spirit, and the spirit of her little girl. But I also was angry. I was angry to think that she had to hold a fundraiser to get her little girl that wheelchair, while the drug dealers who did this to her are getting their lawyers paid for by the taxpayers. So I am very, very happy to announce today the creation of a new program, the Special Fund for Victims of Violent Crime, which will provide families like the Manchesters with funding for wheelchairs, physiotherapy, sports programs, special training and education, whatever they need to give their kids every chance in life that other kids take for granted."

He paused for applause.

"This permanent federal program will be funded with a one-time federal grant of $4 million," he said. "But in the future it will be funded out of the federal government's Proceeds of Crime Recovery Fund."

Simms's BlackBerry buzzed on her hip. It was Murphy.

She stepped away, from the riser, plugged one ear and took the call.

"Hey Scoop," said Murphy. "You ready for the Q-and-A?"

"Yeah," said Simms. "You still want to go ahead with it? This announcement makes him look like a hero. Any chance we'll look cheap by hitting him with this?"

"No," said Murphy. "If he wants to announce his candidacy with some poor kid in a wheelchair as his backdrop, that's not our problem."

"Cochrane said he wouldn't announce today, but he would respond to questions in the Q-and-A," said Simms.

"What's he gonna say?" said Murphy. "'People are asking me to run, and I'm giving it serious consideration.' Right? After he says that, ask him if he would open the Constitution to grant Quebec special status. Then right after the Q-and-A, we go to you for a stand-up, then play the tape."

Flanagan set up the computer on a table next to his desk while Ashton went to fill Zwicker in on the result of their interview with Sophie. He booted it up, typed in the password, plugged in an external drive and started to copy over the contents of the hard drive. While the computer made the duplicate, he opened the documents folder and took a quick glance at the list of files: mostly personal business correspondence, tax files, resumes and letters to landlords. He opened the pictures folder, and clicked through snapshots, holiday pictures and party pics. He took a quick glance next at the history folder, and clicked on some of the most recent web pages, taking a quick look at the sites that Sophie had visited since Sawatski was attacked.

Sophie had checked the weather, some news and gossip sites and had spent a lot of time visiting web sites with information on brain damage. She read several pages, in both English and French, with reviews of *The Diving Bell and the Butterfly*, a book that a French writer managed to write although he had locked-in syndrome, and was able to communicate only by blinking.

Sophie had also repeatedly visited an online forum for people with family members with locked-in syndrome. When Flanagan went to the site, it automatically signed her in as Gaspegirl, and he was able to search the forums for her contributions.

The most recent was titled Disappointment.

> **Gaspegirl:** I felt great after yesterday, when my boyfriend communicated with me and a friend for about five minutes. We had good eye contact, and he responded to my questions with clear blinks, but today he seemed not to want to talk at all. I had the feeling he could hear me but didn't want to respond. It was so hard to lose him again.
> **Zitherwoman:** Don't give up so easily. It took six months after my husband's accident before he was able to consistently have long chats with me. But now he can blink at me all the time. We have long chats every day, and I thank God that my husband has come back to me. Remember, we're in His hands.

Flanagan made a note to show Ashton this exchange. Sophie might not be saying everything she knows, but it was clear from the forum messages that she cared about Ed and was doing what she could to help with his recovery.

He flicked back through the history folder to the days before Ed was found in the canal. There was a lot of news and a lot of porn. Sawatski appeared to visit online video sites every day, and watch short, free pornographic films, mostly orgy and group sex videos. Flanagan grimaced and clicked on one at random and sat to watch. A colleague sitting behind him said, "Shouldn't you save that kind of thing for home, Flanagan?"

The other cops chuckled. Flanagan turned to his colleague and grinned. "Wayne, will you ask your wife to stop sending me these links," he said. "At first it was funny, but now I'm starting to wonder what she's trying to say."

Still, Flanagan decided it was time to see what kind of videos Ed made himself.

He looked for a video file folder, and found one, but it had nothing in it but some vacation videos. He did a hard drive search for videos, to see if there was dedicated folder for web cam videos, but it came up blank. So he looked into the device driver, found the camera and double clicked. A recording program – Security Master – booted up. He selected the camera and turned it on and pressed record. Immediately, there was a video on the screen showing the camera's feed – a picture of the squad room. Flanagan hit save. It saved the video in a sub-folder inside Security Master's directory, named for the date.

He looked at all the subfolders in the directory. There were dozens, each one titled with the date of the recording, dating back six months.

Someone had quite a little hobby, thought Flanagan.

He decided to start with the most recent recordings, and clicked on the top folder.

A password window came up.

"Shit," he said, aloud.

After he finished researching the story of Rena Redcloud, Jack spent a while doing Internet searches, following leads that came up as he went along.

He searched the newspaper web site for all the mentions of Sergeant Earl Gushue, and found he was often quoted as a spokesman for the local RCMP detachment, although he was also on the Major Crimes Unit, and was quoted as the lead investigator testifying in murder trials.

He did a search on Redcloud, and found out that Mike, Rena's brother, was a pretty good hockey player on the men's senior league in Fort McMurray. He read a couple of features on Rena's father, Dennis, who organized powwows and traditional hunts in Fort MacKay. He was once arrested for illegal moose hunting, a charge that was dropped when he showed up with a lawyer prepared to argue that he was exercising his Aboriginal rights. He was quoted in several stories complaining about the environmental impact of the oil sands developments, and had led several protests after a university study found a strange pattern of rare cancers in the residents of Fort MacKay, cancers that he and other Dene attributed to the air pollution from the refineries.

He did a search on Ling Cho Wi, and found nothing beyond the murder stories and a few business stories from when he came to town to negotiate the project.

SinoGaz, Jack learned, was one of the world's biggest companies, a state-owned Chinese oil company that had a virtual monopoly on petroleum imports to China. It had been trying to buy a piece of the oil sands for years, and had finally started work on the $3-billion project, eighteen months after Wi's death.

SinoGaz had had to jump through several hoops before the project could go ahead. First they had to get cabinet approval of the buyout of PanPetroDev, the American company that owned the parcel of oil sands they wanted to develop. Then a federal-provincial environmental assessment panel had reviewed the project, and recommended against it, because of the massive amount of greenhouse gases that would be produced. The Stevens cabinet had quietly overturned that decision, along with several similar decisions, and given the project the go-ahead.

When Jack finally couldn't think of anything else to research, he transferred all his files to a memory stick and walked down to the coffee shop where Peggy worked.

He found Fort McMurray depressing. There were some nice new buildings, but many of the older buildings downtown were shabby, built in some long-ago boom and never looked after properly. There were plenty of big trucks whizzing by, most of them covered in brown dust. The drivers were mostly young men, with ball caps and moustaches. There were few people on the sidewalks, and the ones who were looked worn down by life. In the parking lot outside the Happy Stop, the restaurant where Peggy worked, a gap-toothed old man in sweat pants, a torn parka and paint-stained work boots tried to stop him to ask him for change, but Jack brushed past him and got himself out of the cold.

Happy Stop was bright and warm and cheerful. It was at the end of a busy mini-mall, with a couple of dozen old plastic booths, specials on a chalk board and a long counter by the kitchen with rotating stools.

"There he is," said Peggy when he arrived. "Have a seat. Have you had your lunch?"

The lunch rush had ended but there were still a couple of tables full of customers that Peggy was looking after.

"I wouldn't mind a bite," said Jack. He nodded his head at a TV in the corner that was showing a hockey game that nobody was watching. "Mind if I sit over there and switch the channel, catch up on the news?"

"No, b'y," she said. "You go ahead. Wait while I gets you a menu."

The menu was a typical greasy spoon, with hamburgers and chicken fingers and a lot of frozen fried items, but there was a Newfoundland special every day. Jiggs dinner on Sundays. Fish 'n' brewis on Mondays.

Peggy brought him a coffee.

"Menu's just like home," said Jack.

"That's what they like," said Peggy. "Half of them are Newfies here."

"How's the chowder?" asked Jack.

"Not bad, b'y," she said. "Best in town, but not as good as you gets at home. Fish and chips is good."

"Gimme a two-piece then," he said, closing the menu.

"Dressing and gravy?" she asked.

"Why not? I haven't had fish and chips with dressing and gravy since I last ate at Ches's."

She gave him the remote and he switched from TSN to NTV Newsnet. He watched the news until his fish and chips arrived. He was halfway through his greasy fish when Ellen Simms appeared on camera, standing in front of a community centre in Toronto holding a microphone. Jack scowled and turned up the volume.

"Lorne," she said to the anchor, "I've just come from an event with Justice Minister Jim Donahoe, where he opened the door to a run for the leadership of the Conservative Party."

The TV showed a clip of Donahoe saying, "I am getting calls asking me to run." He was standing in front of a black girl in a wheelchair.

"I am giving it serious thought," he said. "I'm talking to my family, and to people across Canada, asking them what kind of country they want. I'm thinking about stories like Grace's, about finding new ways to draw Canadians together, whatever their backgrounds. I'm thinking about Canadian citizenship, about what it means to be Canadian, about what kind of leadership we need now. Those are big questions, and you'll forgive me if I haven't come up with all the answers yet, but I'm thinking and I'm listening."

Then Jack could hear Simms shouting a question. "If you were prime minister, would you open the Constitution to recognize Quebec as a distinct society?"

He tried to ignore her at first, but she shouted the question again and he had to respond.

"Ellen," he said. "This is an announcement about victims'

rights, about a program that will really change the lives of people affected by violent crime, so I don't know if I want to distract from that with a discussion of hypotheticals."

Ellen shouted something else, which Jack couldn't make out but which prompted Donahoe to say, "I have no plans to do anything like that." He paused and looked thoughtful. "Quebec's unique place within Confederation should never be discussed casually, and Quebec's traditional desire for formal recognition isn't the kind of thing that we should discount out of hand. I have too much respect for Quebecers to stand here and say no, never anything like that, the Constitution can never be changed. I don't want to present a closed hand to my friends in *la belle province*, but I think most people who have been through that process would say, certainly, that it is not easy and not the kind of thing for which there is an appetite now or any time soon."

The anchor's handsome face appeared on the screen. "It sounds like he's saying no there, doesn't it, Ellen?"

Simms nodded. "That's right, Lorne. It sounded like a polite but firm no. But NTV News has learned that in a closed-door meeting with Quebec Tories last week, Donahoe delivered a very different message."

The screen showed a picture of Donahoe, with a quote superimposed in white letters while he spoke in French.

"To mend this rift, they say, we need to make a new place for Quebec in the constitution, and formally recognize what is a fact of life, the distinct and rich cultural life of the province. Call it Meech II. I am with these people."

"That sounds a little different, Ellen," said the anchor.

"Well, Lorne," said Ellen, "it is different. Behind closed doors, Donahoe said that he would consider reopening the constitution to provide special status for Quebec, if he had a majority government. The Conservatives met at the elite Champlain Club, in downtown Montreal." The screen showed a shot of the elegant stone building. "Donahoe actually said that it would not be wise to discuss such a plan in a campaign, but if he were elected he would try to open the Constitution, trying to, in a nutshell, recreate the Meech Lake Accord, which led to the rise of the Bloc Quebecois. That alone would be controversial, but Donahoe's answer today gives the impression that he is saying one thing in public and another in the back rooms. Lorne?"

"Very interesting," said the anchor. "Thank you Ellen. With reaction, now, we go to Ottawa, where Fred Murphy is standing by. Fred?"

Murphy was in the lobby of the House of Commons.

"Well Lorne, this revelation is sure to put the fox among the chickens," he said in his gravelly baritone. "A lot of the current crop of Conservative MPs come from a Reform party background, which grew up, in part, in opposition to the Meech Lake accord. Now, Donahoe is a former Progressive Conservative, who served for one term as a backbencher in Brian Mulroney's government, so this story could remind everyone of old divisions in the Conservative family at a time when the party is looking to find a new leader to take it into the future. It will be interesting to see what other Conservative MPs have to say as they arrive for Question Period."

Murphy looked away from the camera. "Here's someone we don't often see in the lobby, former Reform MP Ben Watson," he said, stepping in front of a tall grey-haired man. "Mr. Watson, you came here with Preston Manning. What do you make of the idea of a Meech II?"

Watson squared his shoulders and looked surprised. "Not much," he said. "What's the expression? Let sleeping dogs lie. I think we ought to let sleeping dogs lie on this one, and I think my constituents would agree."

Murphy stepped back. MPs were arriving in ones and twos, streaming behind Murphy into the House.

"Ben Watson, one of the original Reform MPs, being clear there. Not interested in a Meech II. I see Public Safety Minister Greg Mowat approaching. Lorne, many people think Greg Mowat is considering a leadership run."

Murphy stepped in front of Mowat. "Mr. Mowat," he said. "I want to get your reaction to the idea of a Meech II, somehow reviving a version of the Meech Lake Accord."

Mowat smiled into the camera. "Well, I spend a lot of time talking to people around the country, and nobody ever comes up to me and says, 'You know what the government should do, you should open up the Constitution.' I think that's pretty far from the concerns most people have. I hear about taxes, crime, and especially the economy, and that's the focus of this government, not constitutional adventures. But –" and he paused to smile "– I would say I've been fortunate enough to visit Meech Lake on occasion, just over the border from Ottawa, and I can tell you it is very beautiful. Every Canadian should make the trek to Ottawa at least once, and if you have time it is well worth the side trip." He smiled again at Murphy and went into the House.

"Do we see a division here, Fred?" asked the anchor.

"Yes, Lorne," said Murphy. "And a division along the old lines, east and west. Greg Mowat was pretty clear there, that he's not interested in negotiating a new constitutional deal, and he looked confident in –" The anchor cut him off.

"Fred, we're going back to Ellen now, in Toronto, where Jim Donahoe spoke recently, and she has some fresh news," he said.

"Yes, Lorne," she said. "I've received a statement from Jim Donahoe's team, and they are saying that Donahoe is, in fact, not in favour of opening up constitutional talks to give Quebec special status. They say his comments in a speech to a backroom group of Quebec Tories have been taken out of context. His people are saying, quite firmly, that he at no point told anyone that he would reopen the Constitution."

"So somewhat of a new position, then, Ellen?" said the anchor.

"It would seem so, Lorne," she said. "In a recording obtained by NTV News of a meeting with Quebec Conservatives, just last week, he appeared to endorse the idea, although he said it was not the kind of thing that could be discussed during a campaign."

"Thank you, Ellen," said the anchor. "We now go back to

Ottawa, where Fred Murphy has Liberal Leader Evan Pinsent with a comment on this developing story."

"Mr. Pinsent," said Murphy. "It appears there is a division between Conservatives here, with the public safety minister saying he is not interested in opening the Constitution to make a special deal for Quebec, and Justice Minister Jim Donahoe apparently reversing himself, floating the idea and now backing away. Your reaction?"

Pinsent squared his shoulders. "What we have here," he said, "is the Conservative government clearly showing disrespect for the traditional position of the Quebec provincial government. It's another example of the way this government, this right-wing government, is out of step with the province of Quebec, and –" Murphy interrupted him.

"I'm sorry, but are you saying that a Liberal government would open constitutional talks with the aim of creating a Meech II?"

"No," Pinsent said. "No. That's not what I'm saying." He blinked and said, "Uh."

"So a Liberal government wouldn't be prepared to consider that?" said Murphy.

"What I'm saying, Fred," said Pinsent, "what I'm saying is that this government, two cabinet ministers of this government, are needlessly, uh, showing a lack of respect for Quebec."

Murphy turned to the camera. "So no clear answer there from Liberal Leader Evan Pinsent on whether a Liberal government would reopen the constitution for a Meech II type deal, Lorne."

The piece ended, and Peggy came over to sit down with a coffee, so Jack killed the volume..

"Don't you get enough of that?" she said.

"Aunt Peg, it's like crack," he said. "Once you're hooked, they got ya."

"My dear," she said. "Don't be joking about crack. There's enough of it in this town."

"Yeah?" said Jack. "We got it in Ottawa, but I wouldn't

think you'd find it way up here."

"My dear, they call it Fort Crack, sure!" she said. "It's rotten with it. These young fellas up here, away from their families, nothing to do, money burning a hole in their pockets, some of them get lost. Lost, me son. They fall in with these girls, these women comes up here looking to party all the time, find some stunned bayman to pay for it. It's shockin'."

"That sounds like the story I'm working on," said Jack. "This girl, Rena Redcloud. She was from Fort MacKay, seems like a good family, got mixed up with coke, turning tricks, ended up getting murdered by a john. Sad story."

Peggy arched an eyebrow at him. "Is she anything to that fellow Mike, that Vern works with?"

"I think that's her brother," he said. "I want to ask Vern if I can talk to him."

"Sure, I'll call him." She got out her cell phone and called her husband. "Vern, I'm here with Jack," she said. "Yes. He just had a two-piece with dressing and gravy. Yes. We'll fatten him up, eh. Now, he tells me that he wants to talk to that fellow you work with, Mike. Yes. Says it's her brother. All right. Talk to you soon."

"He's going to check," she said to Jack. "See when Mike's working. They goes all night up there.

Ashton and Flanagan ventured down to the office of Sgt. David Gaston, the computer forensics guy, to sweet talk him into cracking the password right away, not in a week, which is what he'd promised on the phone.

He was sitting in front of a wide-screen monitor, in a windowless room crowded with computers and parts of computers. Steel shelving units, loaded with hard drives and circuit boards, lined the walls. Many of them had evidence tags hanging from them. More partly dissembled computers – old and new – sat on several big wooden tables, a warren of cables, connectors and power bars strewn among them.

"I don't like to bug you, Dave," said Flanagan. "But Zwicker is on us. It's bad. He swore at us. In two meetings. You ever hear him swear? Told us to get the fuck out of his office. Somebody is shitting on his head, and he doesn't know what else to do, except to sit down and have a big, stinky dump on our heads. On poor Mallorie's head. Forget about my old head. Think of Mallorie. Do you want to see this nice head all covered in Zwicker's shit? Because that's what you're saying here. You are saying you don't give a fuck if Zwicker shits on Mallorie's head. And I didn't think you were that kind of guy. Don't be that guy. Hook a brother up."

Gaston swivelled on his old computer chair and glared at Flanagan, then turned to look at Ashton, who was trying not to grin. "Is that true, Mallorie?" he asked. "Is Zwicker gonna dump shit on your head?" He lowered his glasses and looked at her.

"I can't have that," he said. "I am very busy here. I would normally tell you both to go fuck yourselves, which is what I tell everyfuckingbody else, and get in line, but Flanagan here says Zwicker's gonna shit on your head. Is that right?"

Mallorie couldn't help laughing. "That's right. If you don't help us, Zwicker's going to shit on my head."

Gaston pushed his glasses back up his nose and held his hand out for the hard drive in Flanagan's hand.

"What is it?" he said.

"Security Master," said Flanagan. "It was used to run one small web cam." He held up the little lens. "Looks like a program for stores or whatever. It can run lots of cameras, but only one camera was hooked up to this one. It was in the boudoir of the guy they pulled out of the canal. It's password-protected."

"Fuck," said Gaston, as he took the zip drive and plugged it in to his main computer. "Security Master. Fuck."

He opened a web browser, went to a hacker web site and typed in "Security Master." A screen came up with a brief description of the device, in hacker shorthand. It looked like gibberish to Ashton and Flanagan.

"Unix-based," said Gaston. "Okay. Sebastian.ru. Okay."

He typed a bit.

"About five years ago, some Russian kid built a password cracker that really strips the panties off this generation of Unix encryption," he said. "Better than lemon gin. Let me try it."

He booted up Sebastian.ru and steered it to the folder on the zip drive. He tweaked the settings and pressed enter. Security Master started up. He clicked on the top folder, and hit enter. The hacking program started trying combinations of letters and numbers, faster than the screen could redraw, so the program looked jammed.

"There are twenty-six characters in the alphabet," said Gaston. "With upper case and lower case, plus ten digits and punctuation marks, you have ninety-six characters. You've got 782 billion possible combinations of characters in a six-character password. If we don't know, as we don't, whether it's a six-, seven- or eight-letter password, there are trillions of possible combinations. Sounds tough, eh?

"Luckily for us, a lot of people use passwords that have some meaning to them, all lower case. This Russian kid built an algorithm that orders the possible combinations from most likely to least likely, using names and words from the dictionary. The program just types the shit out of the damn thing, trying combination after combination in the password window. Sooner or later it will match. Or it should do."

He glanced up at Flanagan. He and Ashton were staring at the unchanging screen.

"Boudoir, eh?" said Gaston. "Is there a girlfriend?"

"Sophie Fortin," said Flanagan. "Very impressive young woman."

The computer chirped and suddenly a folder popped open. Gaston clicked on sebastian.ru. The password was Sneak.

"Wow," said Ashton.

"Is that it?" said Flanagan.

"Yup," said Gaston. "Let's see what we have here."

In the open folder there was a single video file, with no name, just a date and time stamp: 2011/07/18.

He double clicked on it and suddenly there was a video of

the empty bedroom. It was surprisingly clear.

"That's their room," said Flanagan.

Gaston clicked ahead on the space bar, toward the end of the file. The lights were out and Sophie and Ed were asleep under the covers. He clicked back and the lights were back on, and Ed was on top of Sophie. They were both naked and her legs were wrapped around his waist. She was groaning rhythmically and Ed was grinding his pelvis into her. Sophie's fingers gripped his back.

"That is our victim and his girlfriend," said Flanagan.

The three of them watched Sophie and Ed have sex for a moment.

Ashton cleared her throat.

"Well," said Gaston, "I guess that worked. "

He sat there watching for another moment. Sophie lowered her hands to Ed's ass.

"Well," said Gaston. "I guess I'd better shut this down."

He stared for a second longer and then clicked stop.

"There you go," he said, and handed them the hard drive even as he turned back to his computer. "Have fun."

After dinner, Vern and Jack put on white hard hats, got into the truck and headed north to call on Mike Redcloud. They drove for forty minutes on a four-lane highway that abruptly turned to dirt when they turned off to the Syncrude site. Vern had told his boss that his nephew was thinking about working there and wanted to see the site, and arranged a visitor pass for him, which got them through the security gates.

Vern drove him around a bit, showing him the massive settling ponds, lakes of poison filled with a mixture of oil by-products and water, dotted with noisemakers and scarecrows to keep away the birds. There was a surprising beauty to the scene. The sun was setting over the softwood forest, and the reflection of the vermillion sky shimmered on the surface of the toxic ponds.

They drove past the massive upgrader, where acres of high-tech equipment refined the oily sludge to light crude. Plumes of smoke and steam poured out of smokestacks into the vast northern sky. Jack stared at the massive hills of yellow sulphur next to the refining equipment. The air was dusty, and smelled odd and unpleasant.

A broad dirt road through the woods took them out to the mine site, where Vern stopped the truck on a lookout. They got out and walked through the snow to the edge of a four-kilometre wide hole in the ground, an artificial canyon that was so big it was hard to take it all in.

"Holy fuck," said Jack.

"She's something, eh, b'y," said Vern.

In the darkening sky, it looked like a blot of nothingness spreading out from their feet, a hole 100 metres deep that stretched out a good way to the horizon. In the distance, Jack could make out buildings, earth-moving equipment and dump trucks working under massive halogen lights.

"They started at this end in '82," said Vern. "And the hole's been getting bigger ever since. I'd like to have a nickel for every tonne of dirt they've hauled out of here."

They got back in the truck and drove around the hole, and then down into it and across it, to a trailer sitting in the sticky, black mud.

From here, Jack could see how the mine worked. Five-storey cranes rhythmically gouged enormous scoops of black sand from the wall of the canyon, and dropped them in the back of dump trucks the size of houses.

Under the glare of the halogen lights, the colours were intense and strange – the yellow trucks gleaming, the dirty snow banks spectral, the sand underfoot so black and dull with oil that it reflected nothing, like a night sky without stars.

"They say there's more oil in Alberta than in Saudi Arabia," said Vern. "But it's just a bit harder to get at, eh."

Jack bent and picked up a handful of the stuff, and rubbed it. It stained his hand black.

"Jeez b'y, you'll have to scrub a bit to get that out," said

Vern. "Let's go in where it's warm."

The white industrial trailer was for the crew, with bath-rooms and a lunch room with a coffee machine, snack machines, a sink, a microwave, plastic chairs and a couple of tables. It was lit by florescent lights. One of them flickered and buzzed.

Two men in blue overalls were sitting over coffees.

"How's she going, b'ys?" said Vern. "You haven't seen Mike, have you?"

"Who, the chief?" said one of the men.

Vern stared at him.

"Mike Redcloud," he said. "What do you mean, the chief?"

The guy grinned and looked away.

"He should be on break in ten minutes," said the other guy. "We're the relief." He looked at his companion. "The comic relief."

Vern stared at the two of them for a moment longer, then turned away, shaking his head.

"You want a coffee, b'y?" he asked Jack.

They sat at the other end of the lunch room from the relief crew.

Mike arrived soon after, walking in with a short blonde woman. Both of them took off their hard hats as they came in.

"Mike!" said Vern. "How's she going?

Mike came over and introduced the woman he was with as Bonny

"Well hello, Bonny," said Vern, smiling and shaking her hand. "This is my nephew, Jack, wants to talk to Mike about something. What do you have for supper? Have enough to share?"

She laughed and he steered her over to the other end of the trailer. The relief crew headed out.

Jack and Mike shook hands.

"I'm glad you could take a few minutes to talk to me," said Jack. "It's about your sister."

Mike smiled and laughed nervously. He was tall and ath-letic-looking, with mahogany skin, a wispy moustache and liquid brown eyes that somehow seemed both happy and sad.

"Sure," he said. "Vern told me. Let me get my dinner going."

He went to the fridge and took out a plastic tub and popped it in the microwave and sat down to wait while it heated his dinner.

"So, why are you interested in Rena's story?" he said.

Jack gave him his card.

"I'm a political reporter in Ottawa," he said. "And a source, someone I have promised not to identify, has reason to believe that there's something odd about her death, or the investigation, something with a link to some powerful people in Ottawa. We don't know what exactly is strange about the death or the investigation, but the source is a very serious person, and we have reason to believe it's worth looking into."

Mike stared at him. "So you don't know what you're looking for."

"No," Jack said. "Not really. I don't know what I'm looking for. You're right."

"Because it's sad, eh, for me to get talking about it," Mike said, avoiding Jack's gaze. "I mean, Rena. Maybe you should talk to my dad, eh? He is more used to talking to reporters and that. For an interview. Maybe you should talk to him."

"I'd like to do that," said Jack. "I read some articles about him. He sounds like quite a man."

The microwave dinged.

"There's my supper," said Mike. He got up and took out his dinner.

"My dad made this," he said. "Moose stew. Want a taste?"

Jack was going to say no thanks, but changed his mind.

"Jeez, it does look good," he said. He got a plastic fork from the counter and took a bite. It was rich and the moose meat was tender and falling apart.

"Damn, that's good. It's been a while since I had moose stew," he said. "My old man makes it too. Adds salt pork."

"My father cooks it with bacon and adds a bit of wine, eh," said Mike.

Jack pulled out his notebook. "I can't imagine how hard

it must have been to lose your sister. I'm sorry for your loss," he said. "I won't quote you, or use your name without your permission. If I do write a story, I'll interview your father for any quotes. All I want is to know what happened. There are no court documents, since the guy who killed her never made it to trial."

"That was the Indian Posse," said Mike.

"Indian Posse?" said Jack. "What's that, a gang?"

Mike looked at him as if he were dumb. "Yeah," he said. "Big gang. Operates in Edmonton, Calgary, Vancouver, Saskatoon, Winnipeg. They're on every rez in western Canada."

"They killed this Chinese guy, Ling Cho Wi? Why? 'Cause he killed a native girl?"

Mike laughed. "Man, they don't give a fuck," he said. "No. My cousin runs with them in Edmonton. He told me they got a contract to do it. Couple of Chinese gangbangers from Vancouver came to Edmonton, paid the Posse to kill the Chinese guy."

"Why would they do that?"

"My cousin didn't know why." Mike shrugged. "Posse doesn't care why."

"You don't know who the Chinese guys were?" said Jack.

"You not gonna say I told you this, right? I can't talk about any of this shit in the paper."

"No," said Jack. "No. No. No. No way. Don't worry."

"Okay then. I don't know who the Chinese guys were. I bet the Indian Posse doesn't know either. Chinese guys with money. That's who they were."

"What happened to Rena?" Jack asked. "The newspaper stories don't say anything about the crime."

Mike put down his fork. "It's sad, eh? We thought she was turning her life around. She was, too, but every now and then she'd want to party. Loved to party, rez-style, all the fucking way, man." He bit his lip and looked away. "She didn't have no pimp or nothing. She'd just decide she had been a good girl too long and she needed to have a party, and she'd go down to the Oilman with some of her bad girlfriends."

He stared right at Jack. He wasn't touching his stew.

"So she picked this guy up at the Oiler. They have a few drinks, go back to his room. It looks like she did him, right, and then he wanted her to go. She wanted more money than he gave her. That is what the cops think. And my sister, boy, you don't fucking fuck with her if she's been drinking and try to rip her off. She was a tough lady with a bad temper. So I guess they started to fight or whatever. He probably tried to slap her around, and then she went fucking bananas, and it got out of hand. He was all bruised, like she got in some jabs, eh? But he stabbed her twice, once in the arm and once in the eye. She died right away. Was all bloody in there, eh?" He spoke in a flat, mechanical tone. Jack could see a vein in his temple throbbing and his jaw muscles working but his face was expressionless.

"How do you know all this?" asked Jack.

"The Mounties, Gushue and Brecker, they told me and Dad some, but after Brecker left the force, started working down Showgirls, he told my cousin the nasty stuff."

"Same cousin?"

"No," Mike said, and laughed again. "I got lots of cousins."

"Who's Brecker?"

"Dwayne Brecker, was a Mountie until last year. He left the force and went to work down at Showgirls, the big strip bar here. I think he got in trouble, eh, and had to get out. Drugs or something."

"And now he works at a strip bar?"

"Showgirls, baby!" said Mike. "Big deal up here. Owned by the Hells Angels."

"This guy used to be a Mountie and now he works for the Angels? He investigated your sister's murder?"

Mike picked up his fork. "Yeah," he said. "Funny, eh?"

Flanagan transferred half the video files – the more recent ones – to Ashton's laptop, and they moved to a conference room and started watching them, trying to figure out what they had.

There were thirty files, dating back over six months, roughly one a week. Most of them were long recordings – more than eight hours, sometimes longer – with static shots of the empty bedroom, or the darkened room with Ed and Sophie sleeping. The angle never changed, and there was no sound. In most of the recordings there was a single sexual encounter before they turned out the lights and went to sleep, then, near the end of the recording, footage of them getting ready for work.

Flanagan and Ashton sat side by side, clicking ahead through the videos.

"It looks like he turns it on before they go to bed and turns it off in the morning," said Flanagan. "Probably while she's in the shower."

"I think she was being honest with us," said Ashton. "I don't think she had any idea he was recording this stuff. Look at this."

Ashton had found a recording where Sophie went into the room by herself, lifted her skirt and inserted a tampon.

"I don't know how far to believe Mlle. Fortin," said Ashton. "I don't like the fact that she won't tell us who her gentleman caller was. But there's no way she knew the camera was there. I don't think a girl would ever do that if she knew she was being recorded."

Flanagan looked at the scene.

"Christ," he said. "Poor thing. She picked a winner. Secretly taping himself with his girlfriend so he can admire himself later and jerk off. Little fucker."

"If I found out some guy I was seeing was secretly recording me, I'd cut off his nuts," Ashton said. "With a butter knife."

Ashton's jaw was set and her eyes were hard as she watched Sophie tidy up the bedroom.

"So what are we looking for?" said Flanagan. "There are what, a hundred hours of video here."

Ashton turned from the screen. "We should make a catalogue, a list of all the recordings, watch them all on fast forward, note the times that anything happens, see what we have."

Jack had to wait in a line to get into Showgirls, shivering and smoking on the sidewalk in the glow of the flashing neon sign. In front of him were three young men in ball caps and ski jackets, chatting in thick outport accents about how much money they were making, and how much they wanted to get laid. "My son, the crack of dawn better watch out around me," said one of them.

Before long, a group of very drunk men came out the door and staggered to their trucks. The bouncers let Jack and the baymen into the bar, where they paid five bucks each for the coat check and stepped into the steaming main room. There were a couple hundred men inside, sitting at cheap tables covered in drinks and spilled booze. Waitresses carrying loaded trays, and strippers in tiny outfits moved through the crowd.

Jack squeezed up to the bar, ordered a beer and leaned back against the bar to take in the scene.

A statuesque black girl was finishing her dance on the stage, naked, sprawled on her back, touching herself to a rap song.

"Ladies and gentlemen, put your hands together for Crystal," said a muffled voice over the loudspeaker. Jack clapped.

A stripper in a florescent blue bikini smiled at him. "Hi," she said. "Where you from?"

"Ottawa," he said. "How about you?"

"I'm from Edmonton. What's your name?"

"Jack," he said. "What's yours?"

"Carrie," she said. "Want a dance?"

She was in her early twenties, with a lithe, athletic body and bright blonde hair, but her eyes were glassy, with enlarged irises, and her smile came out of a pill bottle. She put her hand on his shoulder and rubbed her breasts lightly against him.

"How much is it?" he asked.

"Thirty dollars a dance." That was ten dollars more than at Pigale.

"Jeez," he said. "You girls must be making out pretty good up here. How much of that do you get to keep?"

She frowned, pulled away and glanced at the back of the room, to the entrance to the VIP room, where dancers and customers did their private dances.

"Hey, how long you been in town?" asked Jack. "Do you know Rena Redcloud?"

She smiled at him vaguely and wandered off to approach a group of young guys at a nearby table. She was soon sitting on one guy's knee.

Jack took his beer and walked back to the entrance of the VIP area, where a massive, bearded guy in a T-shirt and leather vest stood guard.

"How's it going?" Jack said to him. He had to holler to be heard over the music, and lean into the guy.

"Very good sir," the bearded guy said. "You looking for a dance? You have a girl in mind?"

"No," said Jack. "I'm looking to have a chat with Dwayne Brecker."

The guy's smile froze. Jack took in his massive arms and chest, and the tribal tattoos on his forearms, and the ghost of an old scar on his cheek. Jack was standing close enough to smell him.

"If it's about business, you should call during business hours to make an appointment," the guard said.

Jack smiled and nodded. He stood beside the guy, looking at the room. A new girl – a curvy blonde – was on all fours, stripping out of her thong and leering over her shoulder at a row of guys sitting next to the stage.

Jack leaned in to talk to the guard again, and tucked a twenty-dollar bill into the breast pocket of his leather vest. "Tell you what, I'd really like to talk to Dwayne tonight if possible," he said. "I'll go have a beer at the bar. You tell him a guy named Jack Macdonald is here to see him about Rena Redcloud. Mike Redcloud sent me. If he can find a minute,

I'll be at the bar. If he can't, I'll call tomorrow. Okay?"

The bouncer looked at him for a minute and nodded. "Don't hold your breath," he said.

Jack laughed and walked back to the bar. He ordered another beer and tried to drink it slowly. When a gap-toothed brunette in lingerie came up to chat with him, he said, "No thanks. No dance for me. Tell me, do you know Rena Redcloud?" She left quickly.

Jack watched the dancers, and the knots of drunk men in their party shirts. The girls would approach them, flirt a bit, then lead one off to the room at the back. Jack tried to amuse himself by guessing which guy would go for which girl, but it was a depressing spectacle. The customers and dancers all pretended to be interested in each other as people, when they were all engaged in a base, impersonal exchange of money for a pale imitation of sex.

He was not immune from desire, himself, and pondered taking one of the girls into the back. Maybe he could see where Brecker's office was. While he was thinking about that, the best-looking stripper he'd seen all night walked up to him. She was wearing stilettos, a miniskirt and a black silk top that left her midriff bare. Her breasts were high and plump, and her stomach taut but slightly rounded. He found it hard to tear his eyes away from the top of her miniskirt, where the irresistible slope of her belly inclined to her groin. She smiled at him coolly from a distance and tossed her hair back. She didn't look stoned.

Yes, I will have a dance, thought Jack, smiling at her.

She leaned in to him and said, "Jack Macdonald? You want to see Dwayne?"

He nodded and followed her swaying hips to the back of the room. They walked past the enormous bearded guard, into the hallway to the VIP room. She pressed a buzzer next to a heavy steel door and waited. The man who opened the door was tall and rugged-looking, with a salt and pepper goatee and shoulder-length hair. He was wearing a black sports jacket, black jeans and an open-necked white dress shirt. The jacket looked wrong on him somehow, because his upper body was so large, even though the cut was right, it gave him a boxy, exaggerated look. His brown eyes were hard. His mouth was a narrow slit.

"Jack Macdonald?" he said.

"Yeah," said Macdonald, stretching out his hand. "Dwayne Brecker?"

He ignored the hand and nodded to the girl, who smiled, nodded back and turned and walked elegantly away.

"All right," he said. "Come on in. Pull the door shut."

The room was furnished with a heavy oak desk below a window with one-way glass that looked out into the barroom. Next to it was a bank of flat-screen TVs, with scenes from throughout the building: the front entrance, the bar, several angles on the VIP room, the parking lot, the street. There was a heavy safe on the floor, and what looked to be a gun locker, a coffee table and leather couch against the other wall, and another steel door, which likely led to the parking lot.

"So," said Brecker. "You want to talk to me."

"Yes," said Jack. "About Rena Redcloud. I just came from talking to Mike, her brother. He told me you were on the case. I'm a reporter. Came here from Ottawa to look into it."

"Who do you work for?" said Brecker.

Jack dug out a card. "*The Telegram,*" he said. "The daily in Newfoundland."

"Why should I talk to you?" Brecker said. "Why should I give a fuck?" He fixed Jack with an unblinking stare, totally relaxed, bored-looking.

Jack puffed out his cheeks and thought for a minute. "First of all, because you have nothing to lose," he said. "I undertake never to tell a soul I've even talked to you, if you want. When I make a promise like that I keep it. In your case, I have extra motivation, because I have a, uh, healthy respect for your associates in the Hells Angels Motorcycle Club. I think if anything ever comes back on you, you could arrange for them to make me sorry.

"Secondly, I suspect there is more to the story of Rena

Redcloud than anyone knows, and I think you know some things that the public should know. I don't know what those things are, but I have the idea they're important."

Brecker stared at him.

"Okay," he said after a few seconds. "I might talk to you, but I want you to know I don't work for the Angels. I wouldn't work for them. That's an organized crime group, and I am a former officer of the Royal Canadian Mounted Police. I work for a private company in a legal business. It's not in anybody's interest – least of all that company's owners – to allow anything illegal to happen here that would jeopardize a profitable company."

Jack smiled. A sickly smile. "Okay."

Brecker smiled back. It was not friendly. "You're right. If there's anything I don't like in what you write, you could easily find yourself getting a visit from some associates of mine in Ottawa, or wherever the fuck you are." He stood up and stuck out his hand. "All right?" he said. "We got a deal?"

Jack shook Brecker hand and met his eyes, then pulled his hand back, wincing. "Easy," he said. "That's my typing hand."

Brecker sat down. Jack stood, shaking out his hand.

"Okay," said Brecker. "No recording but you can take notes. I'll tell you the story. I don't care if people guess it came from me, but you can't use my name. All right?"

"I won't use your name," said Jack, and he took his notepad and pen out of his coat pocket. "I'll refer to you as a source close to the investigation."

"Fine," said Brecker. "Call me that. But don't use my fucking name."

"I won't," said Jack. "We have a deal."

"Alright," Brecker said. "It was August 13, 2008. Sergeant Earl Gushue and I were called to a disturbance at the Great Western Motel. Dispatch had several calls from guests and the guy working the front desk. They all said the same thing. Screaming and yelling. Sound of furniture breaking, then one terrible scream, from a woman, then quiet. We get there, about five minutes after the first call.

"We pound on the door, no answer, so I kick it in," he said. He was staring at the coffee table as he spoke, reciting the story carefully. "Sergeant Gushue had his sidearm drawn. The room was dark. We switched on the light. It was like an efficiency unit, with a little living room. Redcloud was on the carpet, with a knife sticking out of her eye. She was prone, on her back, blood all over the place, furniture overturned. TV screen broken. Bottles and broken glass all over the place. Cigarette butts. The place smelled of liquor. Coffee table was broken. There was nobody else in the room.

"Gushue steps in with his sidearm drawn, looking down the little hallway to the other rooms. Calls out. 'Come out with your hands up. This is the police.' I check on Redcloud. She has no pulse. She's dead. One eye staring, the other with a knife buried in it to the hilt. There is no point giving her CPR.

"There is no sound from the other rooms. I draw my sidearm. We both have our flashlights out. We move down the hallway. I turn on the light. We hear something from the bedroom. Gushue calls out again. No answer. I open the bedroom door. The perpetrator – what was he called, Ling Wing? – was sitting there, little Chinese guy in his underwear, blood all over his hands, sitting there at his desk, working at his laptop.

"We come in, he looks up. 'She try kill me,' he says. 'Bitch try kill me. Sef defence. Sef defence.'

"I put the cuffs on him, and Sergeant Gushue reads him his rights. He kept babbling. 'She rob me. She try kill me. Sef defence.' It was ugly. I got her blood all over me.

"So I take him out to the cruiser and Gushue goes back in to see what he was doing on the laptop. His email program was open. Bunch of messages in Chinese. But Gushue checks the Deleted Items folder, there's a bunch of emails in there in English. Looked like the Chinese guy just deleted them but didn't empty the folder."

He looked up at Jack, who was scribbling frantically. "You following me?"

Jack nodded.

"Okay," he said. "We take the laptop back to the station and while I'm processing the guy, Gushue is reading the emails he was trying to delete, and loading a backup onto a memory stick. Later on, he shows them to me.

"It was an email exchange, between the Chinese guy and an unknown party," he said. "It had to do with their project here, with a decision by the Canadian cabinet to approve or reject the project. This little Chinese guy was getting reports. They were memos, descriptions of who said what at a cabinet meeting. Said some of the cabinet members thought the Chinese should get the okay, some said no. There were a series of messages like that, and for every message, there was a reply, from the Chinese guy, with details about a wire transfer to an account in Panama, each time $100,000 U.S."

Jack stiffened and stopped writing. Who were the messages from?"

"That's the thing," said Brecker. "They were from a Hotmail account. I can't even remember the address. A random bunch of numbers and letters."

"Do you have the emails?"

"No," said Brecker. "I never did. They were in the file on the case. It was more Gushue's interest than mine. It bothered him. He said someone had violated the Security of Information Act. Said, basically, there was a spy in the cabinet. Told me to keep my mouth shut about it, but he started a new file, starting working it, wrote to Hotmail, looking for the IP address of the person who set up the Hotmail account. And he reported it up the chain of command."

Jack looked up from his notepad. "And?"

"And very quickly two guys came in from Edmonton, senior guys. Inspector Duncan Wheeler and Assistant Inspector Emil Dupré. Brass. They call us in, tell us this is a national security investigation, way above our pay grade, point out that we would be violating the Security of Information Act ourselves if we ever said a word. Said that senior Mounties and CSIS agents would take over the investigation and we did a great job, and congratulations, and that was it."

"Fuck," said Jack.

"A couple months later, cabinet approves the project. Was a big story up here. Now they're building it," he said. "And I never heard anything about any arrests. If you check the records, you'll find that Gushue, Wheeler and Dupré all got big promotions. Gushue got promoted to Ottawa. Wheeler was made deputy commissioner, and yours truly got pushed out the fucking door."

"Why were you pushed out?" asked Jack.

Brecker laughed. "Is that for your story?"

"Well, I can find out, but I'd rather hear it from you. I don't want to go around asking about you."

Brecker narrowed his eyes.

"They didn't like the way I handled a cocaine bust," he said. "Okay? Is that good? We had a disagreement over the whereabouts of some cocaine and some cash. That dispute ended with me leaving the force very quietly and moving down here, where I make a shitload more money."

Jack nodded at him.

"That'll do 'er," he said. "What was Gushue like?"

"Good Mountie," said Brecker. "Great Mountie. Old school. A believer. When he was posted up north, he'd have all the Eskimo kids playing hockey, get gear donated from down south. The league he set up is still going. You remember Andy Mahonik, Eskimo kid cracked the AHL? Scored some goals for the national junior team? He's one of the kids Gushue coached. Jesus, he was a good Mountie. He'd go visit crime victims, criminals, years after he handled their cases, see how they were doing."

Brecker's eyes had softened. Jack was suddenly looking at a very different person.

"I was glad he was gone by the time I had my little trouble," Brecker said. "He was good to me, and I wouldn't have liked to face him when . . ." All the warmth suddenly vanished from his eyes, and he was standing. "Got enough? Ready to go bother somebody else?"

"Yeah," said Jack, and he made for the door. "Thanks so much. You did the right thing telling me this shit. I'm onto something here, something weird, and I'm going to do my best to get it out."

He was at the door. Brecker pressed a buzzer and it unlocked.

"And don't worry about getting dragged into this," Jack said as he stepped into the hallway. "I'm not going to ever mention your name to anybody."

"You'd better fucking not," said Brecker. And he slammed the door in his face.

After a couple of hours in front of the computers, watching Sophie and Ed have sex, Flanagan found something interesting. It was on one of the last recordings, dated just a month ago.

It was obvious from the beginning that something was different. While most of the recordings started with an empty bedroom, or sometimes while Sophie was undressing, or in bed waiting for Ed, in this recording, she was on her knees, in her underwear, performing fellatio.

"Hey," said Flanagan. "That's not Sawatski."

Ashton slid her chair over and looked at the screen.

"Holy fuck," she said. "Who is it?"

"I don't know," said Flanagan. "It just started. You can't see his face."

The man was wearing nothing but an unbuttoned blue dress shirt. He was significantly heavier set than Sawatski, a bit pudgy around the middle. He was sitting on the edge of the bed nearest the camera, and his face wasn't visible on the screen.

The screen showed the back and side of Sophie's head, which was bobbing quickly up and down. After a few minutes, Ed stepped into the doorway, a strange smile on his face. Sophie pulled her mouth away from the man on the bed and looked toward him, still holding the man's penis in her hand. She smiled and said something. Ed responded and she turned back to caressing the other man with her mouth.

"Holy fuck," said Flanagan. "This is some kinky shit. Look at the dude, standing there watching his girlfriend with another guy."

"People do some funny things when they think nobody's watching," Ashton said. "Check it out, he's getting into it."

Ed was staring from the doorway, apparently mesmerized. He rubbed the front of his pants.

Sophie stopped again, and turned to look at Ed, speaking to him, smiling and laughing, and Ed started to undress as she turned back to the other man. When he was naked, Ed walked toward the bed and stood there, touching himself in front of her. Ashton and Flanagan could no longer see his face.

Sophie pulled away from the stranger and reached for Ed's penis. She spoke to him, smiling.

"I wonder if we could get a lip reader to figure out what she's saying," said Ashton.

"Geez," said Flanagan. "We'd need a pretty open-minded lip reader."

"Is this bugging you?"

"No. It's no big deal, but she seemed like such a nice girl when we interviewed her."

"You might be surprised at some of the things nice girls get up to, Devon."

"I might be," said Flanagan, nodding at the screen.

Sophie was now performing oral sex on Ed, and masturbating the other man's penis at the same time. Then she switched back.

"We still haven't seen his face," said Ashton. "Maybe we can do a printout of his unit. Show it around the Hill. See if anyone recognizes it."

Flanagan frowned and looked at her over his glasses.

"Just saying," said Ashton, grinning. "Look. He's moving. Maybe we'll get to see now."

The man stood up from the bed, and took off his shirt. Sophie looked up at him, and then at Ed, and took off her bra.

The man tossed his shirt aside, toward the camera, and suddenly the screen was filled with a closeup of a blue cotton weave.

"Fuck," said Flanagan. He jabbed at the remote and clicked forward. An hour farther in, the shirt was removed from the shelf as the man got dressed. But he got dressed off-camera. The screen showed Ed and Sophie under a sheet on the bed. They were talking and laughing, obviously engaged with the man as he got dressed.

Then Sophie jumped out of bed and stood naked close to the camera, so the screen was filled with a closeup of her pale, slim belly. She turned as the man's body came into view, they embraced and she remained standing there as he left the room, her ass blocking the view of him as he passed by the camera. Then she jumped back into bed and snuggled up with Sawatski.

Flanagan clicked ahead. The recording ran through the night and finished after the two of them got up in the morning.

"We need to look through this more carefully and see if we missed something," said Ashton. "Maybe you can make out his face and we missed it."

"Or maybe he's in another video," said Flanagan.

He clicked on the next folder – 2011/11/13 – and typed in the password, but there was no file inside.

"Hey," he said. "This is funny. There's no video in this one."

He clicked through the remaining folders.

"Every other folder has a file in it," he said.

"So it looks like he deleted this one file," said Ashton.

"I wonder why he would do that?" said Flanagan.

"Perhaps their guest made another appearance," said Ashton.

Peggy and Vern were curled up in front of the TV when Jack got back to their mobile home. They looked as though they had nodded off on the couch, although they denied it when he came in, but they would do that, he thought.

"How was your adventure?" said Peg. "Vern tells me you

went to the show." She muted the TV.

"Yes," said Jack, taking off his parka. "I popped into Showgirls. Had to talk to a fellow works there. By the Jesus, I think that might be the worst bar I've ever been in. What a sad bunch of b'ys there, drinking their wages."

"I don't doubt it," said Peg. "Poor shaggers."

"I don't know who to feel worse for," said Vern. "The b'ys or the dancers. Makes me glad I married Peg here. I don't have to chase after all that foolishness." He winked.

"So did you learn anything for your story?" asked Peg.

"I did," he said. "I got something good. I'd better not tell you about it just yet, but I did get something good. Do you mind if I go online? I've got to book a ticket back to Ottawa."

"You leaving already?" said Peg. "Your mom's gonna think we didn't treat you good."

"That's what I'm gonna tell her," said Jack. "It's shocking the way you two treated me."

Vern and Peg laughed. "Go way with ya, b'y," said Peg. "You complain to your mom and I'll tell her we hardly saw you 'cause you was always at the strip bar."

Jack gave her a hug. "You two have treated me finest kind," he said. "But I got to get back to Ottawa and try to save my career. What time's the first flight tomorrow?"

Chapter 9 – Rats

JIM GODIN WOULD rather have been at his girlfriend's apartment on Avenue du Parc la Fontaine, in the heart of Montreal, sipping coffee on the little table in front of the window, looking out at the snowy park, taking his time going through *La Presse* and the *Globe*, as he did most weekend mornings, but an old friend of his father's had insisted on meeting for breakfast at 7 a.m. at La Binerie, so he had bundled up in his parka and fur hat and walked through the slushy streets of the Plateau.

Godin had known Jean-Fred Charbonneau as long as he could remember. Some of his earliest memories were of happy afternoons when Charbonneau and his father would drink beer and talk politics on lawn chairs behind his parents' little house in east-end Montreal, while their wives cooked and he and the other children played in the little backyard.

The men were both riding-level political operatives then, Godin a Liberal and Charbonneau a Tory. They grew up together in the working class neighbourhood, and although they were members of different political tribes, they were both passionate federalists and good friends, drawn together by their common experience in the cutthroat world of Montreal politics and street-level battles with the sovereigntists, which they lost more often than they won.

After Godin's father died four years earlier, Charbonneau started calling him up and taking him out for lunch or a beer whenever he was in Montreal, trading political gossip with him and asking him about his life, never giving advice but gently posing questions that often led Godin to some insight.

The old fellow was sitting in a booth when Godin arrived. He was still wearing his parka in the overheated little restaurant, sipping coffee and peering through his reading glasses at *Le Journal de Montreal*, the city's colourful tabloid. La Binerie – a holdover from the days when the Plateau was a working-class Québécois neighbourhood, not an artsy enclave – was steamy and crowded. Customers were hunched over greasy breakfasts at the long wooden bar, and jammed into tiny booths.

"Salut, mon gars," Charbonneau said, when he spied Godin. "Ça va bien?"

"Pas si mal," said Godin as they shook hands. "Mais il fait pas chaud pour la pompe à eau. Osti."

"Tabarouette," said Charbonneau. "I should be in Florida with my sister and her kids, eh? but I can't tear myself away from the politics."

"Ouf," said Godin, taking off his parka and sliding into the booth. "Haven't you had enough of that shit? You should leave it for us young fellows."

Charbonneau smiled. "And let you fuck it up," he said. "Sacré monde osti. Did you see this shit?"

He held up the newspaper. It was open to a column by Henri Leblanc, a sovereigntist. The headline read, "Les conservateurs montrent leurs propres couleurs."

"What's Leblanc have to say?" said Godin.

"It's all bullshit," said Charbonneau. "They are making hay out of this Meech II thing. It's like a wet dream for the sovereigntists. You couldn't write a better script for them if you tried."

"Tremblay is hammering you guys on this," said Godin. "But what did you expect? I like Donahoe, but you can't go around promising to reopen the Constitution and then taking it back."

The waiter arrived and brought coffee for Godin. They both ordered big breakfasts.

"I shouldn't be eating this shit," said Godin, patting his tummy. "Marie-Claude is after me to lose a little bit of this."

"I think you should do whatever she says at all times," said Charbonneau. "You're lucky she puts up with you. I find it a source of never-ending surprise. I'll call the waiter back and order you a fruit salad."

Godin laughed. "I think she'll forgive me this one time. Or maybe I'll tell her I had the fruit salad."

Charbonneau peered over his reading glasses. "I wouldn't do that if I were you. They don't serve fruit salad here. She'll know you're a lying sack of shit. Better let her just suspect it. Tell her the truth, ask for forgiveness and go for a long walk with her this afternoon."

"Good advice, as always, Jean-Fred," said Godin, bowing his head. "But I have to drive to Ottawa after breakfast. Pinsent's got an interview on NTV. I've got to hold his hand."

Charbonneau puffed out his cheeks and exhaled. "They're going to be talking about this Meech II shit?"

Godin nodded.

Charbonneau suddenly looked older, grey-faced and tired. "It's a piece of shit," he said. "This is a real piece of shit."

"What is it, Jean-Fred?"

Charbonneau lowered his voice and leaned forward. "Well, you know that *petit con* Balusi?"

"Sure," said Godin. "Of course."

Charbonneau leaned back and pursed his lips, then leaned forward again. "A couple of weeks ago he calls me. Tells me he hears that Donahoe is going to make a speech at the Champlain Club, asks me if I am going."

"Okay," said Godin.

"I tell him of course I'm going, I tell him Donahoe is going to be a great leader of the Conservative party, that we've had enough of the goddamned Albertans running the country, although they're better than the goddamned Liberals."

Godin laughed. "That's good for him," he said. "He's so full of himself, that guy. Give him shit."

"Yeah, well. He tells me that Donahoe is great, he wishes he could go to the event, but he can't make it, and asks me to record it for him and send him the tape." Charbonneau looked at Godin sorrowfully. "He asked me to do it on the sly, eh? Not let on that I was recording it."

"You didn't do it," said Godin.

Charbonneau frowned down at his coffee. "I'm sorry to say I did," he said. "Look, I'm going to support Donahoe, but you and I both know that Mowat is more likely to win, and there's no point burning bridges."

"Tabarnac," said Godin.

"These *osti de* Reformers are clumsy," said Charbonneau. "Everything they do in Quebec is clumsy. They want us to help them run their campaigns, find sign-pounders, but they don't listen to us. You know that. I'm often tempted to give it up, but we have been hoping that things will change when the leader changes. Whether it's Mowat or Donahoe, Quebec needs people on the winning team. The fucking teenage MPs in the NDP won't get anything done."

He sounded like he was trying to convince himself, and failing. He looked down at his coffee cup.

"So you recorded the meeting?" said Godin.

Charbonneau nodded his bald head. "*Oui.* I sure did. I wasn't born on the last rainy day. I have a little recorder with a tiny mic. I put it in my breast pocket, and I transferred the file to my computer later and emailed it to Balusi."

Godin laughed. "Well, you've been in the game for a while," he said. "Donahoe should never have said that shit. It's not your fault that he's stupid."

Charbonneau wasn't laughing. His face was turning red. "Donahoe isn't stupid. He didn't say it. That's what I'm telling you. He was very careful. He said he didn't believe it was possible to do a Meech II. He was explicit."

Godin scowled. "I heard the tape. I had to hold Pinsent's hand while we worked out how to respond."

Charbonneau laughed. "You say Donahoe is stupid, but you work for Pinsent! I can't believe he came out and attacked Mowat and backed Donahoe. What potato truck did he fall off?"

Godin smiled ruefully and sucked his lips. "He doesn't

always take my advice," he said.

"No," said Charbonneau. "I hope you didn't tell him to say that. *Câlisse*. Between Donahoe and Pinsent, Tremblay has an easy job. The *maudite séparatiste* just has to point out what a bunch of goddamned lying idiots the federalists are. Christ." He shook his head in disgust.

"Someone doctored the tape," he said. "They edited what he did say, and cut off the end of his speech, where he explained the practical steps he would take instead of opening the constitution."

"Who?" said Godin.

Charbonneau pulled a memory stick out of his pocket and put it on the table just as the waiter arrived with their plates of eggs and sausages.

"Is this the original recording?" said Godin.

"Yes," said Charbonneau, spearing a sausage. "Go ahead. Take it. Use it. Get it out."

"It won't help you with Balusi. They will know it came from you."

Charbonneau dropped his fork. "Fuck them," he said in English. "Fuck those cocksuckers." He switched back to French. "I don't give a Christ what they think of me. This is dirty tricks. Okay. I'm not a virgin. Fine. A little ratfucking is part of politics. But this is shitty. They are helping Tremblay and putting a good man in the shit. Fuck them."

He bit into a sausage and smiled as he chewed.

"Believe me," he said. "I'll sleep better at night. A lot better."

Ida Gushue was surprised to find Jack Macdonald on her doorstep shivering in the cold at 10 a.m. on a Sunday morning, holding a cup of takeout coffee, with his suitcase and laptop bag next to him on the doorstep.

"Sorry to show up without calling," he said. "And don't worry, I'm not here to ask for room and board. I'm just arriving from the airport and I wanted to tell you what I found out in

Fort McMurray before I went home."

She stood in the doorway and stared at him for a moment, then looked out at the curb. "How did you get here?"

"I took a cab," he said. "I'll have to ask you to call another one for me after we've had a chat. If you would be kind enough to spare a moment for a chat, that is."

She looked at him again, and looked away and he thought she was going to close the door in his face.

"All right," she said. "Come in."

He sighed with relief and thanked her and stepped inside.

"You're lucky I decided not to go to church this morning," she said, leading him into the living room. "Otherwise you'd have been stuck in the cold with nobody to call you a cab."

"I'd have to have pestered one of your neighbours," he said.

She stopped and frowned at him. "Yes. Well. So you were lucky. I don't know that I'm going to be able to help you with anything else though. As I told you last time, I haven't decided what to do about my husband's files."

Jack took off his coat and sat down and dug through his laptop bag.

"I know," he said. "I understand that. All I want is to show you what I learned in Fort McMurray. Maybe it will help you make your decision. I may be stunned, but I'm not stunned enough to think I could sweet-talk you into doing something you don't want to do."

She sat down and appraised him coolly. "Okay," she said. "I'll have a look at what you found."

He opened his laptop. "Do you have wireless?"

"Yes," she said. "Erin set it up."

"Can I have the password?" asked Jack. "It would be easiest if I can show you some things online."

"Hm," said Gushue. "I'll have to call her to get it."

She stepped out of the room to call her daughter and got the password.

"Gaga012," she said when she returned, and then spelled it out. Her expression suggested she would rather not hear any comment about the password.

Jack smiled and typed it in, then turned the laptop so that they could both see the screen. He opened his web browser and a series of tabs opened up.

"I was up all night putting this together," he said. "Then I caught the first flight out of Fort Mac. Jeez, I was glad to get out of there."

The first tab came up. It was a story from *Fort McMurray Today* about the Second Chance program, with the picture of Redcloud laughing as she made a dream catcher. He told her about the girl, clicked through the murder stories he'd collected, and then opened an *Alberta Report* story about the SinoGaz deal, showing bulldozers clearing stunted spruce.

"The project had to clear two sets of hurdles, a foreign investment review panel and a federal-provincial environmental panel," said Jack. "Both rejected it, but Stevens overturned both decisions. That's not particularly noteworthy in itself. Stevens is very close to the Alberta oil people, and he has given a number of oil sands projects the go-ahead after regulators said no. Stevens likes the oil sands."

He opened the next story, illustrated with a picture of two Mounties posing with some children in a classroom, part of a crime prevention program.

"What's strange is what your husband and his partner, Constable Dwayne Brecker, found on Wi's computer when they investigated the crime scene."

He explained the emails, and the secret payments, then clicked to the story about Wi's death.

"Wi was killed in remand in Edmonton a couple weeks after he murdered Redcloud," he said. "It was a hit, carried out by the Indian Posse, a First Nations gang, contracted by some Chinese gangbangers from Vancouver. I suspect that SinoGaz ordered the hit to silence Wi."

He clicked next on a group photo of the Stevens cabinet. "One of the people of this photo is a traitor, basically, someone who sold out his country. Your husband knew this, and was investigating it until two senior Mounties came to town, Inspector Duncan Wheeler and Assistant Inspector

Emil Dupré. They showed your husband and Brecker a letter from the deputy commissioner, praising their investigation, and informed them that any further investigation would be handled by CSIS and senior Mounties. They reminded them of their legal obligations to keep quiet about the case, and they took all the case files with them."

The next tab showed a number of photographs of men in full dress Mountie uniforms, standing at attention during a promotion ceremony.

"Three of the men – your husband, Wheeler and Dupré – received promotions within the next few months, and all three of them were transferred to headquarters here in Ottawa," he said. "Brecker was drummed out of the force last year."

"Oh my," said Gushue. "He seemed like such a nice man. Earl had him over to the house a few times. What happened?"

"He was pushed out," said Jack. "The suggestion is that there was some impropriety on his part, involving a quantity of cocaine and cash. He's now the chief of security at Showgirls, a strip bar in Fort Mac."

For the first time since he met her, Gushue looked rattled. "Oh my," she said. "I hope Earl never heard about it. He would have been so disappointed."

"I don't think he ever did," said Jack. "Brecker said he was glad your husband didn't know."

Jack clicked on one of the promotion pictures. "This man on the left is Emil Dupré," he said. "He is now an inspector based here in Ottawa at RCMP headquarters, working for Wheeler, who is now the deputy commissioner of the RCMP."

He zoomed in on Dupré's face. He had a dark moustache and a scar on his eyebrow. "Did you ever meet this man?"

Gushue shook her head.

"Well, he tried to kill me," he said. "I suspect he is also the man who tried to drown Ed Sawatski, although I don't know exactly why."

Jack pulled out the police report and the business card that Dupré gave him, and quickly told her about the fake story he'd fallen for and the attempt on his life.

"I suspect that Dupré wants to silence me. I don't know if he will try again, but I'm afraid he will."

He handed her the business card. "Do me a favour and call the number on the card," he said.

She looked at him blankly, then picked up her phone and called, and held the phone out so that they both heard when the voice mail at the bowling alley answered.

"I need your help," he said. "Your husband knew there was something funny about this file, and he kept a copy. Right now I have no evidence that I can use to show what these guys tried to do to me. My reputation is completely ruined. Everyone thinks I'm an idiot. I can't go to the police, because they are the police. I don't know who to trust."

He clicked back on the photo of Stevens' cabinet, standing with frozen smiles in Rideau Hall.

"It is very possible that Dupré was acting on the instructions of one of the members of cabinet," he said. "Ed Sawatski worked for Jim Donahoe. He handled natural resources files, including oil sands files." He zoomed in on Donahoe's face. "Donahoe, the justice minister, could be the guy. It doesn't look good for him right now, but funny things happen in leadership races, and he could be prime minister in three months."

He moved the cursor over to Greg Mowat.

"Or Mowat could become prime minister," he said. "As public safety minister, he could easily be directing Dupré or Wheeler." He zoomed out. "Or it could be any one of the people in this picture, or maybe, maybe, one of their senior staff members, although I doubt it."

He clicked another tab, and came back to the picture of Gushue and Brecker posing with a group of children.

"If you let me see the file," he said, "nobody will be able to assume that I got it from you. They might wonder, but it could also be someone else in the Fort Mac detachment, or here in Ottawa, or they might think it's Brecker." He leaned back in his chair. "Brecker has nothing to lose. He likely has hard feelings about the force, or at least people might think that."

Gushue looked overwhelmed. She slumped in her chair.

"Mrs. Gushue," he said. "Please show me the file. I swear that I won't do anything until we talk again, and you've had a chance to think it over, but if I know what it is I can talk to a friend of mine at the *Globe* and see if they're willing to run a story."

"You wouldn't run it in the *Telegram*?" she asked.

Jack shook his head. "They suspended me," he said. "And they have been burned already. This story is too big for them. I would go to my friend Dennis Burkley at the *Globe*. I would ask for a double byline, and let them check everything I've done. It would be up to you whether you meet with Dennis or not. You might prefer not to, so that only me and maybe a very senior editor at the *Globe* would know your identity. If I had a copy of the file they might not even insist on knowing where I got it."

"Would they agree to go with the story?" she said.

"A story showing that a member of the cabinet sold secrets to a Chinese oil company?" he said. "I think they would have to go with it. It's the kind of story reporters spend their careers hoping to uncover."

"And you undertake not to do anything unless I give you the okay?" she said. "And to never reveal who showed you the file?"

Jack looked at her soberly. "I undertake to not go with the story unless I have your okay," he said. "And I further undertake to never reveal who showed me the file, without explicit instructions from you."

Gushue got to her feet and headed for the hallway. She stopped and looked back at him.

"I have a feeling somehow I might regret this," she said. "But I'll show it to you."

Jack sighed with relief. "I don't think you'll regret it. I'll do everything in my power to make sure you don't."

She came back in a few minutes with a manila folder. She sat down on the couch and held it in her lap.

"As I think I told you before, my husband never brought anything home that he shouldn't have," she said. "Except this once."

She put the folder on the table and held her hand on it. "He loved being a Mountie. He loved the uniform. He loved the history." She laughed. "I think he actually liked the rule book. He liked knowing it and following it and, I guess, he liked the way that it made things clear. Some of the guys would complain about the rules, but Earl would tell them they should have gone to law school if they wanted to be judges. So I was shocked when I found this in his papers. There's a letter in there, signed by him, that explicitly states that the whole file is all covered by the national security provisions of the Security of Information Act."

She tapped her finger on the file. "The letter says that he understood it would be a violation of the law to disclose anything about the investigation. So I find it very surprising that he brought the file home. He would have had to smuggle it out of the office."

"Perhaps he wanted to protect himself," said Jack.

Gushue turned quickly to him and her cheeks coloured. "My husband was not one to cover his arse," she said. "More's the pity, but that was not his way. No. No, sir. He brought this home, I'm convinced, because he had misgivings." She pushed the folder toward him. "That's the reason why I'm agreeing to show it to you. My husband and I were very close, but he never spoke to me about this. I felt, at times, after he was promoted, that something was bothering him. But he never talked to me about it. So now I want to know why he did what he did."

Jack smiled at her. "I can tell how much you miss him."

She shot him a sharp look and got to her feet.

"Never mind that, boy," she said. "I'm going to make us both some tea while you look through the file."

As soon as she left the room, Jack reached into his laptop bag, pulled out his digital camera, and, as quickly as he could, photographed each page of the file. His hands shook.

He was reading quietly when she came back with the tea tray.

Fred Murphy liked to get his makeup done before any guests arrived, so he could sit in his office and go through his script for the show while they were awkwardly waiting with one another in the windowless makeup room, partisan foes making small talk or working their cell phones and ignoring one another.

Godin knew that Murphy was in his office, so he left Pinsent in the makeup chair and walked through the cubicle farm. He knocked on the door frame.

"Jim, how are you?" said Murphy, looking up from his computer. He had a white bib tucked into the collar of his shirt to keep the foundation on his neck from staining his shirt collar.

"Good, Fred," said Godin, leaning in the doorway. "How about you?"

Murphy turned back to his computer, typing last-minute notes to the script put together by his young producer.

"Good, Jim," he said. "Just finishing the damn script."

"Look, I know how busy you are before the show," said Godin. "But I want to have a quiet chat later." He reached into his pocket and pulled out the memory stick that Charbonneau had given him. "I have something for you. Something on the Meech II thing."

"Sure, Jim," said Murphy, looking up again from his keyboard. "Let's have a coffee after the show." He looked up and smiled. Godin thanked him and left.

Sunday Politics didn't have the best ratings, but it did far better than anything else on the dial in Canada at noon on Sunday, and it was important to Murphy. During the week, political reporters were lucky to get a two-minute story on the nightly news. For an hour every Sunday, Murphy was able to go deeper and explain two or three stories thoroughly, and that mattered, whatever the ratings, because the politicians, staffers and journalists who made Canadian politics function all tuned in. Murphy was dedicated to making it count.

This week, the show was going to hit the Meech II thing hard. It was the first action in what was so far an undeclared leadership contest between Mowat and Donahoe.

Murphy had covered the Meech Lake accord, the Charlottetown accord and the referendum that followed, and he wouldn't let anyone tell him that Donahoe's position wasn't news. He knew that the issue made the average person's eyes glaze over, but once again he was watching a politician who had been foolish enough to open a Pandora's box by suggesting to Quebecers that the federal government would find some way of recognizing their desires in the Constitution. Murphy found it hard to believe that Donahoe was serious about that, but if the guy wanted to be prime minister, he shouldn't be able to say one thing behind closed doors in Montreal and another in Toronto, and he certainly shouldn't be able to get away with lying about it. Murphy was looking forward to pinning him down.

Jack took a cab home, dropped off his luggage while the taxi waited, and then went to Dunn's, a smoked meat sandwich shop on Elgin Street, not far from the NTV studio. He asked the waitress if he could sit near a TV, and if he could change the channel from hockey to NTV.

She didn't look impressed, but she let him set up camp in the back corner, under a TV.

He ordered bacon and eggs and watched *Sunday Politics*.

Murphy had both Donahoe and Mowat on the show, Mowat from NTV's Toronto studio, Donahoe sitting next to Murphy in Ottawa.

"So," Murphy started. "Mr. Donahoe was good enough to tell us this week that he is considering applying for a pretty big job, leader of the Conservative Party of Canada, a job that carries with it the office of the prime minister of Canada. How about you, Mr. Mowat? So far you haven't said whether you're interested in the job. Here's your chance to let us know. How about it?"

Mowat smiled into the camera. "Well, Fred, I hope you

know I'm not being coy." He chuckled. "This is not an easy decision to make. Anyone who following the news this week got some insight into the pressure this puts on your family life. I think entering a political race is like jumping in a swimming hole. You better make sure you really want to get wet, because you can't change your mind once you're in the air."

"And you can't look for rocks in the water from the air," said Murphy, who didn't give Mowat a chance to respond before asking his next question.

"Mr. Donahoe, you told voters this week that you're trying to make up your mind about whether to run, but then you hit a pretty big rock. NTV's Ellen Simms had a story this week where it looked like you were telling Quebec Tories one thing behind closed doors and some else thing publicly. Here's your chance to clear it up. Do you believe in opening the Constitution to recognize Quebec's distinctiveness?"

Donahoe smiled. "Fred, I've been in politics for long enough to know that some questions have no simple or right answer," he said. "The short answer is no, I don't believe that we should reopen the Constitution, but I also don't think we should be slamming the door on those Quebecers who have a legitimate desire to renew the federation. I'd like to point out that my comments have been taken out of context and distorted, and I'd also like to note that I was secretly recorded at a private meeting –" Murphy interrupted him. "Hold up there, Mr. Donahoe. I've heard the clip. We can play it again and let viewers decide what you actually said."

Donahoe wore a sour-looking smile. "Well, if you want to, go ahead, but I'm not really sure you want to be focusing on a secret recording of a private meeting when there are a lot of issues out there, really important issues, that voters would rather hear about."

The screen was filled with the English translation of Donahoe's comments, superimposed over his face while the French audio clip played. Donahoe looked pained. He actually squirmed in his chair.

"How about it, Mr. Donahoe?" said Murphy. "Do you stand

by those comments? Do you have a secret plan to renegotiate the Constitution with Quebec? That seems to be what you're saying."

Donahoe struggled to smile. "No, Fred, I have no secret plan. Not at all. No. Fred, this comment has been distorted and twisted. There is no secret plan here, but what we really should be talking about are the issues that Canadians are telling me they're concerned about. They are talking about crime, taxes, the economy, not this constitutional arcana."

Murphy turned to Mowat.

"How about you, Mr. Mowat?" he said. "Do you think the government should reopen the Constitution?"

Mowat looked somber. "No, Fred. Jim is right to say that we should never slam the door shut on Quebecers and their aspirations, but I can tell you that I don't think the way to address those concerns is through the Constitution. We've been down that road, and it was a bit bumpy. I wasn't surprised this week to hear Mr. Tremblay accusing us all of being a bunch of bad apples. He's a separatist, and we can expect that kind of thing from him. But I was surprised to hear Mr. Pinsent say that we should consider opening the Constitution. I think that's unbelievably reckless, and I think it should give voters pause. Let the Liberals go down that path if they like. I think the Conservatives should make it clear what we stand for and what we don't."

Murphy smiled. "Mr. Donahoe, do you agree?" he asked.

Donahoe wore a sickly smile. "Sure, Fred," he said. "I think Mr. Mowat is right on this. We don't need to get mixed up in this kind of divisive question."

The camera cut to Murphy. "I think we've just watched someone swallow himself whole here folks," he said. "When we come back, our political panel handicaps the race for the Tory leadership."

Jack jammed a piece of toast in his mouth, put a twenty-dollar bill under his plate and walked quickly through the empty streets to the entrance of the big glass building where NTV had its studios. He waited there, leaning against a pillar across the street, smoking a cigarette. When Dave Cochrane and Jim Donahoe stepped outside, Jack crossed the street, calling out. "Mr. Donahoe," he said. "I have a question for you, sir."

Donahoe had a scowl on his face, and his mood wasn't improved by seeing Jack.

He kept walking. Jack ran to catch up with the two men, then walked beside them, his recorder extended. Cochrane tried to get between Jack and Donahoe.

"Who are you working for?" he asked. "Why don't you call the office tomorrow and we'll have a talk then."

Jack walked faster and stepped around Cochrane, putting his recorder in Donahoe's face. Cochrane's face was fixed in a scowl, with his eyes on his car ahead – a silver Toyota Camry.

"Sir, did you sell cabinet secrets to SinoGaz?" Jack asked. "Did you send emails to Ling Cho Wi? Did you receive payment from him in a Panama bank?"

Donahoe's face twisted as Jack spoke, and he stopped and turned to him, as if to speak. Cochrane stepped between them and steered Donahoe toward the car.

"Sir, I have the emails," said Jack, as the men got into the Camry. "I need to ask you about this."

He stood on the snowy sidewalk. "I need answers," he bellowed. "I have the emails."

The car took off down the empty street, spinning its wheels, sending jets of snow flying. Jack switched off his recorder and stood on the sidewalk, breathing heavily, his body shaking.

The car stopped halfway up the block and reversed toward Jack. Cochrane rolled down the window. Jack could see Donahoe staring straight ahead.

"Jack, meet me in the Bridgehead in fifteen minutes," he said. "Okay?"

Jack nodded.

"We need to talk," said Cochrane.

Fred Murphy was picking up an Americano and a cappuccino

at the counter of the coffee shop when Jack came in the door, rubbing his hands against the cold. Murphy took the coffees over to a corner table, where Godin was waiting for him.

"That kid Macdonald just came in," he said, nodding to the doorway. "The guy who messed up that Mowat story."

"Jack?" said Godin. "I thought he moved back to Newfoundland."

"He's right over there."

"I'm going to go say hi," said Godin, getting up.

He walked over and slapped Jack on the back. "Hey Jack. You're back in town? I thought you moved to Newfoundland."

"I'm back for a few days anyway."

"Did you get a job?"

"No," said Jack. "Haven't started looking yet. I'm not sure I smell good to employers after that Mowat thing."

"Email me if I can help," said Godin. "You're a good reporter and you deserve another chance."

"Thanks," said Jack. "Maybe you can help me figure out how I got fucked."

Back at the table, Godin sat across from Murphy.

"I'd like to know what happened with that Mowat story," he said. "There's no way that kid forged that police report."

Murphy emptied two packets of sugar into his coffee. "It would've been pretty stupid of him. But it was pretty stupid to go with the story without checking it."

"Yeah," said Godin. "But sometimes there's more to the news than meets the eye." He pulled a memory stick from his pocket and put it in on the table in front of Murphy. "This is a recording here of Donahoe's Meech II speech," he said.

Murphy picked it up. "We already have one of those. We've been running it for days."

"I know," said Godin. "Tell me, do you know the source of it? Would it happen to be Ismael Balusi?"

Murphy smiled at him. "You know I never discuss my sources."

Godin smiled back. "Well, this recording is different from the one that you played on the air. In this recording, Donahoe brings up the idea of Meech II only to say that's not what he would do." Murphy placed the stick back on the table and nudged it away with a finger.

"Listen to it. You'll find that someone edited the version they gave you to make Donahoe look bad," said Godin. "I have reason to believe that Balusi did it to fuck Donahoe coming out of the gate."

Murphy pursed his lips. "Correct me if I'm wrong, but hasn't Pinsent's position been that we should do a Meech II? He keeps attacking Mowat for rejecting the idea out of hand."

Godin laughed. "I'm not here on behalf of my guy," he said. "Look, Greg Mowat is headed for 24 Sussex. I doubt very much that Pinsent will ever get there. If you ever quote me saying that, I'll wring your neck, but it's true. Greg Mowat, on the other hand, will likely be prime minister in a matter of months. I find him scary. If I'm right, someone working on his behalf ratfucked Donahoe, who I think is a decent politician, and would probably be a good prime minister, for a Tory. I'm giving you this because I don't think that's the way our politics ought to work."

Murphy leaned forward and spun the memory stick while he thought.

"Have you given this recording to anyone else?" he said after a moment.

"No," said Godin. "And I don't plan to, not without talking to you anyway."

Murphy nodded and put the stick in his pocket. "Thank you for bringing it to me. If you're right, we have a problem on our hands, the kind of thing I might have to handle very delicately."

"I can imagine," said Godin.

Murphy took a sip of his cappuccino. "I don't think I have to tell you that if I find out that NTV has been manipulated into running lies, I'll do what I can to get to the bottom of it and expose it."

"No," said Godin. "You don't have to tell me that."

Murphy nodded over his shoulder. "There's Donahoe's man there, having a chat with Macdonald."

Godin looked over his shoulder.

"I wonder what they're talking about," he said.

Cochrane was all business. He sat down across from Jack and leaned toward him, speaking low, looking out the window.

"I have a few things to tell you, but first I have some questions. First off, are you recording this?"

"No," said Jack.

"Okay," said Cochrane. "Second, do you agree to talk on deep background? I want to talk to you but I don't want to be quoted in any way. If you eventually go with a story, you can't mention this conversation at all. Agreed?"

"All right," Jack said. "I agree to treat this conversation as deep background."

"Now, who are you working for? I understand that you are suspended. Has that suspension been lifted?"

"No," said Jack. "I am pursuing this story as a freelancer. I have, as I think you know, some significant information. I anticipate that I will find someone to publish the information. I will contact you again after I've made an agreement with a media organization."

"So, you have to shop the story?"

"Yeah. You could put it that way."

"That makes all of this more difficult. My boss is concerned that people could easily get the wrong impression about this. He thinks you likely have the wrong impression, and the consequences of that misunderstanding are significant. That's why I'm here."

"You're afraid I'll go blabbing around town."

"I'm afraid you'll spread a bullshit story."

"Is it bullshit? I have read the emails."

"What emails? Who are they from? What do they say?"

Jack pursed his lips. "I think it would be unwise for me to go into detail at this time," he said. "That's the kind of conversation we should have after I have arranged for publication."

"That makes this difficult," said Cochrane. He laughed, a short angry burst. "You have some half-baked accusations, which I don't think I have to tell you are defamatory, and you want us to respond without knowing what documentary evidence you have? I'm not sure I should even be sitting here with you."

Jack's face coloured. He leaned forward and spoke quietly but quickly. "Why are you sitting here, then? You're here because your boss needed you to talk to me, because he knows what I have. Don't fuck with me, Dave. I'm not letting anyone bully me. I've been put through the fucking wringer in the past week, and I'm not playing games with you. I have evidence that suggests your boss was selling secrets to the fucking Chinese. As a journalist, as a Canadian, I have a clear responsibility to get to the bottom of it."

Cochrane sat back and laughed. " Okay. Whatever. So, do you want to know what I have to say, or not? How about if it kills your story?"

"Yes, I do. What have you got?"

"Okay," said Cochrane. "I had no idea what you were talking about when you approached us on the street, but the boss did. Once we got in the car, he told me to set up this meeting. He said, and I quote, 'That kid doesn't have a fucking clue what he's getting into.' "

Jack nodded for him to continue.

"He says he knows of an email exchange between someone with cabinet-level access to Mr. Wi. I didn't know anything about this, but CSIS does, and the prime minister's office does, and it is well above my pay grade, and yours, and you had better tread very carefully."

"Are you threatening me?"

"No. I'm not threatening you. I'm just telling you that certain elements of our national security apparatus will be very concerned that you have top-secret information. The minister's responsibility is clear. He has to inform them. Their responsibility is clear. They have to try to figure out who knows what. And my minister asked me to make it clear to you that you can only have the wrong idea about the meaning of the emails."

Jack glared at him. "What do you mean?"

"Let's say," said Cochrane with a small smile, "just as an example, that a member of a foreign intelligence service tried to induce a senior official in the government of Canada to provide certain information. In a circumstance like that, the Canadian security services might ask that a Canadian official provide a false story, as an information-gathering technique."

Jack frowned and shifted in his chair. "Are you saying that Donahoe sent the emails with the knowledge of CSIS?"

"That is a strong possibility."

"That might be an even more interesting story," Jack said. "If someone wanted to tell me that on the record."

Cochrane spoke sternly. "If a public office holder spoke about such an exchange, he would be in violation of the Security of Information Act. So any story would just unfairly smear a faithful servant of the Crown. You might be able to live with that, but I wouldn't if I were you."

Jack thought for a moment.

"Listen," he said, his anger rising. "I started investigating this story after someone tried to kill Ed Sawatski. I don't want to talk about it, but the same people who tried to kill Ed are also after me. I have no idea why. I have evidence that they are Mounties, but I don't know if they are acting on behalf of the government." Cochrane looked genuinely surprised. "They planted a fake story with me that was calculated to damage Greg Mowat's campaign. I'm not going to just accept your word that Donahoe had nothing to do with it. I may be fucking stupid, but I'm not that fucking stupid."

Jack spoke slowly to stop his voice shaking. "Look, I don't know what the fuck is going on, who's doing what, but I do know that when I start publishing what I have, the truth will come out. I don't have to nail down every detail before I publish. I'm a reporter, not a judge."

Cochrane started to say something then stopped and looked around. He stood up. "Let's go for a walk."

They bundled up and walked down Sparks Street toward the war memorial. The freezing wind whipped at their faces and they walked side by side hunched over, without looking at each other.

"Listen to me," said Cochrane. "If you think my guy had anything to do with what happened to Sawatski, you're fucking crazy."

"Well, somebody tried to kill him," said Jack. "You got any idea who?"

Cochrane stopped but Jack didn't notice for a moment and kept walking. He turned back and they faced each other on the sidewalk. The wind broke on Jack's back and twisted at his coat.

"Listen," said Cochrane. "I don't know that anyone tried to kill Sawatski, but even if it is true, Donahoe wouldn't be at the top of my list of suspects. I'd start with the guy who was fucking Sawatski's girlfriend."

Jack glared at him. "Who was fucking Sophie?"

Cochrane stared at him, blinking in the cold wind. "I'm not a gossip."

"Who?" growled Jack. "Who's fucking Sophie?"

Cochrane set his chin. "Not the minister of justice."

"Who? Another minister? What? Mowat?"

"No comment. Okay?"

Jack turned into the wind and let it tear at his face for a moment. He turned back to Cochrane. "Do you have reason to believe that Mowat tried to kill Sawatski?"

Cochrane shook his head. "Look, no," he said. "But I know that my guy wasn't banging her. And someone else was. If I was looking for a suspect, that's where I'd start."

"How do you know that Mowat was banging her?"

"I don't have proof. But we have pretty good reason to believe. We have all Ed's emails and PINs, you know." He looked up and down the empty street. "I shouldn't be telling you this shit. If anyone finds out I did, I'll be out on my ass."

"You don't have to worry about that," Jack said. "I won't tell anybody. I'm going to ask Sophie. She and I are pretty good friends. I won't tell her where I heard it."

"Don't even tell her you've been talking to me," said Cochrane. "She's a smart cookie. She might guess I told you."

Jack nodded. "I've got to track her down first," he said. "She's been ignoring my messages."

"She has a new phone," said Cochrane. He pulled out his BlackBerry. "I'm not going to email it to you," he said. "I don't want any email exchanges with you, at all. I'll tell you her number."

Jack pulled out his BlackBerry, took off his gloves and typed Sophie's number into his address book. "Give me your cell number as well," he said.

Cochrane recited his number. Jack's fingers got cold as he typed.

"I want you to tell me what you find out," Cochrane said. "Christ, I must have rocks in my head to trust you. You haven't got much to lose, have you?"

Jack laughed. "You're right about that. Look, somebody tried to ruin me. Fuck. They did ruin me. I'll be lucky to get a job taking obits in Goose Bay. I don't have anything to lose, but I have a lot to gain. I'm looking for a story, a really good story, something so good that I can get back in the game. I thought I had it until we sat down for a coffee."

"And now you're not sure?"

"Yeah, I'm not sure. I believe you, though. I might be wrong, but I don't think you would be helping me, even a little bit, if you thought your boss had anything to do with what happened to Ed."

"That wouldn't make sense, would it?"

"I don't think it would. And it's possible the same people who are fucking me over are fucking you over too."

Cochrane nodded. "It's possible. Look, I've got to go. You won't do anything with the SinoGaz story without talking to me?"

"No," said Jack. "I have one guy to talk to, a reporter, but I'm going to swear him to secrecy before I say a word. And I won't tell him anything about who might have sent the emails unless I have some pretty good assurances. So don't worry. I'm not going to go shooting off my mouth about this shit."

"That's all I can ask," said Cochrane. He nodded at Jack's phone. "Call me if you want to talk to me. No names. No emails."

"All right," said Jack. "Now I need to talk to Sophie."

Jack went into the heated Royal Bank machine kiosk nearby and called Sophie.

"I need to talk to you," he said.

"Oh my God," she said. "Where are you? Are you in Newfoundland?"

"I didn't go there. I went somewhere else, and I learned some things. I have to see you."

Sophie was quiet.

"I learned some things that might have to do with Ed," he said. "And with you. It's really important that I see you."

He heard a rustling, like she had covered the phone with her hand, and the muffled sound of her voice, talking to somebody else. He waited.

"I don't know, Jack," she said. "Look, this is a very difficult situation for me right now. My lawyer has told me not to discuss Ed's case with anyone. And anyway, I'm going skating right now."

"You're going on the canal?"

"Yes, I'm supposed to be meeting Marie-Hélène," she said. "Look, let me think about it and call you later, okay? I should probably talk to my lawyer. I got to go. I hope you're okay. Okay. Bye."

Jack tried to call her back, but it rang through to her voice mail.

Chapter 10 – On thick ice

JACK JOGGED TO the canal, head down, into the wind, his boots squeaking on the packed snow, across the triangular plaza where the massive war memorial stood against the grey, freezing sky, to the bridge over the locks. He glanced up at the Chateau Laurier. It was so cold that the steam pouring out of the chimneys atop the hotel was twisting in frantic, swirling plumes. It had started to snow, but the flakes were small and hard, like pellets, and stung his face.

Jack waited for a pause in the traffic, jogged across Elgin Street and down the slippery concrete stairs to the canal, south of the bridge and the locks. Where only a week before the canal had still been liquid, now it was frozen solid, and filled with skaters in parkas. Along one wall, a row of low, temporary cabins had already been erected on the ice. One sold hot chocolate and Beaver Tails – hot, deep-fried pastries covered in sugar. Another rented skates. Jack skittered across the ice on his boots and waited impatiently behind a young francophone couple who didn't know what sizes they took and acted as though they had all the time in the world.

After they got their skates, Jack thrust his Visa card at the kid behind the counter and got size ten skates. He sat down on a bench, tore off his boots and pulled on the skates, his cold fingers tightening the laces. He stashed his boots under the bench and took off south down the canal, skating quickly, bent at the waist, hands locked behind his back, kicking his feet out behind him, weaving around the families and couples moving slowly on the rough ice.

Jack skated along the west side, looking for Sophie at the

canal entrances near her apartment. He slowed down when he got to the entrance nearest Cooper Street, scanning the crowds, looking for two girls among the crowds of skaters.

He pulled his BlackBerry out and tried to call her but it rang through to voice mail again. He started south again, moving fast, keeping his head up, his eyes scanning the hundreds of people huddled against the cold on the canal. The snow was coming down heavily and hard. Jack wasn't properly dressed for a cold skate, and he was sweating under his clothes from the exertion, while his head and hands and feet were becoming numb.

He skated down to Dows Lake, where the canal opens up to a broad rink, and a dozen people were playing hockey. Jack skated past them, then turned and skated back north again, in the direction of the bridge. He was halfway back when he caught sight of them. They were moving slowly, chatting to each other. Jack knew Sophie at once. She was wearing her Kanuk parka, with a fur hat and a thick green wool scarf bundled around her neck. Her cheeks were pink from the cold. She skated gracefully, holding her stride to keep pace with Marie-Hélène, who was not a good skater.

Jack slowed to keep pace with them, straining to hear their conversation, but the wind was too strong. He caught his breath, then skated up beside them.

"Sophie," he said.

She started when she turned and spied him.

"Jack," she cried. "Oh my God. What are you doing here?"

She stopped, and so did Jack and Marie-Hélène, the two women looking at him with surprise as the wind and snow whirled around them.

"I need to talk to you," said Jack. "I need to talk to you about Ed."

Sophie's eyes darted back and forth. The wind pulled at the wisps of her hair peeking out from under her hat. "I can't," she said. "Jack. I'm sorry, but my lawyer says I can't talk to anybody about it."

Marie-Hélène pushed herself between the two of them,

trying to keep Jack away from Sophie with her stout body. She was unsteady on her skates.

"You'd better go," she said. "Sophie doesn't want to talk to you. Leave her alone."

Jack ignored her. "Do you know a big scary guy with a scar on his eyebrow?"

Sophie just stared at him.

"They tried to kill me, Sophie," he said.

Marie-Hélène pulled Sophie away and they started to skate. Sophie looked over her shoulder at Jack.

"I'll talk to my lawyer and call you," she said.

He skated beside them. "He'll tell you not to talk to me," he said. "We need to talk. They will kill me."

Marie-Hélène started to speak to Sophie rapidly in French. Jack couldn't understand what she was saying. She skated faster, her legs pumping, trying to pull Sophie away. Jack easily kept pace with them. Ahead of them, there were four young people skating together – two young black men teetering unsteadily on their skates, their legs straight, first-time skaters, each clutching a white girl. Students, Jack assumed. They were all laughing. Jack and Sophie and Marie-Hélène had to slow down to avoid running into them.

Jack skated around Marie-Hélène and approached Sophie from the other side.

"You need to tell me what you know," he said, grabbing her arm. "They are going to fucking kill me like they tried to kill Ed. What's wrong with you? You don't give a fuck?"

Marie-Hélène launched herself at him then, putting her mittened hands on his arm and shoving him away from Sophie. "Va chier!" she said. "Get the fuck away from her! Leave us alone."

Caught off balance, Jack tried to pull away from Marie-Hélène. His skate caught in a hole in the uneven ice and he fell hard, banging his knee and sprawling forward. At the same moment, one of the black students in front of him crashed to the ice, clutching his arm.

As Jack pulled himself to his feet, he saw blood on the

snow under the black student. His friends saw it too, and froze in their tracks, their laughter dying. One of the girls screamed. The man's eyes bulged out and he gritted his teeth as he twisted onto his backside to try to get to his feet. He noticed the stain on the snow, then looked down in horror at his hand, which was covered in blood dripping down from inside his coat sleeve.

Marie-Hélène and Sophie turned when the girl cried out. They took in the fallen student, Jack scrambling back to his feet and a third figure – wearing a black parka and balaclava – standing behind the fallen men on his skates. His hand was straight in front of him, holding a pistol with a long black silencer on the end. It was pointed at Jack.

Sophie screamed, a high, piercing cry of fear and alarm, and it startled the man as he fired again, so the shot went just wide of Jack, hitting the snowy ice beside him. Jack turned at Sophie's scream, and saw the man aiming at him, and saw the muzzle jerk as he fired. He thought he'd been hit in the shoulder, but quickly realized it was only an ice splinter sent flying by the bullet.

Jack launched himself upright, clawing at the ice, his heart pounding with fear, willing himself away from the masked man. In his desperation, he knocked over one of the girls standing over the bleeding student, and then he took off, skating as fast as he could, furiously working his arms and legs, bent at the waist.

He snatched a look over his shoulder and saw that the masked man was pursuing him, skating fluidly, swinging his arms elegantly, like a speed skater.

Jack knew the masked man couldn't fire the pistol accurately without stopping to steady his aim, so he tried to make himself a difficult target, veering from side to side. He skated past a slow-moving family group, and then cut in front of them. He bent at the waist and accelerated as hard as he could, thinking hard about what he knew about skating, trying to find the magical balance between gliding and propulsion that made you move fastest. Jack had played hockey all winter for years, on frozen ponds and in rinks, and he'd even taken power skating courses, but stopped during university and was out of shape. His lungs burned as he moved, weaving among the slow-moving skaters. He brushed past an unsteady couple and they fell to the ice, and some people called out to him to be careful.

He glanced quickly behind him again but couldn't see the masked man among the throngs skating along in the falling snow, but he felt him, felt the danger as if he had a target painted on his back, expecting at any moment the hot impact of a bullet.

Ahead loomed the bridge, where the rink ended, just before the locks, where a stage was set up. There, Jack thought, I will be cornered and shot. He'll put a couple of bullets in my body to stop me and bring me down, then finish me with one through the head.

He glanced over his shoulder again and spotted his pursuer well behind him, skating with languid grace, his left hand behind him, the long pistol swinging in his right hand. He knows, thought Jack, that he doesn't have to catch me, because I'll run out of ice soon enough. Ahead were the skate shack and the Beaver Tail hut, where dozens of people stood in line.

Jack veered to the other side of the canal and as he passed the end of the Beaver Tail line, he saw the masked man gliding quickly toward him, standing ramrod straight, his legs spread and his arms out, his left hand bracing his right, the pistol pointing straight at Jack.

Jack dodged around the line and made a hard right, heading for the concrete steps up to the bridge. The slippery stairway was clogged with people, skates hanging round their necks.

"Look out," Jack bellowed as he launched himself at the steps. Some of the people on the stairs turned, startled, and saw him hurl himself into the air, vaulting the first four steps with his legs pulled up under him, like a barrel jumper. He hit the fifth step hard, smacking his right shin and knocking over a woman and her daughter, but he kept upright and forced himself up to the landing halfway up the steps. He could see the people ahead of him look at him in surprise, and then look to the bottom of the stairs and dive for cover.

Jack's skates clattered as he launched himself up the second flight. He bent double and scrambled up these steps. In his shooter's stance at the bottom of the stairs, the gunman had a clear shot at him, but Jack was bent low enough that he was protected by the concrete railing. The skaters huddled in terror on the stairs watched as the gunman lowered his pistol and raced up the steps himself, taking them two at a time.

Jack was exhausted when he reached the top of the stairs and fell onto the sidewalk. Across the street, at the Chateau Laurier, two porters in wool coats and fur hats were ushering guests into taxis. One of them caught sight of Jack as he ran out into the traffic on Wellington, forcing cars to stop, skidding in the snow, the drivers gaping at the madman running across four lanes.

Both porters were staring, open-mouthed, when the second man on skates came up and assumed his shooter's stance at the top of the stairs, legs spread, both hands on the pistol, and levelled it at Jack's back. He fired, but he was breathing hard himself after his long skate, and his hands and arms were freezing, and his aim was badly off, and the bullet went well over Jack's head, smacking into one of the stone pillars in front of the Chateau.

He held his stance, lowered his arms, drew a deep breath, released half of it, and focused, willing his arms to stop shaking, and drew a bead on Jack, who was running in front of a city bus. The bus driver, seeing a lunatic on skates running in front of him, hit the brakes and the bus went into a skid. The masked man held his arms steady, closed one eye, pulled the trigger and saw Jack run out of sight behind the bus. The bullet smacked into the engine block of the bus.

The porters watched, mouths agape, as the man in the mask unscrewed the silencer, put the gun in one parka pocket, the silencer in the other and clattered back down the stairs to the canal.

Jack ran past the startled porters, through the Chateau's

beautiful wooden revolving doors and into the lobby, where his skates skidded on the waxed stone floor, and he fell on his hands and knees, chest heaving, eyes wild with fear. Everyone stared at the apparition. A valet started towards him, calling out: "Sir! Sir! Please! Your skates will damage the floor."

Jack ignored him and launched himself to his feet again, driven by terror and adrenalin, and dashed across the lobby. He turned right down a hallway, running past a bank of elevators and down to the side entrance. The valet pursued him. He left a trail of scars behind him on the burnished stone floor.

He burst out the side door that led onto MacKenzie Avenue, and sat down heavily, his back against the wall. He tore off his gloves, and with frozen, trembling fingers set to work on his skate laces. As he struggled, someone stepped out through the door. Jack started, fearing it was the masked man, but it was a heavyset man in a blazer. "Sir," he said. "I'm Daniel Davis, hotel security, and I'm going to have to ask you to wait for the police. You may have been having fun, but you've done a lot of damage and the police need to talk to you about that."

Jack looked up at him as he tore off the first skate.

"Do you have a gun?" he asked him and bent to work on his second skate.

"Sir, I'm not allowed to discuss the hotel's security arrangements," said the man. "Would you mind telling me your name please?"

Jack pulled off his second skate and got to his feet. "If you don't have a gun, I'm not sticking around, because the guy chasing me has one."

He left the skates on the sidewalk and ran across the street in his socks, through the slush, toward the Rideau Centre Mall.

Marie-Hélène had first aid training, so as soon as Jack and the masked man disappeared, she dropped to her knees and went to work on the injured student. She unzipped his parka and yanked his injured arm out of it so she could examine the wound. He had been hit from behind, halfway between his elbow and his shoulder. There was a tiny entrance wound on the back of his arm and a much bigger exit wound through his bicep. His arm was sticky with blood and more was oozing out of the wound. She clamped her gloved hand on it and the man yelped in pain.

"You're going to be okay," she said to the guy. "What's your name?"

He stared up at her, his face contorted with pain. "Miko," he said.

"Miko, you're going to be fine, but we have to stop this bleeding. You're going to have to be brave for a minute, okay?" She turned to Sophie, who was staring toward the bridge. "Sophie! Câlisse! Sophie!"

Her friend started and turned to her.

"Donne-moi ton foulard!" she yelled, and Sophie skated over and gave her her scarf. Marie-Hélène folded it into a square and pressed it against the oozing wound. She tied her own scarf around the guy's arm, tightening it with an efficient knot.

"Sophie," she said again. "Appele 911!"

Sophie yanked out her BlackBerry and got set to dial, then stopped. She turned to one of the girls standing there staring at Marie-Hélène and Miko.

"Hey," she said. She tapped the girl on the arm. "Call 911."

The girl, who was in a daze, started and looked at Sophie. Then she dug her phone out of her purse and jabbed at it.

"Why don't you do it?" she asked Sophie.

Sophie looked down at Marie-Hélène. "Marie-Hélène, Il faut que j'y ailleaie. Désolé, mais je dois partir avant que les police arriver. Je dois immédiatement parlez avec mon avocat, immédiatement. Désolé."

Marie-Hélène looked up at her, her face suddenly hard.

"Marie-Hélène," said Sophie, who was starting to cry. "Je dois partir tout de suite. Je vais tout t'expliquer plus tard."

Marie-Hélène nodded. She looked very angry. "Oui," she

said. "Allez-y. Attention, hein."

Sophie skated towards the steps where she had left her boots. Her neck was cold without the scarf.

She tried calling Jack, but there was no answer. She dialled another number.

"Hello," said the man on the other end. "I can't really talk right now. I'm in a meeting."

"Listen to me," she said. "Did you tell anyone that Jack was trying to get in touch with me?"

"What?" said the man.

"Listen," she said. "I need an answer. Who did you tell? Did you tell anyone that Jack was looking for me?"

"I'm sorry," the man said. "I really can't talk right now."

"Just tell me who you told," she said. "It's important."

"I didn't tell anyone," he said, lowering his voice. "Why? Did you see him? Did he harm you? What's going on?"

"Are you sure?" she said. "Are you sure you didn't tell anyone?"

"Of course I'm sure," he said.

"Okay," she said. "Thanks. I'll call you later and explain what's going on."

She got to the bench where she left her boots and changed into them as quickly as she could, shivering in the cold. She had just finished putting on her boots when her BlackBerry buzzed. It was Jack.

"Oh my God," she said. "Are you okay?"

"I've been better," he said. "Do you believe me now?"

"Oh my God. Who was that? What happened?"

"I don't want to talk about it over the phone. Let's meet. We need to talk."

"Where are you?"

"Buying boots. Can you meet me?"

"Yes," she said.

"Okay," he said. "Remember that place where Ed tried to pick a fight with one of the Senators? Don't say the name."

"I know where you mean."

"Meet me there in twenty minutes."

"Okay. I'll be there."

"Do me a favour," he said. "Take the battery out of your BlackBerry now and don't use it until you see me. Okay? I'm gonna do the same."

"Okay."

"And don't tell anybody where you're going."

"I won't."

Ashton slept late, then went to a neighbourhood gym for an hour on the elliptical machine. She had been working such long hours since she caught the Sawatski case that she had neglected her workouts, and she could feel the difference. Her body felt bloated and she had more aches and pains than she liked. She stopped at Starbucks on her way home, bought a huge macchiato, then picked up the paper. She planned to spend a happy hour doing not much at all, then crack open her laptop and work on the Sawatski case.

She still didn't have a working theory to investigate, but there were enough loose ends that she felt if she pulled them all something might turn up in the next day or two. If nothing did, Zwicker would likely insist that they move on, and she wouldn't be able to say he was wrong. So the next day or two would be crucial, and she hoped to steal a march by sending a series of Sunday afternoon emails, and drawing up a plan of attack for Monday morning.

She needed to convince Zwicker to let her put pressure on Sophie Fortin, at her workplace if necessary, to find out who she'd been sleeping with. Fortin had ignored several calls on Saturday, and late in the day a defence lawyer named Jonah Chisholm had called. He'd said that he was representing Sophie, and expressed the hope that they could sit down soon to see how Sophie could help with the investigation, as soon as he'd had a chance to thoroughly debrief his client.

Ashton was curled up on the couch, flipping through a day-old *Citizen*, sipping her coffee, when her phone buzzed.

The call display showed it was Zwicker.

"Ashton," he said. "We have an odd situation here. Have you heard the news from the canal?"

"No," she said. "What is it?"

"There was a shooting, about an hour ago. Some guy in a balaclava tried to shoot someone, and winged a bystander, an African kid, Miko Wamala, the son of the Ugandan ambassador."

"Bizarre," said Ashton.

"It sure is," said Zwicker. "The kid's been taken to hospital. Is likely going to be okay."

"Why are you telling me this?" said Ashton.

"Well, we have a witness at the scene, a Marie-Hélène Bourassa. Does that name ring a bell?"

Ashton's mind raced. "Does she work with Sophie Fortin?"

"That's right. She's a receptionist or some damn thing in Mowat's office. Anyway, she was skating with Fortin today when Jack Macdonald skated up, wanted to talk to Sophie. They tried to brush him off. Bourassa says he said someone was trying to kill him. Sophie said she couldn't talk to him, but he keeps trying. They're trying to get rid of him when the African kid suddenly gets hit. They turn around, see a man in a balaclava, holding a pistol with a silencer on it. Macdonald takes off."

"Holy cow," said Ashton. "I need to come in right now."

"Yes, you do," said Zwicker. "I just got a report from Jack Vierra, the weekend duty officer. He didn't see the link to your case right away."

"Oh, it's linked," said Ashton.

"I know," said Zwicker. "Here's how I know. About ten minutes ago, 911 gets a call. Male caller with a disguised voice, a fake accent. Won't identify himself. I'm going to read it to you: 'Tell Detective Mallorie Ashton that the canal shooter is RCMP Inspector Emil Dupré.' He repeats the message word for word and hangs up."

"Holy fuck."

"That's right. And it gets better. The call was from 613 555-0139. You know who that number belongs to?"

"Ed Sawatski," said Ashton.

"I want you in here right now," said Zwicker.

Rupert Knowles didn't like going to meet Fred Murphy on a Sunday afternoon. He didn't like giving up time with his family, and he didn't like reporters. He saw the parliamentary press gallery as, at best, a troublesome filter between the prime minister and voters. Journalists were an unpredictable, unprofessional bunch of egotistical slackers who frequently missed the point and messed up the message and just as often petulantly refused to deliver it, despite the best efforts of the prime minister's stressed out media staff.

So when Murphy called him at home – God knows how he got his unlisted number – and asked for a chat, Knowles said, no, sorry, he couldn't, but maybe they could get together for a coffee sometime soon. He'd ask his assistant to find a time this week if that worked for Murphy.

Murphy laughed. "It's not like that. Sorry, Rupert. I need to see you. For your sake as much as mine. It's very important. I could see Naumetz instead, I guess, but I think it would be better if I saw you. I assume he's busier than you are. Would you say that's right?"

Rupert agreed. Yes, he said, he was very busy but the chief of staff was even busier.

"That's what I thought," said Murphy. "This won't wait. And I'm telling you it's very important. I don't want to track down Naumetz to tell him that you told me to call him instead, but I will. This matter is very important and it won't wait. I'm repeating myself, aren't I? I already told you that it's very important and that it won't wait."

Knowles took it in. "I'm thinking."

"How's three o'clock?" said Murphy. "You name the place. It won't take long."

So Knowles was uneasy as he entered the little tea house in Rockcliffe.

Murphy was waiting for him, sitting in the rear of the empty place – a faux Victorian nightmare of lace curtains and ornate wallpaper, chosen only because it was close to Knowles's house. Murphy was wearing a frayed green sweater, and warming his hands around a cup of coffee. His laptop was open beside him.

"Kind of you to come, Rupert," said Murphy, standing to shake his hand.

"No bother at all," said Knowles, amused that they both started with lies.

"Rupert, I've been in the business for a long time," Murphy said, when Knowles was settled and served with coffee. "And I've never blown a source. I've always been very, very careful. However, I intend to reveal a source to you today. I suspect it will cost him his job, but unless I am sorely mistaken, the information he gave us was a malicious lie, and I will not protect a source who tells a malicious lie, who induces us to report something false for the purpose of hurting a rival."

He sat back and fixed Rupert with a steady gaze. "Do you get that? Do you see the ethical code here?"

Rupert nodded. "Of course."

"I like the system," said Murphy. "I don't give a good goddamn who the prime minister is, who's in power, who's out. Couldn't care less. I don't even care that half the stuff you tell the voters is nonsense. Not my fault if they're stupid enough to believe it."

Murphy wore an odd, twisted smile. Knowles grew uneasy. He wondered if Murphy had been drinking. Then the smile was suddenly gone.

"I wish we'd met for a drink instead of a coffee," Murphy said. "I have no choice but to give you this information, and I'm going to ask for some in return, which I ask you to provide to me as soon as you get it. You can't really agree to that until I tell you what I have to tell you, but there you go. Nothing I can do about that. I think you'll be smart enough to do what I want."

Rupert tried a half smile. "I don't know if I can agree to

that, Ed," he said. "I don't have the foggiest idea what you're talking about, but I expect this is the kind of thing that would be more fruitfully discussed with our communications people. It sounds more like Ismael's bailiwick."

Murphy ignored him. He pulled earphones from his pocket and plugged them into the laptop.

"Here's how this is going to work," he said. "I'm going to play you a bit of audio. Then I'll ask you a few questions."

Jack was huddled in the doorway to Chez Lucien when Sophie pulled up in a taxi. He was very cold, but was afraid to wait inside, where he wouldn't be able to run if Dupré showed up. He had retrieved the BlackBerry from the nook in the men's room where he had hidden it, powered it up and made his 911 call. Then he shut it down and went outside to wait for Sophie.

He jumped into her cab and asked the driver to take them to the Nicholas Street entrance of the Rideau Centre.

Then he turned and hugged Sophie.

"Oh my God," she said, pulling him tight. "I'm so glad to see you."

He kept his arm around her and put his lips next to her ear. "I am so glad to see you. You have no idea." Then he pulled her in for another hug and they stayed that way until they came to the mall.

Jack paid the driver and they went inside, Jack leading her by the hand.

"Where are we going?" asked Sophie.

"Did you turn off your BlackBerry?" he asked, striding along so quickly she had to trot to keep up.

"Yes. Where are we going?"

"I want to make sure we're not being followed. I'll explain soon."

They went up the escalators, and he led her on quick circuit of the third floor of the mall, then ducked into the hallway that led to a pedway that crossed Rideau Street to the Bay. He led her along, constantly looking behind him, beside the racks of women's fashions, then up the escalator, through the house-wares department, then down the elevator to the first floor and out the side entrance to the cab stand across York Street.

They jumped into the first cab, out of breath, and Jack pulled Sophie close to him.

"We're going to Gatineau," he said to the driver. "To Pigale."

Sophie looked at him, startled.

"Okay," he said so quietly that only Sophie could hear. "This is what I think we should do. We get out at Pigale, go next door to the motel there and get a room. Pay cash. Nobody will know we're there and we can do four things." He held up his hand and raised a finger. "One: I will tell you everything I know, like, for example, that I have Ed's BlackBerry." He pulled it from his pocket and showed it to her. Her mouth dropped open in astonishment. He raised a second finger.

"Two: You tell me everything you know." He pulled away, looked at her, waiting for a reaction.

"What are three and four?" she asked.

He pulled her close again, put his hand on her thigh and whispered in her ear. "Three, we have sex, and four, we make a plan to sort everything out."

She pushed him away, gave him a skeptical look.

"Whoa, la," she said. "Let's start with number one and take it from there."

Ashton and Flanagan parked down the street from Dupré's house.

By the time they had both made it to the station, Zwicker had researched the inspector and he quickly laid out what he learned about him for Ashton while they were waiting for Flanagan to arrive.

He was a twenty-year veteran of the force, a family man, by all accounts a by-the-book, no-nonsense Mountie on a typical career path, with a modest string of commendations.

Then, after a career spent policing in small Canadian towns, while he was working in Edmonton, he and his boss there, Duncan Wheeler, both got big promotions and got moved to Ottawa. Within a year, he was divorced. His two kids lived with their mother in Gatineau. He lived in a townhouse in Old Ottawa South.

Ashton and Flanagan strolled up to his car, a black Buick, and peeked through the windows. In the backseat was a balaclava and a pair of skates. There was still a bit of ice on the blades.

"You see what I see?" said Flanagan. "He's our guy."

Ashton called Zwicker. "There's a balaclava and black skates in his car. The skates still have ice on them. That's evidence in plain view. I think we have enough to bring him in."

"Okay," said Zwicker. "Bring him in then. But handle this very carefully. I'm going to call Wheeler. Tell Dupré that. Tell him he can come in right now, ride in the back of the cruiser, but no cuffs, and we can all have a little meeting. Tell him if he doesn't want to play it that way we'll arrest him and formally charge him with aggravated assault on Wamala, put the cuffs on him."

"All right," said Ashton. "I think that's about right."

"Be careful," said Zwicker. He paused, thinking. "Jesus, be really careful."

Dupré was smiling when he opened the door. He was wearing jeans and a sweater.

"Hello," he said. "What can I do for you folks?"

Ashton and Flanagan were unsmiling. She was in front, Flanagan behind her, his hand close to his revolver.

"I'm Detective Sergeant Mallorie Ashton, This is Detective Sergeant Devon Flanagan. We're with the Ottawa Police Service. Are you Inspector Emil Dupré?"

"That's right," said Dupré, his eyes darting between them. "What's this about?"

"We just want to ask you a few questions," said Ashton. "Do you mind if we come in, have a look around?" She started to step forward but Dupré held his ground.

"Well I don't know," he said with confused-looking smile. "I'd like to help you but I'm kind of busy right now. It would be easier if I knew what this was about."

Flanagan leaned forward. "Is that your car there?"

"Sure," said Dupré.

"Can I have the keys?" he said. "Mind if we take a peek."

Dupré looked perplexed. "I don't know. What's this about?"

"This is a police investigation," said Ashton. "And we are seeking your assistance. Are you refusing to help us?"

"No," said Dupré. "Oh boy. We are getting off on the wrong foot here. I don't like the sound of this. I know it's a little bumpy sometimes, eh, between our two forces, but I've never had anything but great experiences working with the Ottawa Police Service. So why don't you tell me what case you're working on, and I promise you I'll do everything I can to help."

Ashton didn't budge. "Can we step inside, Inspector?"

Dupré laughed nervously. "This is really not the most convenient time. It's a Sunday! We all have our little hobbies. Can this wait till Monday?"

Ashton stared at him coldly. Flanagan stood with his hands by his sides, his eyes on Dupré's hands.

"Inspector Dupré," Ashton said. "I'm prepared to charge you right now with aggravated assault in the shooting this afternoon of Miko Wamala. I have been instructed to do so by the director of investigations for the Ottawa Police Service, Inspector Wayne Zwicker, who, as we speak, is trying to make contact with Deputy Commissioner Duncan Wheeler, your superior."

Dupré said nothing but his smile was gone.

"Inspector Zwicker is of the opinion that we may be able to sort this out in a friendly way," Ashton continued. "He would prefer that you agree to come down so we can have a meeting, figure out if we have our wires crossed. We have a set of facts that led us to some tentative conclusions that we find confusing. You and Duncan Wheeler may be able to explain them in some way that we have not contemplated."

Dupré smiled. He looked relieved. "Well, okay. I can see

how you might be confused. I know what happens in investigations. Half the time you don't know your ass from a hole in the ground until you see the whole picture. I'll tell you what. Give me an hour. No. Two hours. I'll take care of a few things I've got to do and then I'll drive myself down to the station and we'll have our little meeting."

He started to close the door. Flanagan stepped forward and jammed his foot in the door. "Don't even think about it," he said.

Dupré let go of the door and backed into the living room. Flanagan followed him, his teeth bared, hands by his sides.

"Hey," said Dupré. "You do not have permission to enter my home. This is a forced entry. Come on guys, back off. Believe me, I know my rights."

Ashton stepped up beside Flanagan. "You are going to walk out the front door right now and you are going to get in the back of the cruiser," she said. "You are not going to take anything with you. You are not going to make any phone calls or send any emails until we get to the station."

Flanagan and Dupré were staring at each other, ignoring Ashton. Both of them had their hands by their sides, their fingers flexed, eyes moving over each other.

"Inspector Dupré," said Ashton. "This is your last chance. We don't want to arrest you but that's what's going to happen."

Suddenly Dupré relaxed. "Hey," he said, turning up his palms. "I can make time. Sure. Why don't I come with you and we'll get this all sorted out right now? Let me just get my coat."

He turned toward the closet and Ashton stepped in front of him.

"No," said Ashton. "I'll get it for you. You go straight out the door"

Dupré's eyes were hard.

"Okay," he said. "Fine. I'll come with you, but I'll go without a coat. You do not have permission to touch anything in my house or my car. You do not have probable cause for a search, or you would have done it already. If you attempt an unauthorized search I will have my lawyer so far up your ass he'll be looking out your mouth, and you won't be able to use anything."

"Fine," said Ashton. "No coat then. You may find it chilly."

He stepped outside. "The cold doesn't bother me."

Jack and Sophie decided to skip number one and go directly to number three, having sex on a bumpy bed in a room that stank of stale cigarette smoke as soon as they arrived. They didn't talk about it. They just started to kiss and then they were undressing each other, and then he was on top of her, holding himself above her, looking at her beautiful face as he pushed himself inside her, her wetness delicious against his bare skin. He watched as her cheeks flushed and she bit her lip, and he moved slowly until she urged him, with her hands, to go faster. And then they moved together quickly and she cried out, and it was over, and he collapsed on top of her and kissed her neck over and over, and told her how much he cared about her, and she kissed his forehead and listened to him.

Then they sat in the tangled sheets. He smoked a cigarette and she talked.

"God," she said. "I'm such a slut."

He laughed.

"Don't laugh," she said. "You're my second man of the day. I was with Greg this morning."

"Greg Mowat?" he said.

She smiled at his look of surprise. "Yes. Pastor Mowat.

"I know," she said. "I'm bad, eh? I've been sleeping with him for two years. It started when I staffed him on a trip to Quebec City. His French is better now, but it was lousy then, and I was translating for him for the whole weekend, and I sort of fell for him.

"You have no idea what he's like, what he's really like. When we got on the plane I had been working for him for months, and I thought he was a boring old guy, a born-again Christian, a typical *tête carrée*, not a bad guy but dull. I spent two days translating for him while he talked to all these Quebec municipal politicians, and I couldn't believe how sharp he was. He got these old warhorses eating of his hand. He charmed them, understood them, always acted with respect and intelligence. It was amazing.

"Then I had a little too much to drink at our dinner. It was a banquet for Quebec Tories, at the Chateau Frontenac, so I sat next to him to translate the speeches, and after a while I was full of wine and started to make jokes in English as I translated all the boring speeches, making fun of the pompous old fuckers. Everyone was watching him so he couldn't laugh, no matter what I said. I got spicier and spicier. One mayor – this fat little bald guy with a big moustache – was making a very long, boring speech and I started to do a fake translation, pretending that he was coming out of the closet. Greg had to bend over to laugh under the table. Oh, I was bad." She laughed at the memory.

"You have no idea what he is really like," she said. "He comes across as Mr. Folksy, but he is very witty, very sharp."

Jack couldn't take his eyes off her as she spoke, sitting naked with the sheets around her waist.

"After dinner, we both went to bed, our own beds," she said. "I must have been pretty drunk because after a few minutes, I got up, pulled on my dress again. Just my dress, hey, if you get me. I went up to his room, and knocked on the door. Poor man. He tried to say no but he really had no chance. I like to get what I want, and I wanted him."

"Wow," said Jack.

"Yes," she said. "And I've been doing it every week, every couple of weeks since then."

"It would destroy his career if it ever got out."

"Oh, I know. It would end his marriage too. Poor Maude. She is such a lovely, lovely woman, and it would kill her if she knew."

"Wow," said Jack.

"I told you I'm a slut," she said.

He crawled across the bed and pulled her into his arms

and kissed her.

"I find you irresistible," he said. "I've wanted you since the first moment I saw you, and I can barely believe we're together now. I don't care if you're a slut."

She kissed him back, then pushed him away. "I'll never get through the story if I don't keep going," she said.

"Eventually I had to tell Ed," she said. "He was going to figure it out, and I couldn't lie to him. He knew I was seeing somebody, and had been before we started dating, but he didn't know who. I was afraid of losing him, but I didn't want to stop seeing Greg. So I got really drunk when we were at Tremblant one weekend. We had a nice place, with an outdoor hot tub, and we were wrecked on champagne, naked, with the snow falling in the tub and the bubbles all around us, and I told him then, and swore him to secrecy, and then we made love."

"So he accepted it?" said Jack.

"Oui, oui, oui," she said, nodding. "He knew, absolutely knew, that I loved him and he trusted me, and knew I would never leave him for Greg. And, uh, it was exciting for him. It's kinky, but I would tell him about my adventures with Greg and it would turn him on. Oh boy. A lot."

"Tabarnac," said Jack.

"Exact," said Sophie. "Tabarnac."

"Then Ed had the idea we should do a threesome," she said. "He really wanted it. And so did I. And I managed to persuade Greg, and he came over, twice, and we did it. In our bed. It was really fun. Weird, but fun."

"Did you know there was a hidden camera?" he asked.

"No," she said. "When the cops found it I couldn't believe it. I still can't believe it. I have to assume that Ed was recording us."

"Do you think he recorded the threesomes?"

"I don't know. But the cops have the computer, so if he did, the videos would be on there."

"You think he tried to blackmail Mowat with the recording?"

"No. No. He wouldn't do that. Ed wouldn't do that."

"Did you think he would be the kind of guy who would set up a secret web cam and record you having sex with him?"

"No," she said, and she leaned over and smacked him on the top of the head. "Okay? No. I'm a stupid slut, okay?" She smacked him again. Jack put his arms up to protect himself and pulled her to him and they kissed, grinding against each other. She pulled away.

"*Attends*," she said. "Enough."

Jack sat back down. "Was Greg with you the night that I came to your apartment?"

"Yes," she said. "There was no way I could let you in."

"Have you told him everything, all along?"

"Yes. He is worried about the cops having the videos, and he doesn't want me to tell them that I've been fucking him. He told me that if I wanted to tell them, if I felt that I had to, he would understand, but he wants twenty-four hours' notice, so he can resign from cabinet."

"Holy fuck," said Jack.

"He would do it," said Sophie. "I told him no. I told him that he has worked too hard, and has too much to offer to wreck his life for a piece of tail. I told him I would keep my mouth shut."

"Was he with you this morning when I called?" asked Jack.

"Yes," said Sophie. "He told me to stay away from you, told me you might be dangerous. Then, after that guy tried to kill you, I called him to ask if he'd told anyone that you were trying to contact me. He said no, but I don't know if he was telling the truth. It's the first time I've ever thought he might have lied to me."

"Cochrane also knew I was looking for you," Jack said. "He gave me your new cell number."

"Cochrane and Donahoe both pushed me for information on Ed's BlackBerry," said Sophie. "They told me to try to get it and to give it to them, not the police and not Mowat, if I found it. Said there might be secret national security information on it that nobody else could see."

"Did Mowat think I had Ed's BlackBerry?"

"Yes," said Sophie. "He kept asking me to push you for it, said it was very important that he get it. I promised I'd give it to him, not the police or Donahoe. I really didn't think you had it or I would have told him."

"Did Ed work on the SinoGaz file?"

"That's about all he worked on for eight months, right up until it was finally approved."

"Did he tell you whether Donahoe wanted it approved?" he asked.

"Donahoe pushed it very hard," said Sophie. "He rode Ed hard on that file. Ed was afraid he'd lose his job if he didn't do what Donahoe wanted. He was stressed. There was no reason for Justice to be so involved in a Natural Resources file, but Donahoe kept pushing him to press the Justice lawyers at Natural Resources. He wanted it to be approved."

Jack sat in silence for a minute, then he said, "So Ed might have had something on Donahoe?"

"I don't know," said Sophie. "I guess so."

"So we still don't know who tried to drown Ed," he said. "I'm pretty sure that Dupré is the guy who held him under the water, but we don't know who gave the order."

Sophie got out of bed, naked, and walked over to the ugly bureau where Jack had left Ed's BlackBerry. He watched her move, and suddenly stopped thinking about his predicament.

She picked up the cell phone and weighed it, and turned to Jack. "We need to know what's on this," she said.

Jack jumped out of the bed onto his knees in front of Sophie. "I have a plan for that," he said, and wrapped his arms around her, pulling her to him. He kissed her belly.

"It had better be a good one," said Sophie.

"I'll tell you in a minute," he said, and ran his tongue down her belly to her loins.

She stepped back. "Whoa, la," she said, pushing his head away with her hand. "How about you tell me your plan, then we take it from there?"

Dupré didn't say a word during the drive to the station, and he said little as they got out of the cruiser and rode the elevator up to a meeting room on the third floor.

Zwicker came in as the three of them sat down. He shook Dupré's hand and introduced himself.

"Nice that you've agreed to help us out here, Inspector," he said. "Duncan Wheeler is arriving shortly and he and I are gonna chew the fat a bit."

"My pleasure, inspector," said Dupré. "Always glad to lend a hand to Ottawa's finest."

"Why don't you help Ashton and Flanagan here," said Zwicker. "Tell them what you know, and I'll have a little chat with Wheeler. We'll look in on you in a few minutes."

Dupré was smiling and nodding. "I'll do everything I can, within the limits of operational security, to help your officers, sir," he said, with the big smile again. "A pleasure."

He sat down across from Ashton and Flanagan. He smiled up at the video camera in the corner of the room.

"I want to thank you again for coming in," said Ashton. "I don't like to interrupt your day off, but we think you might be able to help us with our case."

"Anything I can do, I will," said Dupré. "Shoot."

"Okay," she said. "To start with, can you tell me your whereabouts this afternoon, between one and three?"

Dupré smiled. "You know, I can see where we might have a bit of difficulty here. Oh boy."

"How's that?" said Ashton.

"Even as we get started I see that I run into questions of operational security."

"Does that mean you won't tell us where you were this afternoon?" \

"Put it this way," said Dupré. "Until I get a chance to talk to Deputy Commissioner Duncan Wheeler, I can't be sure – not completely sure – what might constitute operational security and what might not. It's just not my call. Chain of command."

Ashton smiled and looked down at her notepad. "Well, if you were off the clock, building a birdhouse in the basement, that wouldn't be operational security, would it?"

"Let me put it this way," said Dupré. "That's a call that I wouldn't be comfortable making. Okay? That decision – to tell you about my birdhouse – I don't think I should make that call. For example, if I was on an anti-terror stakeout this afternoon, that would be classified, right? Follow me? Under no circumstance could I share that information with you. That would put me in violation of the Security of Information Act. As much as I might like to help, I could say nothing."

Ashton kept smiling. "So are you saying that you were engaged in anti-terror surveillance this afternoon?"

Dupré grinned. "You see? You see where my problem is? How can I answer these questions without getting clearance? I need permission from Duncan Wheeler, who is having a chat, maybe a coffee and a doughnut, what have you, with Inspector Zwicker right now. If he were to give me the thumbs up, give me the clearance, no problem. But it's not my call. Not on that kind of question, if you are asking about anti-terror surveillance."

Ashton stretched and flexed her fingers.

"Okay," she said. "Tell you what. Why don't you wait here and we'll wait out there, and when Zwicker and Wheeler are finished, maybe we'll have another go."

Dupré's grin turned cold. "Hey," he said. "You're the boss."

Ashton and Flanagan left him in the meeting room, asked a uniformed cop to keep an eye on him and went to find Vierra, the officer putting together the pieces on the Wamala case.

"Have you got anything?" asked Flanagan. "Any way we can link Dupré to the masked man?"

"Fuck all," said Vierra. "We had lots of guys down there, looking for witnesses. We found a lot of people who saw the guy in the balaclava, but nobody who saw him without it. The people who saw him shoot the bus say he went back down the stairs and skated down the canal like a bat out of Hell. My bet is he got out of sight and pulled off the balaclava."

"Then he put it in the Buick," said Flanagan.

"What's he say?" said Vierra. "Was he skating today?"

"Said he can't tell us anything without the say-so from Wheeler," she said. "Operational security. He's laughing at us."

Vierra rolled his eyes. "I got to tell you two, this all puts me outside my comfort zone. Know what I'm saying?"

"You and me both," said Flanagan.

Then Zwicker called Ashton and asked her and Flanagan to return to the interview room where Dupré was waiting.

Wheeler was sitting next to Dupré. He was short and pale, with grey hair, sharp features, heavy glasses and an air of bureaucratic resignation. Both he and Zwicker were dressed in nearly identical Sunday casuals: khakis, button-down shirts and crew neck sweaters.

Zwicker introduced them.

"Inspector Dupré is going to leave with the deputy commissioner," he said. "He assures me that he will debrief him and get back to us as soon as possible to see whether the RCMP can be of any help to our investigation."

Flanagan said, "What?"

Zwicker cautioned him with a look.

"We found a black balaclava and skates in his car, director," said Flanagan. "We have a 911 caller naming him as the perp. He has refused to co-operate with our queries and would not consent to a search of his car. The skates still had ice on the blades."

"I know," said Zwicker. "That's why we asked him to come down here, Detective Sergeant. I've explained that to Deputy Commissioner Wheeler, who feels, because of operational security matters that he is not free to discuss with us, that the RCMP should immediately initiate their own investigation. The chief agrees with him. Do you read me, Detective Sergeant Flanagan? The chief is of like mind."

Ashton put her hand on her partner's arm. He was shaking his head angrily.

"Inspector Dupré," she said. "On behalf of the Ottawa Police Service, I'd like to thank you for your help here today."

"Oh no," said Dupré, rising to his feet. "It is no bother at all. I'm sorry I couldn't be of more help." He moved around the table, and extended his hand. Ashton shook it. Flanagan turned his back. "Believe me, I look forward to sharing with you all the information that operational security allows."

Mr. and Mrs. Sawatski told Sophie they didn't think Ed would feel like chatting this evening, since they'd pushed him hard in the afternoon, but he'd only blinked a bit.

"I'll try my best," said Sophie. "It will just be nice to be with him, and you two need a break."

They embraced, and Sophie turned off the Newfoundland music, which was starting to drive her crazy, and went out to talk to the nurse.

"Salut, Sophie," she said.

"Salut, Elizabeth," said Sophie. "J'ai une question pour toi, mais c'est un peu délicat."

"Oui?" said Elizabeth.

"Ben, je me demande si je pouvais passer un peu de temps avec Ed maintenant, tout seul," she said, and she blushed.

Elizabeth, a matronly franco-Ontarian, also blushed when she realized what Sophie was getting at.

"C'est ton chum, n'est pas? C'est normal. Aucun problème. Ferme la porte et je vais surveiller ça pour toi."

"Peut-être que ça pourrait l'aider," said Sophie.

"Et toi aussi," said Elizabeth, and gave her a saucy wink.

Sophie closed the door firmly, and put her own iPod in the little stereo, and put on "Wake Up," by Arcade Fire, which Ed loved. She went to the side of the bed and spoke to him softly. His eyes were closed and they remained closed when she kissed him and whispered in his ear. Then she pulled back the covers, pulled up his hospital gown and took his penis in her hand.

"Ed," she said. "Ed." She started to stroke him. He hardened and his eyes popped open.

"Hi, sweetie," she said, and gave him a beautiful smile, then kissed his limp lips, pushing her tongue into his mouth.

He was awake now, staring straight at her. He blinked.

She pulled open her blouse, and climbed onto the bed, straddling him.

"I love you," she said. "Je t'aime."

He blinked.

"You love me?"

He blinked again.

She crawled backwards down the bed, and caressed him until she could feel his excitement build. Then she stopped, climbed off of him and sat by the side of the bed.

"Ed," she said. "I want to fuck you now. Okay?"

He blinked once.

"You have to do something first, though," she said. "It's very important. I need the password to your BlackBerry."

She reached down and stroked him.

"Stay with me, Ed," she said. "Please."

He blinked.

"Do you remember it?"

He blinked again.

She squealed with pleasure and kissed him. "Okay," she said. "Blink when I get to the right letter." She started to recite the alphabet.

Some time later, Elizabeth blushed when she heard – quite clearly through the door – the sound of Sophie crying out with pleasure.

Chapter 11 – Good news, bad news

ISMAEL BALUSI PASSED the morning alone in his office, trying to keep one step ahead in the perpetual media war with the opposition: going through clippings, sending emails to communications staffers, imagining problems that he couldn't see coming, working his way through an extra large coffee. He was an hour into it, and the coffee was mostly gone, when Suzanne, from Knowles' office, called to say that her boss wanted to see him.

Balusi traipsed down the hall, a little nervous, as always when Knowles wanted him.

"Hi, Ismael," he said, shaking his hand and gesturing to the couch. "Tell me. How's your day look?"

Ismael blathered for a few minutes about media lines and ministerial newsers before Rupert cut him off. "Doesn't sound like anything that Geoff couldn't handle, if push came to shove," he said.

"No," said Balusi. "I suppose not. Why? What's up?"

"Well," said Knowles. "The prime minister would like you to go over to the party office today. The election readiness team there has worked up a Campaign Rapid Response Kit. You know about this thing?"

Balusi nodded. He hoped it wasn't an impatient nod. "I helped Chris and the kids debug an earlier version," he said.

"Great," said Knowles. "Great! So that means it won't take you forever to figure out what the fuck they're talking about. Those kids are smart but they aren't always very good at explaining their treacherous computers to lesser mortals. Anyway, someone must have been whispering in the boss's ear about it over the weekend, because he comes in this morning and wants to know exactly how it works, whether it works, everything. You know what he's like."

"Sure," said Balusi. "I can do that. I like the idea of CRRK, but I was never convinced it could stand in for experienced political operatives. It's like a logic tree. Pump in the variables, answer the questions, and it finds the appropriate media lines for an issue. If it works, it could save a lot of time for all of us during an election campaign. What I'm afraid of is someone starts using it –"

Knowles cut him off. "Okay," he said. "Why don't you run down there now, put the fear of God into the kids, and be ready to give the boss a thorough report on it tomorrow."

"Sure," said Balusi, getting to his feet. "Are they expecting me?"

"They will be. I'll call as soon as you leave," said Knowles. " Just one other thing." He picked up a white cardboard box from his desk. "I've got you a new BlackBerry here. We need to take yours, likely just for the day, for a security thing. So this one is ready to go." He slid it across the desk to Balusi.

"A security thing?" said Balusi. He pulled his phone off his belt, placed it on Knowles' desk and picked up the cardboard box.

"That's right," said Knowles, ushering him to the door. "See you tomorrow."

Balfour was drinking coffee in front of his computer screen at home when his BlackBerry buzzed. It was an urgent alert – another one – informing him of the location of the missing BlackBerry.

He opened the map screen on his computer and found the dot, flashing at 88 Peel Street, which, he recalled, was the residence of one Jack Macdonald. He checked the log. It had been online for two minutes. While he was watching, it pinged again.

Twice in the past twenty-four hours the Berry had been briefly activated. The first time, in the afternoon, it had been used in the Byward Market, at York and Parent, for a bit more than a minute. He had called his contact, then had to tell him that it had gone off line while they spoke. The second time was later last night, when it was activated, again for about a minute, on the Queensway. It pinged three times, each time a bit north of the previous ping, suggesting someone briefly used it in a moving vehicle. He had again called in to report the phone had been turned off.

This time, it was holding. He called his contact.

"The Berry's been online now for three minutes," he said. "You can check it on the program I loaded on your phone. It has been stationary, though, at 88 Peel Street."

"Macdonald's place," said the voice.

"That's right."

"Good. Keep tracking it, please, and call me if it moves."

Ashton was at her desk, drinking coffee and going through the witness statements from the canal shooting, when Zwicker called.

"We have another 911 call for you," he said. "Same thing as yesterday. Muffled voice. Refuses to identify himself. From Sawatski's BlackBerry."

She sat bolt upright. "What's he say this time?"

"I quote: 'Tell Detective Sergeant Mallorie Ashton that an armed and dangerous perpetrator is about to break and enter at the residence of Jack Macdonald, 88 Peel Street, apartment 3.' Then he repeats it word for word."

"Jesus," said Ashton.

"I want you and Flanagan there as soon as you can. Call me from the scene. I'm sending a backup car."

"Roger that," she said, hanging up, standing and grabbing her coat all at once.

"Hey, Flanagan," she said. "You're going to like this."

Wheeler and Dupré were going over the investigation report from the night before when the call came in. Dupré listened carefully, nodding, hung up the phone and ran to his office to change out of his uniform. He was in black civvies in under two minutes, behind the wheel of his Buick in four and in front of Macdonald's building in ten. He ran up the stairs, then stopped and listened at the door. There was no sound. He pulled his pistol from his jacket pocket, screwed on the silencer and picked the cheap lock.

He pushed the door open and stood in the doorway in his shooter's stance.

There was nobody in the living room. He darted to the bedroom, the den, the kitchen and the bathroom, clearing the apartment as he had been trained.

Back in the living room, he approached the coffee table. The BlackBerry was sitting on it, in front of an open laptop. He unscrewed the silencer, put the pistol in his parka pocket, pulled out his phone and dialled in. "Apartment is empty," he said. I'm looking at a BlackBerry."

"Good. Grab it and get the fuck out of there."

"Roger that," Dupré said.

When he reached for the Berry, the laptop screen suddenly came to life. Jack Macdonald's face was on the screen. "Inspector Emil Dupré," he said. "What are you doing in my apartment? Why are you stealing my property? Why are you breaking and entering?"

Dupré froze in his tracks.

"You are being recorded by web cam right now," said Jack.

Dupré could see the camera now, resting on the coffee table, a round plastic eye, out in the open. How could he have missed it?

"Please put down the BlackBerry, leave my apartment and call your lawyer, because I intend to have you charged with attempted murder," said Jack.

Dupré froze for a moment, staring at the computer, unable

to process what had just happened.

"Who were you just talking to on the phone?" Jack said. "Who's directing you? No matter. I bet the police can find out from your phone records!"

Dupré scowled and sprang into action. He slammed the laptop shut, yanked the web cam from the side of the computer and called in.

"Dupré reporting," he said.

"What is it?"

"I have the BlackBerry, sir, but I have been recorded taking it," he said. "Jack Macdonald left a web cam set up, and he has filmed me taking the phone. He accused me of breaking and entering and theft, and says he intends to have me charged with attempted murder."

"Oh dear God."

"Yes," said Dupré.

"Get out of there."

"Yes," said Dupré. "Should I bring the BlackBerry or leave it here?"

"Bring it. And get out."

Dupré jammed the phone into his pocket, cursed and ran out into the hallway. As he turned to go downstairs, he froze for the second time in as many minutes. Flanagan and Ashton were on their way up. Flanagan had his gun drawn.

Dupré's mouth dropped open. He slid his hand into his pocket.

"Don't even think about it or I'll shoot you where you stand, motherfucker," said Flanagan.

Dupré pulled his empty hand out slowly. He tried a smile.

"What's this about?" he said. "We seem to have another mix-up."

"Inspector Dupré," said Ashton. "You are under arrest for break and enter. Turn around, please, and put your hands behind your back. We're going to put the handcuffs on you now."

Marie-Hélène had spent Sunday night brooding over the events of the afternoon, and she still couldn't decide whether to stay angry with Sophie when her friend eventually apologized. She was sure Sophie would tell her she was sorry for the way she'd behaved the day before, running away, leaving her to perform first aid and explain the situation to the police. And Sophie's explanation, that she needed to see her lawyer, well, that was beyond weak.

Marie-Hélène kept composing what she would say to Sophie about that, after she had apologized. Something sharp: "Oh, by the way, did you see your lawyer after all?" Or maybe: "I guess the important thing is that you got to see your lawyer." Or maybe laugh it off: "Well, hey, we all know how hard it is to get an appointment with a lawyer."

She was surprised, then, when Sophie breezed into the office with Jack Macdonald at her side, at 9:05 on Monday morning, dressed in a black business suit, the one with the skirt that Marie-Hélène thought was a bit too short, really, for Parliament Hill. Jack, for once, was wearing a neat suit, and his hair was combed. He had Sophie's laptop bag over his shoulder.

"Good morning, Marie-Hélène," Sophie said as she breezed past. "I'm taking Jack in to see the minister."

Marie-Hélène sat with her mouth open. She closed it, then opened it again.

Sophie stopped and turned as they entered the hallway to the minister's office. "By the way," she said. "Thank you for yesterday. You were amazing."

They were halfway to the minister's office before Marie-Hélène realized that she ought to have stopped them. The minister was in a meeting. Sophie couldn't just walk in with a reporter. She jumped to her feet and called out, but it was too late, they had already opened the door and entered. Marie-Hélène stopped in the hallway and tried to decide what to do. With the journalist there, she couldn't go in and eject her colleague, she supposed. She decided to wait by the door, in case she was needed when the minister sent Sophie away.

She was surprised again when the door opened and Bouchard came out with Doug Amos, the deputy minister, neither of them looking pleased.

"Is everything okay, Mr. Bouchard?" said Marie-Hélène, falling into stride with them as they headed for the exit.

He gave her a little smile and nod. "Everything's fine thanks, Marie-Hélène."

The deputy minister didn't even look at her.

Sophie had ejected them by walking in and holding the door open.

"I'm sorry gentlemen," she'd said. "I wouldn't dream of doing this normally, but something urgent has come up that demands the minister's attention immediately."

Greg Mowat raised his eyebrow at Sophie's interruption, stood, smiled apologetically at Amos, promised to call him soon, and turned to hear what Sophie had for him, wearing an expression of polite curiosity. His mouth tightened and his eyes widened when Jack followed Sophie in and he froze, awkwardly, half sitting, half standing, with his hands on his desk.

Jack frowned deferentially and leaned on the closed door. Sophie stood in front of the desk.

"I'm sorry, sir," she said. "But this is very important. If you disagree with me, if you think I have overstepped my bounds by barging in here, I'll resign today without complaint, but you are going to have to give us a few minutes first."

Jack stuck out his hand. "I'm Jack Macdonald, late of the St. John's *Telegram.*"

Mowat looked at Jack's hand as if someone were offering him something unpleasant to eat. He sat down heavily without taking it. "What's this about, Sophie?" he said.

"Jack has a presentation for you, minister." she said. "It'll just take a few minutes"

Mowat nodded and his expression said, this had better be good.

Sophie pointed Jack to the projector, and he plugged in his laptop. Sophie pulled down a screen on the wall, and closed the blinds, one after another, blocking the view of the Ottawa River, until the room was half-dark.

Jack checked the projector and nodded at Sophie. She switched off the lights and leaned against the wall. When Jack clicked on an icon on the desktop, the screen was filled with a video of Mowat and Sophie and Sawatski in Sophie's bedroom. They were naked. The men were on their knees on the bed, with Sophie between them. Ed was in front of her and Mowat was behind her. He wore an animal grimace of pleasure.

After staring in silence for 30 seconds, Mowat spoke. "That's enough," he said in a cold voice.

Jack clicked pause. "That's the video we retrieved last night from Ed Sawatski's BlackBerry," he said. "I have had that Berry since the night that Inspector Emil Dupré put Ed in the canal and left him for dead, but we just got the password last night."

He shut the video program and opened a PDF. "This is an affidavit, describing how I came into possession of the BlackBerry, and the various attempts to get it from me. Twice Inspector Dupré has tried to kill me."

Jack clicked the file shut. "Sophie's lawyer, Jonah Chisholm, is in possession of this affidavit, in a sealed envelope, and of the preceding video," he said. "He also has a copy of the following video." He clicked an icon and the screen showed Dupré entering Jack's living room, taking the BlackBerry, and Jack's voice over the webcam.

"I recorded this video remotely about ten minutes ago," he said. "I set up a web cam in my apartment. I set the alarm on the BlackBerry, so it would go off at 8:30 this morning, with the goal of catching Dupré breaking and entering my apartment, in the hopes that the evidence, along with the evidence on the other video and in my affidavit, would provide sufficient cause for the authorities to take action and stop Dupré from killing me as, I suspect, he tried to kill Ed." He let his words sink it for a minute. "I also informed the Ottawa

Police Service about the potential break and enter and they likely have Dupré in custody now."

Sophie switched on the lights and sat down.

"Greg," she said. "This man tried to kill Jack, and he turned Ed into a vegetable. Did you ask him to do those things?"

Mowat's face was still and expressionless.

"Sir," said Jack, taking out his BlackBerry. "If you don't give us answers, the truth, I will call Chisholm and ask him to open the envelope and distribute the contents to the Ottawa Police Service, the Commission for Public Complaints Against the RCMP, and to the Ottawa Press Gallery."

Sophie repeated her question: "Greg, did you ask Dupré to kill Ed? Did you ask him to kill Jack?"

Mowat finally reacted. He spoke very quietly. "Are you recording this, right now?" he asked.

"No," said Sophie. "I would never agree to that."

Mowat turned to her, searched her face and turned to Jack. "Is this an interview? Will you use this conversation in a story?"

"Under no circumstances," said Jack. "I don't know if I will ever write about this. But I need to know."

Mowat turned in his chair to stare at the closed blinds. He sat upright and spoke without inflection.

"On Oct. 18, there was a reception in the West Block, for the Canadian Television Fund," he said. "I stopped by after work to have a Coke and say hello. Ed came up to me then and grabbed me by the arm, quite hard, and leaned in and whispered in my ear. He said: 'There's a video. Sophie doesn't know it, but I have a video of the three of us.'

"He gave me a funny, kind of manic smile. I managed to get away from him, but he emailed me the next day, asking for a meeting. Against my better judgement, I invited him to pop by here, before work, a week ago today. He didn't mention the video, but he told me he wanted a job. He told me he wanted to be my principal secretary after I become prime minister. He offered to help me win, by sabotaging Donahoe's campaign from the inside, and he said he had a guarantee that I wouldn't double-cross him, which he would surrender to me after the election, if I honoured my commitment."

"Oh my God," said Sophie, under her breath. "Ed."

"When he told me he had a guarantee, he patted his BlackBerry and winked at me," Mowat said, turning back to face her. "I told him I admired his work for Donahoe, and I would very carefully consider his offer, and I hustled him out the door."

He sat in silence for a moment.

"Then what did you do?" said Jack quietly.

"I was very upset, as you can imagine," said Mowat. "I decided to resign. I drafted a letter to the prime minister, which I did not send."

He lapsed into silence again.

"What did you do?" said Jack, almost a whisper. But Mowat was lost in thought, and Sophie had to say his name before he would respond.

Jack repeated his question.

"I spoke to Duncan Wheeler later that day," said Mowat. "I had got to know him pretty well since I took over the portfolio. I like him. Trust him. We see eye to eye about a lot of things."

"And?" said Jack.

Mowat turned to him.

"He was sitting where you are," he said. "Just the two of us in here. I broached the subject with him. Told him I was being blackmailed. Told him I was thinking of resigning. Told him I didn't want to do that, but I'd be damned if I let some little punk blackmail me. No way of knowing where it would end."

"What did he say?" said Jack.

"He told me not to do anything in a rush," he said. "He told me to see if the blackmailer could be reasoned with. 'I have a fellow,' he said. 'A very good man, someone I would trust with my life, very psychologically astute character, good with people. Name of Emil Dupré. Let me send this fellow to have a chat with the punk. See if he would give up the video right now. Explain to him that we don't play that way. Get him to see the light.' "

"So you said yes," said Jack.

"I said, 'Yes, thank you, let's give it a try. Christ. I can always resign tomorrow.'"

"But something went wrong," said Jack.

"Yes," said Mowat. "Early the next morning, Wheeler called me, insisted that I see him. He arrived in a big rush, out of breath, told me that Dupré had accidentally killed the boy. He trailed him all night – the two of you, I suppose – and then waited for him at his building, your building, Sophie. Ed was completely drunk. Dupré grabbed him easily enough, put him in the car, told him he was charging him with blackmail. He parked on Sparks Street and walked with him up to the Peace Tower, past the East Block, and then onto the path that loops down to the locks. He was trying to reason with him, telling him how politics works, telling him he was in too much of a rush, telling him, I suppose, that he would be looked after, if only he would give us the video, not after I become prime minister, but right away.

"Ed must have been scared, but he wouldn't say where his BlackBerry was," said Mowat. "I don't know. I wasn't there, but I suspect that Dupré misjudged him, thought he was hiding something when he wasn't. I think Ed was just too drunk to remember what he'd done with it.

"Evidently, Dupré marched him down by the locks, under the bridge, and decided to persuade him by dunking his head in the water there, and holding him under for a spell. He put handcuffs on him and forced his head under the water. He thought that would be persuasive. God knows what happened, but Dupré miscalculated and drowned him. When he realized what he had done, he removed the cuffs and dumped him in the canal. He believed he was dead. He was sure of it."

Sophie made a small choking noise and Jack turned to notice that she was crying quietly, and appeared to have been doing so for a while. Her cheeks were wet and her chin was trembling. Jack stood to comfort her, but she waved him off. He turned back to Mowat, gathered his thoughts.

"Then later you found out he was still alive," he said.

"Yes. And we thought you had the BlackBerry, or might have. Wheeler told me to let him handle it. He didn't tell me how he was going to handle it, but he said he would. I didn't know they tried to kill you. I didn't think they would do that."

"No?" said Jack.

"No," said Mowat. "Honestly, by that point I was so rattled I didn't know what to think. It has been a terrible, terrible week. I wish so much that I had resigned straightaway." He smiled slightly. "I guess that's the good news now. I can resign now. That's the bright side. Ha."

Sophie stopped crying. "No," she said. "No you can't resign."

"You're making a big mistake," said Dupré, when they slapped the cuffs on him. "I have identified myself as a Royal Canadian Mounted Police officer. I am here on police business, on a national security investigation."

"Do you have a warrant?" said Flanagan. "If you have a warrant to search that apartment, I'll release you right now. Otherwise, you're under arrest for breaking and entering."

Flanagan patted the Mountie down, took the BlackBerry, pistol and silencer.

"I am an officer of the Royal Canadian Mounted Police, here on police business," said Dupré. "Please release me immediately."

Flanagan passed the weapon and the phone to Ashton. She put them in plastic evidence bags while Flanagan hustled Dupré down the stairs.

"If we get a ballistic match on this, you're fucked," he said. "You shot an ambassador's son."

"You are making a mistake here," said Dupré. "You're going to regret this."

Ashton called Zwicker while Donavon put Dupré in the back of the cruiser.

"We arrested him," she said. "We caught him leaving Macdonald's apartment. He has a pistol, a silencer and a cell phone belonging to Ed Sawatski."

"What's he saying?" said Zwicker.

"He has identified himself as an officer of the Royal Canadian Mounted Police," said Ashton. "He says he is here on police business, on a national security investigation."

"Fuck," said Zwicker. "What did you charge him with?"

"Breaking and entering," she said. "He failed to produce a warrant."

"Okay," said Zwicker. "That's good enough to bring him in. I think we're okay there. Bring him in. Tell him I'm calling Wheeler."

"Minister," said Jack. "Sophie and I think you should hear us out before you reach any decisions before your future."

He resumed his presentation. "This is a recent picture of the SinoGaz site near Fort McMurray, Alberta," he said. The screen showed a picture of a scrubby spruce forest being cleared by bulldozers.

"Cabinet, as you know, approved the takeover of PanPetroDev and overruled the federal-provincial environmental review panel to allow this project to proceed."

Next an image of Rena Redcloud filled the screen.

"This is Rena Redcloud," he said. "She was a prostitute who was murdered by this man on August 13, 2008." An image of Ling Chi Wi came up. "Ling Chi Wi was a SinoGaz executive who was sent to Canada to make the project happen. He was killed in custody in Edmonton on August 29, 2008. In the course of the investigation into the killing, RCMP officers uncovered an exchange of emails." The screen filled with PDFs of the emails. "These emails are from someone familiar with the cabinet discussions about the SinoGaz project. They appear to have been written either by a member of cabinet or a very senior official in the Privy Council Office. They are detailed and show an intimate knowledge of the innermost workings of the highest level of government.

They were retrieved from the Deleted Items box of Mr. Wi's email account."

Jack clicked to the next image. More emails appeared. "These emails, Wi's replies, contain details of wire transfers to a numbered account in a Panamanian bank. In total, we have records of about $1 million in transfers."

Next to show was a single letter. "This is a PDF of a letter from Hotmail, in Seattle, to Sgt. Earl Gushue, the investigating officer on the case," said Jack. "It identifies the ISPs that accessed the Hotmail account. There are three locations. Two were Internet cafes in Ottawa. One was an Internet cafe in Lunenburg, Nova Scotia."

An audio file opened. "This is part of a longer recording between me and Dave Cochrane, who, I think you know, works as chief of staff to Jim Donahoe. I made the recording yesterday. Cochrane acknowledges that Donahoe is aware of the emails."

He hit play and Cochrane's voice said, "He knows of an email exchange between someone with cabinet-level access to Mr. Wi. I didn't know anything about this, but CSIS does, and the prime minister's office does, and it is well above my pay grade, and yours, and you had better tread very carefully." Jack stopped the recording. "After uncovering this apparent connection to Mr. Donahoe, Sergeant Gushue of the Fort McMurray RCMP detachment reported it up the chain of command. Wheeler and Dupré visited him and Constable Brecker in Fort McMurray and took over the investigation, telling them it had national security implications. Wheeler and Dupré were both subsequently promoted to Ottawa. Mr. Donahoe, as you know, was public safety minister at the time. I don't know if he was really communicating with Mr. Wi at the behest of CSIS, as Mr. Cochrane suggested, but I think somebody, such as the current public safety minister, for example, should find out."

Sophie cleared her throat and pushed herself away from the wall. "So, you see, minister, you need to deal with this, and with Wheeler and Dupré. You really can't afford to resign today. If Donahoe spied for the Chinese, he wouldn't be an appropriate prime minister, would he?"

Mowat looked at her, and then at Jack. He leaned forward, his shoulders hunched, and thought for a long minute.

"Mr. Macdonald. Are you willing to share all this evidence with me, with the government?"

Jack cleared his throat. "Under certain circumstances," he said. "Yes."

Mowat leaned back in his chair. "Sophie, I need you to do me a favour now. I want you to go have a chat with Claude, fill him in, give him the broad strokes. We need to figure out how exposed we are." He turned back to Jack. "And I will have a chat with Mr. Macdonald here."

Dupré wouldn't say anything except: "You're making a big mistake."

He said it several times during the short drive to the station when they asked him what he was doing in Macdonald's apartment.

Zwicker intercepted them in the lobby as they were about to take him downstairs to be fingerprinted and photographed.

"Take him to Interview Room Number 2," he said. "We need to talk. You can process him later." In the elevator on the way up, Dupré whistled "Three Blind Mice."

They left him in cuffs in the interview room, locked the door, asked a uniform to watch him and rode up to the fourth floor. Zwicker took the evidence bags holding the pistol, silencer and BlackBerry, and all three walked back to his office, where Wheeler was waiting. Zwicker tossed the evidence baggies on his desk.

"Deputy Commissioner Wheeler, you've met detectives Ashton and Flanagan," he said. "I wanted them to sit in our meeting. They have just apprehended Inspector Dupré, as you know, in the act of committing a break and enter."

Wheeler glowered at them. "I think it would be better if

we met alone," he said.

"I don't give a fuck what you think," said Zwicker. "Excuse my French. But these two have been working their holes off to investigate the attempted murder of Ed Sawatski, the shooting of Miko Wamala, who has diplomatic status, and now we have a break and enter. Inspector Dupré is a person of interest in these investigations, and he has refused to co-operate with our officers. When they apprehended him today he had a pistol with a silencer – which is a prohibited firearm, as you know. Why would Inspector Dupré be carrying a silencer, deputy commissioner?"

Wheeler looked at Zwicker and sighed. "This is a national security investigation," he said. "We went over this yesterday. We have launched an investigation to make certain that the appropriate procedures were followed."

Flanagan's laugh sounded like a bark.

"Detective Sergeant Flanagan finds that amusing, Deputy Commissioner Wheeler," said Zwicker. "So do I. We all find it amusing, and also confusing. What was Inspector Dupré doing with this cell phone? Where was he on the night that Sawatski was drowned? Why does he have a silencer?"

Wheeler said nothing. Zwicker got to his feet. "In the course of what kind of national security investigation would an inspector, an inspector with the Royal Canadian Mounted Police, have cause to have in his possession a silencer?" he asked.

Wheeler glared at him.

"Maybe it is evidence," said Zwicker. "That might explain it. Maybe Inspector Dupré apprehended the man who shot Miko Wamala. Is that right Deputy Commissioner? That would explain it. I wonder if that's right. I wonder if we test this pistol if we will find a match with the slugs we pulled out of the canal." He started to laugh. "I bet that's what we're going to find. I am willing to bet my two saggy old balls that we're gonna get a match. So what I'm fucking wondering, you bag of shit, is where's the suspect? What kind of deputy commissioner of the Royal Canadian Cocksucking Mounted

Police would keep the suspect from us, the officers with juris-diction over the case?"

He turned to Ashton. "Detective Sergeant Ashton," he said. "Where do you think the suspect is?"

"Sergeant, I believe he's in Interview Room Number 2," she said.

"Thank you, Detective Sergeant," he said.

Wheeler stood up. "I think this exchange might better take place at a higher level," he said, and walked out.

Zwicker walked over and slammed the door shut as hard as he could then sat down behind his desk.

"You want to stick around?" he said to Ashton and Flanagan. "The chief will call soon."

He drummed his fingers on the desk. "I should actually call him," he said. "Maybe you should leave, now that I think of it."

Ashton and Flanagan got up to go.

"Good work, you two," he said. "Excellent work. I'm proud of you."

He spoke again when they got to the door. "Bottom line here, just between us, I'll likely have to let them spring the Mountie, at least until we get the ballistics results, but there's no fucking way I'm letting them have the gun or the phone."

Ashton and Flanagan looked at each other and Ashton cleared her throat to speak. "Thanks, boss," she said.

"They can have my fucking badge first," said Zwicker.

Mowat folded his hands in front of him and smiled brightly at Jack. "You've been through the wringer, young man, and come out the other side no worse for wear," he said.

"I don't know about that," said Jack. "I don't have a job, for example."

"How long have you been a reporter?" said Mowat.

"Five years"

"Well, you've certainly got quite a story on your hands now. Several stories, in fact. Huge stories. I'm impressed."

"Thanks," said Jack. "Yours alone would be explosive, no doubt. I keep thinking of the headline: 'Sex Tape Blackmail Linked to Drowning.'"

Mowat chewed that over, the ghost of a smile in the corner of his mouth.

"It would be quite a thing," he said at last, and pushed himself to his feet and walked toward the window. He pulled up one of the blinds, and winter sunshine filled the room. He stood for a while, looking at the frozen Ottawa River, across to Parliament Hill, where the Maple Leaf atop the Peace Tower whipped in the wind.

"So the police likely have the BlackBerry now?"

"Yes," said Jack. "But they don't have the password."

"Are there any other copies of the video?"

"Not to my knowledge," said Jack. "Just the one on the BlackBerry and the one on this laptop. One with Sophie's lawyer."

Mowat walked back to his desk. "So what are your plans now? Back to journalism?"

"I'm not sure," said Jack. "I think this story would be hard to tell, in many ways. There are a lot of national security implications. I'm not sure what to do. In fact, I've been thinking about a change."

Mowat smiled. "Really?"

"Yes, minister," he said. "I've been thinking about politics."

Mowat laughed. "You want to come over to the dark side? Well you wouldn't be the first reporter to do that. Are you interested in communications work?"

"Well," he said. "No. Not exactly."

He inhaled, puffed out his cheeks and exhaled. He felt himself blushing.

"Sir, in April, Senator Barry retires," he said. "It will be the first Senate vacancy the new prime minister will fill."

Mowat furrowed his brow. "Senator Barry," he said, searching his mind. "Senator Barry."

He walked to the window again and looked out across the river.

"How old are you Jack?" he asked.

"I turn thirty next month, sir."

"Are you a conservative?" he asked, turning so his back was to the window, gesturing with his hands. "Philosophically, I mean. I know as a journalist you have been non-partisan, but what are your political views, on a personal level?"

"I would describe myself as a small-c conservative," Jack said. "But I'm not the type to seek publicity for my views. I'm more of a low-profile type."

"I see," said Mowat. "You like to stay below the radar, eh?"

"That's right," said Jack. "I'm interested in public service, but I'm not the type to seek the limelight."

Mowat nodded, as if deciding something.

"You know," he said, "the next prime minister would be lucky to have a fellow like you working for him in the Senate. And you could be a valuable addition to my campaign team. I think I'd like you to spend some time with Claude, see if we could use your research skills, behind the scenes, on the campaign, maybe in our Toronto operation. What do you think about that? How about we fly you out there tonight? Put you up in the Royal York?"

"That's a very appealing offer," said Jack. "And at the end of the campaign?"

Mowat went back behind the desk and again laced his fingers together and stared at Jack.

"I could see you as a senator, but I have to tell you, Jack, people will wonder why I'm appointing you," he said. "You see the problem, do you?"

Jack nodded. "It won't make sense to them."

"That's the kind of thing we need Claude to handle," said Mowat. "It's a delicate problem and he's got a deft touch with delicate problems. I rely on him greatly."

He stared until Jack grew uncomfortable. "I understand, sir," he said.

Mowat scowled suddenly and so fiercely that it made Jack start.

"For instance, if one of your reporter friends asks you

about your appointment, what would you say?" said Mowat.

Jack bit his lip. He could feel the force of Mowat's gaze boring into him. It was unpleasant. "Whatever Claude tells me to say."

Mowat nodded at him, still scowling. "What will you do if the Ottawa police want to interview you again?"

Jack shrugged. "Whatever Claude says I should do." He spread his hands out, palms up. "I am a neophyte. I would consider myself very fortunate to have Claude guiding me. He tells me to jump, I'll say, 'How high?' "

Mowat nodded again and suddenly the scowl was gone and he was on his feet and smiling and his hand was extended.

"I'm going to get Claude in here now, get him to take you to his office and debrief you thoroughly while I go over a few things with Sophie. What do you say?"

"Thank you, minister," said Jack. "I would be very happy to work for you, until April 15, when Senator Barry resigns."

Mowat laughed and took his hand.

"Of course," he said. "After April 15, you're going to have other things on your plate, Senator Macdonald."

Fred Murphy gestured to Ellen Simms to stick around after the morning news meeting. "Something I have to talk to you about," he said, after the other reporters left his office.

He walked behind his desk, opened a folder, pulled out a sheaf of papers, placed it on the desk in front of him and spread it out so that she could see what it was.

He sat down to wait while she leafed through the printouts of the emails and PINs she had exchanged with Balusi about the Meech II speech, and the transcripts of both versions of the speech, with the Meech II section highlighted. It took her about five seconds to realize the importance of the documents.

"How did you get this?" she asked. "You have no right to access my PINs!"

He looked at her with concern.

"Ellen," he said. "This is tough for both of us, but long story short, you're out of the bureau."

"Oh my God," she said. "This is such bullshit. You've never liked me. You see me as a threat. How did you get access to my PINs?"

Murphy closed his eyes briefly, put his fingertips together, as if in prayer. "No, I'm very fond of you, on a personal level. This has nothing to do with that," he said. "But I have evidence here that you deliberately misrepresented the facts to our viewers. You can't work in my newsroom anymore. And your buddy, Balusi, is out over at PMO." He tried a warm smile. "This must come as a shock, but you might be better off seeing it as an opportunity. We want you to go to Toronto. We want you to stay with NTV, just not reporting politics."

"What do you mean?" she said.

"We want you to do on-air stuff from Toronto, the weather to start, but eventually we'd like to have you anchoring newscasts for us there, after you complete an ethics course. Or you could take a leave of absence and return as an anchor, after you take the course. The camera loves you and we don't want to lose that. We think, really, that you have a bright future at NTV."

Simms's nostrils flared. She threw the papers down on his desk.

"You want me to do the fucking weather?" she said. "You can talk to my fucking lawyer."

"That's fine," said Murphy, and he nodded at the printouts. "Give him that and ask him to give me a call."

She stomped to the door, hauled it open and strode outside, livid. She looked around at the busy newsroom, then took a deep breath and went back in.

"Fred," she said. "I don't want to do the weather in Toronto. Come on. Give me a break. Let's talk."

"I'm sorry, Ellen, but that's not really possible," he said. He pointed to the printout on his desk. "I can't live with that."

She sat down and started to cry. He stepped behind her and patted her back.

"It's a just a misstep," he said. "You'll get over it. You have an amazing career ahead of you."

"I knew it was wrong," she said. "Damn. I'm so stupid."

She looked up at him. A tear ran down her beautiful cheek. "I need help," she said, taking one of his hands in hers. "I know that I'm not there yet. I come across as cocky because I'm afraid I'm a fraud, and everyone will find out. But I know I can learn."

She stood up and pulled his hand to her breast, imploring him with her eyes. "If you worked with me closely, you could train me. You could mould me."

"Ellen," Murphy said, backing away and pulling on his hand.

"I just need the right teacher," she said. "I could be such a good student."

"Ellen, that's not going to work," he said, and he yanked away his hand.

Her face was suddenly very angry.

"Look," he said, "you want my advice, you should go home, call Toronto, confirm that they have my back on this, which they do, and then think hard about whether you want to sue us or put your tail between your legs and go to Toronto, which is what I think you should do."

She stood, fuming, staring at him.

"But either way, I've got to ask you to leave," he said. "I have to go break a story. Donahoe is about to announce he's pulling out of the race, and I have the scoop."

Sophie and Bouchard met Eric Pothier, the commissioner of the RCMP, and his deputy, Duncan Wheeler, at the elevator. Marie-Hélène sat at the reception desk, looking busy.

"There you are," said Bouchard when the two men got off the elevator, looking immaculate in their perfect dress uniforms. "Nice to see you!" He reached out to shake their hands. "Let me introduce Sophie Fortin, our new senior policy adviser," he said.

Sophie smiled and shook hands with the two men. "Such a pleasure to meet you," she said. "The minister is very grateful that you could find time to come at such short notice."

"We're happy to be here," said Pothier, and he gave her a warm smile, nodding his handsome grey head and crinkling his blue eyes. "And let me congratulate you on your promotion, Ms. Fortin. If I recall correctly, the last time we met you were in communications."

"Thank you, commissioner," she said. "The minister would like to see you in his office to discuss the Strategic Review Process."

She glanced at Bouchard.

"And you, Deputy Commissioner Wheeler, are stuck with me," said Bouchard. "There are a few operational details the minister would like me to go over with you."

The smile froze on Wheeler's face as he learned he was going to a different meeting. "Great, Claude, great," he said, his voice too loud and too cheerful. "Lead the way."

Bouchard showed him to his office, and they sat at a little coffee table.

"I have some good news and some bad news for you," said Bouchard, and he put a single sheet of paper in front of him. It was a civil service job posting. The heading read Director, Security, Via Rail.

Wheeler's smile disappeared instantly when he saw what it was. For a second he looked confused, then he understood. He covered his mouth with his hand, then pulled his hand quickly away from his face and looked up at Bouchard.

"I'm sorry, Duncan," said Bouchard. "But that's the good news."

Wheeler closed his eyes, took off his glasses and covered his face with his hand. He bowed his head and stayed like that for a long minute.

"I'm sorry, Duncan," Bouchard said, very softly. "We have no choice."

Eventually, Wheeler put his glasses on, stuck out his chin,

sat up straight and squared his shoulders.

"Okay, Claude," he said. "I'm ready for the bad news."

Bouchard picked up the job posting and held it in the air.

"The bad news," he said, "is there's a bit of tricky paddling ahead of us before we can make this happen. It's not a sure thing, Duncan. Far from it."

Pothier and Wheeler spoke urgently in low voices in the back of the car on the way back to RCMP headquarters. Pothier waited in the car, reading documents from his briefcase, while Wheeler ran into the building. He came back ten minutes later, jogging out to the commissioner's car, carrying two paper evidence bags.

"Thank you, Duncan," said the commissioner. "I'll see you soon."

Peter O'Malley, chief of the Ottawa Police Service, met Pothier in the lobby of the station and rode with him in the elevator up to Zwicker's office.

Zwicker greeted them politely, but his jaw was set and he was formal and brisk as he invited them in. Three evidence bags – one holding a pistol, one holding a silencer and one holding a BlackBerry – were sitting on his desk.

They sat down across the desk from Zwicker.

"I want to start by apologizing, Inspector Zwicker," said Pothier. "I have only just learned, this morning, the details of this operation. I want you to know that Inspector Dupré and Deputy Commissioner Duncan Wheeler were acting without authorization, and they have made a terrible mess. On behalf of the Royal Canadian Mounted Police, I offer my apologies."

O'Malley looked at Zwicker. Zwicker bent his head an inch. "Thank you, commissioner. I appreciate that."

"Second," said Pothier, "I want to let you know that Wheeler and Dupré have been suspended, effective immediately, and I have ordered an investigation into the events of the past week. They are off the force. We are going to do it quietly, but make no mistake, they are out. Neither of them will ever wear the uniform again."

Zwicker nodded. "I think that's wise, commissioner. Do you mind if I pass that on to Ashton and Flanagan?"

"Not at all," said Pothier. "I'd ask them to be discreet, but I'm sure they would feel better knowing that their excellent police work has had a desired effect. Honestly, I feel the RCMP owes the two of them, and you, a great deal. I hope to have the chance to repay that debt eventually."

"Thank you," said Zwicker. "They worked damned hard on this case."

"I wonder if both of them wouldn't be good candidates for the courses we run at the investigative centre in Regina," said Pothier. "It's a six-week training program for mid-career officers. Recharge the batteries, learn the newest tricks from the best in the business. Normally, it's only for members of the force, but we can invite officers on exchange. I imagine both of them could benefit from that."

O'Malley whistled. "That's a great idea," he said. "Very thoughtful of you, Commissioner."

Pothier took out a business card and handed it to Zwicker. "Send me an email this week, Inspector, and I'll get the ball rolling on that."

Zwicker nodded. "I appreciate that," he said.

"Okay," said Pothier. "Now, I am also looking for a bit of help from you."

"Is that right?"

"Yes sir," he said. "As I mentioned, we're going to conduct an investigation into what happened with Dupré and Wheeler. We need to figure out how the controls broke down. How could two senior officers go rogue on us? It's very strange and I can tell you we'll be wrestling with this for a long time."

"How can we help?" said Zwicker.

"Well, two things," said Pothier. "First, I'd like to ask you to forward us, informally, a report on the state of your investigation. This would be eyes-only, for me and the senior investigator handling our internal investigation."

Zwicker nodded.

"That sounds reasonable," said O'Malley. "All things considered."

"What's the second thing?" said Zwicker.

Pothier puffed out his cheeks, put his briefcase on the coffee table, turned it to face Zwicker and opened it. Inside, there was a copy of the Ottawa Citizen and two evidence bags. He put the newspaper on the coffee table, then lifted one of the evidence bags and upended it. A BlackBerry slid out of the bag, landing with a gentle thump on the newspaper. He dumped the second, and a nine-millimetre Smith and Weston, exactly like the one sitting on Zwicker's desk, slid onto the paper.

"I think your investigators ended up with the wrong gun and phone, director," said Pothier. "I think there was a mix-up. This is the right pistol. This is the pistol that you have to send for ballistic testing."

Zwicker stared at Pothier for a moment as he absorbed what the Mountie was saying. He turned away, shook his head, pinched the bridge of his nose and exhaled noisily. He stared down at the gun and BlackBerry. He didn't make eye contact with the other men.

O'Malley leaned his head close to Zwicker's. "Wayne. If we get a match, we would have to charge a member of the Royal Canadian Mounted Police with shooting a foreign national on a diplomatic passport. Think about that for a fucking second, would you?"

Pothier cleared his throat. "Director, a charge like that would present very significant challenges to the RCMP, to the office of the minister of public safety and to the prime minister of Canada," he said. "Very significant challenges." He fixed Zwicker with a sharp look. "It's just, uh, not the kind of thing that can happen. You might think I'm just covering my ass here, which I am, but tell me what you think we should do. Tell me the alternative."

Zwicker didn't trust himself to speak. He folded his arms over his chest and leaned back in his chair.

O'Malley stood up. He took the pistol and BlackBerry from Pothier's briefcase, walked over and placed them on Zwicker's desk. He removed the other pistol and cell phone, sat back down and placed them in Pothier's briefcase. He closed it and rested it at Pothier's feet.

Pothier kept his eyes on Zwicker. "I can see you don't like this," he said.

"Yeah," said Zwicker. "That's about right."

"I don't blame you. To tell you the truth, I don't like it too much myself." He held his hands open, palms up, and shrugged.

"Christ," said O'Malley. "You two look like a couple of old maids at a priest's wake. Wayne, get that goddamn bottle of rye out of your desk and pour us all a fucking drink, will ya? Jesus Murphy. None of us shot the goddamned African."

Casse-Croûte Chantal is a roadside poutine joint in Templeton, a working class French neighbourhood on the edge of Gatineau. When Bouchard arrived, Dupré was already hunched over a small poutine, picking at it with a wooden chip fork. Far from downtown Ottawa, this was the kind of place where neither man was likely to run into anyone they knew. The dining room had a worn linoleum floor, four small booths and a takeout counter. It was busy at suppertime, but by the time Bouchard arrived, the dinner rush was over, and Dupré was the only customer.

Bouchard walked over to Dupré's table with an evidence bag in his hand.

"I got something for you," he said, tossing the bag on the table. It landed with a heavy thunk. "It's a parting gift from Pothier."

He went to the counter and ordered. When he walked back to the table with a poutine and a coke, the bag was gone.

"So, you're out," he said, sitting down.

"I'm out," said Dupré. "I gave Wheeler my badge this afternoon."

"What are you, twenty years in?" said Bouchard.

"That's it," said Dupré.

"Well, too bad," said Bouchard. "You didn't do anything except what we asked you to, and you did it damned well, but there's nothing we can do. We have to bury this shit."

"I know," said Dupré. "I understand that. But I need to make a living."

Bouchard put his hands up. "I told you not to worry about that," he said. "I've been working on it. There are still some wrinkles to sort out, but we're almost there."

Dupré took a bite of poutine and raised his eyebrow. "And?"

Bouchard pulled a business card out of his breast pocket and put it on the table. It was for a Laval lawyer named Henri Savard.

"This is your new lawyer," he said. "Tomorrow, you are going to Montreal to sit down with him. He will have documents ready for you to sign, first of all hiring him as your lawyer, and second of all, registering you as the sole proprietor of DigiService Information Technology Systems. You will be president. Savard will be secretary. You will both be directors."

Dupré wiped gravy from his mouth and raised his eyebrows.

"Next month, Via Rail will issue a request for proposals for an information technology security contract, to be granted by Via's new director of security," Bouchard said. "Wheeler will see to it that DigiService is the successful applicant."

"And what will I do for Via Rail?" said Dupré.

"You will submit a bill for $50,000 every month," said Bouchard. "That's $600,000 a year. From that, you will make a monthly payment of $2,000 to a subcontractor – I don't have the name of his firm yet, but Savard will. The rest of the money is for DigiService operations, less Savard's fees, which should amount to $50,000 a year."

"That seems like a lot," said Dupré.

Bouchard shrugged. "He's going to do a lot. He'll handle all the paperwork for DigiService, including book-keeping, taxes, all that shit. You can expect to clear about $200,000, after taxes. I'm not an expert on this, but I think Savard can arrange it so that most of it lands in the bank account of your choice, so it's up to you what you tell the wife. But you better pay attention to the details, because if you run into trouble with Revenue Canada we can't lift a finger to help you.

"If you need extra help with an operation, an extra pair of boots, you file a contract amendment, Via pays it on a costs-plus basis," said Bouchard. "Like on this job. Who was the guy who helped you? What did you say his name was?"

Dupré laughed. "I don't recall telling you. That's an operational detail."

Bouchard winked at him and Dupré laughed again. "I like it so far," he said. "So far, it sounds like a clever setup."

"Savard will handle all electronic communication between us," said Bouchard. "He has set up a forwarding service, so every email we send to each other moves through his server, meaning it's covered by solicitor-client privilege."

"I like that," said Dupré.

"I thought you would," said Bouchard.

"So who's the subcontractor?" he asked.

"Tim Balfour," said Bouchard. "He's been working for me for six months, but I think it would be better at this stage if he works directly for you. He's at CSIS. He's the guy who was feeding us the co-ordinates on the BlackBerries. He can do a lot of things already, and I think if you push him, he has the potential to develop. I hope so, because a lot of my plans depend on that. We need, uh, communications intelligence, and if he can't get it for us we need to find somebody who can."

Dupré finished his poutine. "I'm very impressed. But, what do you want me to actually do?"

"A lot of things, my friend," Bouchard said. "You're going to earn every goddamned sou. All national security operations. Surveillance. Intelligence. Security. Maybe some banking."

He leaned back in the little booth and a look of pleasure spread across his face.

"You are going to serve your country."

Chapter 12 – Whoa, la

JACK FLEW TO Toronto, checked into the Royal York, bought himself two nice suits with the credit card Bouchard gave him and, a few days later, moved into a condo high above York Street, with a breathtaking view of Lake Ontario.

Every morning, he donned one of his new suits and made his way to Mowat's Toronto leadership campaign office, and, following Bouchard's instructions, kept his eyes open and his mouth shut. He attended important meetings, took notes on his laptop and sent detailed daily accounts to Ottawa.

"You're a reporter, so report," Bouchard had told him.

What he didn't do was explain to anyone what he was doing there.

"I'll take care of that," Bouchard had said, and he kept his promise, looking for every opportunity to show, at least to people in the party, that Macdonald was doing crucial work, so it would be less of a shock when he was appointed to the Senate.

"We'll appoint a hockey player or somebody at the same time, so voters won't pay attention to your appointment," he said. "But we don't want it to look too weird to people on the Hill."

Every day, Bouchard would call him and he'd close his office door and recite every little thing he had seen or heard, and Bouchard would ask him questions and give him instructions. After a few weeks, he started to give Jack instructions, asked him to call people, pass along messages from him, and advised him to speak up in meetings to tell everyone what Bouchard wanted. And he would coach him, on the phone, regularly, about what to say if someone asked about Sawatski.

"Look like you don't want to talk about it," said Bouchard. "Look sad, but not bothered. If they press, tell them you visited him in the hospital, hope he's getting better. If somebody really presses, say that he was very drunk and, so far as you know, he fell in the damn canal."

They would practise his lines on the phone. But nobody asked about it until Jack ran into Dave Cochrane at the Drake, and Bouchard's lines wouldn't have worked. Jack was leaning against the bar, eyeing some girls, nursing a Grey Goose, waiting for his date, when Cochrane called out to him, a shout of happy surprise, and he turned to see him shambling up, his tie loosened, his shirt half untucked, wearing a big smile. He slapped Jack's back and they shook hands.

"Hey, you motherfucker," said Cochrane. "How you doing?" He stepped back and checked out Jack's suit, head to toe. "Somebody has come up in the world!" he said, and he laughed and slapped Jack's back again. Jack smiled weakly.

Cochrane hoisted himself on the stool next to Jack and waved to the bartender. "Give me one of whatever this bad motherfucker is having."

"How you doing, Dave?" said Jack. "You still working for Donahoe?"

"Yes," he said. "For, what? Another three weeks. Donahoe's not running again. I just had a job interview up here. Aiming to make some goddamn money."

"How'd it go?" said Jack.

"You know," said Cochrane. "Good, I hope. I'm finished in Ottawa. The Mowat boys . . ." He made a chopping gesture with his hand.

"No good?" said Jack.

"Not for me," said Cochrane, and he took a mouthful of his vodka martini. He suddenly looked a little soberer. "Looks like it might be a bit better for you."

He stood up from his stool so he could stand closer to Jack, elbows on the bar, his face close. Jack leaned back but there was a brick wall behind him.

"I hear you're in pretty good with the Mowat boys," Cochrane said. His eyes searched Jack's face. Whatever he saw in Jack's blue eyes didn't seem to trouble him, and he leaned back, licked his lips, looked down, and had another drink of vodka.

"Funny thing," he said. "The day after you and I talked about those emails, the boss decided he'd had enough, decided he wasn't going to run for the leadership, was going to pack it in." He let loose an angry bark of a laugh, and then he raised his glass in a toast. Jack clinked glasses with him and watched him gulp the rest of his drink and call to the bartender for another, slapping the bar and smiling.

"He didn't tell me until the next day, but I could tell that he had decided," said Cochrane. "We were in his office on the Hill, meeting with two organizers from here, couple of sharp young Indo dudes, won some municipal elections, had juice at a couple big Mississauga temples. They're telling him how they can deliver a bunch of riding associations for him. He was having a great time, listening to these hotshots pitch him, kind of buying it, kind of not buying it, having a laugh.

"He was having such a great time, finally running a leadership campaign. We knew Mowat was way ahead, but the boss was having the time of his life." His drink arrived and he paused to take a decorous sip.

"So my BlackBerry rings," he said, now addressing the row of bottles behind the bar. "Bouchard calling. I excuse myself and step out to take it. First time he's called me since Stevens announced, so I figure I should hear what he has to say."

He pursed his lips and blew a soundless whistle. "As soon as I heard his voice I knew he was calling about those fucking emails. He didn't mention them to me, but I knew. He said his boss wanted a few minutes with my boss. Wouldn't say why, but said it was important and wouldn't take long and sooner would be better for everybody."

A little more vodka.

"So sure. I set it up. Mowat and Bouchard come in two hours later. Bouchard and I sit in my office while our bosses have a chin wag. Bouchard is friendly, but quiet, then he takes a long call in the hallway. I expected he would maybe banter a bit, try to ferret out a bit of info about our campaign, but then, why would he do that?" He turned to Jack, to see if he was following. "Why would he do that, eh? He knew the boss was done, because he had the emails, eh?"

Cochrane waited for Jack to nod, to show that he was following, then turned his bleary face away. "They come out, friendly with each other, Mowat says hello to me, Bouchard comes back from the hallway, and poor old Jim says goodbye to them. He was cheerful enough, but I've worked for him a long time, and I could see it. He was done. Waited until the next day to tell us, but I knew then. Fuck. I think I knew as soon as Bouchard called."

He frowned deeply, stared at the bar, then tilted his head and knocked back the vodka. His eyes were watering from the liquor when he turned to Jack again. He gripped Jack's shoulder with his left hand, squeezed Jack's right hand in his and spoke into his ear.

"All's fair in love and war and politics," he said, and Jack felt the grip tighten. "No hard feelings. But just so you know. There's no way Jim Donahoe would betray his country. No fucking way. I don't know the deal with the emails, and I don't need to know." He kept the iron double grip on Jack but leaned back to look him in the eyes. "You know that, right? You know that Jim Donahoe is no traitor, right?"

Jack met Cochrane's bleary eyes and nodded his head, but he could see that Cochrane needed him to say it. "I know that, Dave," he said. "Jim Donahoe is no traitor."

That was enough, apparently, because the grip loosened, and Cochrane was smiling and backing away, and telling Jack he was happy for him, and they should stay in touch, and he was gracious when Jack's date arrived, and said nice things about him to the girl as he took his leave.

Jack could tell that the girl sensed his unease, but after Cochrane left he asked her about her political opinions, and told her about life in the game in Ottawa, and the dinner was great and she let herself be coaxed back to his condo afterwards.

Jack was starting to feel important, he was wearing some sharp suits, and nothing was stopping him from romancing the many young volunteers and staffers on Mowat's leadership campaign. As he became more comfortable in his new role, and Mowat's operation expanded and took on an air of inevitability, Jack became accustomed to taking home young women to his condo, where he would ply them with champagne in the living room, show them his view of the city, then seduce them on the couch, so that he could look out at the inky waters of Lake Ontario as he took his pleasure, and admire the reflection of their naked bodies in the glass.

But even while he was delighting in the erotic shadow play against the night sky, maybe especially then, he found himself missing Sophie. He spoke to her when she had time, but she was busy with her work in the department, busy with a special leadership-related project she wouldn't talk about, and busy with her visits to Ed, who was making little progress.

Bouchard wanted Jack to stay clear of Ottawa until he was appointed to the Senate, so that he could avoid his journalist friends, and Sophie didn't have time to go to Toronto, so he didn't see her again until just before the leadership convention in Montreal.

They met for dinner at her favourite restaurant, Au Pied de Cochon, where they started with glasses of champagne and deep-fried cubes of foie gras. Sophie looked more beautiful than ever, in a simple, low-cut black dress, and it made Jack so nervous that he dropped his fork and knocked over his water glass. When their appetizers arrived, she quizzed him on what he'd observed in Mowat's leadership office, and asked about his love life.

"Is there anyone serious?" she asked.

He took a big slug of wine and rolled his eyes.

"No one the least bit serious," he said. "They're all sort of the opposite of that. How about you?"

"God," she said. "I have no time for that shit."

She told him about Ed, who had moved into a downtown long-term care facility, where she visited him every day.

"Are you still seeing Mowat?" he asked.

"Shhh," she said. "We're not supposed to talk about that."

"Fine," he said. "I won't talk about it. But are you?"

She shook her head.

"No," she said. "That's over for good. We never even discussed it. The minister and I are enjoying an excellent professional relationship."

Jack was on his fourth glass of wine by the time he'd finished his appetizer. Sophie had barely touched her champagne.

"You're not drinking much tonight," he said. "Are you planning to get me drunk and seduce me?"

She laughed her high, tinkly laugh, and he beamed at her.

"I can tell you," he said. "You don't have to do that. You can pretty much just tap this shit anytime you want."

Sophie blushed and laughed and told him to not be such an idiot.

He sat back and looked at her. Their eyes locked, and he suddenly realized why she wasn't drinking.

"Sophie?" he said. "Are you pregnant?"

She set down her knife and fork and composed her face.

"Well," she said.

Jack grinned. "Holy fuck," he said. "Congratulations."

"I didn't say yes," she said. "You can't tell anyone. I'll be showing in a month or so, but I want to be in my next job before anyone knows."

"Wow," said Jack, closing his eyes. He was surprised to feel a tear run down his cheek. He wiped it away and took Sophie's hand in his.

"Will you marry me?"

She pulled her hand away and slapped his. "Ferme ta gueule," she said. "That's not funny."

He reached to take her hand again. "I'm not joking," he said. "I'm crazy about you. I can't stop thinking about you.

If you knew how much I look forward to our phone calls …"

She let him hold her hand.

"Thank you, Jack," she said. "No. You can't marry me. I'm a Québécoise, remember. We're not really into marriage."

Jack searched her eyes for a moment, then leaned back in his chair.

"I will ask you again later," he said. He took a drink of wine.

"Wow," he said. "Fuck. So, uh, who's the father?"

She raised an eyebrow, and sat back with a little smile.

The waiter arrived then with their main courses: steak frites for him, and for her, a whole pig's foot, glistening with maple syrup, atop a mound of buttery mashed potatoes.

"I'm eating for two," she said, and tucked in.

Jack cut a piece of steak and lifted it, then put his fork down.

"Who's the father?" he asked again.

She swallowed her first bite and started on a second, and looked at him, chewing.

"I can't say for sure," she said. "It's either you or Ed."

She sat back and watched his face as that sank in. "Two to one it's you, though," she said, and she laughed.

He looked confused.

"You remember that shitty motel?" she said. "We had sex twice there. Then later, at the hospital, I had sex with Ed once. So I figure that makes you the odds-on favourite."

Jack's mouth dropped open.

"It's how I got the password. I got his attention, then after he gave me the password, I had sex with him."

"Wow! And you slept with Mowat that morning."

"Yes. Three men in one day. I can't believe it." She shook her head in honest astonishment at herself.

"So, how do you know he isn't the father?" he asked.

She shrugged. "I guess he could be, but he used a condom. You didn't, and I let you, didn't I? Either time. I don't know why."

Jack shook his head.

"So," she said with a little wink. "Do you still want to marry me?"

"Yes," he said. "Yes. Maybe I am stupid, but I still want to marry you."

He put down his knife and fork and peered at her. "That's not the kind of thing you would do all the time, is it? You don't need three men every day, do you?"

She laughed, and Jack's heart swelled at the merry sound.

"Think about it," he said. "We can afford a house, have a nursery and a room for Ed, get home care for him. That would be good for him, having a house full of people to look in on him. Both of us could spend time with him every day. I'll likely have a lot of time on my hands. I'm hoping this whole being-a-senator thing will be sort of a part-time deal. They tell me that's up to me."

They both laughed at that. Then he took her hand in his again.

"So," he said. "What do you think of my plan? Will you marry me?"

She laughed, pushed his hand away and took a bite of pork.

"Whoa, la," she said, chewing. "Tell you what. How about we go back to your place after dinner, and then we'll take it from there?"

Acknowledgements

I would like to thank friends who read drafts of Deadline and gave me valuable advice and encouragement: Tisha Ashton, Andrew Balfour, Mark Bourrie, Carrie Croft, Susan Delacourt, Camille Labchuk, Christina Lopes, Don Martin, Glen McGregor, Jordan Owens, Elizabeth Pigeon and Gaby Senay. Andrew Coyne corrected some errors in English, Daniel Leblanc kindly corrected my French. I'm especially grateful to fellow novelist and old college friend Julianne MacLean, whose advice was crucial in helping me turn the manuscript into a publishable novel.

I'd also like to thank cover designer Tim Doyle and photographer Dan Brien, whose image of the Peace Tower appears on the cover, and patient proof reader Sylvia Macdonald.

Made in the USA
Charleston, SC
23 February 2013